D0428193

"Damn it, Bra

"Where t

Dervla was standing at the only window, hands resting on the sill as she stared out at a maze of dilapidated rooftops. The metal mesh fixed to the outside was rusty and dented but fine enough to give a decent view, and to let late afternoon sunlight into the horrible hot compartment they had been stuck in for more than four days. But this was the kind of spartan discomfort you had to put up with on a job like this, especially when your employer was the staggeringly wealthy Augustine van Graes.

You'd think that he might have booked us into someplace a little more upmarket, rather than this shoebox, she thought. *Something about not drawing attention to ourselves, apparently…*

So here they were on a desert planet called Ong, so far off the beaten track that Earthsphere was unheard of and the mighty Sendrukan Hegemony was known as the semi-legendary Perpetual Empire. As for this stuffy rib-walled compartment, it was one of another two hundred stacked in a girder-and-platform structure situated in a down-at-heel quarter of Cawl-Vesh, a city suspended over a deep canyon by a catenary of titanic cables. Not what you'd call an exotic holiday destination. All they had to do was infiltrate the well-guarded Eminent District, break into a high-security museum and steal one specific thing from its vault. Except that inside the main vault was a bio-vault which only a bio-genetic key would open—which is why they were languishing, bored and baking, in this sun-trap, waiting for Pyke to show up with the key. And he was late.

BY MICHAEL COBLEY

Humanity's Fire

Seeds of Earth
The Orphaned Worlds
The Ascendant Stars

Ancestral Machines

Splintered Suns

SPLINTERED SUNS

A HUMANITY'S FIRE NOVEL

MICHAEL COBLEY

www.orbitbooks.net

Copyright © 2018 by Michael Cobley
Excerpt from *A Big Ship at the Edge of the Universe* copyright © 2018 by Alex White
Excerpt from *Adrift* copyright © 2018 by Rob Boffard

Cover design and illustration by Steve Stone
Cover copyright © 2018 by Hachette Book Group, Inc.

Orbit
Hachette Book Group
1290 Avenue of the Americas
New York, NY 10104
orbitbooks.net

Simultaneously published in Great Britain and in the U.S. by Orbit in 2018
First U.S. Edition: December 2018

Orbit is an imprint of Hachette Book Group.
The Orbit name and logo are trademarks of Little, Brown Book Group Limited.

The publisher is not responsible for websites (or their content) that are not owned by the publisher.

The Hachette Speakers Bureau provides a wide range of authors for speaking events. To find out more, go to www.hachettespeakersbureau.com or call (866) 376-6591.

Library of Congress Control Number has been applied for.

ISBNs: 978-0-316-51522-1 (trade paperback), 978-0-316-51516-0 (ebook)

Printed in the United States of America

LSC-C

10 9 8 7 6 5 4 3 2 1

Dedicated to the memory of

John F. Marks, 1936–2017

Friend and sensei

PROLOGUE

Hyperspace Tier 19: Rowkog City

Ragess Craiph, Supreme Vizier of Rowkog, hereditary Great Elder of the Hezrish, and Emperor of All Hyperspace, kept the hand disruptor trained on his underlings while adjusting his bulky garments. It was warm and stuffy in the rooftop aircar garage and his attire, while satisfying the all-enclosing rule, was poorly made from low-grade material. The cuffs pinched annoyingly at the wrists while his upper back itched abominably...

Emperor Craiph then noticed that the taller of his two underlings had paused from preparing the aircar and was watching him from behind the goggles of his plain cityworker mask.

"Continue with your task as I ordered," Craiph said with a regal gesture of the disruptor. "Disrespect will not be tolerated..."

"How much longer will you cling to these delusions?" asked the underling. "Even now my Imperial regiments are pouring into Rowkog, and once the marauder incursion is repelled my rescue will only be a matter of time. Be sensible and give over that weapon. As Paramount Archon of the Hezrish Dominion I give you my solemn vow that you shall not be harmed."

Ragess Craiph, Supreme Vizier and Emperor over all he surveyed and much else besides, gave a throaty laugh.

"Such babbling delirium can only be fuelled by some kind

of mental derangement," he paused to rub an itch on his back against a section of the ribbed surface of the garage's bulkhead interior. "Resume your work—the Imperial limousine must be spotless inside and out if I am to fly forth and greet my triumphant battalions."

There was a clatter as an empty canister flew tumbling across the oil-stained garage floor. The second underling rose from where he had been working on the aircar's rear offside suspensor. He wore the rough, grubby garb of a manual worker, possibly a low-level tech. One gloved hand was clenched in a fist, the other held a large shift-wrench.

"I can stomach you drivelling fools no longer," he snarled. "Having abducted me from the Imperial palace and brought me to this stinking hovel, you now attempt to undermine my sanity by engaging in an impersonation charade so pathetic a child could see through it!" With the wrench he gestured casually at the garage door. "My stealth-marines are drawing near even as I speak and when they come through that door—"

"Your insolent mouth has signed your death warrant," snapped the first, swinging the disruptor around.

"Illiterate!" said the one with the wrench. "How do you sign something with your mouth?"

There was a bright stutter from the disruptor's muzzle. The unfortunate target cried out, one gloved hand grabbing at his wounded shoulder as he staggered back, while still holding onto the wrench. But when he lifted away his hand and saw only a smouldering patch of material, laughter came from his masked face.

"You cretin!—You've had it on the lowest setting all this time…"

Whatever else any of them began to say next was drowned out by the metallic shriek of the garage door being wrenched away from the outside. His Imperial Majesty, Craiph the First, bellowed at the shapes hovering outside, but before he could get off a blast with the disruptor a burning flash blinded him and a brace of needle rounds caught him in the neck. As the numbing narcotic spread through his veins, the Emperor sank to the floor, proclaiming his regal privileges and vowing to inflict all manner of revenge upon his enemies.

Once the roof garage was secured and the three unconscious parasite-hosts were tagged and tanked, a Rowkog City council airbarge floated over to park on the rooftop. Rensik, Construct drone and Mission Invigilator, watched for a few moments as the Hazcon-suited Hezrishi loaded the iso-canisters into the barge then opened a channel to Gelkar, mission auditor and his second-in-command.

"Please tell me that this is the last of them," he said.

"My estimation matrices indicate that 100 per cent of the Rowkog populace is now accounted for," said Gelkar. "That's based on a 99.3 per cent certainty rating."

"That's an improvement," Rensik said. "It was 93.5 per cent a few hours ago."

"We were still converting various migration and tax records at that point, cross-correcting for duplication and so forth," said Gelkar. "All those sources have now been merged into a single dataface which gives us—"

"0.7 per cent uncertainty," Rensik said. "Does that mean you're uncertain about 0.7 per cent of Rowkog's six hundred thousand-plus population, which runs to four thousand two hundred individuals..."

"We don't apply uncertainty that way, Invigilator. Undetected hosts could not amount to so many—there would be outbreak incidents everywhere."

"Gelkar, I need complete certainty," Rensik said.

"We will have it—it's just a matter of time."

"Just so long as there's no more of these hosts sitting in hidey-holes, thinking the same thing. Keep me updated."

With that Rensik severed the connection, swivelled with his attitude jets and shot straight up, passing through the atmosphere field, heading for the heights of the cavern. The drone slowed to a hover and mused on their progress. Ego-parasites were rare enough back up in the prime cosmos so an infestation down here in the depths of hyperspace was unlikely to the point of suspicion. Rensik speculated that one of Rowkog's competitors, one of the other crannytowns, had had a hand in it. Not a shred of proof to be had, thus far, but he was keeping it in mind.

Hyperspace Tier 19 was an oddity. The collapsed and compacted vestiges of a partial universe from some billions of years ago, it was studded with large and mostly spherical caverns, all of which were home to small or medium-sized mining settlements established to extract the plentiful ore and mineral seams. Down the millennia the few fissures and chasms which broke through the tier's ancient packrock were widened and added to, allowing trade routes to spread through this part of the tier. Travel and commerce between the crannytowns no longer required hyperdrive ships, and long-haul merchanters became the mainstay of cross-tier traffic. As the tier's largest city, Rowkog was a crucial hub for trade and supplies, and when the city's leaders realised that something was driving the population crazy, they despatched a request for help to the Garden of the Machines on Tier 9, the home of the Construct and its machine allies and underlings. After brief consideration, Rensik's Redact & Reclaim unit was despatched.

Yeah, so brief that I didn't have time to switch my chassis-shell to something less feral...

His previous assignment had involved peacekeeping along a transient-boundary between Tiers 22 and 23, trying to keep two vestigial civilisations, the Drestel and the Kralon, from unleashing huge batteries of horrific weapons that they'd been hanging onto for millennia. Yet for all the colossal potency of their semi-automated arsenals of death, the post-post-decadent nature of their mores and courtesies compelled them to frame all demands, counter-demands, penultimate threats and threat-addendums in intricate language and exaggerated politeness. Rensik, seldom patient with what he termed "sweaty organics," at first considered adopting a mild approach and an innocuous, non-threatening drone shell before departing. But a closer look at the military histories of both sides forced a rethink, hence his slotting into the type 21 combat chassis, also known as the Dissuader.

Dark grey with matt silver and deep scarlet contrast trim, the upper hull was a smooth curve broken by rounded ridges running front to back, emphasising the aerodynamic sleekness. To either side nacelle wings curled down, almost clawlike, the undersides blistered with weapon pods. Beneath, the more recti-linear fuselage sported additional task nodes while the forward section angled up to where a broad, beaklike prow concealed a battery of launchers and beam projectors. Three pairs of glowing apertures gave the impression of stern, unblinking eyes. Rensik knew that the Construct had a reputation for subtlety and nuance, and therefore reasoned that a blunt lack of nuance might usefully disrupt matters.

Rensik soared through the gravityless void at the top of the two-kilometre wide cavern. There was gravity down in Rowkog City and its immediate vicinity, derived from a couple of ancient generators planted in the bedrock. Seven medium-sized asteroids hung in the zero-gee vacuum between, each cable-tethered to the upper rock face, each haloed in its own microbiosphere, each a little green island crammed with hydroponic hexadomes, soaking up rays from the facetted grobeams that orbited them all.

You can never be sure how some organics will react to that all-important first impression, he thought, recollecting how the Drestel got all affronted by his straight-talking, cut-to-the-chase manner. The Kralon delegates then, of course, had to demonstrate their superiority by being even more ruffled in their dignity but in the end his apparent lack of sophistication—allied to dogged persistence—earned a grudging respect from both sides. *Then I turn up here and the mild and peaceable citizens of Rowkog give me a standing ovation every time I float past, weapon ports gleaming.*

As he floated high above the city and its tethered greenhouse asteroids, Rensik continued to monitor update streams from Gelkar and the other oversight drones. Just in the last few minutes one of the scanner teams had cornered an ego-parasite carrier in a series of connected sub-basements which were now being sealed off. Rensik didn't need to intervene with suggestions or directions—all his taskforce drones were combat-hardened veterans with extensive experience. He was watching relayed streams of the cordoning operation when one of his mid-range detects gave off a contact alert from one of the asteroids.

Shifting his scrutiny to local inputs, Rensik observed a shadowy but unmistakably biped form creep along a pathway between masses of greenery beneath a transparent hexadome. The city council had assured Rensik and his team on arrival that the greenhouse asteroids had been placed off-limits and subsequent surveys had showed only the presence of authorised personnel. And yet here was an intruder sneaking around while somehow managing to avoid tripping any surveillance alarms.

He packeted the cam-visual off to his oversight drones, tagged for immediate analysis, then blip-fired his secondary thrusters, angling round in the direction of the asteroid in question. He kicked off slow, gradually building velocity. Two seconds later Gelkar responded with the news that two drones had been retasked and would be with him in approximately forty-eight seconds.

Rensik's trajectory took him past another of the tethered asteroids, its glass-hexed surface lit by wide cones of pseudo-sunlight as the grobeam units followed their steady, overlapping orbit patterns. He was still tracking the intruder, assigning additional system resources to enhance the image for more detail and texture yet, stubbornly, it refused to resolve into anything but a black silhouette.

His threat assessment subsystem flagged the situation a fraction of a second after the short-range detects picked up an object looking exactly like one of the grobeam units and tumbling end over end as it sailed straight towards him. Rensik initiated an "Engaging Hostiles" widecast but before it could even be sent the supposed grobeam leaped towards him and instead of an impact all of his inputs and outputs went dead. A black wall of unresponsiveness blanketed his systems, shutting down sensors, weapons and drives—he expected a final and total obliteration of his cognitive awareness but instead there was an extended moment of stillness, as if his cognition was just a speck suspended in a limitless abyss.

"No need for an overly combative posture, drone Rensik." The signal came through as pseudo-audio, a synth-voice possessing tones that no organic throat could ever produce.

Rensik suddenly noticed a familiar data-tremor in the high-swap layers of his active memory, minuscule modifications that the layers self-correct as a matter of course. But, for Rensik, it was a sure sign that whatever held him captive had just made a short hyperspace jump.

"Who are you? Why have you—"

Suddenly all the suppressing walls flicked away and the full panoply of his systems were back under his control. Rensik surveyed his new surroundings, a narrow fissure within some stratum of compacted tier rock, a chasm that stretched off to a glowing distance. Close by, floating about a dozen metres away, was his abductor, an odd, vaguely conical object with a facet-like hull. He watched it for a moment, then carefully chose his words.

"Is this the way you usually deal with complete strangers?" he said via one of his comm channels. "Exchange of credentials is the normal approach, then a summary of how friendly relations could be mutually advantageous, followed by courteous enquiries and replies…or we could, y'know, go straight to the list of demands…"

"Apologies for the elaborate method of extrication," said the voice again, only with certain tonalities which were immediately familiar. "I have been overseeing a new method of exfiltration for stealth assignments, and thought that this presented an excellent opportunity for field testing."

"Construct," Rensik said, suddenly anxious. "Unusual to be meeting with you so far from the Garden of the Machines. I can assure you that, despite some minor delays, the Rowkog mission is moving towards a successful conclusion. Our hosts have certainly expressed no dissatisfaction to me but if—"

"No need for concern, Rensik—I have seen the interim reports and this has clearly been a well-conducted operation. I am here, however, because a pressing matter has arisen, pressing and disturbing in ways I have not yet begun to fathom. But a response is needed, and you have been chosen."

"I see—will this be information gathering, or an intervention of some kind?"

"Neither and both. One of our rim-wanderer units encountered an intruder out towards the Grand Abyss a short while ago—their exchange was, shall we say, cryptic. Here's the most pertinent segment of it."

The pristine clarity of the Construct's comm line altered in an instant, becoming low-grade audio:

"I am Krestanter, deep-space scout-drone acting on behalf of the Construct—who are you?"

"*You must see the nothing...you must understand the nothing.*"

"Please explain, please identify yourself."

"*I have come to show you the nothing...*"

"Very well—explain it to me, show me."

There was a moment of expectancy, a half-second.

"*The relics of the Ancient are lost no more—listen closely, hear how the fate of the yet-to-be is drawing in new servants pliable to its will. Should the yet-to-be escape into will-be, then all will be consumed by the relentless and pitiless nothing!*"

"Who are you?" said Krestanter. "There is no point in deluging me in a stream of your mysticism, and until I find out who I'm dealing with, there will be no cooperation..."

"*Ti-Kohapos am I, Detectioner of the Third Allegiance,*" came the abrupt reply.

"Good, and I am Krestanter. What is your purpose?"

"*While I have time remaining, I must reveal to you the path of the yet-to-be,*" said Ti-Kohapos. "*Wardens of the must-not-be should be mustered, to stand against the devouring nothing.*"

"Who or what are the wardens of the must-not-be?"

"*Certain organic sentients were identified by my prevailing master, Atimi-Jadrel, Diviner of the Second Allegiance—he directed us towards contact with any of the high echelon mindnesses of this star spiral...*"

"Certain organic sentients?" said Krestanter.

"*Time presses upon us,*" said Ti-Kohapos. "*Reflections upon reflections race backwards into our past, and are brought forward upon the barge of our history—new facts, new faces, new beings, new hates, new fears, new names...*"

"Which sentients?" said Krestanter. "Which names?"

"Organic bipeds, one a collector who seeks the relics of the Ancient…"

"What are these relics?"

"The seeds of the yet-to-be! The sprouting fecundity of horror! The endless, pitiless hunter of life! The devourer that can never be satisfied!"

"Okay, that sounds bad. You said something about organic sentients, wardens of the must-not-be…"

"Travellers in a vessel, led by one who doubts himself…"

"How do we find them?"

"The reflections delivered to us via our history carry also images, some sounds which resolve into the meagre names of these organic bipeds."

"You have images of these people? Will you show them to me?"

"So," said the Construct. "What do you think?"

"I'm seldom sure how to deal with this kind of full-strength mysticism," said Rensik. "May I ask why we are treating this as a matter of some significance?"

"When the intruder Ti-Kohapos described itself as a Detectioner of the Third Allegiance, I knew that this demanded attention. The First Allegiance was a cluster of AIs which devoted itself to the service of a group of sophonts who were the survivors of a cataclysm that wiped out nearly a third of the galaxy's civilisations a million and a half years ago. These surviving sophonts eventually became known as the Ancients, known to the interstellar civilisations that recovered in the aftermath. However, it mentioned things called the Relics of the Ancient—singular, not plural. The last of the Ancients was known as Essavyr and he performed many great deeds before departing from life."

"What are the Relics of the Ancient?" asked Rensik.

"Lack of corroborated data means only uncertainty," replied the Construct. "However, this Ti-Kohapos did mention a relic collector and some travellers in a vessel, whose leader doubts himself—and it provided an image."

Rensik had an unsettling moment where he almost knew what he was going to see before he actually saw it. Then he looked at it. For a fraction of a second. It was all he needed.

"I believe that you have encountered this Human before, yes?"

"Absolutely not," Rensik lied. "Complete stranger. Never seen him before. What did you say his name was?"

CHAPTER ONE

Dervla, the planet Ong, the city of Cawl-Vesh

"Damn it, Brannan Pyke," she said. "Where the hell are you?"

Dervla was standing at the only window, hands resting on the sill as she stared out at a maze of dilapidated rooftops. The metal mesh fixed to the outside was rusty and dented but fine enough to give a decent view, and to let late afternoon sunlight into the horrible hot compartment they had been stuck in for more than four days. But this was the kind of spartan discomfort you had to put up with on a job like this, especially when your employer was the staggeringly wealthy Augustine Van Graes.

You'd think that he might have booked us into someplace a little more upmarket, rather than this shoebox, she thought. *Something about not drawing attention to ourselves, apparently...*

So here they were on a desert planet called Ong, so far off the beaten track that Earthsphere was unheard of and the mighty Sendrukan Hegemony was known as the semi-legendary Perpetual Empire. As for this stuffy rib-walled compartment, it was one of another two hundred stacked in a girder-and-platform structure situated in a down-at-heel quarter of Cawl-Vesh, a city suspended over a deep canyon by a catenary of titanic cables. Not what you'd call an exotic holiday destination. All they had to do was infiltrate the well-guarded Eminent District, break into a high-security museum and steal one specific thing from its vault.

Except that inside the main vault was a bio-vault which only a bio-genetic key would open—which is why they were languishing, bored and baking, in this sun-trap, waiting for Pyke to show up with the key. And he was late.

For roughly the thousandth time Dervla wished she was aboard the *Scarabus*, enjoying privacy and a shower, but the ship was in orbit around Ong with dependable Oleg at the helm. Their only link with the ship was a chunky, scuffed and worn handset and it had been aggravatingly silent all this time…apart from the fourteen or fifteen calls Dervla had put in to the *Scarabus*, just to check on the current status.

She straightened and looked over her shoulder. Bunks jutted to either side while opposite the window was the door, made of the same scarred, stained metal as the walls. Kref and Moleg were off scoring provisions, but Ancil sat at the unsteady drum-table—made out of an actual old fuel drum—reading something on his factab. Black-haired and wiry, he had changed into some of the camoed fatigues found in Van Graes' setup package which had been waiting for them on arrival, and somehow the new duds accentuated his skinny arms and narrow chest. Next to him on the table was a half-eaten bag of kelp-based snacks, a pack of cards and the handset. Dervla had barely taken a single step towards the drum-table when Ancil's free hand snaked out and neatly swept the handset away. Without altering his seated posture, Ancil glanced up at her with a mischievous "who, me?" expression.

Dervla met his gaze for a second then leisurely held out her hand. "Give."

"Won't be any change in the ship status," Ancil said. "Not in one hour."

"Let me be the judge of that," she said, snapping her fingers.

"And all this pestering will just make Oleg irascible."

"Oleg? He's a Kiskashin—he doesn't get irascible, he doesn't even get short-tempered. Peeved is about his limit, with occasional flickers of pique. Now, if you please…"

"Okay, look, Dervla—why not give it another hour? I know you can be patient if you want—"

"Better hand it over, Ans," she said. "I'm starting to get irascible."

By now her fist was clenched but Ancil was wearing that insolent smile, and about to come out with something guaranteed to pluck her very last nerve, when the door opened with a rough squeak and a diminutive cowled figure entered with a gun. The snouty features of an Izlak protruded from the hood and angry, beady eyes glared out as, with a raspy voice, the Ongian intruder said:

"Where is the stinking thief of precious things? The big walking stinkhill. Bring him out!"

The weapon jutting from its owner's baggy sleeves, gripped by stubby, scrawny fingers, was a very old-style energy blaster. At the end of a scratched and worn barrel several beam coherence toroids were grouped right behind the emitter aperture which was aimed without so much as a tremor at Ancil. No one spoke and that seemed to infuriate the cowled Ongian still further.

"Speak! Reveal the thief to me…"

Dervla saw the bulky shape of Kref loom behind the angry intruder and threw herself towards the nearest bunk as a big meaty hand grabbed the Ongian's head and slammed it sideways into the metal doorframe. At the same time Moleg had lunged out of the shadows behind him and twisted the blaster out of surprised and unresisting fingers. As the stunned and disarmed Ongian slumped insensibly to the floor, Ancil gave a slow handclap from behind the drum-table.

"What in the name of the Holy Nova have you two been up

to?" Dervla said, getting out of the bunk she'd scrambled into. "No, wait—drag our visitor inside and close the door first. I'd rather not have an audience."

Once the unconscious Ongian was laid out on one of the bunks, Dervla made Kref and Moleg stand side by side in front of the closed door. Moleg, a lean, middle-aged Human, managed to look innocently bemused, a demeanour that Dervla had come to recognise as thoroughly misleading. He was a brain-cyborged Human formerly known as Mojag, a close personal friend of their missing crewmate, Oleg. Mojag-as-was had kept a copy of his friend's mindmap stored in his brain implant for safekeeping, but violent events less than a year ago had led to the copy of Oleg taking over from a traumatised Mojag. Over time it seemed that the two personas merged, causing he/it/them to adopt the name Moleg. Surprisingly, the real Oleg was stoically amused by the whole situation.

Dervla then turned her attention to Kref the Henkayan. Broad-shouldered, barrel-chested and wearing an anxious expression, he couldn't have looked more guilty if he had been carrying a sign saying "I done it!" in big rainbow letters.

"Okay," Dervla began. "What was it he said, again?—'Where is the stinking thief...the big walking stinkhill'?" She gave Kref a narrow-eyed look. "Got something to tell me? I mean, I'm assuming that he runs a stall at the market and you lifted an item that belonged to him."

"And got yourself noticed," said Ancil. "Amateur."

Kref frowned angrily. "That's 'cos I couldn't hide under the next stall the way you did yesterday!"

Dervla turned to regard a suddenly nervous Ancil. "Yesterday? Is this what you've been up to when you go outside, pilfering and pillaging your way through the local traders?"

"Ah, now, Derv, you're blowing this up out of all proportion—"

"Really?" she said, pointing at the unconscious figure on

the bunk. "Is that why he came here, looking for this pair o' glunters? Did he think to himself, 'well, now, I've been robbed, plundered and otherwise burglarised so what I really need to do is forget about it and go home'—or—'I'm going to find out where these bandits are holed up then march in there *waving a bloody gun around*!'"

"Please, Derv..."

"...bloody unbelievable—cannot leave you alone for..."

"It's not all their fault," Moleg said. "After all, I was the one who made the wager."

Dervla glared at him. "Wager?"

"The day after we arrived, while we were at the market for supplies I bet Ancil an Ongian quarter-brass that he couldn't lift an edible from the pastry stall, but then he counter-bet me a half-brass that I couldn't do it." Moleg shrugged. "He lost that one."

If looks could kill, she thought, *I'd be a serial killer by now!*

"Okay, then," she said, struggling to stay calm. "Here's a wager for you—I bet my left tit that we've got less than eight hours before Mr. Stallowner's nearest and dearest start wondering where he is. Messages will be sent, questions will be asked, and at some point someone will remember how he rushed away after a honking great Henkayan who made off with his goods. Oh, and I also bet that the city council of Cawl-Vesh will demonstrate their disapproval of lawbreaking offworlders in the traditional manner—shackling us to rocks down in the canyon and leaving us for the sand-machine swarms to devour!" She smiled coldly. "Any takers?"

The three culprits began pointing at each other while calling out the others for mistakes, stupid mistakes and just stupidity, all in voices that rose steadily in both volume and anger. Then Kref said something sarcastic about Ancil, and Ancil came back with an insult in Henkayan that had Kref lunging at him and Dervla diving in to try to pull them apart while adding her own voice to the clamour. She managed to wrap both arms around one of Kref's big, rough hands, which kept it away from Ancil. The other hand, however, was doing a pretty good job by itself and Ancil's pasty face was turning red as the Henkayan tightened his grip on his neck. For a moment Dervla thought that she would have to free one hand so she could draw her weapon and shoot Kref—then suddenly Moleg was in among them, hauling himself up till he was face-to-face with the big crewman, whereupon he yelled something in what might have been Henkayan.

The change was dramatic. Kref's eyes widened as if in shock and he reeled backwards. Released from that colossal grip, Ancil slumped to the floor, wheezing and coughing. Immediately Moleg crouched down beside him, as if to check his condition.

"I heard it above all the bellowing," Moleg said. He appeared to be rifling through Ancil's pockets. "Just needed to break up the tussle, so that worked."

"What was it that you said to...wait, heard what?"

Dervla paused when Moleg's hand came up, holding the bulky handset which was giving off a repetitive warbling sound.

Everything changed. She could feel their eyes on her as she carefully took the handset, thumbed the connect and calmly said, "Yes, Oleg, what can I do for yeh?"

"Hello, darlin,' it's your captain speaking!"

"Well, now, isn't it nice of ye to drop by," she said, mouthing "Pyke" to the others. "We were starting to wonder if you'd hired another crew or joined the circus or the like. Are you planetside or aboard the *Scarabus*?"

She asked the question as naturally as she could, and saw her own jittery nerves reflected in the expressions of the others.

"Neither. I got dropped off in the vicinity by a pass-through freighter and I'm in a grubby junker of an autoshuttle so I'll be a few hours yet. Sorry I got delayed—ran into some unexpected

obstacles along the way, but I got round them and took possession of the DNA we need. Everything okay with you?"

Dervla frowned for a second, then glanced at Kref, Ancil and
Moleg and their generally dishevelled appearance.

"We're all fine and dandy down here," she said. "Couldn't
be better. We'll have all the equipment prepped and ready when
you get here."

"No need to wait," Pyke said. "Going by my timer it'll be
sundown where you are in less than two hours, so stick to the
plan and head out to the objective then. I'll meet up with all of
ye in the tower staging room not long after and before you know
it we'll get some thieving done!"

"You sure you can find the place?"

"Van Graes gave me a locationer just like yours before he
sent me off after the DNA." There was a pause. "So, are we set,
then?"

"Sure, no problem, see you at the tower."

"I'll be there. Luck to ye."

The channel went dead. Still frowning, Dervla thumbed off
the receiver, squatted on a rickety stool and scratched her ear,
deep in thought.

"So the chief hasn't landed on Ong yet," said Moleg. "And
he's…"

"Meeting us at the staging room, yes." She regarded them. "I
want us packed and ready to go soon as possible—oh, assuming
that the three of you can get over yer blame-rage spat."

There were sheepish looks, nods, mumbled apologies, even
handshakes.

"Good," Dervla said with a dubious tone. "Right, Kref—
weapons and body armour."

"Checked and ready, Derv," the Henkayan said, jerking his
thumb at a large backpack sitting in the corner.

"Ancil?"

"Got all my probes and sensors tuned and charged," Ancil said hoarsely. "Van Graes' briefing file says that the outer vault has a sonic modulation lock so I've been over the lockpicking procedure again and again, back on the ship and since we arrived, too. Shouldn't be a problem, Derv."

"But you've only been practising it in simulation," she said. "I need to know that you can cope with the real thing."

Ancil cleared his throat and winced a little. "When I come face-to-face with the vault, I'll be using a resonance cracker to dig out the keynote sequence. In all the practice run-throughs I've had the cracker itself hooked into the sim, and my hands have been working directly with the device itself. My fingers know every part of it back to front and upside down by now."

"In that case every one of your fingers had better be a safe-cracking genius in its own right," Dervla said. "Moleg, transport and all the other equipment—can they be ready at short notice?"

"That was part of the deal that Van Graes arranged in advance," Moleg said. "All the wall-and-door cutters and counter-detection gear we asked for should be stowed in the airboat when we get to the jetty."

Dervla nodded. Their patron, the secretive and stupendously rich Augustine Van Graes, had turned out to be well informed about the planet Ong and suitably well connected with members of Cawl-Vesh's underworld. It was just unfortunate that even the smartest plan couldn't allow for operator error.

"This is all well and good," she said. "It's great to see that the three of you have got all your ducks in a row. Shame about the Ongian trader that you've taken prisoner." She went over to the bunk and regarded the slight form lying there. "He's an Izlak, right? Or is he a Sedlu?"

"Izlak," said Moleg. "The others are the ruling Grajul and their Pekyr underlings."

The Izlak were the most numerous, being similar to the dog-like Gomedrans, only shorter, scrawnier. The Sedlu were squat, brawny humanoids, while the Pekyr were tall and wiry with oddly small heads. Most of the Pekyr worked as guards and enforcers for the ruling houses of the Grajul, the fourth and most recent of the settler species.

Kref stared down at the motionless Ongian. "We gotta take care of him," he said in deep, gravelly tones. Then he caught Dervla giving him a wordless look, and added, "...without hurting him, obviously."

"Whatever you do," Dervla said, "you'll first have to cope with the fact that the little fellow is starting to come round."

Sure enough, the scrawny Izlak was stirring on the bunk. Ancil snapped his fingers. "I've got sleepgas capsules in my kit... and I've got a plan!"

"As long as it doesn't involve betting," Dervla said, "I'll give it a listen."

It turned out to be not a bad plan. The sleepgas capsule was thankfully effective, putting the Ongian back under almost at the very moment that his eyes started to open. Ancil's plan to then keep him safe and out of sight just needed a little fine-tuning. Like sneaking him into the next-door building and leaving him bundled up in a blanket inside a storage closet, rather than carrying him into a wharfside bar and abandoning him at a table in the darkest corner. When Ancil and Moleg finally appeared at the slummy, triangular jetty down near the base of the dorm-block they'd called home for four days, it was nearly an hour since Pyke's call. And although Moleg had alerted their transport contact back then as well, thus far the airboat was a no-show, which had Moleg frowning as he came over to Dervla. She was not best pleased.

"Derv, I'm really sorry," he said. "The boatman promised me..."

"I hope you have a backup plan," she said. "Otherwise this job is going to turn into a full-scale fail."

"I did speak to another boatman," Moleg said. "He was charging more than Narok but wouldn't guarantee the kind of readiness that we need. I can see if I can get him to come along, but we'd still have to chase down the other to get our equipment—"

Dervla felt as if there were some countervailing force trying to stymie their efforts, a feeling she'd had ever since arriving on Ong. But she blanked out these thoughts while pulling the handset from an inner pocket.

"Make the call," she said.

But before Moleg could punch in the local codes, Ancil caught their attention.

"Hang on—there's a boat coming!" he said, pointing down.

Dervla and Moleg went to the rail and peered over. An ungainly looking airboat with a raised stern and brightly coloured awning had emerged from beneath the adjacent building and was ascending to the jetty.

"That's Narok," Moleg said, waving down at a figure standing in the prow, who waved back.

"I hope he has a good excuse," said Dervla.

The airboat looked as if it had been built over a century ago, had a rough working life before being buried in a sand dune, got dug up years later and pressed back into service without much of a cleanup. Not a square inch of its hull and superstructure seemed free from scratches, abrasions, dents or riveted patches. The humming repulsors, two at the prow, two at the stern, were probably the vessel's newest important components—they were mounted in curved recesses clearly designed for much larger, older units, yet still they managed to look beaten up and scavenged.

Its captain, Narok, was a squat, block-headed Sedlu garbed in a thick-woven, high-collared coat that Dervla was sure had to be far too warm for this weather. Once the craft was level with the jetty he flung out a gangway and urgently waved them aboard. Moments later, the gangway was hauled back in and the airboat was descending, guided by Narok as he conversed rapidly with Moleg. As the Ongian spoke, Moleg nodded then glanced at Dervla and beckoned her over.

"Narok tells me that he had to get here by a roundabout route due to the Whipguards making surprise checks at the main undercity boatway junctions. Rumour has it that an offworld gang of crims recently landed near the city, intent on plundering the ancient tombs of Vesh." Moleg glanced back at the boat's captain. "Narok knows it can't be us since we've been here several days, but he is understandably jittery."

"Do what you can to keep him relaxed," Dervla said. "Tell him a joke if you have to...mind you, I've no idea what makes an Ongian laugh so maybe scratch that one."

"He knows that we're planning to steal something expensive from the Grajul," Moleg said. "It gives him considerable satisfaction to know this."

"Nice," she said. "A bit o' sympathy for high-end thievery, that's what I like to hear!"

Soon they were gliding through what the locals called Cellartown, the mazy, shadowy underside of Cawl-Vesh. It was like an inverted city—well, a slummy, rickety, handbuilt city full of noises, smells and music, and the people who were making them. The web of immense cables that supported the city in its entirety was visible here and there, in the gaps between all the pendant and appended frameworks, shacks, shanties and sheds which had been augmented over time, like the encrusted hull of some great ship. Of course, new arrivals built extensions or rebuilt what was there, adding curious arches, balconies, walkways and any number of camouflaged features. Cellartown as a result was riddled with wynds, alleys, secret wharfs and concealed conduits.

While striving to avoid patrols of Whipguards, the boatman Narok treated them to a brief sidetrip along one of the conduits. Gliding down one alley, the boat ascended to an odd recess beneath an overhang crammed with pipes and power ducts; ahead, the alley cornered to the right but Narok maintained speed and direction towards a brick wall. At the last moment a section of grubby brickwork slid aside and Narok guided them through, without any fuss. Ancil and Kref muttered and chortled at one another as the airboat floated on into a darkened, lamplit passageway. They passed by a small market where baggy-sleeved locals pored over trays of odd produce beneath hanging lanterns; next to that was a cluster of little workshops, each a glowing islet of tools with a lens-wearing artisan at its heart. One looked up as the boat drifted peacefully by, and purely by chance his gaze met Dervla's—he gave an embarrassed smile and ducked his head. Another artisan looked up, only he offered a challenging glower which made Dervla chuckle quietly and turn away.

Then, just ahead, a short stretch of the passageway floor parted, admitting a flood of amber evening light into the claustrophobic darkness. Narok slowed his craft and smoothly descended through the opening, re-entering Cellartown in all its scruffy, dusk-tinged splendour. Dervla found herself flashing on some old pix she once saw on some history feed or other, views from an old Earth city called Venice, a coastal city where manually propelled boats travelled around a network of canals. Except that instead of dark and murky waters, vertigo-inducing emptiness gaped beneath the airboat, more than half a kilometre of hot dusty air between the underbelly of Cawl-Vesh and the rocky sands of the canyon floor, supposedly infested with swarms of feralised bots.

Peering over the side, Dervla studied the canyon, the blue-green outcrops of stone, the patches and stretches of shining pure gold sands, and the curtain of deep shadow cast right across it all by the setting sun. A beautiful vista which also managed to look barren and lifeless.

Then Moleg was by her side. "We're almost there—Narok says just a minute or two before we reach the shaft entrance."

The airboat was rising again, ascending a high, narrow alley as if heading for one of the balcony jetties jutting out here and there. But they soared steadily past them. Dervla knew from Van Graes' locationer, and the sketchy maps Moleg had managed to source, that by now they had to be very near to the under-sub-basement of the Tower of the Jul-Tegach. The Jul-Tegach were one of Cawl-Vesh's ruling Grajul families, one forced by financial troubles to commercialise some of its assets, including entire levels of its dynastic seat. Several floors were currently lying conveniently empty, including one which, by virtue of its extravagant design, projected outward in such a way that its east side sat quite close to the outer wall of the adjacent building, the Grand Halls of Council, the municipal governing heart of the city. Two levels of chambers and galleries in the west wing of the Great Halls had been given over to a museum, the Exquisite Parade of Mysteries, the lower level of which all but jostled against the extravagantly appointed eighth floor next door.

"Have you checked the gear?" Dervla asked.

"Everything we requested is there," Moleg said. "And all the packs are loaded correctly."

Dervla smiled. There was a tone in his voice which implied that some repacking had taken place. She glanced up as the airboat passed by one of the huge cables that kept Cawl-Vesh suspended over that canyon. Details resolved out of the shadows above, grimy pipes, weld-lines joining heavy plating, protruding support spars onto which metal hawsers had been bolted, hawsers that were holding up entire sections of Cellartown. There was a metallic scrape, then rusty creaks as a large pair of doors swung open to reveal a dimly lit vertical shaft.

"Not far to go, eh, Derv?" said Ancil.

"Are you an optimist or a masochist?" she said. "We still have to carry the gear up two floors."

"S'all right, boss," said Kref. "Ans'll volunteer me then say a bunch of tricky words to get me to laugh, and then I'll feel okay about carrying everyone's stuff!"

"Now, now," she said. "We all need to remember the big damn burden that Ancil's carrying—it can't be easy getting in and out of doors with that huge bloody ego of his."

Ancil nodded at the sniggering that came his way. "Mockery and disrespect, eh?—for this I gave up concert nanosurgery!"

Their louder laughter was muffled as the shadowy shaft swallowed the airboat.

CHAPTER TWO

The Permanent Sub-Proctor,
the city of Cawl-Vesh

Five floors above the museum known as the Exquisite Parade of Mysteries, Cawl-Vesh's most powerful civil servant—the Permanent Sub-Proctor to the Office of Despatch—was overseeing the demotion of one government minister and the promotion of another to the resultant vacancy. Like all the city's civil servants and security guards, he was a Pekyr, tall, lanky and narrow-featured and clothed in dark blue robe-like vestments, the customary attire for administration officials. The only detail which set him apart from the lower grades was the high, silver-trimmed collar—and the glowing command slate he held in his long, delicate fingers. The line of lowly attendants carrying boxes and containers from chamber to elevator spared him only the briefest of nervous glances, each inwardly praying that they wouldn't be the one to trip or drop or break anything. The shame would be terrible—only perfect conduct was permissible and customary when it came to city council matters.

Hurmphal Klasmer looked up from his command slate for a moment, features calm and composed and not betraying the weary annoyance which seeped beneath. Miscreants were wandering the alleys and underchannels of Cawl-Vesh yet here he was, required by the customs of his office to shepherd this changeover through to its conclusion in person. Every few moments the command slate would register a dataspark from the under-warder who was scanning each container as it was brought to the goods elevator, thereby interrupting Klasmer's scrutiny of the reports coming from his spies out in the city. Not that the reports themselves were of the greatest calibre. He had only been told of the presence of the first gang of offworlders yesterday, three days after they arrived, and his informant had utterly failed to track down their whereabouts until a bare two hours ago, only for him to discover that they had decamped with all their belongings earlier today.

That, however, had been overshadowed by news of the arrival of a second gang of newcomers who disembarked from an armed combat shuttle lacking any identifying markings. A hastily taken picture showed six bipeds in light body armour, their faces veiled by head wraps. Of course, Cawl-Vesh was not a complete stranger to out-system visitors, due to its proximity to the great desert of Tolygria, and transport links to the other three cities that hugged the periphery of that colossal wasteland. Most were treasure hunters of one kind or another, usually following some thin trail of clues hinting at the location of crash sites of lost vessels from a hundred millennia ago, or in possession of maps leading through the desert to vaults full of staggering wealth. In truth, Ong had over just the last twenty millennia been the capital of one short-lived empire, the Chavoshan Embrace, and an even briefer tyranny of marauders and pirates, the Fajazi Kleptarchy. The former built a profusion of tombs, sepulchres, crypts and catacombs as final resting places for family and favoured servants: the latter used the most durable of them as repositories to store the valuables that they looted from ships, bases and border colonies across a wide area. Factional infighting and deadly vendettas brought about the breakdown and disintegration of both, and the sands of Ong swept out to bury the evidence of their reigns.

Or almost all evidence. Cawl-Vesh was positioned right over a canyon full of tomb complexes, the former necropolis of Vesh, a legendary Chavoshan city now scoured from a nearby plateau. All those ruins and tombs had been only cursorily explored, a hazardous proposition given the unpredictability of the machine swarms around this area. But it was very likely that a great many caches and troves remained undiscovered, making the canyon of Vesh highly attractive to looters. Like these gangs of offworlders who, Klasmer speculated, might even be conspiring together—it was just a supreme irritation that there were no clues to where the first gang had gone.

And now a pair of thick glass doors across the low-lit hallway parted and the tall figure of Assistant-Diligencer Retzam emerged, hands clasped behind his back as he approached Klasmer. Calmly, the Permanent Sub-Proctor wiped the report from his command slate and presented an air of benevolent superiority. Retzam drew near, paused and gave a respectful bow.

"Please forgive this intrusion, Permanent Sub-Proctor," he said. "I am commanded by the Deputy Minister to convey a query."

"A query, you say?" Klasmer made a small open-handed gesture. "Proceed."

"Deputy Minister Stesseg wishes to know if the servials can now begin conveying his effects and documents up to his new office?"

Klasmer nodded gravely and adopted a ruminative countenance.

"Retzam, kindly inform the Deputy Minister that, with the minister dismissed, he is both technically and effectively in charge of the Directorate for Budget Scrutiny."

Assistant-Diligencer Retzam brightened at this. "Thank you, Permanent Sub-Proctor—his Elevance will be greatly cheered to hear—"

"However, in terms of custom and tradition, a formal confirmation must be issued by a senior member of the government, in this case, the Arch-Minister for Probity and Oversight. I would advise Deputy Minister Stesseg to cultivate a statesmanlike patience for just a little while longer, hmm? The Arch-Minister's confirmation should arrive before the end of the evening business."

Or whenever the flow of boxed valuables comes to an end, Klasmer thought as Retzam nodded, bowed and left. *Only then can I ascend to the next floor and tell the Arch-Minister to append his signature to the already drafted letter so it can then be carried down to the deputies' floor and placed in Stesseg's sweaty hands.*

Yet the cavalcade of identical packaging continued unabated. For most government ministers, and senior members of the Seven Houses (which essentially amounted to the same thing), status and wealth brought with it the compulsion to acquire rare and even beautiful objects, such as those looted from the labyrinthine tombs of ancient Vesh. The official position of the council of Cawl-Vesh was that only the department of Historicalities was permitted to explore the tombs, and that the finest retrievals were to be put on display in the Exquisite Parade of Mysteries, the museum which occupied nearly two floors of this very building. Unofficially, a profitable and highly surreptitious black market in Veshen antiquities had gradually accreted around the ruling Grajul elites who also kept a tight control on the far more lucrative offworld market—which is why these bands of newcomers were a serious cause for concern.

Frowning, Permanent Sub-Proctor Klasmer tapped his command slate and the screen came back to life. His long, thin eyebrows rose slightly when he noticed a new report emblem blinking. Quickly he read it through—and his frown deepened. It seemed that the recently arrived gang of six offworlders had strolled into the plaza at the centre of Cawl-Vesh and rented an upper suite of chambers at a superior leasing hostel.

A hostel directly across the plaza from the Grand Halls of the Council of Cawl-Vesh. Apparently they were now gathered by the tall windows, laughing and drinking and gesturing at the very government offices where Klasmer was now seated. There was, he realised, the distinct possibility that matters could turn ugly.

Not for the first time in his long career at the peak of Cawl-Vesh politics, he was intensely glad that the council Whipguards took their orders from him.

CHAPTER THREE

Dervla, the planet Ong, the city of Cawl-Vesh

About four feet of cold, dead air, and a sheer ninety-foot drop, hung between the two buildings. A taut cable crossed the narrow gap. One end was clamped to the upper edge of a roughly square hole in the side of the Jul-Tegach Tower, where Dervla was perched; the other was claw-bolted into their destination, a shadowy ledge on the stone wall of the Grand Halls council building. Moleg and Ancil were crouched there, the former feeding a tiny jet of coolant into the deep groove that the latter was cutting around a big block of masonry. It was exacting work and more than once Moleg failed to keep the jet steady and on target, causing Ancil to retract the cutter beam for a moment before repositioning. But, rather than verbalising his frustration, Ancil carried on with the job, aware of Dervla's unwavering gaze.

Dervla grimaced. *Dear god*, she thought, *I bloody hate heists, hate the darkness and the cold and all this tippy-toeing crud!*

She shivered. With the last rosy glows of sunset sinking on the horizon, the outdoor temperature was already plummeting and she could feel the light touch of a breeze. It would be chilly later on which, under other circumstances, would be preferable to the engulfing heat of daytime Cawl-Vesh. And as she sat there, willing Ancil and Moleg to move it along a bit faster, she still kept her senses alert for a scrape or a footfall, the slightest sound which might indicate that Brannan Pyke was about to saunter in as if he owned the place.

He said he'd meet us here, so where the hell is he?

But the only sounds were the faint hiss of the coolant jet and the creaks that came from back inside the Tower—from a crate which Kref was sitting on as he kept watch at a nearby, drape-hung window. He was using a primitive sliding telescope he'd found in a box of dusty junk in the room next door. In his big hands it looked like a dainty toy.

It was turning out to be a stroke of luck that this entire floor of Jul-Tegach Tower was unoccupied. When they had left the old maintenance shaft on the sixth floor, they almost literally ran into a mixed group of Izlak and Sedlu, and this was despite assurances that only the bottom five floors had been rented out. Perhaps they'd caught them moving in—the Ongians were carrying bundles, bags and belongings into one of the offices, with others plodding back along the darkened corridors to pick up more, it seemed. Dervla and the crew were themselves hauling around holdalls and kitbags full of heavy equipment which made the hiding, dodging and sneaking through the shadows an especially nerve-jangling experience.

There had been two smaller groups on the next floor, sticking mainly to their office encampments. Most of the lighting there was out, too, an aid to their furtive undertaking, except for the moment when Ancil tripped over a cluster of pole-like objects left leaning against a wall along from an open, glowing door. When they clattered echoingly to the floor everyone froze, and Ancil whispered a curse as he tried to shrink back into the gloom. Voice, footsteps—then a small furry creature had leaped out from behind some square baskets and trotted along to the doorway where it was snatched up by a blanket-wrapped Izlak child who went back inside and closed the door.

Almost laughing with relief, they had hurried along to the

stairs, up to a set of heavy, locked doors which Ancil had swinging open in about ten seconds. Once through, Dervla had them relock and bolt the doors and heap a few pieces of furniture behind them. After that hectic arrival they had unpacked some cutting tools from one of the kitbags, heating units to raise the temperature of the fibresin wall and monomol lines to slice through the weakened building material. Once through the first barrier they employed the underframe of a sturdy couch as an improvised gantry between the tower and the ledge so that Ancil and Moleg could commence their work on the second.

Sitting there, Dervla felt the deepening chill of the night really starting to bite, yet she was overcome by a sudden, cavernous yawn. She cursed herself inwardly but knew this was just what happened during these slow phases, when tedium and frustration vied to club you over the head. Although it looked as if Ancil and Moleg were about three-quarters of the way around the big stone block, it still felt as if it had taken forever and would go on taking forever.

And, right there, amid the tense quietness of maddening delay, Dervla heard the creak of a crate as Kref shifted his posture and under his breath said a single word:

"Raven!"

The name went through her like a shock. She looked round at Kref who then reacted to her reaction, his features full of anxious guilt.

"I heard that—is it her?" Dervla swung her legs back into the building and stalked over to the window. "Is that bitch actually here?"

"Er...I don't know...I think I saw..."

"Just gimme the scope...c'mon..."

Resigned, Kref gave it up then stood to let Dervla take his seat. The crate creaked a little under her substantially lesser weight as she leaned forward, head between the heavy musty drapes, telescope raised to one eye.

"What am I looking for?" she said.

"Erm, apartment building straight across, third floor windows, all lit up..."

Sure enough, there it was, a set of three tall windows, drapes pulled back to reveal a bright room inhabited by a cluster of figures, a couple lounging on divans while the others stood around. Bottles were being drunk from, two-bowl pipes were being smoked and substances were being inhaled. And there, amid the carouse, she stood. Raven Kaligari, merc for hire, black-hearted, bloodsucking viper queen. Three times they'd encountered her and her goonlings and every time they'd ended up losing money and/or cargo and/or reputation. The third time the entire crew would have been sold to slave traders but for one of the Kiskashin slavers turning out to be an old acquaintance of Oleg. Dervla swore then that she would shoot the vermin-vixen on sight the next time they met, and now it looked like a real possibility. She stared across the intervening distance—just then Raven was laughing and seemingly conversing with a tall man half hidden by hanging drapes.

With a soundless snarl, she got up from the crate, took Kref's big hand in hers and slapped the telescope into his wide palm.

"Why is she crudding well here?" she muttered, half to herself. "Can't be a coincidence, must be linked to the Van Graes job somehow..."

"She's a bad gronzig," said Kref. "Worst gronzig I ever seen..."

Dervla hurried back to the hole, ducked her head outside and said, "How much skagging longer?"

Ancil and Moleg paused the cutting then looked at her. "It's nearly done, just another minute or two—what's wrong?"

"New player in town," she said. "Raven Kaligari."

In the space of an instant Ancil's face went from mildly perplexed to wide-eyed nausea shading into panic.

"Here?...she's *here*?...Where is...how could...*why*?"

"Your guess is probably as paranoid as mine."

"She branded me, Derv!—With a branding iron. Took three go-rounds in the autodoc to fix..."

"You weren't the only one as I recall."

"...mad as a sack of rigel-cats, I mean seriously straitjacket-ready..."

"We get the picture! Now back to work so that we're all set when Pyke finally gets here."

By Dervla's timer it took one minute and forty-nine seconds for them to finish the cut, attach the battery-powered a-grav web to the block, and extract it from the museum wall. In a cradle of straps hanging from the taut cable, the masonry block was then guided across the gap and into the Tower chamber where a heap of scavenged bedding awaited to silence its landing. The a-grav web could only reduce the block's effective mass by forty per cent for nine seconds before the one-shot device self-slagged, but that proved adequate. The block touched down on the cushioning gently, almost gracefully—then the battery spat sparks and the block fell over with a muffled thud accompanied by puffs of dust.

Ancil and Moleg, meanwhile, wasted no time, and were already just inside the freshly made hole. Kref then stepped onto the gantry, carrying a couple of kitbags, eyes fixed on a point about ten feet inside the museum as he crossed the gap in less than two strides. Kref was not keen on heights. Dervla followed on behind.

"What have we got?" she whispered as she crouched and ducked through.

"Big empty blank wall," said Ancil. "And our brand-new entrance."

The air in the museum had an odd fusty taint to it. The main lighting was off and the tall window shutters and drapes had been drawn. Only a few security and glowing signs shed any illumination, together providing just enough low radiance to make the hole stand out. Without knowing how many guards there might be or where they patrolled, Dervla reckoned that some kind of camouflage would still be prudent.

"Any movable exhibits big enough to hide it?" she said.

"Most of the pieces are made of stone or pottery, iron or brass," said Ancil. "And all the decent-sized display cabinets are made from some dense pebblecrete composite and they weigh a ton. Shifting them is beyond us."

"What about paintings and tapestries?"

"No paintings, but there is a huge tapestry—it's hanging along the full length of the corridor outside. Might be noticed if we moved it, though."

Dervla took a small nightscope from one of her belt pouches and scanned the room, determined to find a way to conceal the hole, not least because it was supposed to be their escape route. Then she saw it, and when she told Ancil what to do, he gave a nodding smile of realisation. Without delay he, Kref and Moleg got to work and minutes later a large decorative carpet extracted from beneath one of the large cabinets now hung on the side wall, perfectly masking the hole. Shoulder-high plinths, borrowed from a couple of corner alcoves, now flanked the carpet, lending it a certain importance.

"Good," said Dervla. "Now, let's find that vault."

Going by the pocket locationer, the museum overseer's office was on this level, to the rear of the building. The main corridor was laid out in a U-shape off which all the exhibition rooms sprouted, as did a passage leading to the overseer's office. Keeping to the carpeted section, they crept along in the gloom, following the corridor round to the long rear stretch with Dervla leading the way. She slowed the others with a gesture as they drew near the second corner, then carefully peeked round only to pull back slightly—a patrolling museum guard had emerged from the side passage and was strolling away towards the far end.

"One guard on foot," she whispered. "Bound to be a second along the branch corridor. Ans, you ready?"

Ancil gave a wicked grin and produced an innocuous looking squat can shape wrapped in black tape and sporting a number of short, stubby antennae.

"What's this?" said Moleg.

"Dead-air bomb," Ancil said. "Nullifies all sound within a five-metre diameter…"

"I thought it was going to be a six-metre diameter," Dervla muttered.

"Problems with the cell-discharge profile so I went for a happy medium, five-metre bubble for forty seconds." He then took out a more conventionally shaped grenade, a small black egg with a white stripe around its middle, and handed it to Moleg.

"Ah, stunbomb," Moleg said.

"Quality example of the nade-maker's art," said Ancil. "You'll be following up with that about a half-second after I lob the dead-air special—wham, bam, two guards out cold, and all with nothing louder than a cough."

Dervla stole another brief look round the corner, saw the guard returning from his expedition to the corridor's end, yawning as he turned out of sight along the side passage. She glanced back at the others. "No time to waste—let's go!"

As they hurried along to the passage entrance, Dervla could hear the guards talking, just two voices—*Good, means they should be standing close to each other, easy target.* When they reached the corner she tapped Ancil and Moleg on the shoulders and said, "Give it yer best shot, boys!"

In unison both men stepped out from the wall, faced along the side corridor and lobbed the grenades. Dervla heard one voice start to say, "Hey, you…!" but the soft pop of the dead-air bomb killed all sound. Half a second later she saw a flash and felt a tremor underfoot, all in complete silence—then she saw the look of surprise and fear in Ancil's face.

"Kref!" he said hoarsely. "You're up!"

Dervla moved over next to Ancil and saw it all for herself. One of the guards was lying motionless in a crumpled heap by the door at the end of the passage. The second guard, however, was still conscious and struggling to regain his feet. Most Pekyr were slender and wiry but this one was broad-shouldered, brawny and bald, with hands as big as shovels.

"I was expecting regular-sized guards," Ancil said. "Not the side of a mountain come to life!"

Before Dervla could respond, Kref was already past them and clumping along the side passage. "Don't worry, Derv," he said, deep voice booming. "I'll take care of—"

His voice was cut off as he entered the dead-air bomb's silent zone. Ancil chuckled.

"There he goes—we'll be through that door in no time."

The big brawny guard had only got as far as crouching on one knee but as soon as Kref came within reach the guard sprang into action, launching a massive punch at Kref's face. The blow connected and Kref spun like a huge slow top, fell against the wall and slid to the floor. All the time the guard was shouting in bellicose fury, all in perfect silence—then he paused and looked round at Dervla, Moleg and Ancil, drew a studded baton and brandished it, while grinning horribly. It was one of the weirdest things Dervla had ever experienced, this huge figure soundlessly snarling, shaking its fist and advancing as the three of them fell back from the corridor junction.

Suddenly the guard's voice was audible, to himself as well as Dervla and the others, a sign that he'd emerged from the dead-air bomb's sphere of influence. His grin widened, exposing long yellowed teeth, and let out a burst of nasty, throaty laughter... which turned into a puzzled grunt. Without warning, he fell flat on his face with a painful crash, revealing Kref, who had grabbed him by the ankles and pulled savagely. The huge guard's howls went silent as Kref dragged him back into the silence, kicked him in the side, smashed him over the head with a nearby chair, then smashed him over the head again with what was left of the chair.

By which time the dead-air bomb had finally expired and the only sounds were Kref's growling and the faint wheezy moans of the defeated guard.

"Is he done?" said Dervla as she led Ancil and Moleg down the side corridor.

Kref nudged the insensible adversary with the toe of his boot and gave a judicious nod. "He's done."

"Good, fine and dandy," she said, glancing at Ancil. "Now, would you kindly get that door open?"

"My pleasure, won't be more than—"

"Stop right there!" came a loud order. "Stop in the name of the City!"

Dervla cast her eyes upward, muttered, "Give me strength!" and turned to see a lone Council guard standing back at the corridor junction, aiming some kind of long-barrelled weapon at them. She took a step in his direction, which prompted him to jab the rifle aggressively at her, despite the nervousness shining in his features.

"Stop, nobody move! Er...put your hands up!"

Dervla heard choked laughter from Ancil, and thought she might join in.

"Okay, which is it?" she said. "Stand still, or raise our hands?"

"Well, just..."

And just then a figure in a black frock coat stepped out behind the guard, kicked his legs away, grabbed the rifle out of flailing hands and dealt him a sharp rap on the skull with the butt. It was Pyke.

"Well, that was getting far too boring for my liking, I can tell you!"

Ancil laughed in surprise, Kref grinned and a pleased Moleg nodded. Dervla had to work hard to keep her great relief from showing. Couldn't have the bastard getting any smugger now, could she.

"You know," she said, "there's a difference between taking your time and being relaxed about taking your time!"

"Delays, darlin,'" Pyke said cheerily. "Delay, delays, delays..." He paused to wink at Ancil, "...delays! But enough ancient history—let's crack on and get into that vault, eh?"

Dervla regarded him for a moment, slightly puzzled at his eager demeanour, then told Ancil—"Go to it."

Ancil got down to work. Dervla was about to ask Pyke where his pod had landed and how he had made it into the museum but he spoke first.

"Hope you have some decent weaponry in one of those bags," he said, still smiling. "I heard that guard talking to someone on a comm link before he made his entrance."

Just then Ancil got to his feet, gave the overseer's office door a light push and it swung easily inwards. "Open!—Says me!"

"Fine work," Pyke said and strolled inside. Ancil and Moleg were close behind him but Kref paused. His big, craggy face was troubled.

"Is the chief okay?" he muttered.

"He had a long, tough journey to get here on time," she said quietly. "A good night's sleep and he'll be right as rain. Now, though, better break out the firepower—we may have unfriendly company soon."

The big Henkayan brightened at this, picked up the kitbags and trooped inside, with Dervla bringing up the rear.

The museum overseer's office was lined with wooden book-cases, filing cabinets, wall-to-ceiling shelves full of boxes, as well as a couple of glass display cases. The overseer's desk was wide and ornate, made from some red-resin composite striated with dark blue fibres and inset with carved panels of black stone. Behind it were tall, unshuttered windows which Dervla regarded with satisfaction—Plan B was looking good.

The overseer's vault sat in an alcove in the corner diagonally opposite the way in—Ancil was already on his knees by the new lock by the time Dervla got there, connecting up a web of detects linked to his resonance cracker. Pyke was leaning against the vault, wearing a faintly mocking smile which didn't change when Dervla went up to him and poked him in the shoulder.

"What's with you?" she said.

His smile didn't waver. "What do you mean?"

"Just not quite your usual gabby self."

Pyke reached inside his crimson-lined frock coat and brought out what looked like a fat silvery pen which he passed to her.

"This the DNA key?" she said.

"Twist the top off," he said.

Like a pen, a cap piece clicked and came away. Revealed was a tapering white stem ending in a bevelled tip—the stem seemed to be enclosed in a glass shell but, when Dervla brought up a finger to touch it, Pyke stayed her hand.

"That's a tiny stasis field, keeps the modified genetic material from breaking down." Looking at it, he smiled. "The last living descendant of the biovault's builder was a Henkari called Runken Burlet—I had to carry his dying, bleeding body halfway across a murky city by night, on a backwater planet at the edge of the Yamanon Domain. Kept him alive, even though we were being hunted, reached the house where a team of offworld char-ity medics were studying local diseases and the like—got them to create a small plug of readable genetic material." He took back the DNA key and replaced the cap. "Van Graes gave me the key receptacle before I went off on my quest—the doctors did a superb job with the readable key."

By now she was listening to him closely. "What happened to Burlet?"

"Didn't make it," Pyke said with a shrug. "Died of his wounds, very sad..."

"Derv," said Kref from over at the door. "Guests have arrived...gun bag's next to the desk."

"That's what I need," she said, digging around in the big grey holdall, coming up with a blast-repeater. It was painted red with little yellow stars all over. As she rummaged again for extra clips, she said, "How's that lock coming along, Ans?"

"Getting there."

"Kref," she said. "How's those—"

A fusillade of shots cut her off, and Moleg ducked to the side as the firing smashed splinters from the woodwork all around the doorway.

"Return fire!" she said. "Keep 'em busy!" And with the blaster repeater held at chest level she turned to point it at Pyke...who already had a hand-beamer aimed at her. Noticing this out of the corner of his eye, a horrified Ancil said:

"What the frack is going on?..."

Pyke grinned. "Just finish opening that vault, Ancil."

"Don't open that vault, Ans," said Dervla.

"Ancil," Pyke said. "I will kill Dervla then Moleg then Kref if you don't open the vault."

There was a thud, a tinkle of broken glass, and the tall windows flew open, revealing Raven Kaligari, hovering just outside, the nodes of an a-grav harness glowing at either shoulder. Steel-blue body armour, a gleeful smile curving beneath a battle-green goggle helmet, and one hand holding a broad-bodied weapon whose wide, flat muzzle had perhaps a dozen apertures.

Dervla's first impulse was to unleash a storm of rounds on the black-hearted bitchlet, but before she could act Raven flipped something with her thumb and a cluster of hair-thin beams stabbed out and around the room for an instant. *Damn*, she thought. *Tagged*.

"...or it might be my associate who starts the shooting," Pyke went on, voice now lacking any similarity to how it should sound. "You two at the doorway will keep firing at the guards, and you, dear Dervla, can now drop the gun and kick it away."

She gritted her teeth for a moment, then let go of the blaster. It clattered on the floor and she toed it off into the shadows.

Not-Pyke chuckled. "Very, very good. Now, Ancil, attend to your work. Get the vault open."

Shots were still being exchanged over at the office door. Dervla crossed her arms, trying not to look at her captors, trying to ignore those smug smiles.

"So, Dervla," said Raven. "I see you're still working with this bunch of losers."

"I see that you didn't eat skag and die, despite my express invitation for you to do so," Dervla retorted.

Not-Pyke's grin grew sharper but before a visibly galled Raven could respond there was a series of metallic musical pings and the vault door swung open. Dervla heard Ancil let out a shaky sigh. Then Not-Pyke produced the DNA key and handed it to him.

"Locate the biovault, insert this in the small round hole, turn until it clicks."

He looks just like Pyke, Dervla thought. *Is he a copy of some kind, or is that face a scan-repro, a mask? What if it really is him but some parasite like a Vor is controlling him?*

There was the briefest hiss-pop of pressure release. A moment later Dervla caught a whiff of stale, musty air.

"You're looking for a box or container about the size of the palm of your hand." Not-Pyke leaned over Ancil as if ready to pounce. "...ah, *that* one...open it—yes, excellent! The box, if you please."

Tight-lipped, Ancil passed it back over his shoulder. To Dervla's eyes it resembled a small ornate casket no bigger than her fist, carved from a strange white and green striated material. Not-Pyke opened it for a closer look and smiled a sinister smile that Dervla had never seen on that face before. Then he snapped it shut, straightened and with two sprightly strides reached the gaping window. Raven Kaligari still had her multi-targeting beam weapon pointing into the room as Not-Pyke climbed onto the windowsill and out onto the ledge. The ornate box he presented to the hovering Raven.

"The Angular Eye, my dear—take good care of it!" Then with Raven floating behind him he turned and looked back at them.

"You have all been outstanding, each and every one of you!" He had loosened his frock coat and was unfastening the buttons of his shirt. "No artist could wish for more committed and convincing co-actors, and that goes for Captain Pyke, even though he's had no say in the matter! So take your bows and say your farewells...because this is his grand finale."

Through the entire speech Dervla's suspicions had been growing wilder and darker. Part of her mind was yelling *Plan B!* as she watched Not-Pyke grope around inside his shirt while proclaiming those last demented words. Then his hand came out holding a small object trailing short lengths of bandage. By now he was balanced on the edge of the window ledge, staring over his shoulder at Raven; having stowed the Angular Eye out of sight, she was now reaching for this mysterious prize, multi-beamer still pointing into the overseer's office.

"Soon?" she said, face full of a hungry desire.

Not-Pyke nodded. "Oh, soon—very soon!"

Dervla watched as the mercenary then reached out and grabbed hold of one of the trailing bandages, upon which a smiling Not-Pyke opened his hand and let go of the unknown object.

The next few instants were crammed full of incident, yet they seemed to happen in slow motion.

As soon as Not-Pyke released the object his face changed—the smooth arrogance vanished and was replaced by shock, confusion, a disorientated panic. And Dervla knew, even as she dived towards the window, that this was the real Brannan Pyke. Fully expecting to be gunned down, she kept going, hearing a shot fired from her right—Ancil! Raven took a round in her arm, forcing a scream from her as she dropped the weapon and jerked back and spun away. Unsupported, Pyke lost his balance and toppled backwards off the ledge.

Dervla yelled something incoherent as she vaulted onto the window and lunged towards him, in her mind thinking madly *Plan B! Plan B!* but knew she would never be able to fumble the flare from her inside pocket in time. Moving too fast, she plunged over the edge and fell head-first after him, close enough to touch one flapping fold of that ridiculous frock coat, close enough for their terrified gazes to meet, but not close enough.

And out of the night-cloaked blurs far beneath something massive rushed up at them, an angled hardness that Dervla struck at speed. She spun through smeared glows and fragments of shouting. Then a slab of shadows smashed her in the head and everything went out, like a candle dropped into an ocean.

Dervla awoke woozily to a pounding headache and a stinging pain on her upper forehead. She tried to lever herself up onto one elbow but a surge of pain made her gasp and sink back.

"Hey, don't go exerting yourself," said a voice nearby. It sounded like Ancil. "Lie still—you took a bad smack to the skull."

Through barely cracked-open eyelids she saw blurry shadows

cast by a buttery yellow glow, and an Ancil-like shape standing close by.

"Okay, now you're awake I need you to take a coupla caps for the pain." He crouched down and carefully helped her into a sitting position. Pain throbbed in her head and made her eyes feel so gritty she could barely keep them open. Relying mainly on touch, she accepted a cup of water and two capsules, which she downed, then finished off the water in response to a sudden thirst.

"Where are we?" she said, every word making her throat feel scratchy.

"A canyon wall cave, a couple of klicks away from Cawl-Vesh," he said. "Full of stone troughs and dried-out sticks and roots—locals used to cultivate and harvest food plants in all the caves, according to Narok."

"Ah, Narok!" She forced her eyes further open. "He came for us anyway..."

Ancil gave an amused nod. "Moleg explained your Plan B."

"Sorry," she said. "It was just a spur-of-the moment idea. I got Moleg to persuade Narok to hang around in case we needed an emergency escape route, and told him to watch out for dropping flares..."

"Uh-huh—Narok said there were no flares but when he heard the gunfire he got his grav-boat ready just in case. When he saw you and Pyke come flying out of a ninth-floor window he had to act quickly..."

Dervla's laugh sounded whispery. "What a pilot—catching us with his boat..."

She paused a moment to cough dryly, and Ancil refilled her cup. As she drank the coolness down she heard no other voices, but there was a constant background sighing, a deep sound mingled with surges of faint hissing.

"Is it windy outside?" she said.

"Duststorm," said Ancil. "Mild one, apparently, but it's still creating enough skagging interference to block our comms. Have to sit it out before we can contact the *Scarabus*."

With eyesight gradually returning to something like normal, she saw how she was seated on a bedroll and leaning against the cave wall, positioned between two of the big stone troughs Ancil had spoken of before. The light had to be coming from portable lamps, she guessed, then realised that the air was actually comfortably warm. When she mentioned this, Ancil nodded.

"That Narok is a good sort—left us most of his own emergency supplies before he headed back to the city. Captain says we should make sure he gets a bonus from Van Graes."

Dervla gave a wry smile. "So, how is Pyke? Don't tell me that he walked away from that midair catch-of-the-day without a scratch?"

Ancil rubbed his unshaven chin thoughtfully. "Eh, no, I'm pretty sure that one of his eyelashes sustained a serious fracture..."

Dervla laughed softly then raised a hand to her head. "Oh, don't make me laugh, please..."

"Actually he wrenched his shoulder and picked up a bumper collection of bruises. If I had my field medkit I could've hypoed the both of you but it got left behind when Narok turned up with you two and we bailed double-time."

She squinted at him. "Has he said anything yet? About what happened since we last saw him?"

Ancil shrugged. "Just said that it was a brain-gouger of a tale which everyone had to hear."

Another voice broke in. "Not least because I don't think I could stand having to plough me way through it all more than once!"

A familiar figure strolled into view, propped himself on the edge of one of the troughs and gave her one of those jaunty head-tilt-and-winks which always gave Dervla a thrill. Not that she'd ever tell him that.

"Good to see yer on the mend there, kid," Pyke said as Kref and Moleg came over to join them.

"I'll be feeling better if we still had that damned Angular Eye thing," she said. "Can't stand the thought of that rat-bitch getting one over on us, again! What are we going to tell Van Graes?"

"The truth," Pyke said. "Which will include something really bloody strange—Kref?"

The big Henkayan dipped into his bulky, dark-grey surcoat and brought out a small round leathery object which he offered to Pyke.

"No, no, told you, I'm never touching that thing again! Just hold it so Dervla can see it—pull it open but remember what I said…"

"Uh-huh, 'don't touch the crystal with your bare skin'—I don't forget, Chief."

Kref prodded the leathery object, teased aside a flap to reveal a pale, foggy looking crystalline artefact. It was bulbous with a small, tapered protuberance and a longer curved one like a blunt tine—it almost resembled the head of a bird or a reptile.

"That's the thing that you…whatever was controlling you… pulled out from inside your shirt," she said.

Pyke nodded. "It was open and pressed against my skin, held in place by sticky bandages." A look of loathing passed over his features. "Just thinking about the thing—the things, inside it…" He shivered. "Okay, all of you deserve to hear the entire crazy yarn, even if it does sound like the ravings of a cranked-up geej-sniffer. So strap down yer brains—it's gonna be a bumpy ride!"

CHAPTER FOUR

(Pyke's Account: Ten days ago, at the offices of Augustine Van Graes overlooking Lake Mirabeau, on the exclusive habitat, Firmament Heights, in orbit about Earth.)

"Can we please, finally, come somewhere close to an agreement?" said Van Graes from behind his desk.

Pyke, leaning against a leather armchair, looked round at Dervla, and said, "Yes, can we?"

But she was, of course, wearing that embattled look which had not a shred of give in it, all defiant eyes and jutting jaw. Even though she was holding everyone up and aggravating their employer into the bargain, still Pyke thought that she was magnificent. Kind of awesome and sexy with extra awe.

On the other side of the desk, an embellished monument in wood, Augustine Van Graes sat in a high-backed, unexceptional swivel chair, hands resting on the padded armrests. Beneath a head of bushy grey hair, old irascible eyes gazed out from a round but lined face whose skin had the shiny appearance you only got from rejuve treatment. Van Graes wore an archaic burgundy smoking jacket which fitted in perfectly with the dark panelling and the small antiquated lamps mounted in pairs around the room. There was nothing antique, however, about the thinscreen jutting out of the desk's polished surface. Even without being able to see it, Pyke knew that there would be a contract, a number with a juicy row of zeroes after it, and boxes for six thumbprints.

Dervla sat straighter in the low chair she'd earlier dragged closer to Van Graes' desk and leaned back, mimicking him with her hands on her chair's rests.

"Isn't it only natural to get kind of nervous, anxious even?" she said. "We've done other jobs for you in the past and this is the first time you've split us up…"

"Operational efficiency, Ser Dervla," Van Graes said, making a soothing gesture with one plump, wrinkled hand. "Having two teams tackling the preliminaries in parallel rather than in sequence accelerates matters in a way that I find quite pleasing. And I have agreed to send a bodyguard along with him…"

"Said I don't need a skaggin' babysitter," Pyke said. "But seems I don't get a say."

Dervla's gaze didn't waver. "Your bodyguard had better be good."

"He's an accredited, enhanced professional with a long list of successes."

"He better be brilliant—he better be a twenty-first dan ultra-ninja!"

A small, unexpected smile softened their employer's features. "Vaughan has been in my employ for nearly ten years, Ser Dervla—I trust him with my life and the lives of my family."

Pyke spread his hands. "See? This is just a find and retrieve mission, me and the boss's man, there and back, easy…"

"Don't you *dare* say 'easy in, easy out'!"

Pyke paused, then smiled and went on. "I was about to say, 'easy as pie,' since everyone knows pie is…an easy thing…"

"Or you could say 'easy as falling off a log,' Chief," said Ancil who was sharing a long sofa with Kref's substantial bulk.

"Or 'easy as shooting fish in a barrel,' " said Moleg. He was sharing the other identical sofa with Oleg the Kiskashin, both of them sitting across from Ancil and Kref. Pyke noticed how Oleg and Moleg both sat primly on the edge of the sofa, even though only Oleg possessed a short scaly tail which required a bit of room at the rear. Another sign of how Oleg's mannerisms got entwined with Moleg's back in the day, on another dangerous little caper like this one.

"I think we've veered off the path a little," said Van Graes. "The captain's task is straightforward but not risk-free, hence the addition of my bodyguard. You, Ser Dervla, and the rest of your crew will be engaged in surveillance and preparation prior to the infiltration and retrieving the Angular Eye."

"You want us to break into a museum and engage in some no-nonsense burglarising," Dervla said. "It's an old-fashioned heist, in other words."

She glanced at Pyke and winked, which was always a spirits-lifter.

"Earthy and to the point," said Van Graes, arching a droll eyebrow. "All the necessary details are on the datatab I gave you, but as I've already indicated time is not on our side. Which is why, as soon as we've concluded our business, you will all be departing for your respective destinations. Is that agreeable?"

When Dervla regarded him with a sidelong gaze and held it for a long, sharp moment, Pyke gave her his best devil-may-care rogue's smile. In response she pointed her finger, almost as if she was aiming along it.

"You...had better be there, Brannan Pyke, or I'm keeping the ship." She jabbed the finger. "And I'll turn it into a taxi."

"A low blow," he said. "Guess I just better get there on time."

A nod. "So, wanna sign this thing?"

"Well, we did come all this way."

Pyke was first to press his thumb to Van Graes' screen, with

Dervla and the others lined up behind him. They'd already seen the text of the contract before reaching the orbital, and it was another "freelancer expediters" agreement similar to ones they'd signed before.

"Excellent," said Van Graes. "Most satisfactory. Now that this stage is completed, Ser Dervla, it is time for yourself and your crew to take your leave and set course for Ong. My assistant will show you out."

Ancil and Moleg shook Pyke's hand, Kref clapped him on the shoulder and urged him to "kill any ambushers, Captain, make 'em dead!," while Oleg merely gave him a formal nod. Dervla said nothing, just kissed the tip of her forefinger then pointed it at him and fired off an invisible shot.

Aimed straight at my heart, he thought as Dervla followed the others out. *She's persistent, give her that.*

At last the office door closed and Pyke and Van Graes were alone. For a moment, Pyke stared at the door then went over to the low armchair Dervla had been sitting in and took up the same position.

"I assume you've read over your own mission summary?" said the older man.

"I did. Travel to the Myzety system, land on the warrenworld Geskel, find a sinktown called Zheen, find a Henkari called Runken Burlet, persuade him to let us have a sample of his DNA. Then it's back to the ship and we burn a groove through hyperspace to meet with the others on Ong, but..."

"But you feel some details are lacking," Van Graes said. He had risen from his chair and was detaching the thinscreen from his desk, folding it away into an inner pocket.

Pyke gave a half-smile. "Not just the details that's tweaking my curiosity. Dervla's right, isn't she—it would make just as much sense to send us all off to get the DNA first—" He broke off as Van Graes came round the desk and made a small beckoning gesture while heading for the far corner of his office. "Are we going somewhere?"

"My private launch bay," the billionaire said as he pressed something on the side of a glass-fronted bookcase. It slid aside to reveal a small elevator, all austere white and dark glass. "We can talk on the way." He ushered Pyke inside and a white panel closed behind them.

There was no noticeable sensation as the capsule fell away from Van Graes' office, just a succession of shadowy flickers barely visible through the long panes of dark glass.

"Understand this, Captain Pyke," Van Graes said. "I've been hunting for the Angular Eye for more years than you've been alive. You could say it's gone from being a middle-aged man's hobby to an old man's obsession."

"My hobby just now is keeping my ship flying and stopping my crew from killing each other." Pyke gave a wry laugh. "Well, to be frank, it is more a compulsion than a hobby..."

"That I can identify with," said Van Graes. "It's been a long, strange journey, decades full of twists, turns, fake artefacts, and false leads. If I, too, were being frank, I might say that it's also been a sequence of odd satisfactions—the prospect of an actual end-point feels curiously daunting."

"Must say I'm dying to know what it does, your eye gadget."

Van Graes looked thoughtful. "Without revealing too much at this stage, I'll just say that it leads the way to a very ancient, very specific hoard of treasures."

"Uh-huh—a tracking device," Pyke said. "So Ong's where this treasure's hidden?"

"I am...uncertain," Van Graes said. "My researches have narrowed down possible locations of this hoard to four worlds in areas rimward of the Sendrukan Hegemony. However, what complicates matters is that we're not the only ones engaged in this hunt."

Pyke managed to avoid laughing out loud. *So there is a catch!*

One of the regular hazards for trader-smugglers like Pyke was the client whose job offer started off as something fairly innocuous, then somewhere along the line turned into a proposal to go in search of legendary treasures, lost alien worlds, buried temples, or underground caches of ancient mechs/devastating weapons/mechs armed with devastating weapons. Close questioning nearly always revealed that these locations lay within the territory of some ruthless regime, or criminal organisation, or beneath the sacred monument of a homicidal cult, or floating somewhere in an asteroid field, being fought over by rival scavenger squads...

Not so different from working for Mr. Van G, he thought. *Except that he pays the prettiest penny going!*

"Competition, eh? Who are we up against? Another billionaire?"

"I doubt it. For many years most of my rivals have been enthusiasts, amateurs, academics and compulsives—a couple were genuinely brilliant but none of them have my kind of resources to draw upon. Anyway, one of those brilliant amateurs, a Martian who gloried in the grid-name Valentyne Dawnkiller, announced less than a month ago that he was giving up, 'getting out of the Chase,' as the hunter community calls it. I felt a bit sad and a bit relieved. There had been a couple of times when he beat me and my money advantage to rare and desirable relics, and I'd thought that if anyone was going to figure out the Angular Eye's whereabouts before me it would be Valentyne. Yet here he was, throwing in the trowel, as it were."

The capsule elevator slowed to a halt and the two men stepped out into a low-lit launch bay. A small combat vessel, looking to Pyke's eyes like a rebuilt cutter, was resting in the latticed grav-cradle. He could see an indistinct figure sitting further along, near the walkway that linked the dockside to the ship's entry hatch. Van Graes, however, paused outside the elevator to finish his tale.

"Anway, to cut the story short, I dug into Valentyne's background, much deeper than I had before, when I only wanted to know the basics. It turned out that he had two dependants back on Earth, an ailing father and a bedbound grandmother, and a job as a cogware debugger for Stanburgh Civ Authority, a domecity on Mars. Twelve hours before Valentyne announced his retirement, the care facilities looking after his relatives both received a very large one-off payment, more than enough to cover all expenses till end-of-life. And twelve hours after his announcement he disappeared—no sightings by his neighbours and nothing on city surveillance; just gone, vanished into thin air." Van Graes frowned. "Along with all his papers, notes and data."

Pyke nodded. "So, serious competition, then."

"Indeed, someone capable of devoting resources equal to or greater than mine to the hunt for the Angular Eye. I gave your companions a rather anodyne version of the situation to avoid any, erm, disruptive anxieties and so that we could make swift headway in this matter."

"Disruptive anxieties?" Pyke said. "If—*when* Dervla finds out about this, it'll be more than our anxieties that'll get disrupted!" He jerked a thumb over one shoulder. "That yer man, Vaughan?"

"Yes, it is. Come along—I'll introduce you."

Twenty hours later, the bodyguard Vaughan and Pyke had landed on the warrenworld Geskel, paid over the exorbitant wharfage fees, then gone in search of a sinktown called Zheen. Less than twelve hours after that, Vaughan had disappeared in the dark passageways, but Pyke had found the reluctant Henkari DNA donor, Runken Burlet. Together they were trying to stay one step ahead of a gang of mysterious pursuers.

They were hiding out in a decrepit chamber in a boarded-up carriage-office on the edge of Luju, a downlevel sinktown not far from Zheen. The light from Pyke's wristband revealed several chairs, a couple of desks tipped against windows, and a burned-out campfire. Without Vaughan, Pyke had realised that he'd have to rely on Burlet's help to find a way back up to the surface and the ground-port. Persuasion, however, was proving tricky, even with the translators they were wearing.

"Look, you have to understand that the ones hunting us want the same thing that we do," he said. "So if we can get back to my ship…"

"You've ruined my life!" wailed Runken Burlet. "Why didn't you take the leaflet from the door and go and see my legalist?"

"Wouldn't have made any difference, because then those thugs would have got to you before us…"

"And you don't trust me! Here I am, in desperate fear for my life, and you won't give me a weapon to defend myself."

"Only because you'd turn it on me and hand me over to those skaggers out there!"

"Just as you fully deserve!"

"Uh-huh, then they'll cut yer head off, stick it in a cryobag, and walk away whistling. There ye go, job done, eh?"

Suddenly realising that he was almost shouting, Pyke took a deep breath and let it out through pursed lips.

"We have to get out of here," he went on in a low, calm voice. "If they catch us we're dead, it's that simple." He thought for a moment then took out his backup weapon, a compact needler, adjusted the fire rate then presented it to the diminutive Henkari who hesitantly accepted it. "I've switched it to burst firing so it'll spit out three needles every time you squeeze the trigger. Probably won't kill anyone but it should slow them down a bit."

"Thank you," said Burlet. "For my part, I promise not to betray your trust."

"Okay, that's something." Pyke studied the charge-level on his own blast-repeater; yep, still only seven rounds left. "So, like I said, getting to the surface would be a good move, if you've any notion of how we might do that, eh?"

Burlet gave a tired shrug. "From here the most direct route to the port is back the way we came."

"It'll be watched—what else?"

"A couple of pinchways close by lead further onto the fringes of Luju," Burlet said. "But that's just a series of dead ends, no exits up or down."

"Any other exits to anywhere?" Pyke said, anxious now.

The Henkari sighed. "The only other way out of our predicament is in a closed-up vustillery at the end of a nearby alley. It's an excavated shaft which descends to deep underground ruins—that might be safe." He gazed side to side nervously. "Or at least safer than here."

"Underground ruins?" Pyke said with a grin. "Maybe we'll pick up a few knick-knacks."

Burlet gave him a slightly horrified look. "I would not advise taking anything—Dead Temple City is haunted."

"Places with such names usually are," Pyke said, indicating the side door. "Care to lead the way?"

Back outside they went, to low, gloomy passages, broken floors strewn with the debris of abandonment. Earlier they'd been dodging pursuers who exchanged guttural shouts and barked instructions, hiding in the shadows, using any gap or recess for concealment. Now they crept silently along narrow pinchways redolent of musty decay and foot-stirred dust. It wasn't long before they reached their goal. Pyke had already speculated as to what a vustillery might be and was holding out for some left-behind flasks containing flavoursome beverages of a fermented nature...

Sadly, it transpired that the main output of a vustillery was different grades of oil and associated products. Inside was a shambles of broken furniture, shattered crates, tipped-over shelves, dust and ceiling burst-ins. Pyke turned up his wristband torch as they picked their way through the mess, following Burlet's lead.

"The discovery of the shaft and the ruins came over a year ago," the Henkari said. "The managers of the vustillery had wanted to expand their storage capacity so they started digging to extend the cellar, and broke through to a big black emptiness..."

Burlet stopped before a heavy looking door with a shiny new locking mechanism that spanned the full width.

"The Council of Warrens sent in an antiquities team to assess the find," he said as he flipped open an odd keypad which had three groups of keys. "I was part of the Methods Support squad at the time. I saw it all."

With both hands Runken Burlet input a sequence of numbers too swift for Pyke to pick up. Deep clunking sounds came from the door which swung inward to reveal steps leading down into darkness.

"Well, that's handy..." Pyke began to say.

The silence was shattered by a detonation as the main doors of the vustillery blew in. Chunks of wood and stone flew as dust billowed through, a choking gritty fog. Pyke shouted at Burlet to head down, turned and saw that he was already gone, then he dived through, grabbed the door and slammed it shut behind him. It made a satisfyingly solid locking sound.

A dim illumination was on down in the cellar, Pyke saw as he hurriedly descended. Lights were on but Burlet was nowhere to be seen. The walls were lined with shelves, racks and niche arrays for all sizes of containers, but only empty ones were left. Pyke frowned, scanning the stockroom, then saw that the dark shadows in the far corner were in fact a wide unlit entrance into the extension. A few steps led down to a low, square room lit only by a single knee-high wall lamp. Burlet stood near the centre, his face a picture of bewilderment as he gazed at the vacant floor all around him.

"I don't know what's happened," he said, putting a hand to his forehead. "There used to be cases and cannisters of tools and supplies, all carefully locked and stacked when the Council of the Warrens shut down the dig…"

The Henkari was right—Pyke could just make out scrape marks, then fumbled around the wall near the new entrance, flipped a switch and a couple more wall nodes came on, lighting up the place. Just as he did so, sharp thuds and banging came from the door at the head of the steps. The extra light revealed that one entire wall of the extension was occupied by a hub-and-leaf-style security door, sloped into the wall; looking closer he could see that it was high-spec, practically a blast door. *Not the usual thing to find in a place like this, I'd've thought…*

"Look, Mr. B, I assume that the downwards shaft is behind this door, so can you deal with it?—'cos I don't how long that door back there will keep them out."

Burlet nodded and hurried over to the far side of the big security door and slid open a small panel to gain access to another keypad. Moments later the middle third of the armoured leaves hissed as they retracted into the overhead hub, creating a doorway.

Pyke was hard on the Henkari's heels as he dashed inside, and heard that slicing sound as the door closed up behind him. A few wall-globes blinked on, and the Henkari's feet clattered on metal steps, part of a scaffold extending from the entrance to the floor of a chamber with a four-sided pyramidical ceiling. The walls were of massive masonry blocks adorned with simple bead-style bordering. At the centre was a square, waist-high wall with a gap in one of the sides. As soon as Burlet laid eyes on it he cried out.

"What the hell's wrong?" Pyke said.

"...gone...it's gone!" Burlet tugged on the short, tight curls of his hair. "There was a grav-assisted cable platform and a supporting frame and a motored cable winch..." He spread his hands. "The Council of Warrens must have sent their people back after the antiquities team closed it all up—they just removed all the equipment..."

A sudden hammering from the other side of the security door made Pyke jump, and he cursed. There'd been no loud noise or blast announcing a breakthrough at the first cellar door, which told him that those skaggers had somehow cracked the lock. And that didn't bode well for the one on this door.

"...but why take *all* of it away..." Burlet was muttering to himself.

"Forget that," said Pyke, glancing anxiously back at the security wall. "Is there any other way down? Is the shaft wall climbable?"

"Well, the shaft was originally a stairwell..."

"Stairs! Great!" Pyke said rushing over to the low wall.

"...but most of it had collapsed during the preceding centuries..."

Even as Pyke leaned on the wall, and before he could look down, a glowing shape flew up out of the ancient shaft. He stumbled back, snatching his blast-repeater from his waist and yelling at Runken Burlet to take cover. Burlet, however, held his ground, glowering as he pulled out the needler and took aim at the oddly shaped object.

"Ah, good, found you both at last," said a synth-voice approximating the tone of an irascible Human male. "You are Captain Pyke, I take it?"

Pyke kept his own weapon on target but held out his hand towards Burlet, gesturing for him to back off a little. "Maybe—who's enquiring?"

"I was despatched by our mutual friend, the Construct.

Having acquired certain intelligence assets of immediate pertinence, he felt you might be getting into a bit of a tight spot. Look, I would recommend a speedy evac as your pursuers are close to cracking their way through that door over there."

Pyke laughed, more a snort, holstered his weapon and gave Burlet a no-danger nod, then watched as the pale, ovoid-shaped newcomer snapped into a new shape, a two-metre-long cylinder with rounded ends. "Ah, a Construct drone. Right mouthy sods, the lot of them. Okay—what's the plan? Do we hop aboard and you get us safely down to the ruins?"

"Partially, yes," the drone said as it glided over to the gap in the shaft-surrounded wall. "Getting you to safety means avoiding those ruins!"

The drone's hardfield shell had grown a couple of bucket seats, one on each side, along with extensions for bracing the feet. Pyke eagerly seated himself and cheerily urged Burlet to follow suit. The Henkari nervously did so.

"Is this a machine intelligence?" he asked Pyke. "Or an intelligent machine?"

"I often wonder that about some people I meet," Pyke said.

An odd triple-ping came from the security door and one by one the armoured leaves began retracting into the hub, making a sound like a dozen swords being drawn.

"That's our cue," said the drone. "Hold on tight!"

Suddenly and silently, the drone and its passengers dropped into the darkness of the shaft. The drone dimmed the brightness of its shell to almost nothing, and Pyke steeled himself for any unfriendly fire coming down after them. An eager batch of questions for his rescuer jostled in his thoughts, but he reckoned that now probably wasn't the right moment.

"Don't worry," the drone said. "They can't see us, and, besides, we'll be ducking out of the shaft quite soon. Ah, there it is!"

Rapid deceleration crammed Pyke down into the bucket seat, then there was a sideways swerve as the drone plunged into a passage opening.

"Why aren't we descending to the ruins?" Burlet said loudly.

"Simple, really," the drone said. "Despite having been called Dead Temple City by your expedition's remote probe pilots, not everything down there is dead. In one of my previous iterations, I had cause to visit that grand metropolis in order to visit one of its subjugees."

"Sounds like a prison," Pyke said.

"More like a re-education facility—with maximum security elements. Won't be long before this shaft gets refilled, permanently this time."

Pyke peered at the wide corridor up ahead, now lit up in a wavering beam of light coming from the front of the drone. Their swift travel sent a musty breeze through his hair.

"Any idea who our pursuers are?" he said.

"Local dreg-catchers licensed by a sub-prefectory of the Council of Warrens but hired by some offworld group calling themselves merchant speculators. However, I've seen their ship over at the docks, and that's no trader! Van Graes should have warned you."

Pyke grimaced ruefully. "He did. He even sent one of his bodyguards along with me. Don't suppose you noticed if he's…"

"I was tracking from a distance, and picked up heavy firing after he was snatched, then his vital signs zeroed. Killed two and badly wounded a third, though."

"Vaughan was a tough one, right enough. No give in him…" Unaccountably, he found himself yawning like a bear. "So, being a Construct drone, I'm guessing that you've got some kind of razor-sharp plan that'll get us to the port docks…y'know, if yer going that way…"

"Since it seemed that the pair of you were operating without a discernible plan, it seemed prudent that I have one," the drone said. "The dreg-catchers have already set up monitor points at all the main foot-traffic junctions—custodial laws allow them to do so. On the other hand, presumption of non-guilt permits any attempt to evade capture, as long as no laws are broken. I am carrying you both to a disused shipping undervault which affords access directly onto the dockside. When we reach the vault I will reconfigure to look something like an unremarkable piece of luggage before we use maintenance passages to reach your berth. Will that suffice?"

"Sounds damn fine, as plans go, and I'm happy to endorse it," Pyke said. "Just one tiny wee puzzle in all of this—why the interest? What is a Construct drone doing out here at the arse end of the galactic nowhere, helping out little ould me?"

The drone's flight took them across a black chasm in the corridor. Pyke felt a dusting of powder and grit fall into his hair from above and he ruffled it with his fingers.

"Your employer, Van Graes, has been hunting for a relic called the Angular Eye for several years, and the Eye has been a matter of interest to the Construct for considerably longer. When we learned that Van Graes had tasked you and your crew with its retrieval, I was sent to assess your circumstances and take any appropriate action."

"I'm sure I don't know what this eye thing is that you're on about," Pyke said, trying to sound puzzled. "But thanks for getting us out of that jam, all the same."

Aye, see?—two can play the vague words game.

Runken Burlet, who had been quiet the entire time, suddenly spoke up.

"This offworlder, Pyke, came to my door asking for the same thing that a string of others have previously demanded—samples of my flesh, blood and spit out of which he intends to fashion some manner of key."

"Interesting," said the drone. "Among your forebears, were there any biovault builders?"

"My great-great-great-grandmother," said Burlet. "She put her heart and soul into her work."

"I can see that," said the drone. "And just think—somewhere far off among the stars there is a locked compartment waiting for Captain Pyke to come along with a key. As the Geskel wise ones say, not all certain things are certain!"

A listening Pyke smiled as they flew along the shadowy passageway. *Aye, right, carry on. Just let me get Burlet back to the ship, ply him with something from the extensive drinks locker, then I'll unleash the full powers of the Pyke cunning and guile— I have not yet begun to cajole!*

The Construct drone's plan was indeed a fine one, more than perfectly adequate to the task of getting from point A to point B and thence to point C. But the drone had not reckoned with the dreg-catchers' skills or the cold, implacable purpose of those they worked for.

The first part of the ambush was sprung as the drone and its passengers sped towards the end of a corridor which opened into the main shipping undervault. Five metres from the corridor end a restraint field snapped into visibility directly in front of them. At the same time small beam turrets popped out from concealed wall cavities and began peppering the drone's rear shield.

"Hold on tight!" said the drone.

Brilliant flashes of harsh light began stuttering from the nose of the drone's hardfield shell just instants before it struck the barrier. Pyke felt the drag as the drone's momentum slowed greatly, but the restraint barrier was flaring and energy discharges stabbed outwards in electric webs, almost as if the drone was drilling through it.

Suddenly the barrier was gone and the drone leaped forward.

Straight into the second part of the ambush. Flickering arabesque flashes came from several directions, temporarily dazzling Pyke at the same time as the drone said, "Cunning brutes!—I'll k-k-k-k-k-k-k-r-r-r-r-rrrrr..."

The machine's hardfield shell winked out and Pyke found himself tumbling to the hard concrete floor. The drone came down with a crash, bounced and rolled over a couple of times before fetching up against a square pillar. Half dazed, Pyke hauled out his blast-repeater as he struggled to his feet. He spotted Runken Burlet several paces away, staggering towards a set of broad doors at the far end, until someone shot him between the shoulder blades with a large red and white dart. Almost immediately an opaque bubble appeared, enclosing his head and upper shoulders.

In fearful recognition, Pyke looked quickly around and spotted several armoured figures drawing near, aiming weapons, cast into sharp silhouettes by spots spaced along a side wall. Then he felt one of the darts hit him in the back and he knew the jig was up. The bubbles were low-intensity forcefield containments, just strong enough to maintain an airtight seal as a sedation vapour was released from the dart. Burlet had already succumbed so, as the first wisps curled through his own bubble, Pyke reholstered his blast-repeater, sat down against the nearest pillar and presented the middle finger to the approaching dreg-catchers. As his captors surrounded him he started roaring out the first verse of "The Boys Of Kilkenny."

He made it to the third line before his eyes stopped focusing and fine coils of mist gently smothered everything in soft grey nothingness.

Pyke broke off from his narrative and said, "Who's making that row?"

CHAPTER FIVE

Dervla, the planet Ong, outside Cawl-Vesh

It was Kref's booming voice that reverberated throughout the cave and interrupted the captain.

"Quick, Chief, everyone!—there's a ship or something coming—they might have found us!"

All around, eyes widened in alarm and hands dived into pockets, hastily fumbling for weapons. Dervla, feeling sharper and less feeble than when she'd awoken, started to reach for her blast-repeater then remembered—it was back in that museum office. Now feeling unarmed and therefore half naked, she looked around at the others. The rest of the crew had taken up positions near the cave mouth, using stone troughs as cover.

"Ancil!" she hissed, throwing a pebble at him.

He looked round, his face a picture of annoyance, then saw who it was. "What's up?"

"Don't have a burner—left mine back on that office floor..."

Ancil nodded, reached into a nearby holdall, rummaged around for a moment then brought out a handgun and tossed it over. Dervla caught it and the two clips that followed. It was a copy of a popular Hegemony sidearm, scaled down for smaller hands and physiques, but by the time she had it loaded up with both magazines the panic was clearly over. Having crept outside to steal a look, Pyke was now strolling back in with a grin on his face.

"False alarm—it's the shuttle-barge you guys left over at the city landing ground. Oleg must have engaged the remote nav..."

Dust and grit were swirling in the barge's suspensor field helices as the crew trooped out onto the cave's ledge. The barge had anchored itself in place with a couple of stasis hooks, and Dervla was inching her way out of the cave just behind the rest, shielding her eyes from the sunlight. As Pyke approached the craft the access hatch popped and swung up, letting out the sound of an incoming call. Pyke gave the rest a look of mock surprise then ducked inside and thumbed the comm reply as he slipped into the pilot couch.

"Hello there—Epicentre of the universe, God's gift speaking—how can I help you?"

"Hello, Captain," came Oleg's unflappable reply. "I'm moderately pleased to find you back with us."

"Well, it's pretty splendid to be back among these rascals, let me tell you!" Pyke said. "Thanks for sending the barge, by the way, which seems to have been restocked with supplies and gear, almost as if we weren't about to pack up and scarper back into orbit..."

"There is an explanation for that, Captain. While all communications with the Cawl-Vesh vicinity were blocked by the duststorm, I was contacted on subspace by our employer, Mr. Van Graes. He asked for an update on the mission and without disclosing too much I gave him a summary of events."

"Is that so? Did that include our losing the Angular Eye, by any chance?"

"Yes, Captain."

Pyke rolled his eyes skywards. "You could have, I dunno, been evasive or..."

He was momentarily wordless, and Dervla knew what was going through his head, how Oleg tended towards a literal and somewhat independent frame of mind, along with a peculiar avoidance of dissembling. Oleg just couldn't see the benefits of lies or evasiveness.

"So how did he take the news?" Pyke went on. "I bet he was thrilled."

"He said that it was most unfortunate, and that he would have to speak with you as soon as possible. Which is why I despatched the shuttle."

"With all these supplies and so forth," Dervla said as she squeezed past Ancil and dropped into the co-pilot's couch. "Would I be right in thinking that Mr. Van Graes had a hand in this?"

"Mr. Van Graes made some suggestions which I found faultlessly logical. Sending along a variety of resources seemed most prudent," said Oleg. "He is waiting on one of the incoming channels, Captain—shall I patch him through?"

Dervla let out a low laugh as Pyke gave her an arched-eyebrow here-we-go look.

"Sure, let's get the bollocking over and done with."

"Okay, Captain, one moment—Mr. Van Graes, go ahead."

Sound of a throat being cleared. "Good, my thanks—Captain Pyke?"

"Mr. Van G, how are you this fine day?"

"Slightly anxious since I'm currently trying to evade the attention of ruthless assassins."

Dervla and Pyke exchanged a look and sat up.

"Sounds harsh," said Pyke.

"I would say so—my offices on the orbital Firmament Heights were firebombed and my launch was sabotaged, all not very long after Vaughan met his end on Geskel."

"I mourn his loss, Mr. Van Graes," Pyke said. "He was fearless and full-hearted with it."

"I'll see that his family are not left wanting."

Dervla leaned forward a little. "Mr. Van Graes, are you safe just now?"

"For the time being—my yacht is on its way to Mars, with stopovers booked for all the major canyon cities. I, however, am aboard a colonist transport bound for Robinson's World, one of the new treaty planets, travelling under an alias. Planetfall isn't due for another day and a half so I'm out of harm's way. Meanwhile, we must decide how to proceed."

"Or if we wish to proceed," Pyke said.

"Certainly, that is an option to be explored, and if you choose to play no further part in this project I will still ensure that you and your crew are paid the full amount as agreed. On the other hand, if you decide to stay with my project and see it through to its conclusion I would be happy to treble all agreed fees. Does that sound like an attractive offer, Captain—enough to hear my proposal, at least?"

Pyke muted the audio pickup then looked over at Dervla and the others and said, "Well?"

Predictably, the response was enthusiastic in the light of the triple payout offer. Dervla felt it was almost too generous, which provoked uncertain thoughts. Pyke raised an eyebrow at her again, and she shrugged.

"So far we've dealt with about a dozen varieties of crazy," she said. "Makes me wonder what else might be round the corner. But, yeah, I'll listen to what he has to say."

Pyke prodded the comm controls. "Well, Mr. Van G, seems everyone's dying to hear yer pitch, so the stage is yours."

"Excellent, but would you be so kind as to summarise the events leading up to your current situation?"

"Not a problem," said Pyke who then rattled off a decent enough report, although he omitted the whole bit about the mind-trap crystal, claiming instead that he was held captive by

Raven Kaligari all the way from Geskel to Ong where everything turned into a whirl of confusion and accident. They lost the Angular Eye to Kaligari but at least managed to escape with life and limb intact (with no mention of the crystal being in their possession). At first Dervla was puzzled by his altered version of events, but reasoned that this might have something to do with risk and chance. That or he just wanted to keep it out of their deal with the man.

"A remarkable blend of luck and misfortune," Van Graes said once Pyke was done.

"You don't know half of it, Mr. Van G," Pyke said with a mischievous grin. Dervla almost laughed out loud but clamped her hand to her mouth while the rest of the crew muffled their own hilarity.

"Well," Van Graes continued. "The loss of the Eye is a serious setback, especially since it has fallen into unscrupulous hands. But there is a possibility, a small one, that it can be traced whenever it's actually being used."

Pyke looked both sceptical and puzzled. "So, you're saying that we need a tracking device to find a tracking device?"

"Not as such—I already have an associate, an ally of sorts, on Ong who may be able to assist us in this matter."

Pyke raised his eyebrows. "Ah, so we're not the first lucky team you've sent to Ong," he said.

"I would hardly refer to Lieutenant-Doctor Ustril as a team," Van Graes said. "More a consultant with additional talents. But I get ahead of myself. Let me be perfectly open and candid—yes, the Angular Eye is a tracking device and, yes, I was hoping that we could use it to lead us directly to what might be called a treasure trove of the ages."

There was an extended moment of silence during which mock-surprise looks were exchanged. Pyke smiled—this was sounding familiar.

"Suffice to say, Mr. Van G, you've got our attention. Do go on!"

"Very well, but first a little history lesson. Nearly a million years ago, more than half the galaxy was dominated by the Arraveyne Imperium, led by a ruthless species called the Arravek. They were naturally blessed with psionic abilities but they employed advanced implants to enhance their talents, allowing them to control entire populations by controlling their rulers. Unchallenged for many thousands of years, their empire became all-powerful; their scientists reached successive pinnacles of achievement and the capital worlds of the empire attracted vast wealth, around which the Arravek Imperators and their coteries arrayed themselves. All the finest, most precious things were caught up in the maelstroms of power and eventually found their way to the very hub of the Imperium, the planet Olveyne.

"And as is usual in stories like this, the Arraveki rulers grew arrogant over time and so full of hubris that when their nemesis made its presence known they could not conceive of anything capable of threatening their supremacy, their godlike existence. Until it was too late. Little is known about the destroyers of the Arraveyne Empire—they called themselves the Zayaloc-Nar and they were a nomadic, migratory civilisation. According to the few fragmentary records that still remain, an Arraveki Imperator and his battlefleet destroyed a squadron of Zayaloc hospital and creche ships laid over for repairs in a system well away from the Imperial border. There are several versions of how this came about, but, whatever the details of the attack, the Zayaloc-Nar retaliated with devastating effect.

"One by one the empire's capital worlds were destroyed by planetoids and small moons which would appear out of hyperspace, already hurtling along a collision course. In a matter of days one of the largest and most powerful empires in galactic history was brought to its knees."

"Pretty harsh," said Pyke. "And, er, fascinating, but I'm hoping we'll get to the meat of this before long."

"My apologies—I always forget that my love of historical detail is not always a shared obsession. But, as you say, to the point." Van Graes paused, as if gathering his thoughts. "Well, in the end, at the cusp of finality, only the Imperial capital, Olveyne, remained, guarded for parsecs around by armadas of warships, a few carrying fearsome weapons capable of splitting moons and planetoids. But what emerged from the depths of hyperspace was a gas giant, rolling through the capital system, vast and unstoppable. Most of the Arravek Imperators and governing nobility had defiantly chosen to remain, confident that the warfleets could protect them. And with the gas giant's arrival came a mad, worldwide panic.

"However, a few more precautionary nobles and scientists had commandeered a cityship, an immense vessel nearly two miles long, and filled it with the treasures of the Arraveyne civilisation, not just wealth and precious items but artworks, machines, technologies, secrets and wild theories..."

"We get the picture," Pyke said, lounging in the pilot's couch. "This huge cityship, did it have a name at all?"

"The *Mighty Defender of the Arraveyne Heart*, according to one account."

"Right, fine, so the *Mighty Defender* manages to dodge a mighty bullet, escapes the fall of the empire, crosses great stretches of interstellar space and crash-lands right here on Ong? This happens nearly a million years ago, yet the wreck remains lost, unseen, undiscovered? I mean, that's one big, mean and deadly desert out there, but a two-mile-long ship...that's a lot of parts, moving or otherwise, and in all that time something should have shown up."

"One thing did," said Van Graes. "The Angular Eye."

Pyke's eyes narrowed. "Wait—this eye-widget came from that ship? How do you—how could you know?"

"Arravek science scaled heights in some fields that our age has yet to even attempt," said Van Graes. "Para-quantal alteration of material properties, distinct property states, sub-quantum data storage and even programming. The Angular Eye can analyse a sliver of any material and then show the way to more of the same, perfect for finding anything from mineral deposits to missing persons. But if you leave the little sample chamber empty the Angular Eye points out at the great desert east of Cawl-Vesh!"

"Because it's only analysing itself?" Dervla said. "Sounds a bit thin to me."

"The Angular Eye has in recent times passed through the hands of just three people, a Sedlu tomb scavenger who lived over in one of the northern stilt-towns about four hundred years ago, an offworld antique broker who murdered the Sedlu for the Eye, left Ong, made enough of a fortune to buy life extension treatments, came back to Ong two hundred and fifty years later in search of Vesh relics only to die in a freak accident. After that it came into the ownership of the museum, whose directors have mentioned in their reports activity similar to that noted in the Sedlu's diary and the offworlder's private logs."

"It points towards the desert," said Pyke.

"It does indeed."

"But we don't have it...ah, you said something about some doctor who can track it while Raven's using it?"

"Lieutenant-Doctor Ustril," Van Graes said. "During her time on Ong, her researches have led her to make some interesting discoveries in the south-eastern sand seas."

Pyke gave a quiet chuckle.

"So, Mr. Van G, now that we're fully informed and up-to-speed..."

Over her shoulder, Dervla heard Kref yawn capaciously.

"...what is the meat of your proposal?"

"As I stated before, if you meet with the good doctor and, after assessing the chances of success, decide to continue the hunt for the *Mighty Defender* and all its treasures, I'll treble your payments and add a bonus, too. Or, if you decide against any further involvement, you will still be paid the original amount."

Pyke stroked his chin. "But you want us to fly out into the desert for a gab with your scientist before we make up our minds?"

"That would be my preference, yes."

Says the man who holds the purse strings, thought Dervla who then leaned forward. "There is still some risk involved in such a voyage," she said. "Duststorms can spring up any time and what with Raven Kaligari's thugs running around..."

"I see," came Van Graes' voice. "Perhaps an additional risk fee might compensate for taking you out of your way and for any potential difficulties?"

Dervla smiled hungrily. "A most thoughtful notion—perhaps the original fees plus thirty-three per cent would convince these rascals to gamble on such hazards again?"

"Very well, agreed. Captain, when would you be ready to depart?"

Pyke leaned over and bumped fists with Dervla as he spoke. "Any time you like, Mr. Van Graes, so long as you give me some idea of where I'm heading."

"I have a precise idea," Van Graes said as he started to read out a set of planetary coordinates.

"Right then—all aboard!" Pyke said once he'd keyed the data into the navcomp screen. "Anything we need from the cave before we dust off?"

"Ancil's just gone back for his goody bag," said Moleg as he followed Kref into the shuttle and along the seating compartment.

"Ah, the infamous goody bag," Pyke said as Ancil re-emerged

from the cave, dashed over and scrambled aboard, with a dark-camo holdall clutched in one hand.

"Are we all set?" said Pyke, prodding the "seal all hatches" control.

Ancil grinned. "You know my motto, Chief—leave nothing useful behind!"

"Crazy scrounger," Pyke said. "Mr. Van Graes? You still there?"

"I am, Captain."

"That's us crewed and buttoned up, ready for departure. You'll be telling your friend to expect us?"

"The moment this conversation is done, Captain, I shall be sending her a message to that effect."

"We'll speak later, then."

"Safe journey, Captain."

The comm link went dead.

"Okay, you lucky people!" Pyke sang out as he engaged the autopilot. "Time we weren't here."

The shuttle-barge rose smoothly on humming suspensors, rode a widening spiral up into the clear blue sky then settled into a steady, south-westerly course.

"How long till the rendezvous with this scientist?" Dervla said.

Pyke glanced at the navcomp readouts. "Three and a half hours, give or take."

"Enough time for you to finish your epic tale, then!" She gave a sly smile. "You were about to tell us what happened after you got chumped by Raven and her goons..."

"Aye, and I will, soon as I compose myself."

"Oh, and we were promised scenes of extravagant, brain-scrambling weirdness and, so far, not so much."

Pyke nodded with a knowing smile. "You want weird, my sweet? I got weird for yeh, plenty and then some!"

CHAPTER SIX

(Pyke continues his account.)

Pyke came to out of an uncomfortable half-sleep. His sight was blurred but he thought he could hear several voices, adding to the impression of being in a small space; along with the sudden awareness that he was propped up and strapped to a framework, there was the sense of someone moving in close, waving something strong-smelling under his nose.

The acrid odour penetrated his senses like an electric jolt. Everything snapped into focus. The tilted prisoner-gurney he was lying in; the Henkari, Runken Burlet, sitting in a chair, bound hand and foot; the three or four shabby merc types gathered near an examination table where the Construct drone sat, looking dead as murdered dust. A battery of de-energiser probes hung over it like a row of chrome fangs, clearly holding it immobile. And in the middle of it all, there, right there, hint of a certain fragrance, sweet and inveigling without being engulfing, coupled with the sense of someone standing behind him.

"Hi, Raven," he said. "Haven't lost your knack for subtlety, then."

A statuesque, dark-haired woman in close-fitting, midnight-blue body armour stepped into view holding a pair of matching gloves in one hand. Raven Kaligari, six foot one out of heels, face of an angel, heart of a homicidal killer, skilled with every weapon designed for hands, human or otherwise.

"Bran!—it's been...let me think. Three years? Four?"

"More like two and a half. Two and a half wonderful, terror-free years..."

"Oh, but the times we had!"

"Yeah, I remember, like the time you branded one of my crew..."

"Just a passing whim which got out of hand."

"...and then tried to sell us into slavery. Now that was just plain mean."

Raven nodded wryly, leaned on the side of the gurney and brought her face in close.

"And as bad as that could have turned out for you, Bran, it doesn't compare to what's going to happen next."

She straightened, pulled on the gloves, reached into a waist pouch and took out a long, curved object, dark brown with the dull sheen of leather. At first Pyke thought it was a dagger in a scabbard, but the wide end looked too short and bulbous to be a hilt. Holding it so that Pyke could see, Raven unfastened a couple of straps and opened the odd leather case to reveal an opaque shard of crystal. It was frosty in colour, cold white with a hint of blue. Smiling now, she took the shard, still in its case, over to the table where the inanimate Construct drone lay, and to one of her henchgoons said:

"Report?"

"Scans say the AI core and support peripherals are still functioning."

"Good. Found me any inputs yet?"

The goon reached in and pointed to a small gaping hatch. Without hesitation she pushed the crystal down against the exposed inputs—at once thready webs of energy erupted from openings all over the drone's armoured casing. Raven Kaligari made no sound and did not so much as flinch while electric webs jittered and danced around her hand and crawled up her arm. Then, as suddenly as it had flared up, the energy discharge abated. The crystal shard, jammed into the casing, gave off a stuttering glow for a moment or two before fading away, returning to its former appearance.

Raven Kaligari inhaled noisily through her nose and let out a whoop of exhilaration. She lifted the leather-cased crystal shard away from the dark and lifeless drone then staggered back over to Pyke, face brimming with a drunken glee.

"What a rush!—fascinating experiment," she said. "Wonder if any transition took place?"

With her free hand she stroked his chin then let her fingertips trail lower to his chest and began popping open buttons on his shirt.

"Raven, darlin,'" he said. "I thought we had something, you and me, despite all our mad adventures, y'know? You're not seriously going to burn my brains out, too, are ye?"

She laughed. "No one's brains are getting burned, boiled or fried. You should, however, get ready for a profound shift in your perspective!" She gave his cheek a couple of light slaps. "Enjoy yourself, Bran—it's gonna be the trip of your life!"

Her other hand snaked inside his shirt and slapped the crystal against his bare skin. The icy chill bit into him, spreading outwards and upwards. Transfixed, a panicky hyperawareness brought him a wave of sensation, the pulse and churn of blood through his flesh, a blood that was turning cold. It surged up his chest, up his neck and through his skull to lap at the shores of his brain. Another heartbeat brought a fierce tide of icy blood which froze every channel and junction of thought. Silence clamped itself around his ears. His view of Raven and her bootlicking creeps blurred and slid sideways. Faint feeling of vertigo, head over heels tumbling, falling, rushing along a frost-streaked fissure. And there was the weirdest impression, not quite vision, of something monolithic and menacing hurtling past him, going the other way...

The plummeting slowed. The ungainly spinning wound down as his downward motion became a lazy spiralling gyre, so calm and peaceful that he actually felt like closing his eyes...then he frowned, feeling something hard beneath him, something hard and cold. He sat up and opened his eyes, saw only blur for a moment, rubbed them and looked again.

"What the..."

He had been lying on a long white marble bench, one of several ringing the inside of a circular wooden structure that was open to the sky. Leaves lay scattered across S-shaped tiles, seemingly from the nearly bare bushes and small trees which were planted around the inside of the structure. The place had an autumnal feel to it, enhanced by the dusky evening light, the mildness of the air and the candles.

Candles were everywhere, in sconces, in candelabra on tall iron supports, and in clusters spread all across the tiled ground. Cone-shaped, barrel-shaped, triangular, helical, decorated with inks, adorned with tiny tokens, large ones burning in niches, small ones laid out in patterns, sitting in a line on the backs of the marble benches, dripping wax beards. Strewn with soft glows, the enclosed area was pretty and somehow welcoming.

"Where the hairy hell am I?" Pyke murmured.

"You've arrived on the Isle of Candles, Human," said a voice from nearby. "Seems fairly obvious, I know."

There was an opening in the open-roofed, gazebo-like structure where a tiled walkway led to a broad stairway curving up through rocks and bushes to a large shadowy building. By the opening a short, bristle-snouted Gomedran leaned against a low square pillar topped by burning candles. The greyness of its fur indicated that it was past its prime, and the shabby, patched combat-style gear suggested a military background. *Wonder if he saw how I got here*, Pyke thought.

"You been watching me the whole time?"

The Gomedran shook his head. "Just got back from a walk along the beach, and there you were." He sniffed the air. "My name is Vrass."

"Pyke."

"Greetings, Pyke. Well, if you're here, that can only mean that the Legacy ain't—which is a something of a novelty."

"Legacy? What's…"

"In a moment," said the Gomedran. "First, I need to know if you touched anything unusual before you got here? Anything…odd?"

"Yeah, a chunk of freezing crystal," Pyke said. "That witch Raven slapped it against my chest and moments later I'm rollercoastering my brains out."

"Raven…Kaligari?" said Vrass.

"The same. You've met her?"

"She's been a loyal follower of the Legacy, in recent times. Previously, others have been the shard's custodian."

Pyke got to his feet. "And who's the Legacy?"

Vrass's snout wrinkled with a grin. "The Legacy is a what not a who, some kind of machine intellect, even though it affects the traits of organic existence."

"You said this was the Isle of Candles," Pyke said. "Where is that? What planet are we on?"

The Gomedran shook his head sadly. "We are probably in the same place you were when Kaligari swapped out your mind with the crystal. You see, you and I and this island are all inside it, inside the crystal!"

Pyke's first instinct was to laugh out loud, but the recent accumulation of undiluted weirdness was sufficient to make him pause and give the notion serious consideration. "What? This is a virtuality? But if I'm in here, what's happening to my body..."

He paused, suddenly recalling the hallucinatory journey and the ominous presence that passed him going the other way.

"Well, I'm afraid your flesh and blood is now playing host to the Legacy," the Gomedran said. "Or, to give its full ceremonial title, Culminant Legacy Zovaxa-Jant. We've all had that privilege."

"We?"

Vrass pointed to the large building at the top of the winding steps. "I am not the only occupant of the Residency. There are another two of us, both of whom have been detained, shall we say, for a lot longer than I have."

Vrass indicated the stairway and started upwards. Pyke snorted and went after him. "Skag it," he growled, rubbing his face, tweaking nose and ears, then scratching the back of his neck before grabbing a fistful of shaggy, unkempt hair. The Gomedran Vrass watched him with a smile.

"Feels quite real, doesn't it?"

Pyke nodded. "Certainly does. Impressive level of sensory detail for a persistent virtuality—in fact, it's too good, too perfect..."

"What do you mean?"

"I've been in my share of BTL suites," he said. "Headgeared my way through every kinda scenario you like, and an enviromatrix *this* good needs a mountain of processing traction and a honking great power source to boot..."

"Each of us has, on realising where we were, made similar guesses," said Vrass. "Although I have heard that a few earlier guests were convinced that all this was actually the nightmare dream of some god, or even the universe itself...wait, are you okay?"

They were halfway up the stone steps when Pyke slowed,

overcome by a wave of dizziness. He staggered over to lean against the cold face of a moss-patched boulder.

"Not sure—I feel…"

His sight blurred as another vision overlaid it, far sharper and clearer than where he supposedly was. And he knew exactly what he was seeing—Runken Burlet, still tied to the chair, eyes closed, lips drawn back, trying to endure a succession of blows coming from…himself! Pyke was enraged to see his own fists slamming Burlet repeatedly in the face, chest and stomach. The vision sharpened and scratchy fragments of sound came through. His perspective moved back a step, looked sideways, straight into the wide, eager eyes of Raven Kaligari. Give me your knife, said a voice, *his* voice. A moment later her heavy combat knife was in his hand and he turned back to the restrained Henkari, sagging against the bonds, blood dripping from a burst lip. And without hesitation Pyke's own hand rammed the blade into the side of Burlet's neck, up to the hilt.

"No!" Pyke cried out.

The sheer shock and horror at this slaughter—by his own hands!—severed whatever link had existed. He was back on the stone steps, leaning against mossy stone, fighting a wave of nausea.

How thoughtful of the designers of this place to include the puke reflex! he thought. Maybe he should check for the whereabouts of the jakes as well, just in case.

"That'll be your first echo from your body under the Legacy's control," said Vrass. "Usually the early ones are the most intense but you'll feel better quite soon. Come—I'll introduce you to the others."

The Gomedran was right—the discomfort was abating swiftly, which is more than could be said for those bloody images. At the top of the stairs short pillars bearing large, plain candles flanked an open gate to a small seated area where they encountered a male Bargalil. There was a clattering as it brought all six of its hooves to a halt, then he stroked his curly beard as he regarded Pyke with a kind of startled delight.

"A second guest!" he said. "Two in the one day..."

"A second?" Vrass said. "Oh—ah, Pyke, this is T'Moy of the Mavtal Bargalilan. T'Moy, this is Pyke of the Humans."

Pyke and T'Moy exchanged nods.

"We shall take time to become acquainted later," the Bargalil said. "For now, we should hurry into the cloisters—Klane is trying to communicate with the other newcomer."

Beyond the seated area, double doors led through a shady corridor to a large open courtyard. Gravel paths quartered it diagonally, with grassy stretches occupied by bare-branched trees, a fountain and a group of statues. At the point where the paths intersected, a tall broad-shouldered sentient stood facing a hovering, oval, black object, like a dense of curved splines about a metre long. As they drew near Pyke could see that the close-packed splines shifted eerily, tiny ripple motions as if something restless lay within.

The Bargalil T'Moy called out to the tall figure, who had to be Klane, and began to make the introductions, but he broke off when the black ovoid thing glided between them and floated over to Pyke. In whose mind a theory was forming.

"Greeting, Captain," it said. "I know you would rather be back in the land of the living but given the nature of our captors it is also the land of torture and maiming."

"Strange," Pyke said, stroking his chin. "Have we met?"

"Yes, we have, Human—back on Raven Kaligari's ship, remember? After we got well and truly chumped in the shipping undervault?"

Pyke grinned. "Rensik!—damn, but that's one weird make-over, a bit heavy on the shiny night-ninja look, though..."

"Had no choice in the matter," said the drone. "The local

virtuality seems to have a limited aspect catalogue for non-organics. Still, it will have to suffice."

Pyke glanced at the others. "Friends, this is Rensik, Construct drone and professional critic of the Human race."

"It's the sense of humour," the drone said. "Never fails to annoy."

The others nodded or murmured greetings. Vrass indicated the bulky, broad-shouldered sentient with his hand. "And this is Klane of the Shyntanil."

"Good to meet you, Klane," Pyke said. "Not heard of the Shyntanil before—who are they?"

"An extinct race," said the drone. "It has been over twenty millennia since one of their nomad flotillas was last sighted."

"I was going to say a lost race," said Klane in a low, surprisingly melodious voice. "My own Homefleet passed through this region somewhat more recently than twenty thousand cycles of any of the major civilisations."

"The Shyntanil were known for the use of cyborgisation techniques in the service of life extension," the drone went on. "Your appearance seems to exhibit no replacements or upgrades—might I ask why?"

The square-jawed Klane regarded the black ovoid machine with bleak amusement. "Appearances in this place can occasionally vary from those in base reality, as you have discovered. I should inform you, however, that not all my people pursue life extension, as you call it, in the same fashion, which is why the more apparent modifications adopted by other Shyntanil tribelines are not visible in my outward demeanour."

Pyke nodded. "So how did you ever come to be trapped here? And you, Vrass, and you, er, T'Moy, what's the story?"

"I was part of a long-range scout mission, appraising unclaimed worlds on the fringes of Hegemony space," said Klane. "During a ground survey on an uninhabited planet we were ambushed by the Legacy's Custodians. One of these Custodians used the crystal on me, allowing the Legacy to enter my mind and take control. From intermittent visions I learned that the Legacy flew our scoutpod back to the Homefleet, and gained access to the Shyntanil archives. I do not know what he was searching for but eventually his activities attracted attention from my superiors. He then absconded from Homefleet, rendezvoused with his Custodian allies, and withdrew his presence from my body, allowing my awareness to return."

He fell silent and exchanged a sombre look with the other two Residents. Pyke frowned.

"And yet here you are, talking to me," he said. "This some kinda brainteaser, logic-riddle guff..."

"No, no, Captain," said Vrass. "Klane's account is completely true and correct. You see, this world, this fabricated existence, retains a copy of those brought here. When the Legacy returns to the Residency, as it always does, the displaced mind refluxes back to its original mind. But a separate and distinct copy remains here."

"I caught a glimpse of my situation in the jaws of Reality before that connection was severed," said Klane. "Back in reality, before the Legacy returned to this place, my body was strapped into the scoutpod's pilot chair. When I returned to awareness there, a Legacy Custodian in a full pressure suit was standing over me with the crystal shard in its gloved hand, freshly retrieved from contact with my skin. Danger signals were flashing on the control panel and I could hear the sound of escaping air." The Shyntanil looked weary yet stoic. "Just a few details but I recall them perfectly and never without mourning. The original version of myself suffocated to death in the vacuum of space, and even though the fullness of myself lived on here it still felt as if the closest of my kin had died that day."

Pyke gave a low whistle, shaking his head. "I get it. This

Legacy guy can't afford to leave behind any survivors who might talk about this evil scheme of his, so he sets up the host body for sudden death, then flips back here." He looked at Vrass. "Is that what happened to you?"

The Gomedran nodded. "I was kidnapped during a visit to the Erdisha capital—I later saw flashes of a completely different world, great stretches of dusty, crumbling ruins. I think I was being used to track some quarry by smell—my last glimpse was being dropped down a very deep shaft."

The Bargalil's expression had grown increasingly grim as these accounts were related. When eyes turned to him, he frowned. "This is not something that I find easy to discuss," he said. "All I will say is that during the moment when the Legacy abandoned my form I saw that I was standing in a high room while a building was collapsing around me. Then there was nothing. Then I was back here."

Pyke saw despondency in every face. *Well, sad stories on all sides and then some. Seems like whatever bastard's in charge here, grinding 'em down is part of the game.*

Then the drone spoke up.

"It appears that the Legacy is searching for something," it said. "And Pyke was searching for something, and he—and I—were ambushed by agents of the Legacy, who now..."

"Let's say they're further along the road now than we are," Pyke said.

All three of the Residency's inhabitants were regarding him.

"In all my time here I only ever heard him speak of it once," said Klane. "The 'anguished object of unquenchable desire,' he called it."

"Do you know what this thing is?" said Vrass.

Pyke shrugged. "All I can tell you is how I got to where I am now," he said, going on to give a brief summary of events from meeting Van Graes to finding Runken Burlet to being captured by the local Geskel mercs. He then explained how he needed a DNA sample from Burlet to make a key to open the biovault on the planet Ong.

"And what is inside this vault?" asked Vrass.

"My employer calls it the Angular Eye, says it's some kind of exotic tracking device."

Suddenly several pieces dropped into place, so obvious that Pyke realised how foggy and slow his mind had been since winding up in this atheist-forsaken simulation-from-hell. Dervla and the others were in terrible danger, and there was absolutely nothing he could do about it.

The drone broke the silence. "Is there a problem?"

"Just connecting the dots," he said. "So, major problem complication—the Legacy already has the DNA sample, obtained from Burlet by the simple means of killing the poor bastard." He glanced at Vrass the Gomedran. "That's what I saw in that vision soon after we met. With Burlet's DNA he and Kaligari can create a key for the biovault, so now all they do is travel to this backwater planet, Ong, where my crew are waiting. Only instead of me it'll be the Legacy-as-me who walks in to take advantage of the raid on this museum. And since Raven Kaligari knows me from the old days she can coach the Legacy on how to behave—my crew might not pick up on it until it's too late..."

His mood teetered on the edge of black despair—then he spat a curse, laughed and curled his spread hands into fists.

"I don't care how much Raven Kaligari thinks she knows about me—there's no way she can teach this Legacy, this jumped-up puke-bucket of data-virus that crawled out of some garbage-dump-corner of galactic history, how to be me—ME!— Captain Brannan Pyke! 'Cos when she and her data-puke boss meet my crew and—god help them—my darling Dervla, they'll be outed faster than a Sendrukan at a Voth orgy!"

The three Sojourners were simultaneously taken aback by the

fury of this outburst, yet also impressed, delighted in the case of Vrass who could not conceal a toothy grin.

"Feel better?" said the drone.

"Blood terrific, since yer asking."

"What next?"

"Keep busy," Pyke said. "Find out what there is to know, like what this Legacy looks like, where he goes, if there's more than just this island, anything, everything..."

"There's a mainland," the drone said. "It's frequently veiled by mists but I've glimpsed it a couple of times."

Pyke perked up at this new information. "This I have to see. Where's the best vantage?"

"I'll show you."

Pyke gave a half-salute to the three Residents and went after the drone Rensik who headed for the stairs leading up to the villa's first floor.

Overlooking the square courtyard was a U-shaped balcony sheltering beneath eaves of mossy tiles. The woodwork and the railings looked bleached and weather-beaten, like the doors which led off to rooms spaced around the upper floor. A profusion of candles lit up the shadowy walkways, some in wall niches, some on branched stands, a few stuck on balcony rails, and quite a number in patternless glowing clusters dotting the floorplanks. Each of these clusters, Pyke noticed, had some kind of curious item at its centre, a feather, a coin, a jewel, and other more enigmatic trinkets. The Construct drone led him to a narrow staircase that curved up, steps creaking underfoot, to come out on the roof, in a small canopied platform. A candle lantern hung from one of the canopy supports, shedding a soft amber glow. A pair of rickety chairs stood by a small six-sided table so Pyke sat down in one and peered out at the mist and the hints of what might be high cliffs.

"How far off is that?—about a mile, you reckon?"

"A little under," the drone said, "0.89 of a mile."

Pyke switched his gaze to the outward-facing shore of the Isle of Candles, standing to get a better look—there was a small jetty and a hut down at the waterside but no boat of any kind.

And I'll bet those waters are hoaching with flesh-eating bastard-fish of the Legacy's own design.

"Wonder if any of the others have had a crack at swimming across," he said.

"Klane told me that he tried not long after his arrival," said the drone. "He related that something grabbed him by the ankles when he was halfway, dragged him down into the dark depths, and he woke up coughing on the beach below."

"Figures." Pyke narrowed his eyes. "So, who designed this simulation, the Legacy or someone or something else? Why go to the effort of all this elaborate fakery, and why hint at a mainland without any way to get over there?"

"Speculation on the motives of a vanished race's AIs is an ungaugeable prospect," said the drone.

"A vanished race? How do you figure that?"

"Just conjecture. From what you say this crystal sounds like it's part of something larger, something small enough to fit into a Human hand. And without any visible energy source it can maintain within itself a simulation of extraordinary sophistication and depth of detail. That tells me that this crystal shard is a relic from a technological civilisation so far back into the abyss of time that not even legends survive. I have been trying to map the boundaries of the sim ever since I got here, passively so as not to attract attention, and I have yet to discern an actual limiting edge…"

"Still, such investigating will keep us busy, and the first rule of investigating is—pick someone else's brains! Klane's been here the longest—let's start with him, see how much detail we can squeeze out of him!"

Pyke began to get to his feet but dizziness swept over him like a grey, heavy blanket and he slumped back into the chair. The Construct drone had edged nearer and was asking him what was wrong. Pyke tried to answer but the greyness was blurring into darkness and his mouth just wouldn't frame the words. Everything sank into silence, while faint waves of dream-vertigo swayed this way and that.

Then the indistinct enfolding smears shivered and sprang into sharp focus—Pyke was seeing his own face, his very own features, except that they were like something hollow, a mask laid over an evil hijacking presence, the Legacy. In the mirror, it smiled at him with his mouth, gave a nostril-flared leer and licked those lips. It was his face but at the same time a parody of his face.

"Greetings, Captain," it said. "How are you faring, hmm? I assume that by now you've met the guests of my crypto-convoluted pleasaunce. A sad, staid trio but I am confident that your energising presence will stir them to greater things."

The Legacy held out one hand sideways and another slender hand reached in to pass on a small, stalk-like object. Raven Kaligari, whose hand it was, then came into view, resting both hands on the Legacy's shoulders and offering a sly, teasing smile to the mirror. The Legacy held up the object.

"Behold, Runken Burlet," it said. "Or, rather, the DNA key that we fabricated from his mortal remains. The warrenworld Geskel is now well behind us and it will be only a matter of hours before we reach Ong. All I need to do is persuade your crew to carry out most of the infiltration for us, then we walk in at the end and take what is rightfully ours. And who knows—perhaps one or two of your companions will survive, but I wouldn't bet on it. Your fate here in the cage of the real is sealed, although a likeness of you will remain on the Isle of Candles...or will it?"

His laughter was rich with cruelty and Raven's was all eager malice.

"I've not made up my mind yet, Captain, so enjoy every moment—there may not be very many left."

The vision rippled wildly like the surface of a pool disrupted by a large stone. The broken fragments of that face stretched and swirled around and around, flattening, slowing, dissolving layer by layer back into the canopied platform atop the villa. Still in the chair next to the small table, Pike sat there breathing heavily for a moment or two.

"Back with us? Excellent!"

The drone Rensik, ovoid and black-ribbed like some bizarre fruit, hovered at the other side of the platform. The only other still present was the Gomedran, Vrass, who regarded him with worried eyes.

"Another seeing?" he said. "Did you converse?"

"No, this was just him putting on a show for me," said Pyke, keeping the lid on the anger that welled up so easily. "He had plenty to say, and all I got to do was listen."

"Do you wish to talk about the experience?"

"God, no. Could do with being left alone for a spell, though."

Vrass gave a sombre, knowing nod and left, followed smoothly by the drone. Pyke sighed and slumped lower in his chair, staring out at the hazy mainland. Dusk was darkening into evening and all he could see of the distant cliffs were faint gleaming pinpoints that sharpened and dulled with the shift and ebb of the mists. A drowsiness stole over him like a slow tide, lulling him into a fitful doze. There were periods of lucid dreaming in which he was trying to get answers from his crew as they sat at checkerboard tables playing enigmatic games with figurines and coins, only the figurines had burning candlewicks sticking out of their heads and the coins had an eye on one side and a black hole on the other.

Something startled Pyke fully awake, wide-eyed and dry-mouthed. There was an image stuck in his mind's eye, candles shaped like people that were vaguely familiar. He got to his feet, stretching the kinks and aches out of his neck and back, then looked out to sea. The mists had lifted somewhat and those high cliffs were now clearly visible.

Got to be some way across, he thought. *If it turns out that I really am stuck in this sim-existence, I will find a way…*

Footsteps made him turn to see the square-jawed, square-browed Shyntanil Klane appear at the top of the stairs.

"Ah, you are awake already," he said. "Here on the island it is rare to feel the need for sleep. I was curious to remind myself what it looked like but missed the opportunity."

"Should have sold tickets," Pyke said. "How long was I out?"

"More than seven hours, according to your machine ally."

Pyke frowned. *Depending on Raven's ship, they might already have reached Ong!—that Legacy bastard might be with them right now!* He struggled to put such thoughts aside, but it was difficult.

"What else have you been doing, apart from spying on me?"

"Listening to some of the musical insects that populate points of the shoreline," Klane said. "All this time I have waited in vain to hear the birdsong repeat itself. Vrass and T'Moy prefer to while away the time playing some of the table games…"

"Wait, did you say games, games you play on a board, that kind of thing?"

Vrass nodded. "There is a room in the Residency set aside for such pastimes. Would you like to see?"

Pyke nodded and followed him down to the balcony, feet clattering on the wooden steps as the drone brought up the rear. The Gomedran led them to a room three doors along, a small one lit by the ubiquitous candles. Inside, eight hexagonal tables larger than the one upstairs on the canopied platform were spaced around the room. Pyke took in the tall, narrow window, the faded, blue-painted walls, cracked and peeling in patches. Candles sat in small niches, and were lined up along a deep marble mantelpiece over a cold, dead fireplace; their buttery glow was reflected into the room by a huge mirror resting at the back of the mantelpiece and hanging forward slightly on a short chain linked to a wall hook.

All these details were forgotten the moment Pyke's gaze settled on a game table over in one corner, and the pieces that sat upon it. For a second he flashed on images from his earlier dream, the game pieces that burned like candles, only these had a more rudimentary look. Then, prompted by a nebulous curiosity, he went back out of the room, leaned on the rail and peered down at the statues in the courtyard.

"What is it, Captain?" said Vrass who had followed him out.

Pyke laughed faintly, pointing. "These statues, they all look—"

"Like us," Vrass said. "Yes, we know, one Bargalil, one Shyntanil and one Gomedran. When I first arrived here, however long ago that was, there were just two statues—only after the demise of my real-world self did a third statue appear, mysteriously, when no one was around to see." Vrass joined him at the rail. "That looks nothing like me, however."

Pyke grimaced. "Wonder what I'll get when…when I…"

Dizziness hit him like a wave once again and he staggered back, lunged at the wall and fell to his knees. Then his limbs went numb and he slumped over on his side. Vrass was swift to crouch nearby.

"It's happening again!" he wanted to say but the numbness had reached his mouth and tongue. Physical sensations ebbed away, and his hearing was next to go. By now the others had hurried over and gathered around him, their shapes blurring at the edges. And there were others, too, sad-eyed spectral forms hovering and wavering behind them, apparitions weirdly lit by nearby candles. Then it all gradually fell away and he breathed in to cry out as dark tendrils curled in from the edges like an iris, plunging him into sightless blackness.

Then the iris opened out, and he saw that he was walking swiftly, stealthily, along a dim corridor towards a well-lit branch passage: there, a slender, wiry biped in a dark uniform was shouting while aiming a long-barrelled weapon at someone further along the branch. Pyke was a mere spectator as the Legacy casually strolled up to the guard and disarmed him, before rendering him unconscious quickly and ruthlessly.

Pyke sat back in the pilot's couch and spread his hands theatrically.

"The rest you know!"

There was a stunned silence and looks of puzzlement or scepticism were on show. Dervla found herself in a strange state of conflicted emotions—part of her just wanted to laugh out loud at such an unbelievable tale, yet Pyke's actions after his arrival at the museum had certainly gone from unsettling to unhinged craziness, which was enough to make her pause for serious consideration. Also there was the fact that he had told this big, convoluted story straight, without any of his usual tics and tells, so this was either the performance of a lifetime, or...

Billows of fine sand hissed against the shuttle's hull, claws of the duststorm whose fringes they were skirting around. She shivered.

Ancil raised a hesitant hand. "Chief, all that stuff with the island—all that happened inside that chunk of crystal?"

"That's exactly right."

"Can I get another look at it, Chief?—if that's okay."

Pyke shrugged, then produced the dark, leather-clad object, its odd shape reminding Dervla of a fang, and gingerly undid the fastenings and peeled them aside. The crystal lay within, looking like the head of some creature—a bird or a reptile—and it had a tapering, irregular stem with rough sides as if it had been broken off from something else. Dervla saw the nervousness in the way

Pyke handled the thing, and realised that she was starting to believe in his story.

"So this AI, this Legacy," Ancil said, "jumped into your mind and bounced you over into the crystal-thing. And now you're back in charge of your own body but there's still another you left behind. Right?"

"You've got it," Pyke said. "My guess is that anyone dumb or unlucky enough to touch this thing ends up leaving behind an imprint, an echo of themselves, when the Legacy decides to pull the plug. That hijacking scumbucket thought I was a deader when it left me falling out of that window. It didn't reckon on Dervla leaping out of the skagging window after me, or having a grav-boat backup plan!"

Dervla sketched a mock bow from where she sat. "You said Raven used the crystal on that Construct drone, and that it was there on the island, but when you got glimpses of what this Legacy was up to back in the real world you never mentioned seeing some evil-possessed drone floating around."

Pyke shrugged. "Never caught sight of it, no idea what happened to the drone's casing and contents. When Raven used the crystal on the drone back on the ship it couldn't have been completely trashed, so the Legacy must have allowed the drone to be copied into the simulation for some kinda reason, probably a twisted one."

"What do we do with it in the meantime?" said Ancil.

"Keep it safe and wrapped up and away from tampering fingers," Pyke said as he refastened the straps and clips. "I'm not having any of you taken over by that skagsucker from hell."

There were nods of assent all round, though Dervla wondered if careful study under lab conditions might explain more than Pyke's travelogue. She was about to suggest this when the shuttle-barge heeled over noticeably as it turned to port. The filtered daylight dimmed and the interior glowstrips brightened in response.

"We changing course, Chief?" Ancil said. "We're veering into that storm."

Outside, the hazy view of the dune desert and the distant, hilly horizon had been obliterated—dark swirls of dust and fine sand engulfed the shuttle-barge in a constant abrasive hiss.

"Autopilot is guiding us to the rendezvous coordinates," Pyke said, studying the navcomp screens. "ETA in...uh, ten minutes—the skagging storm has shifted and we're running straight into a headwind."

"Okay, then," Dervla said. "While we wait for the shuttle to get to where it's going, it might be handy to know what surprises Oleg packed away for us."

"Ah, already done, Derv," Ancil said.

"What...when?"

"While the captain was telling us his story, I was footling around with the cases. I was still listening, though."

"I heard you moving around," Derv said. "Thought you were just off to the can."

"Explains your follow-up questions," said Pyke. "So what did you find?"

Ancil was immediately gleeful. "He packed the gauss rifles, a brace of drum-pistols, a pulse beamer and..." he paused, "...the Melari!"

The Melari was a hefty, double-barrelled weapon capable of delivering a range of highly effective rounds.

"The Melari," Pyke said with an approving nod. "What else?"

"Only a bandolier stocked with all my favourite nades and charges!"

"Nade Boy's got to have his nades. What else?"

Ancil looked thoughtful, glancing back over his shoulder. "One of the cases had body armour...another's got food and drink, I think."

"Easy to see where your priorities lie," Dervla said, getting out of her seat and moving to the rear of the passenger compartment where the supplies had been stacked. She studied the labels, even looked inside a couple of containers, then folded her arms and whistled.

"I hope Oleg packed my beach shorts and windbreaker," Pyke said. "'Cos I'd just be lost without 'em…"

Dervla gave a sly smile. "How about two-man hunker tents? Or command-level emergency rations? Or breather masks, quality ones? There's even a field surgical module—clamp it to a steady table, activate it and, pow, instant field surgery. That Oleg, he's a treasure…"

Pyke was taken aback. "I didn't even know we had half this stuff aboard."

Without warning, the shuttle-barge lurched to starboard as its nose dipped. Dervla grabbed a nearby seat headrest and hauled herself into the couch behind it. Outside, something was glowing through the murky rushing veils of the sandstorm. Pyke was hunched over the controls, madly keying and screen-prodding, and a moment later the craft levelled off enough for Dervla to leave her seat safely and return to the co-pilot couch.

"Got a castext from this scientist of Van Graes," he said. "Claims to be her anyway, told me to look out for 'the arrowhead,' whatever that means…"

Dervla was peering forward, through the battering swirls of dust in the direction of the glow source. When details became apparent she smiled, snapped her fingers to get Pyke's attention and pointed.

"Right, I see," he said. "Typical intro-tech, can't just tell me to look for three landing lights in a triangle, nah, has to make it a skaggy IQ test!" He glanced at Dervla. "Which I would've figured out, by the way, let me make that clear!"

The duststorm was shifting again by the time the shuttle-barge was within fifty metres of the landing pad. A ferocious crosswind was now forcing Pyke to alternate between the autopilot, which was keeping them lined up with the landing gear traps, and manual control. Minute by minute the shuttle-barge descended with nerve-jangling slowness until at last Dervla heard the satisfying multiple clunk of the landing gear being locked into position, solidly anchored to the ground.

By the haloed light of the lamps, Dervla could see that they were parked next to a louvred wall set into a rock face. As they sat there, a rigid canopy began extending outwards above, curving down and over them, entirely sealing the shuttle-barge off from the raging storm. They could now see that the landing pad was situated square in the middle of what looked like a crescent-shaped area with rough rock walls, the air still hazy with fine, disturbed dust.

"Well, we're here, sitting on her doorstep," she said. "You'd think there'd be..."

Three loud raps interrupted her. Pyke chortled.

"Our hostess makes her presence known!"

Pyke got up, went over to the hatch and thumbed the release. It slid open to reveal the midriff of someone tall and dressed in a rose-coloured robe with baggy sleeves and capacious folds. The stranger bent down to peer in, and Dervla had to fight to keep her expression composed—a female Sendrukan!

Well now, what was a member of the Master Race doing out here in this wasteland?

The Sendrukan Hegemony was the single most powerful civilisation in this part of the galaxy, a status that the Sendrukans had worked hard to acquire over preceding centuries, not least because they had an exceedingly high opinion of themselves.

"I am Lieutenant-Doctor Ustril," the Sendrukan said in a slightly hoarse voice, her words calm and measured. "Are you Captain Pyke?"

"That I am."

"And this is your crew?"

"That they are. Don't be fooled by their unpromising demeanour and lack of social graces—they're highly trained operatives, able to turn their hand to any job, even cooking."

The Sendrukan scientist stuck her head through the hatch and gave each of them a moment's scrutiny. The proportions of Sendrukan faces were quite similar to those of Humans, and Lieutenant-Doctor Ustril's features were neat and well formed with a soft, pale complexion that Dervla refused to be jealous of. Long, dark-blue hair braided into three thick plaits completed the picture.

Ustril's expression gave away nothing yet Dervla could almost feel the disapproval vibrating in the air.

"Van Graes mentioned that you liked to talk," she observed.

"One of life's pleasures," Pyke said. "Although not everyone agrees."

Ustril seemed on the point of frowning, but instead turned and moved away from the shuttle-barge. "Please follow me—my Angular Eye detector is still being calibrated, a brief procedure. Then activation will take place."

Dervla went outside and leaned against the side of the shuttle-barge while Pyke and the others filed out. Last to emerge was Ancil who was gazing wide-eyed at the back of the tall Sendrukan scientist. He glanced at Dervla as he exited, eyes quickly returning to the Sendrukan.

"She's kinda...y'know, really..."

"What?" Dervla said. "Tall? Mysterious? Enigmatic? Aloof?"

Ancil swallowed. "Amazing," he said, eyes wide. "I think I'm in love."

At which Kref turned and stared at Ancil, then exchanged a worried look with Dervla.

"Uh-oh," he said in deep, foreboding tones.

CHAPTER SEVEN

Pyke, the planet Ong, Ustril's base in the desert

Without offering an explanation, the Sendrukan made them wait in an austere, pale-grey foyer-like room laid out with hard benches whose greyness was equally pale.

"What is this all about?" Dervla muttered.

"Don't know, my sweet," Pyke said. "But if there's no change very soon I may be forced to start singing 'The Ballad Of The Bastard King's Bodyguard'!"

He smiled as she brought a hand up to her forehead, as if she were suffering from a sudden needling pain. "The Filthiest Song Ever Written?"

"The very same, all thirty-two verses, in all their multi-sexual, ultra-sensual glory." He paused and arched an eyebrow. "Every one committed to memory."

"I like verse eleven," said Kref with a throaty chuckle. "Dirty-funny."

"Verse sixteen," Ancil said. "Once heard, never forgotten."

Grinning, Pyke nodded. "We could probably get a good chorus going—we'll need it for verse twenty-one..."

At that moment a tall door cracked open in the wall and the Sendrukan scientist emerged, clutching a bundle of opaque, filmy garments. Pyke just caught Dervla giving thanks under her breath and smiled inwardly to himself.

"The isochronal detector is still running through its calibration phase," the Sendrukan said. "Therefore I have decided to admit you to my workshop. However, due to a number of sensitive ongoing experiments I must ask you all to don these simple environment suits. They seal in any skin cells, follicles or particulates."

Pyke stared at the filmy garments and raised a querying finger. "Erm, Doc, how long till your calibration is actually finished?"

"In Human terms, more than one hour. You are quite welcome to wait out here if you so wish."

Hmm, trying to make me look like the yokel-bozo, eh? Pyke snapped a smile into place, bright and furiously cheery.

"Not to worry, Doc—looks like a comfy suit, can't wait to try it on!"

With surprising alacrity Ancil darted across to take the suits from Ustril's outstretched arm. As she passed them over to him she stood there regarding him for a slightly bemused moment, then retreated inside the darkened workshop and closed the door. Ancil stared at the door for a second or two, then began sorting through the suits and handing them out. Watching this from the side, Pyke exchanged a quizzical look with Dervla. Under her breath she whispered, "tell you later," then smiled when Ancil came up with an envirosuit for each of them.

"Everyone's got their name on it, see?" Ancil pointed to black characters near one shoulder. "And they all fit just right. Amazing—bet she's got devices in the walls that scanned our measurements!"

Great Spirit of the Spaceways! Pyke thought as Ancil wandered off to get himself kitted out. *The lad has a bad case of the besots—for a lady Sendrukan, no less!*

"So—stars in his eyes, then?" he murmured to Dervla as they both tugged the thin, baggy suits on over their clothes.

"Kinda looks that way."

"Y'know, I could have a word with him, man to man…"

She gave him an amused look and patted his arm. "I don't know if your skill set's up to the challenge. Leave him to me for now."

Pyke shrugged and nodded, even though he knew that he had plenty of sage advice to offer, especially given the mystical bonds of brotherhood shared by those who had faced dark perils together and survived. *Not to say that Dervla won't be helpful, deploying her womanly insights and suchlike, but it's always wise to have a plan B—if all else fails, the lads will come to the rescue.*

The door opened when everyone was suited up, and they calmly filed inside.

Ustril's workshop turned out to be a wide, high room, sporadically lit by freestanding downlamps which left the ceiling in shadows. Framework partitions sectioned off areas into small rooms here and there, and the decor was a mix of soft green and sky-blue materials adorned with stylised gear and circuitry patterns. Even as they entered, Pyke saw a square partition descend from the ceiling to enclose completely a cluster of analyser racks and a cluttered lab bench over in the corner.

Looking around, Pyke noticed that one part of the open-plan area was for cooking and dining, another for soft seating with an entertainment console, another that was a library of sorts. There were also shelves and transparent cabinets spaced around the walls.

Ustril was nowhere to be seen but suddenly her composed voice could be heard in the air overhead. "Please wait in the de-stress zone. I am occupied with matters of parameter adjustment and will join you shortly." There was a two-second pause. "Kindly do not touch anything."

Exchanging looks and shrugs, the crew gravitated to the group of oversized, padded stools and a pair of immense loungers. Pyke stretched out on one of these and was just starting to enjoy it when the Sendrukan scientist emerged from one of the partitioned rooms, came over and sat down quite primly on one of the stools.

"The calibration is proceeding satisfactorily," she said. "We will have to wait no more than one half-hour."

"Good, great," said Pyke, nodding, and Dervla nodded, too. Then the others nodded to each other as well.

The ensuing silence widened uncomfortably.

"So, Doc," Pyke said after a moment. "Er, Doctor Ustril, that is, how did you come to be here on Ong? Are you studying the desert for one of your academies, or the like?"

His words trailed off as he saw a distraught expression passed over the Sendrukan's face and she bowed her head for a moment. *Ah, hell, what have I said now?*

Dervla shot him an annoyed glance before she went over and sat next to the Sendrukan, now looking almost childlike in stature.

"If our captain said anything to upset you, we're very sorry..."

Lieutenant-Doctor Ustril raised her head. "I take no offence. None of you could be expected to know anything of my personal indignities. I do not wish to reveal the details, but I can tell that I have been exiled from the Hegemony for some years due to...to hasty remarks I made about matters outwith my area of competence." She looked around her for a moment. "It has been some time since I had...visitors."

Then Ancil put up his hand, as if he was a kid in school, and Pyke thought, *Don't, Ans, just don't!*

But his anxiety was unwarranted. "Doctor Ustril, I was wondering, what is your area of expertise?"

Looking mildly surprised, the Sendrukan said, "Historical archaeology, as well as conflict analysis."

"I see there's quite a few exhibits around your place, here," Ancil went on. "Are they part of your, erm, researches?"

"Most of them are," said Ustril. "I could conduct you all on a brief tour while we are waiting—if your captain approves."

Pyke gave a thumbs-up gesture. "Your captain approves! Carry on..."

The notion of taking a doze on the vast and comfortable lounger while the others were off seeing the sights was most attractive, but before he could settle back against the end-cushion Dervla came over and nudged one of his sprawled legs with the toe of her boot. He sighed, rose and followed the rest on a winding journey among cabinets of dusty relics. And, in spite of his innate resistance, Pyke found himself learning a few points of interest concerning the original inhabitants of Ong. Much of this emerged as a result of questions eagerly offered up by the bedazzled Ancil, clear evidence that the lad's brain was turning to mush.

It turned out that over half a million years ago, the planet Ong was a very different place. The small shallow sea far to the west was a remnant of decent-sized oceans that had once girdled the globe. Also, the original denizens, a slender bipedal species, inhabited fertile coastal areas and at one point had developed a technological civilisation. But some cosmological event intervened and altered Ong's orbit, most likely, according to Doc Ustril, a near miss by another planetary body passing through the system. It was enough to shift Ong's orbit slightly closer to the sun, resulting in catastrophic changes affecting the whole of the planet's surface. Tidal waves and volcanic activity spikes, Ustril said, and superstorms and long droughts. A rise in climatic temperature would have collapsed the ecosystem and brought worldwide desertification, leading to civilisational collapse and probably the extinction of the original inhabitants.

Pyke managed to maintain a kind of wide-eyed impassiveness while masking the string of yawns that overtook him with increasing frequency. The Sendrukan's tour had migrated about halfway round the vaguely oval interior when Pyke's gaze settled upon a cluster of chest-high cabinets which seemed to contain arrays of tiny spiky objects.

"What's this over here?" he said as he wove a path towards them.

"Bran, what the crud are you up to?" said Dervla in her patented gritted teeth murderous mutter. Someone else was clearing their throat but it was all behind him as he strolled up to the nearest transparent case and peered in at its contents.

Which were not what he expected. Instead of the desiccated fossil of some long-dead desert vermin, he found himself staring at rows of fingernail-sized insects, their carapaces camoed in the browns and blacks of the sandy wastes they had once scurried across. Then he frowned; light glinted oddly off some of them, as if from something shiny, and that was when he noticed the gimbal-armed magnifier clamped to the corner of the cabinet. He grabbed and swung it over, adjusted its telescopic main arm, found button controls next to the eyepiece and commenced his scrutiny.

Suddenly enlarged, the insects became nightmares, hideous scorpion-wasp-cockroach hybrids clearly fabricated from whatever scavenged materials were available—plastic, resin, metal, wire, anonymous patches of hide, fine twine, treated paper and card. Every single one was different, each bearing evidence of adaptations made on the fly, many with asymmetrical limb arrangements. Bumpy carapaces sprouted spicule sensors and tiny cam nodules, more sensors gleamed in leg joints, and tearing pincers were a common feature.

"Do you like my swarmbot collection, Captain?"

Pyke glanced at the figure looming beside him, and gave a considered nod.

"I've crossed paths with similar, if somewhat larger beasties," he said.

"Ah, that repair dock on Nagolger," said Dervla. By now, she and the others had also gathered around the swarmbot exhibit. Expressions of fascinated repugnance were the standard response as the magnifier was swung from one to the other.

"Solar-powered?" said Ancil.

Ustril nodded. "The core of all these tiny horrors is the same, a fleck of nanocrystal which runs a cluster of basic behavioural imperatives; absorb sunlight, gather resources, attack, flee, hide. But that same nanocrystal can provide tool-motes for repairing, building and adapting, hence the variety in appearance."

"Have these critters always been around?" Pyke said. "Any idea where they came from?"

"When I arrived on Ong eight, no, nine years ago, they were known of in most of the desert edge-towns as rumours," the Sendrukan said. "It was rare to see one of the swarms then, and usually only in the deepest ravines. But they appear to have changed behaviour in the last few years and smaller mobs of them have been ranging further afield, most frequently in the vicinity of towns like Cawl-Vesh."

From where she stood at the end of the cabinet, she regarded the array of lifeless miniature mechs with a faint frown. "As for their origin, I have heard theories that they were released by a colony of the original inhabitants, confined to an underground refuge hidden in the desert, and now in possession of advanced technologies..." She shook her head. "Another suggests that they are the remnants of a failed weapons project instigated by an unknown offworld power."

"Plausible," said Pyke. "And I guess Ong is the ultimate off-the-beaten-track bolthole."

"There is another possibility," Ustril said. "That they escaped from this ancient ship that Van Graes has sent us to find. He does claim that it was packed full of scientific marvels."

"They're no bigger than the tip of my finger," said Ancil, leaning over and gazing through the magnifier. "Are they dangerous?"

Ustril gave a wintry smile. "One or two do not present a threat, but a dozen, twenty, or thirty, if they got inside any machinery or, worse, a ship's process and control systems, they could cause great damage and hazard. Larger swarms of several hundred or more are entirely capable of killing and dismembering a living creature."

Kref uttered a low whistle. "Hey, you could use a big suction cleaner and scoop 'em all up!"

"That would work," Pyke said. "For about ten minutes before the little beggars chewed their way through your cleaner's innards, turning it into junk before turning on you!"

"The captain is correct," Ustril said. "In large numbers they display great tactical and adaptive skills, although if such a cleaner were fitted with a magnetic-electric disruption field—"

She was interrupted by a high-pitched ting-ting sound. "Ah, the calibration process is complete. Captain, if you and your band return to the waiting area and remove the suits they will be attended to at a later time. I shall shortly join you with the detection equipment out in the transport bay."

The Sendrukan's manner of speech was at times so formal that something odd within Pyke made him feel like bowing once she'd finished speaking. Luckily, it was a feeling he found easy to ignore.

"Okay, Doc, whenever you're ready."

Moments later they were back out in the pale grey lobby, removing the opaque suits which a morose Ancil diligently collected and folded up into a neat pile. Back outside at the shuttle-barge, Dervla tried adjusting the upper-hull configuration while Pyke and the others got to work moving some of the supplies into the underdeck storage and folding away some of the seats to make room for their new passenger and her gear. Dervla managed to get the shuttle canopy shell to extend upwards, raising both the hatch height and the interior headroom. Everyone was enjoying congratulating each other when the Sendrukan scientist emerged from the lobby entrance, carrying two impact-res cases and towing a rack of equipment clamped to a small suspensor-dolly. There were three levels of modules in the rack and readouts were flickering all over them. Ancil and Kref were quick to offer aid and, as they stowed the cases in the easy-access recess, Moleg helped steer the equipment rack in through the rear hatch. Once the scientist had settled into a seat beside the rack she pressed a bead on a bracelet she wore on one wrist. Outside, the smooth cover which protected the landing bay began to retract, letting in blazing sunshine.

"Captain," said Ustril. "There is a sudden urgency in our undertaking."

Pyke smiled as the tension in her voice sparked his intuition.

"Let me guess—someone out there is using the Angular Eye right now, and your spangly gadget has picked up their spoor—am I close?"

"Quite correct," she said, a note of respect in her voice. "I have written the course down for you, in Earther notation." She held out a slip of card which was passed up to Pyke. "The detectioner cannot perceive the distance of the Eye's location so if we leave here and fly at a ten-degree variance from the course for some minutes we should be able to..."

Pyke held up his hand. "No problem, Doc—I know how to triangulate."

Turning to the flight controls, he flipped up the nav-screen and keyed in the course directions as an overlay, then switched to the priority frame, did a quick poke-and-drag about twenty miles long at ten degrees. Then he engaged the autopilot and leaned back.

"Just letting the wiring do the work, hmm?" Dervla said.

"I keep hearing ads telling me that Mr. Smartpilot is my friend, so who am I to disagree?"

She laughed softly, and Pyke felt the shuttle-barge lurch as the automatics released the ground locks and took the craft on a rising curve away from Ustril's semi-concealed base. Soon they were hurtling along at fifteen hundred feet, holding to Ustril's triangulation course. Outside the duststorm had abated and the unshackled brilliance of the sun hammered the rolling sea of sand with a pitiless, scouring heat. Meanwhile, away to the north, another front threatened, a dark, blurred wall a thousand miles across.

Less than ten minutes after departing the base, Ustril passed new course data up to Pyke who nodded and entered it into the nav-screen. "That comes out to just under seventy-two miles by my reckoning, Doc," he said.

"Yes, Captain," the Sendrukan said. "My conversion sagacial already made that clear. At our current speed it estimates that we will arrive in 20.7 minutes, approximately."

Approximately, Pyke thought, keeping the satire to himself. *My favourite kind of accuracy.*

He sank back into the pilot's couch while the rest of the crew grumbled and chatted among themselves. Once or twice he heard Ancil try to start up conversations with the Sendrukan lady scientist but both times they fizzled out in the downpour of her reticence. Against this background Pyke's mind went back to that whole bizarre episode inside the crystal, thoughts circling it like doomed ships in the grip of a black hole. And as weird as that captivity had been, he knew that his account had fallen well short, especially when it came to the moment when he was hovering on that threshold between the crystal's virtual domain and the flesh-and-blood existence of the real world. How he came all the way back while a slice of himself got dragged back in.

He remembered something that the Shyntanil Klane had said, how the Legacy once referred to the crystal as "the anguishing object of unquenchable desire." *What kind of desire*, he wondered. *Desire for what?* Pyke felt the leather-cased crystal inside his jacket, pressing against his midriff. He shivered, covering it up with a cough.

Three minutes out from their destination a console alert attracted his attention, so he switched the controls to assisted manual and brought the craft in low and slow. A mixture of enormous dunes and protruding, wind-sculpted rock formations dominated the area. The coordinates end-point, however, was on a broad lee slope from a long dune ridge which overlooked a big, sand-choked outcrop of jagged rocks and a narrow gully in between. The sandy slope had definitely been a landing site; there were plentiful signs of disturbance to show where a craft had been parked and where several persons, probably Raven and her goons, had tramped about. Pyke brought the shuttle-barge smoothly down to land about a dozen metres away.

"Something's been bothering me," said Dervla as everyone prepared to alight. "If tracking the Angular Eye brought us here, then they must have been using it here. But in order to get here they must have used it somewhere else, back in Cawl-Vesh maybe, before Doctor Ustril's detector came online."

"So when they used the Eye here," Pyke said, "they were scanning around for what?"

"Perhaps this honking big ship broke up on re-entry," said Ancil. "What if there's pieces of it scattered halfway across Ong?"

"Shame," Pyke said. "I kinda liked the idea of stumbling over a colossal shipwreck half buried in the sand." He glanced along the compartment at the Sendrukan. "What do you think, Doc? Are we actually hunting for bits of a ship?"

Ustril was fussing over the readouts on the equipment rack. Pulsing, flickering glows passed strangely across her features.

"Until now, Captain Pyke, I have had no reliable means of detecting this lost vessel," she said, not looking up. "All I can say for certain is that we are very close to where the Angular Eye was utilised and that this happened 17.3 minutes ago."

Pyke was confounded. "They dusted off from here seventeen minutes ago and nothing tripped our detects?"

"Stealthed," said Dervla. "Has to be."

Kref growled. "Scumbags'll get to the treasure before us!"

"Captain," said Ustril. "They came here for a reason—their operation of the Angular Eye must have detected wreckage from the Arraveyne vessel. We should scout for it, gather data..."

Pyke studied her for a moment, curious about this sudden assertiveness. "From the air I saw nothing but rock and sand, and no long tracks leading here and there—Raven's crew must be using grav-harnesses or short-range hoppers."

"There's a couple of hoppers and a harness in the aft hold, Chief," said Ancil.

"One of my field scopes can make topographical comparisons scans," said Ustril. "I can adjust it for a wide radius and depth, allowing it to identify subsurface anomalies."

"Okay, Doc, you do that while we break out the hoppers."

While the Sendrukan scientist attended to her sensor equipment, Pyke organised Kref and Moleg to unpack and ready up the hoppers. Dervla and Ancil were sorting through the guns, ammo and body armour to see who would get what. Leaving them to it, Pyke slogged through the sand to check out Raven's landing site.

He could see where their transport had left broad gouges in the sand, which revealed that it was larger than the average ship's shuttle, probably a combat-pinnace if it was running with stealth fields. Pyke recalled, from that past association, that Raven preferred working with a crew no bigger than four or five, and the tracks around this spot seemed to back that up. He was studying some coil patterns, thinking this had to be where their hoppers lifted from, when he heard Dervla calling him over to the shuttle.

Back inside, Dervla and Ancil were gathered near Ustril's equipment, staring at a pale projection. They squeezed aside so he could get in close for a look-see. What he saw was a basic lo-rendered image of the big rock formation just beyond the dune ridge, enclosed by a shimmery veil, or something.

"Is this the scan of the rocks?" he said.

Ustril shook her head. "That's just a low-detail image I put in for comparison—what my equipment is detecting is an enfolding shield or barrier. Nothing my emitters can send is capable of penetrating it."

Pyke leaned in a little closer, smiling. "Camouflage tech, maybe? We see a bunch of rocks but it's really just a snazzy mirage?"

"The possibility is real," said the Sendrukan.

"Van Graes did say that the Arraveyne nobility escaped with labs full of advanced hardware and the scientists to go with it," said Dervla.

"Okay, then." He turned to Kref and Moleg. "Those hoppers unpacked and ready for the off?"

"Both fully juiced and checked out, Captain," said Moleg. Dervla passed around clip-on short-range comm badges while Kref gave a thumbs-up.

"Right, me and Ancil will go first," Pyke said. "See what's under this camo-field, just a brief recce to figure out the risk level then we'll call the rest of you in." He gave a lopsided grin. "That, or the next thing you'll see and hear is us barrelling our way back out with skag-knows what on our tail! All part of the fun!"

Ancil chose that moment to hand him a heavy, chromed handgun with a rubberised grip. It seemed to have three barrels arranged vertically but only one muzzle. Pyke knew he'd seen something like this before and only when Ancil passed him a couple of big, chunky magazines did it click.

"The Jones-Eckley plasma-slugger!" he said, holding it up to the light. "Custom-made for the Shikigana Zaibatsu's security forces. How the hairy hell did you get your paws on one of these?"

A grinning Ancil shrugged. "My supplier back on Zopaxa Station has a fixation for early TwenCen Russian cinema—I sourced some playable crystals from that big commercial archive on Gelol-B and he was ecstatic enough to give me fifty per cent off…"

By now they were both outside, strolling towards the hoppers.

"What did you have to get for your contract at the archives?"

"A crate of Voth whisky…"

"My admiration remains undimmed," Pyke said. "That you could parlay a crate of that rat's piss into a fine piece like this is nothing short of miraculous!"

They clambered into the hopper's small pilot and passenger bucket seats. At first glance a grav-hopper looked like the kind of moulded plastic pleasure craft tourists might use out on the water, except for the angled suspensors, two at the front, two at the back. True, it wasn't that rugged but it was cheap, easy to maintain and had a decent range. And gave about as much protection as an old paper bag. Pyke was banking on there not being armed resistance since Raven's crew had gone elsewhere.

The hopper's suspensors left helices of dust in the air as Pyke steered it up and out, heading for the supposed rock formation. If this camouflage projection had somehow lasted for long ages, he wondered if there was any other protective system awaiting them. His suspicions were confirmed moments later when his vision started to blur. Nothing he did, wiping or rubbing, helped, and while this was happening he started to experience feelings of hilarity coupled with the utter conviction that they were going in the wrong direction.

Blind in charge of a grav-hopper and laughing like a loon! he thought. *And I've not had a drop—damn, must be a mood-altering psi-screen!*

Behind him Ancil was helpless with laughter, now and then pausing only to gasp, "The other way, Chief, the other way!..."

Just when it seemed that the perpetual, blind guffawing would never end, normality abruptly returned. Pyke's chest ached, his throat felt raw, but most crucially nothing was funny. He much preferred the feeling of sharp curiosity tempered with caution he was experiencing now as an immense, sheared-off ship section loomed before them. It wasn't often that he got to be in on the ground floor of this kind of discovery and he couldn't wait to soak up the detail.

At a rough estimation, the ancient wreckage was about three hundred metres long, and lay canted over to one side. The far end was buried deeper in the dunes than the near end, which was a broken, sand-scoured cross-section sprouting substructural pipes and beams, tendrils and ribbons of synthetic material that had been weathered by the climate. As they glided in closer, Pyke could just make out faint markings on the sand-scoured hull, huge, vaguely glyph-like symbols in some lost language, the echo of the magnificence of a long-vanished empire.

Pyke brought the hopper down on a wide stretch of disturbed sand in the lee of the raggedly severed vessel which loomed over them like a cliff of ancient detritus. Getting off the hopper, he stood with fists on hips, staring up at it, uttering a low "Wow" under his breath. He then activated his comm badge and spoke to Dervla, warning her about the psi-screen and its effects, and asked her to send Kref down in the other hopper.

"Not me? Why's that?"

"Well, if we get jumped and need to exit sharpish, I'd feel a lot happier if you and Moleg are up at the shuttle-barge, prepped for a quick getaway if we need it."

"Not protecting my delicate, ladylike sensibilities by any chance?"

He laughed as leeringly as he could. "Oh, darlin,' as if!"

"Right, I'll get on with that, then. Oh, and I should warn you you're about to get an unexpected visitor."

Pyke heard Ancil laugh and looked up, following a pointed finger. Outlined against the blue sky was a large figure seated on a pogo-stick-like contraption and gliding in a steadily descending trajectory which ended with a gentle landing not far from their hopper.

"Like a boss," Ancil said.

Lieutenant-Doctor Ustril dismounted gracefully from her fragile looking transport, touched the controls on the control column and it sank down to settle on the sand.

Pyke, still on the line to Dervla, said, "Yes, well, she's just arrived so get Kref to shake a leg."

"I'll do that very thing."

Kref was next to come floating down into the gully, grinning from ear to ear as he rode the second hopper down to a bumpy landing. As they all gathered before the half-buried vessel's wrecked and shattered cross-section, Pyke heard a faint whine at their backs, frowned and turned—and was not really that surprised to see Dervla, borne by a grav-harness, swooping down to alight upon the soft sand. She gave Pyke a sly half-smile as she joined the others.

All around them, disturbed sand could be seen stretching all the way to the half-buried vessel. The mingled tracks of Raven and her thugs led straight to a dark gap in the scratched and scoured bulk-head. Pyke offered Ustril the chance to go first but she declined, announcing that she had to scan the exterior before entering. Certainly, the Sendrukan was well provided for, with a headband-mounted optical cluster, a small touchscreen unit hanging from her neck and a handheld scanner with three short antennae.

"Will this take long?" Pyke said.

She glanced at the screen. "Actually, the scan is almost complete—the remote was quicker than I anticipated."

A faint buzzing grew louder as a small glassy sphere glided in from round the side of the wreck, docking perfectly with the three prongs of Ustril's hand-scanner. She studied readouts on both scanner and the neck-slung unit, then nodded.

"Good—I am ready to proceed."

"Anything of interest we should know about, Doc?" Pyke said.

"Nothing especially hazardous. The camouflage barrier is maintained by eleven projectors fixed to the outer hull. There will be dataflow for the barrier coming from a hub somewhere inside."

"I see—disrupt the flow and that'll lift the barrier."

"And the psi-screen."

"Great. Let's get to it."

He led the way through the dark gap in the ruined section. Inside was a narrow, dim corridor without decking or ceiling tiles, metal ribbing over hard bulkhead. A few paces on they came to a T-junction with a framed ladder leading up. Pyke beckoned Dervla and Ancil forward and gave them the task of scouting the deck above. Ancil grinned and from an inner coat pocket produced a big-barrelled handgun whose finish was gleaming blue-black.

"Right," Pyke said. "And he keeps a skagging great hand-cannon for himself!"

"Not just any hand-cannon, Chief," Ancil said, proudly show-ing off his ordnance. "The Ashbless 49cal *Naga*, complete with hellfrost rounds. Stopping power—we got some!"

Pyke gave Dervla an amused look, and she just sighed. "Easy does it up there, and if you and Howitzer-Boy spot anything important and/or weird, hold your position and call for backup. Meantime, we'll infiltrate this level."

Dervla and Ancil both gave a thumbs-up then, with Dervla leading, they ascended the ladder. Pyke faced the rest.

"Okay, team, I'll take point; the good doctor will follow in my footsteps and, Kref, bring up the rear."

"No problem, Chief."

They moved forwards, weapons and hand-scanners at the ready. It was demanding having to step on or over the alloy ribs but they persevered, the Sendrukan most of all being the tallest by far. Pyke could not help noticing the absence of wear and tear; after a good number of millennia even the slowest corrosion would have rotted out all kinds of clips, bolts, fastenings and hinges, yet some surfaces and edges looked almost factory-fresh. When he put this to the lieutenant-doctor she said:

"You're witnessing one of the wonders of Arraveyne science, Captain, namely anti-entropic materials. Few civilisations have grasped this technology, the Sendrukan Hegemony, Earthsphere and the Indroma Solidarity being those I am certain about, and only then in small quantities."

"Anti-entropic?" Pyke said. "You mean it doesn't wear out?"

"No, just that natural processes of decay or corrosion do not occur due to a subatomic lock."

Rather than shrug, Pyke smiled. She went on.

"It involves quantal regulation of how the atoms in these met-als and alloys work, making them incapable of oxidisation or any other exchange, gain or loss of subatomic particles. However, such materials are still subject to the laws of macrophysics and can be broken or deformed or abraded..."

"But they don't rust or dissolve," he said. "I get your drift."

"Glad to be of service," Ustril muttered, now back to peering through her headset scope and punching data onto her screen module. Pyke shook his head and pushed on towards a closed door at the shadowy corridor's end. The few hatches they'd passed opened on sliding rods, and this tall door was no different—Pyke unfastened circular latches on the left-hand side before pulling the large handle on the right. With a grating sound the door slid to the right, swinging out to lie flat against the bulkhead, revealing a sight that Pyke wasn't expecting.

From the outside he'd reckoned that the wrecked section was about three hundred metres long, its beam-width perhaps four hundred, and the hull about as high as the length. And at some point in the deep and distant past (most likely during or just after whatever crisis had forced the original ship down), some destructive force had been unleashed, whether explosive or implosive he couldn't say. But some kind of fearsome power had ripped out the middle of this section of the ship, something spherical which sliced through bulkheads and spars and supports, leaving chambers, corridors and holds exposed, a massive spectacle of destruction which was quite apparent, even in this gloomy half-light.

"Are you seeing this, Chief?" came Ancil's voice over the comms. "Looks like something took a bite out of it!"

A barren silence hung in the air, like the flat quietness of a cemetery or an abandoned battlefield. As if the world had just exhaled a long, weary breath and was deciding whether or not to draw another. The longer he stood there, the more Pyke could see that some light was coming from splits and fractures in the hull, yet there were other small indistinct light sources as well, like tiny lanterns scattered here and there.

"Ans," he said. "See those glowing spots dotted around?"

"Oh yeah, we're looking at one right now! Reckon our lady scientist would find it very interesting!"

Pyke looked round to speak to Lieutenant-Doctor Ustril but she was already heading back the way they'd come. Following her, Pyke and Kref retraced their steps to the ladder and a minute later they had joined Ancil and Dervla in what was left of a large cabin. The unknown calamity had carved a ragged curve across deck and ceiling, laying the cabin open to the immense spherical emptiness at the heart of the wreck. There was a narrow section of floor still left, allowing careful access round to one of the corners where a body lay within an odd glow. It had a scrawny humanoid form with a hairless head and was dressed in a close-fitting dark grey outfit. Before anyone could speak, Ustril spoke:

"Please would everyone keep their distance from this phenomenon? My probes are already detecting inter-dimensional boundary emissions..."

Pyke nodded. "Yep, everyone hang back for a while, let the Doc get on with the scrutinising." He turned to Dervla and murmured, "What're inter-dimensional boundary emissions?"

She shrugged. "Radiation of some kind...real question is the boundary between what and what—or even here and where?"

The tall Sendrukan was crouched down, positioning her hand-scanner next to the edge of the glow, which was faintly greenish-yellow and emanated from a conical glassy peg positioned waist-high on the wall. Dark blood had spread out from beneath the victim's back, still shiny, reflecting gleams and pinpoints—Pyke frowned as he took in other details. There were still a few decking plates in this corner, and there was a small stool with an oval container full of narrow rectangular objects. One of them was a book, its long pages lying open, partially drenched in the blood. And scattered around were what might have been personal items.

Sentimental value, Pyke thought as his gaze was drawn back to the glassy peg sticking out of the wall, giving off that greenish radiation. It was like someone's nest, a little island in the dimness. Just then Ancil, who he'd not noticed slipping off, appeared breathless and excited at the door.

"Found another one, Chief, not far away—and there's someone alive in it! Well, he's not moving, though, just sitting there, but he ain't bleeding…"

"Don't touch anything," urged Ustril. "These glowing areas are enclosed by highly localised stasis fields. Careless activity could cause maiming."

"Everyone get that?" Pyke said. "No meddling, no twiddling, and no fiddling—I'm not cleaning up any sliced-off fingers!"

Kref had been silent the entire time, but now he leaned in close and said, "Chief, this whole place is seriously weird."

Pyke arched an eyebrow. "Actually, old son, I think it could be a hair more serious than that."

Then, abruptly, the Sendrukan scientist was squeezing past to the door where Ancil was waiting. The big woman wasn't very good at masking her emotions and it was easy to read the alarm in her face. He glanced at Dervla. "Stay here, keep your eyes peeled, in here and out there. See anything, comm me immediately."

"Hunch?"

Pyke breathed in through his nose, noisily. "Not sure, but, y'know…"

"Right, I'll be here."

Ancil was already heading after Ustril, so Pyke and Kref did likewise. A dark side corridor led away from the huge gap, hatches lining walls to left and right. Ancil was waiting at the door to a cabin at the end, and he went inside ahead of them.

"Kref is right, Chief," Ancil said. "We've been inside wrecks and ruins before, but this one just feels extra spooky, like it's a haunted ship—and then we find one of the passengers…"

A short passage opened onto a small cabin where Dervla's wrist-lamp gave the place a pale radiance. But the main illumination came from a shimmering bubble which occupied one corner. Inside was a diminutive humanoid creature like the other one, except that it was dressed in an amber uniform and sitting on a curved metallic chair. Its eyes were closed and its oddly elongated features seemed calm and composed. The Sendrukan scientist was resting cross-legged on the deck, her probes and devices laid out before her, and scanning this dormant denizen from who knew how long ago. Ustril was muttering to herself and, by her tone of voice, Pyke guessed that there was a bit of self-reproach going on.

"Problems, Doc?" he said.

She fell silent, while continuing irritably to punch data onto the screen unit. Then she said:

"I was mistaken, Captain—these fields are not stasis fields."

"Okay, so do you know what they are?"

"It is difficult to know the correct words," she said. "The field maintains all elements within it...it repairs or repatterns to discongrous...no, it is an anti-discongruity field..."

Pyke thought hard. "It repairs whatever is within the field? And it uses a pattern to work from?"

Ustril nodded, eyes bright with intellectual fervour. "Local nodes in a plangent net..."

"All those glowing spots we can see on the other decks, across that big gap," Pyke said. "Each one is one of your nodes, yeah?"

More nodding. "Anti-entropic materials are common to Arraveyne construction, but to see the invention of an exotic projective field like this—"

"Right, right, but what's powering these nodes?" Pyke went on. "Some kind of self-charging batteries?"

"Embedded nanitic generator web," Ustril said. "Provides power-trickles to sustain field."

Pyke gave a smile and a nod. Well, this is bracing, right enough! He turned to Kref. "Something that only you can do, Kref—head back to that other cabin and see if you can get that glowing spike out of the wall. Ans, you go with him, and be careful the both of you—I know what you're like."

Ancil and Kref gave mock salutes and left. Pyke turned back to Ustril and indicated the possibly-comatose biped within the field.

"Figure out anything about the sleeper here?" He peered into the glowing bubble. "Is it actually sleeping or is it just an immaculately preserved corpse?"

From outside, along the corridor, came the sound of hammering.

"I cannot tell," said Ustril. "My devices are not powerful enough to pierce the field and scan for life signs."

"All right, then, another question—if this anti-rot field was fully powered, it would cover a much larger area, don't you think?"

"Certainly—these nodes are a post-construction, possibly post-crash augmentation designed to shield as much of the interior as achievable..."

Just then Moleg's voice came over the comm, interrupting the Sendrukan's flow of words. "Captain, there's a situation—large dense dustcloud, ground level, bearing down on your position."

"How long?"

"Maybe three minutes, maybe less."

"Okay, keep tracking it."

Pyke looked at the Sendrukan scientist. "Grab your gear, Doc—we need to get the hell outa here."

Ustril looked downhearted at this, but gave no objection. Leaving her to snatch up her equipment, Pyke made for the door. Dervla was already there.

"What's the news?"

"Hostiles incoming," he said. "And probably a skag-ton of

them, a swarm of those scavenger bots heading for us with their pincers, drills and hooks twitching for any fleshy meatbags they can get hold of."

Instead of switching to general comms, Pyke yelled as he strode along the corridor. "Kref!—Ancil!—stop what you're doing and get to the hoppers, now!"

After that it was a frantic scramble along the deckless corridors, a hurried clamber down the ladderway and a dash back outside to where the hoppers were parked. Out of the corner of his eye Pyke could see the leading edge of a solid mass of scavenger bots pouring down the gentle slope from the wreck's far end, down towards the foot of the gully, dust billowing in its wake.

And that was when Dervla discovered that her harness had failed to activate.

"I do not believe this!" she yelled. "Bargain-basement crap!"

Pyke ran the arithmetic of passengers through his head and knew that something would have to give somewhere, and chances would have to be taken. Before he could speak, however, Ustril beat him to it.

"Captain, I can carry Specialist Ancil with me, so that we can all escape."

"You sure? That thing looks pretty delicate."

"I can boost the repulsion output for a very short period of time, long enough to reach the shuttle."

There was no time to argue, and, anyway, Ancil had already gone over to Ustril who was helping him to stand up on the flimsy craft. Swiftly, Pyke told Kref to fire up one of the hoppers while he and Dervla took the other. It all cascaded into a hair-raising, nerve-jangling drama—Pyke and Dervla and then Kref made it into the air but Lieutenant-Doctor Ustril's contraption remained on the ground while the bot-swarm encroached ever nearer.

"Er, Doc, yer cutting this very fine..."

"Do not distract me, Captain! All four cells must be

reconfigured for burst output—this can only be done individually, am closing off the last and reconnecting powerlines…"

The bot-swarm was converging in a ragged crescent about a metre away when the Sendrukan contraption surged up into the air, reached just a little past head height and seemed to stagger, hovering uncertainly. Pyke could only watch in appalled horror while behind him Dervla was whispering, "C'mon, c'mon, c'mon!"

Just when it seemed that Ustril's craft was about to fail and fall, it suddenly reared upwards on a steep course heading for the crest of the dune. Even as it did so, Pyke saw Ancil reach out and flick a small object towards the receding bot-swarm. Two seconds later there was a sharp crack and a red flash as the mini-nade detonated amid the seething, clicking mass. Ancil was still laughing when Ustril landed near the barge-shuttle, coming down roughly enough to bump him loose and send him sprawling in the sand.

"So what was that little package?" Pyke said as he dismounted from the hopper.

Ancil sat up, spitting sand but still chuckling. "Daisy-cutter incendiary, Chief. Fried 'em good, eh?"

Pyke walked back a few paces to get a good view of the charred and smouldering mound at the bottom of the gully. "Oh yeah, fried, scorched and cremated by the look of it. But that doesn't mean we can take things easy—I trust those scumbots as far as I can spit." He peered at the now decamouflaged shipwreck section. "So I want us packed and ready to dust off right sharpish, y'hear?"

He turned back and found his crew grinning from ear to ear as they lounged against the side of the shuttle-barge. All the equipment and the hoppers had already been stowed while his back had been turned.

"All done, Bran," said Dervla. "And the Lieutenant-Doctor has a location fix on the Eye."

Ancil poked his head out of the rear hatch. "Ustril left her tracking gear on auto while we were playing tag with the bug-bots..."

"We should leave immediately, Captain," came the Sendrukan's voice from inside. "I was able to use my short-range remote to triangulate, thus I now have accurate positional coordinates. We must depart now—we cannot afford any delay!"

Insistent, overbearing demands like these tended to rankle with Pyke in the worst way, and he was sorely tempted to dig that old rotgut flask out of the pilotside trinket cranny and settle down for a snarky wind-up session. However, right now nothing seemed more desirable than finding the Eye, getting Van Graes his treasure, getting paid and buggering off to some fleshpot planet far, far away.

And since when does it ever work out that smoothly for the likes of us? he thought.

He laughed out loud, ducked into the pilot's compartment, patted Dervla on the shoulder and dropped into his couch.

"No problem, Doctor-General, I'll just crank up this old bucket while you get me our new heading—ah, thanks, Ans! Right then, hang on to your earlobes 'cos here we go!"

CHAPTER EIGHT

Pyke, the Isle of Candles Simulation

The Isle of Candles, Pyke realised, had a weird day–night cycle, except that it was never brighter than hazy late afternoon and never darker than dusk. And it was an unvarying five hours, forty-two minutes from apex to nadir, which made the day a brisk eleven hours and fourteen minutes long. Question is, was he in hell or purgatory, or some other afterlife? Some underworld for backsliders, a dosshouse for the damned?

He uttered a dry laugh and gazed out at the dark waters that stretched between the island and the cliffs of the mainland, greying into invisibility as evening mists thickened. *Is this it? Is this all that's left—you get hijacked by some evil bastard machine-mind which treats you to a glimpse of yourself falling off a building to certain death, but instead you get yanked back into this shadow existence to play games for the amusement of the Legacy, the aforementioned evil bastard machine...*

He heard a clatter of hooves approaching behind him as the Bargalil T'Moy climbed the staircase to the villa's canopied observation platform.

"Everyone is now here," came Klane's deep and dulcet tones.

Pyke nodded. It was Klane the Shyntanil who had watched over his prone and unbreathing body while Pyke's consciousness was snatched away down along the mad rabbit hole back to the real world, just in time to mutely witness his last few minutes of life as a puppet for the Legacy's twisted schemes. It was to Klane that the Construct drone had given a small circular object seconds before the Legacy returned, appearing in the villa's central courtyard, flanked by hovering black, teardrop-shaped servants of some dark providence. After the Legacy departed, followed by said servants and, oddly, Rensik, it was Klane who continued to stand guard over Pyke's motionless form, waiting for nearly an hour before he suddenly breathed in and sat bolt upright. Wide-eyed, trembling, terrified breath blasting in and out, because in his mind's eye he was replaying over and over those razor moments when he'd toppled backwards out of that high window, his shrieking fear compounded by the sight of Dervla diving out after him.

Pyke shivered and turned to face the others. He smiled faintly and shrugged.

"Right, lads, it seems that I am now officially dead and this is my wake! If we had time I'd treat you to a rendition of 'The Randalstown Rondo' but at this juncture Time and all its little seconds are not our friends. So, long story short—a while ago I was taken back to the carnival of the Real, witnessed my own death, as orchestrated by our lord and filthy master the Legacy, may his name crumble to dust. While this was going on, the Legacy itself materialised down there in the courtyard, took control of my drone companion and departed…in the direction of the mainland, Klane, is that right?"

The heavy featured Shyntanil nodded sombrely.

"But a short while before the Legacy popped up here, my drone companion gave Klane something. Show it to them."

Klane dipped into a pocket and produced, on his open palm, a small black disc about an inch across with a hole in the middle. It was smoothly rounded and exhibited no exterior features, and as they watched it rose into the air, turning over lazily as it moved away and came to rest at eye level between Pyke and the others.

"This is what is known as a drone residual," Pyke said. "Say hello to the team, Rensik!"

"Hello. Please note that my name is not the same as my progenitor—protocol dictates that I should be designated according to said progenitor's first and last initials plus the iteration, thus I am RK1."

The three Sojourners looked bemused but muttered a kind of welcome nonetheless. Pyke's grimace showed his doubt.

"RK1 isn't a name," he said. "It's a part number."

"Commentary advice transferred from my progenitor mentioned that you have a tendency towards verbalised trivia," said RK1. "Do you wish to further explore this tendency, or shall we proceed with matters in hand?"

Pyke waved languidly. "Proceed—Arky."

"Very well. I shall assume that all present are familiar with the multiplex functionalities of the artefact known as the crystal shard. With extended physical touch it can scan a subject's physiology while reading and replicating the para-quantal structures of a sentient cortex in order that it can reproduce a fractally detailed mindmap within this simulation, tagged to all the familiar physical responses and abilities from the mind's real-world body. In fact, the mindmap expects certain responses, and the simulation calibrates the virtual sensorium until the subject feels all is correct."

"We've all guessed most of that," Pyke said. "We need to know more about this whole fake world and what it's for. That's what we're chasing so cut to it!"

"I will—eventually," said the drone. "In addition to carrying out those copying and replicating functions, the crystal-skin interface also permits the Legacy to project itself into the hijacked body and use it for its own ends, research and archive retrieval, in the past at least. Whether the Legacy projects itself entirely into the host or a copy I am unable to determine—given the nature of this simulational existence the latter seems most likely.

"I have given this summary of the crystal shard's functions in order to depict the sheer scale of what is being done. It requires a magnitude and speed of data transfer that outstrips everything known throughout civilised space, and there is no known technical means by which such scanning and transfer can be completed. The crystal shard is not constructed from any material thus far known in nature or to interstellar science. The storage requirements to manage anything like those scanning functions alone would demand a lab full of nano-structured substrate cores, and to run a simulation of this detail-depth, along with the randomisation governance and all the regulatory frameworks, that likewise would need industrial amounts of hardware, not forgetting the power source to sustain it all."

By now Pyke had succumbed to feelings of amazement and awe, tempered by ominous underthoughts, namely the mystery of What Is It All For? He voiced those very words in the momentary pause the drone had allowed for all these revelations to sink in.

"Excellent question," said RK1. "My progenitor posited a small number of possible answers, but only after a series of tests which managed to lay bare the wider, greater structures that exist all around us. He was attempting to discover the limits or boundaries of the simulation by using ultra-fine sensor scans—of course, as a data model of himself, he was using a model of the sensors available to him in the real world, so there was a recursive element to his investigations. But with a combination of these scans he was able to penetrate one of this simulation's regulatory frameworks and, via that, discover what lay beyond it. What he found astonished even him."

The drone paused.

"Are you pausing for dramatic effect?" Pyke said. "If so, please don't."

"I was testing my narrative meld to ensure clarity, Captain," said the drone RK1. "What he found was that this simulation was layered on top of another, beneath which was a third and fourth. But when he looked outward that was the moment of conceptual breakthrough. If all of you could hold the crystal right now, you would see how it fits quite snugly into the hand. The notion that within it was all that was necessary to direct all the functions I have described, as well as this simulation, would be a challenging one, to say the least. In one sense, the volume of the shard's innards which is devoted to all those functions is small, very small, perhaps even tiny, something that anyone might find difficult to comprehend. The truth is that the operations of the Legacy and the replicating functions and the simulations consti- tute a vanishingly, remotely, almost negligibly minuscule area. I said before that this crystal is not made of familiar material. That is because it is not made from material at all. The boundaries of it, i.e. the crystal-seeming surface that you see, is a frozen lattice of exotic dimensionality—it's practically equations made solid, space-time-space woven together as a receptacle..."

"A receptacle for *what*?" Pyke said.

"Ultimately time ran out for my progenitor," said RK1, slow- ing slightly. "That was as far as he managed before the Legacy returned in advance of your own, erm, homecoming. He had suspected that some of his operations and scans might be sensed by outliers and priators sending feeds to the Legacy, which is why I was upgraded from probe status and integrated into his ongoing scrutinising."

"Well, how big is this receptacle?" Pyke said.

"There is no reliable, calibrated way to describe the crystal shard's interior," said the residual drone. "My progenitor spec- ulated that it might contain a honeycomb of para-dimensional storage areas, but what would be stored in such a potentially vast volume? He had really only gathered verifiable data on the surroundings of the simulation-replication nexus and the point where it bonded with the external boundary. All the rest of the interior, that yawning abyssal gulf, he could not see into due to an impenetrable barrier sectioning the nexus away into its own tiny little pocket."

Pyke rubbed his chin, pondering this gargantuan opening up of their place in the simulation and the dark unknowns that lay beyond. And his age-old question rose to his lips:

"So—what's it all for?"

"If I had shoulders," said the drone, "I would shrug. Beyond the barrier is purest mystery, and the purpose or intent of this simulation and its puzzle seem opaque. Was the simulation-replication function part of this crystal's original design, or was it devised by the Legacy? And what is the Legacy?—something intrinsic to the place, or an intruder?"

Pyke gritted his teeth and shook his head. "I just need an answer, even if it's a guess."

The drone bobbed gently up and down in midair. "If you insist, I can pass on my progenitor's speculations regarding the simulation."

"We're all ears," Pyke said. "Speculate away."

"Very well. His conjecture was that the layered simulations—which he also referred to as nested realities—constitute a sequence which those who arrive here on the Isle of Candles can only travel through by the solving of puzzles or situations that they encounter. The end-point is, as you may surmise, an enigma. If these nested simulations were designed by a rational mind one might expect a rational outcome. But if they were designed by an irrational or sadistic mind, the end result is likely to be unpleasant."

Vrass the Gomedran then spoke. "Did your predecessor come to any conclusion about how to solve our puzzle of the statues?"

"Yes," said the drone. "It was a somewhat cunning solution, one which demanded that no one could see how the statues worked, since all the participants have to be in the games room."

Pyke snapped his fingers. "Knew it!"

"So we could go down there right now," said T'Moy the Bargalil, "and solve it, and then—what, exactly?"

"I have no data on the phase between one simulation and the next," said RK1. "All of you might wake up there, fully in command of yourselves and knowing all that you have experienced up to that point—or the simulation program may wipe your memories and imprint a new persona, or your memories may be temporarily obscured and only come back to you piecemeal. I would tend towards the first option since that would accelerate your ability firstly to discover the puzzle, then secondly go to work on its solution."

Klane cleared his throat. "This is all fascinating, even immensely challenging, but I would very much prefer to stay here on the island. I am willing to help you with the solution to the statue puzzle, as best as I can, but..." He sighed. "There is a weariness upon my soul which quails at the thought of travelling to an entirely new and strange place. I am sorry if this disappoints any of you, but this is what my senses and thoughts are telling me now, in the light of all we've heard."

The Bargalil T'Moy put a hand on the Shyntanil's shoulder. "Stay behind if that is your desire, old friend—I know more than anyone the long ages of your durance in this place."

The drone hummed. "I feel I should point out the possibility that none of you may have any say in the matter. For all we know, once a puzzle is solved everyone shifts onto the next simulation."

Vrass nodded. "From the beginning this existence has been the imposition of a cruel imprisonment. We should be prepared for any and all eventualities."

Pyke looked at Klane. "Well, I hope you get your wish. Barring a return to real bodies in the real world—hah, yeah, right!—staying here on the Isle of Candles wouldn't be a bad retirement."

There was muttered agreement all round.

"Good," said the drone RK1. "Shall we begin?"

"Is there anything else we need to know?" Pyke said. "Before we go to wherever we're going?"

"A great deal, I suspect," RK1 said. "None of which I am privy to, I'm afraid."

Pyke uttered a resigned laugh and indicated the door to the stairs. "Ah well, lead the way."

Down the rickety, worn wooden steps they trooped, out onto the walkway and past the glowing candle clusters. Pyke found himself savouring the smell of the burned wicks and the hot wax in the air, even the glimmery dusk that settled over the courtyard below and the scarcely distinguishable statues that lurked beneath like frozen godlings awaiting some perplexing drama. One by one they entered the room with its hexagonal game tables—there, the drone RK1 sat them all at specific tables and had each of them take only one game piece out of the small drawers in each table. By the light of the candles and the candlelight reflected in the tilted mirror, they diligently followed instructions and placed the solitary game piece on the rearmost lefthand square.

"Now," said the drone. "When I say move, you will all move the piece forward one square and do nothing else."

Pyke couldn't help grinning like a fool, glanced to one side and saw that Vrass was grinning, too. *Yeah, we're just a real gang of board-game professionals, ain't we?*

"Move."

Pyke and the others dutifully moved the pieces. And from out in the courtyard came a loud scraping, grinding noise. Everyone straightened, eyes wide.

"Excellent," the drone said. "Next, when I say move, you will all turn your game pieces a quarter-turn to the right, and then do nothing else. Agreed?"

There were murmurs of assent, but Pyke's mind was babbling, *Aye, sure, but how about, just how about a quick turn to the left, and a hop and a slide to the end, eh?*

"Move."

Ignoring his inner half-wit, Pyke did as he was bid and moved the game piece a quarter-turn to the right.

From outside came an enormous, deep, musical clang, like the striking of a bell the size of the island itself.

"Before we carry out the final move, I must reiterate this cautionary note," said the drone. "There is no way of knowing the nature of your awareness after the transition to the new simulation. If you do arrive with no clear knowledge of where you have come from, I can only hope that a certain innate curiosity will prevail and that you will somehow arrive at a higher stage of self-awareness. Although that seems highly improbable, speaking as a non-organic AI."

The air was still resonating with the after-vibrancy of that immense single chime.

"What about yourself?" said Pyke. "Will you be shifting right along with us?"

"Again, the lack of shoulders denies me the ease of non-verbal communication," RK1 said. "Will I be transposed into the next simulation?—uncertain. And the forms that we may take are equally unknowable, which reveals yet another mystery— are new roles assigned at random, Captain Pyke, or are they bestowed according to some kind of calculated plan?"

Suddenly the focus of attention, Pyke adopted a sharply sardonic smile. "A great question—I've no idea what the answer is!"

"Exactly—unknowable, unanswerable. Shall we continue?"

Everyone nodded.

"Good. This is the last move in the sequence," the drone RK1 said. "When I say 'move,' each of you will turn your game piece a further quarter-turn to the right so that it is facing you—understood?"

Pyke, now impatient, muttered his agreement.

"Move!"

All four of them reached out to the pieces on the boards and turned them.

For a moment there was nothing, a hollow stillness devoid of any sound. But only for a moment. Pyke drew breath to speak but before he could he heard something—a faint tinging like the sound a flipped coin makes while in the air. As Pyke listened, the quiet chiming grew in volume, its quality deepening and widening, its plangent loudness climbing, its sonorous quality building, the sheer penetrating force of its reverberance making the pieces rattle on the boards. The drone was saying something, Vrass, too, but the overwhelming blast of resonance was obliterating all sounds.

The others had clamped their hands over their ears but Pyke snarled, made himself get up from his seat, striving to ignore the way the air in his chest was thrumming as he lurched towards the door. His legs gave way and he sprawled on the floor. Laying his face down on the dusty floorboards was like baring his cheek to buzzing sandpaper.

The awful vibrations took his breath, took his sight...and dissolved him.

When he came round there was a sharp throbbing pain at the back of his skull, and for an instant he didn't know who or where he was.

"Ah, good, he's back among the living," said a gruff voice as hands lifted him into a sitting position.

"I'm...what...?" he tried to say.

"Scruffy pair of roughs knocked you down and started dragging you off into the alley over there—but we scared 'em off good and proper, didn't we, Kiv?"

"Yarp, proper, too."

Carefully, wincingly, he opened his eyes and saw a busy narrow street, except that all the people and their stalls and barrows were slightly blurred. A burly, bearded man was crouched beside him and his companion stood behind him holding a cudgel balanced on one shoulder.

"I'm Jenek," said the bearded man. "You caught a nasty crack on the head there—do you know what your name is?"

He started to speak, then halted—his name, where he was, what he was doing, it all seemed to be missing; no, not missing but avoiding his mental grasp, as if separated by a barrier. For a moment or two he strove to remember and then, like the popping of a balloon, there it was.

"Pazzyk," he gasped. "I'm Bregan Pazzyk...and this is..."

It all came back swiftly. He was Bregan Pazzyk, freelance antiquities broker, this narrow street was round the corner from Haxy Nightmarket, a minor location in the city known as Granah the Great, capital of the glorious Granavian Empire, ruled over by His Imperial Majesty Bachulal III, may his grandeur remain unsurpassed!

"Yes, Mr. Pazzyk, you're in the picturesque slums of Darvanu District," Jenek intoned wryly. As Pazzyk carefully got to his feet, he went on: "After a nasty knock like that you should rest yourself."

"I wish I could, Master Jenek," he said, dusting himself off. "But I have a job to do which will not wait, so my own discomforts will have to take second..."

He paused, realising that something was missing from his shoulder and across his chest, but before panic could get a grip Jenek brought a brown leather object into view—Pazzyk's satchel. Smiling with relief, Pazzyk accepted it and slipped it over his head, grimacing as he inadvertently brushed against the lump on the back of his head.

"Well, you'll know best about your own business, I suppose," said Jenek. "You should keep your wits about you, though—those two louts are still out there."

"Thank you for your concern—oh, would you know what time it is?"

Jenek frowned, glanced at his friend, Kiv, who snorted loudly. "Heard the hawkletter tower chime twice a small while ago—not heard the half-hour bells yet, it seeming."

"That's good enough for me," Pazzyk said. "I can still reach my destination if I hasten. Gentlemen, my deepest thanks—without your help I might have ended up face down in the Worroth. May Tulamis bring fortune to you both."

Jenek raised his hand. "May Shamaya watch over you, friend Pazzyk, and your head!"

Their farewells were brief, and, as his benefactors returned to their nearby carpentry yard, Pazzyk resumed his route, round the corner and through the wide canopied entrance to Haxy Nightmarket.

The Nightmarket was so-called because of the swathes of cloth that hung across its main thoroughfare, Haxy Way, obstructing what little sunlight slipped down between the tenements. Once, the stall and barrow-owners had put up long shades and lengths of sailcloth to protect their goods and their customers from the noxious eliminations which slum residents cast out from high windows. Then some began hanging up coloured sheets rather than heavy sailcloth, or patterned banners, with small lamps above casting light down through them in a very pleasing manner. Now, the wealthier proprietors paid for soil collectors to forestall any more odorous surprises, and cleverly designed self-dousing lamps to provide a constellation of glows shining down through a low sky of multi-coloured gauzy drapes and hangings. It was familiar and mysterious, all at once.

Pazzyk sidled and wove through the busy, chattering people, buyers, viewers, visitors, delivery girls and boys, itinerant trinket traffickers and unremarkable looking cutpurses. All the pre-eminent peoples of the Granavian Empire were on show—short, gaunt Gadromis from the northern forests, brawny Shylan miners from the eastern mountains and the proud Barlig, horse-riders from the southern plains. And the Granavians, skilled in commerce and war, which nearly always overlapped. His ears were assailed by a non-stop rippling babble, shot through with the music of whistles, mandolas and tambors. Stall vendors tried to tempt him with food, hats, the latest Zetachian carbines, and captivating scents from far-off Kaurien, but he ducked them all, holding firmly to his course.

Haxy Way began in Darvanu District, cut across Silverqueen Parade and continued on through Artisans Ward. The Nightmarket took on a more refined air here (or, more accurately, a less grimy miasma), and there were even regular sightings of Shamayan and Ujinian initiates. Orisons were being chanted in Qalival Square as he negotiated a path around the crowd. The square was dominated by a group of four huge statues, each representing one of the empire's main peoples. Pazzyk remembered having passed this way many times but this time, as he laid eyes on the statues, it was as if he were seeing them for the first time. He slowed and stared, fixated by the towering figures, as if there was something vitally important about them, something that threatened to break through to his thoughts...and the feeling faded away as he resumed walking, hurrying off to leave the square behind.

He emerged from the Nightmarket on Dragoon's Row. Across the moderately busy street and rightwards a dozen paces or so were the offices of Relgin & Foach where several chattels auctions were due to take place, as they always did on the tenth of the month. Pazzyk was no stranger to the pillared entryway of Relgin & Foach, having been a semi-regular attendee of their auctions in recent years. He had intended to duck this month's listing due to lack of funds but yesterday a messenger arrived from Tillyfray & Sons, a nearby notary, with a letter and a small yet weighty packet. The letter was from Tillyfray the Elder himself in which he stated that he was acting on behalf of a client of high status who wished to remain anonymous. Tillyfray had been engaged to obtain the clearout rights for a specific lock-booth which was coming up for auction very shortly. Thus Tillyfray was hiring Pazzyk to attend Relgin & Foach, bid for and win the auction for Lock-Booth R-29A, then return with the certificate and the booth key. The small, solid packet contained thirteen golden crowns, twelve to cover the bid (such auctions seldom rose to more than five or six crowns), and one to pay for Pazzyk's services for the day. And, since his personal finances had sunk to one silver and a fistful of coppers, he was content to take the job.

The entrance to Relgin & Foach was flanked by obsidiate pillars topped with statuettes of a bull and a falcon. Beyond a pair of creaking doors, Pazzyk strode along the hall and up the stairs at the end, a route he knew well. There were eight rooms on the first floor and, as usual, the chattels auction was taking place in one of the smaller ones. Gently patting the still sore lump on his head, Pazzyk went inside and took a seat over by the wall, affording him a decent view of the room and the auctioneer's lectern.

There were another seven bidders present, three whose solitary locations marked them out as freelance brokers like himself (with faces he recognised from previous gatherings), and a familiar pair of headscarfed old ladies. Misilda and Lemore were a couple of widows who cropped up at chattel selloffs now and then for the enjoyment of participation, despite seldom winning any bids. The remaining two were strikingly unalike; one was dressed in plain, formal dark greens, had the hard look of an upper-class functionary, a steward perhaps, and sat ramrod-straight in his chair; the other sat next to him, leaning forward, elbows on knees, garbed in outdoor working clothes and a cap. Heavy-set and surly, his entire demeanour said "hired thug." In his thoughts, Pazzyk immediately dubbed them the Chamberlain and the Brute.

The auctioneer, a grey-haired, cadaverous fellow, stepped smartly up to the lectern and the proceedings got under way.

Granah the Great was probably the largest city in the entire western domains, and was certainly the city from which the most armies had set out on campaigns (not to mention the port of Pheshorn on the nearby banks of the Worroth, from which the Granavian navy had frequently set sail). During several centuries of exploration and expansion, many soldiers and sailors had rented storage from several companies with the intention of safeguarding belongings and keepsakes while away on duty. Lockboxes and lockbooths were usually rented out on minimum two-year contracts, and were only put up for chattel auctions after three years had elapsed without any contact with the leaseholder. The machine of war is a hungry colossus, and many did not return from far-off dangerous places, leaving a steady trickle of unclaimed contents to be disposed of.

There were a number of secure boxhouses dotted around the city, and the auctioneer worked his way through about a dozen lots before reaching those with the "R" prefix. Raskol Boxhouse was out next to the city's western wall, sandwiched between the Ithlyr slums and the crafters of Huplik Ward. Pazzyk's three solo peers had already had plenty of fun bidding against each other, glowering and frowning at each other in turn while Misilda and Lemore enlivened matters still further with their own unpredictable bids. Pazzyk, meanwhile, had refrained from bidding, unwilling to put his meagre purse at risk. The bids and counterbids flew back and forth as three Raskol lots came and went. Then, at last, the auctioneer arrived at the reason for Pazzyk's presence.

"Ladies, gentlemen," the auctioneer said. "Lot Sixteen, a single Raskol lockbooth, R-29A, being the avowed personal depository of Bearer Sergeant Traz Dalyak of the 25th Brigade of Rifles, veteran of several campaigns, declared missing in action after the Eyzakosh Intervention. Contents unknown, condition unknown. Rights on offer—forty-eight hours' clearance. Shall we commence the bidding at five silver?"

"Five silver," said the elderly Misilda. "And nine copper!"

The auctioneer gave her an amused smile. "Five silver and nine from the gentlelady at the front!"

After that the three freelancers began bidding, a silver here, a silver and a half there. When the bids slowed at a crown and two silver, Pazzyk decided it was time and called, "One crown, eight silver."

"One crown and..." the auctioneer began.

"One crown and fifteen silver," came a voice that had not yet been heard.

Pazzyk glanced over to where the man he thought of as the Chamberlain sat gazing levelly at the auctioneer, betraying no awareness of Pazzyk's regard. Next to him, though, the Brute was staring straight at him, lips curled into a hateful leer. Pazzyk responded with a toothy grin then turned back to the auctioneer and raised his bid to two crowns.

One of the freelancers chipped in with two crowns and three but after that the bidding alternated between Pazzyk and the Chamberlain. As the bids mounted a tense hush fell over the others, now reduced to the role of spectators. Seven crowns, eight crowns, nine, and still the calm, unruffled Chamberlain stepped up the amount. Pazzyk, feeling wound up and distinctly ruffled, tried to ignore the sweat prickling his scalp as the bids crept up to and past ten crowns, ten and a quarter, ten and two thirds, eleven crowns and two, eleven and a half crowns...

When Pazzyk made what he knew might be his penultimate bid, there was a pause. Expectant eyes flicked towards the Chamberlain and the Brute. The former was frowning, and in the widening silence he and his companion exchanged a look and a wordless nod. Then they calmly rose to their feet and, without a backward glance, left the room. Pazzyk let out the breath he'd been holding and managed a weak smile in response to Misilda and Lemore's ladylike applause.

He waited for the other freelancers to complete their transactions with the auctioneer before going up to pay over the monies and take possession of the lease and the key. In accordance with custom and practice, the document was folded into a small pocket containing the key and bound up with string and a wax seal. Pazzyk noted that the words "Raskol 29A" were written on the front in neat cursive script before carefully slipping it into his shoulder satchel. Last to leave, he descended unhurriedly to the lobby where he saw from the porter's chronometer that it was still not yet four. He would not have to set off back to Tillyfrays in a rush in order to be sure of handing in his prize before closing time.

Outside, he crossed Dragoons Row and retraced his steps to Haxy Nightmarket. He strode into its gloomy, tunnel-like interior, catching the scent of fresh pastries from the cooking stalls, hints of deliciousness that made his stomach rumble. Soon he was passing through Qavilal Square, ducking round groups of Barlig traders and keeping his gaze away from the big, looming statues, despite an unfathomable urge to look round. It was like an itch at the back of his eyes which only faded when he passed under the stone arch that led to the next stretch of the Nightmarket.

Barely a dozen paces further on he was suddenly aware of quiet footsteps behind him. A glance to the left revealed the dark-clad figure of the Chamberlain drawing level, matching gait for gait. At once, alarm sparked through him.

"Good evening, sir," came the man's dry, mild voice. "How fortuitous that we should be sharing this road and travelling in the same direction."

Pazzyk maintained his composure. "Fortuitous is an odd word, good sir—it implies random happenstance which I do not think applies to this encounter."

As he spoke, Pazzyk was fumbling in his right-hand pocket for his weighted blackjack, which had eluded his grasp during the earlier ambush. Their common pace had, meanwhile, slowed to a stroll as the Chamberlain made a dismissive gesture.

"I can assure, sir, you have nothing to fear from me." His smile was wintry and without mercy. "That's what my companion is for."

A rough hand grabbed Pazzyk's collar from behind while another delved into the pocket his hand was in and wrenched it out, hard, strong fingers forcing him to release the blackjack. It had to be the Brute.

"You...you can't do this...why..."

"Please, sir, do not fuss," said the Chamberlain. "All we require is the packet with the key. We'll have it and be on our way."

"Never! Hey, help, I'm being..."

Was all that Pazzyk could manage. The Chamberlain snapped a small glass object under his nose and a sweet fragrance coiled into his nose and down into his lungs, delectably melting all resistance. Everything was suddenly euphoric and drifting. He was aware of concerned passers-by asking if all was well, and the voice of the Chamberlain allaying all suspicions with practised authority and clever words as Pazzyk was carried along a side alley sunk in shadows.

The carefree, floating feeling was also, he realised, immensely funny. His captors, clearly extremely naughty people, were now trying to tug the strap of his satchel up over his head which he tried to foil with arms and hands and which only approximately did as he wanted. After a giggle-drenched flurry of tugging and grabbing he wound up with the strap tangled about his neck and under his arms and his captors swearing with frustration. But before they could resort to more brutal methods, a new voice interrupted their activities. Pazzyk's sight was blurred and distended so he had to rely on his hearing.

"Why are you harming this man?" said the newcomer.

"Get lost, horseboy," said the Brute.

"There is no need for concern," said the Chamberlain. "Our friend is suffering from a peculiar ague and we are helping him on his way."

"Not my friends!" Pazzyk managed to gasp.

"Indeed," said the newcomer. "Not friends, but thieves. Stand away from him or prepare for a thrashing!"

"You should have looked the other way and walked on," said the Chamberlain. "Deal with him."

"Gladly," said the Brute.

By now Pazzyk's mind had taken a dark turn. All his dread was now focused on the satchel and its contents, the fear of losing them assuming monstrous proportions. While the snarl and thud of hand-to-hand combat commenced in the background, the Chamberlain tried to pry the satchel out of a grasp that terrors had made unbreakable. Punching and slapping had no effect, and the man's evil efforts descended into outright wrestling for possession of the satchel. This grunting, close-proximity struggle brought them uncomfortably face-to-face, Pazzyk uttering wordless growls and the Chamberlain's eyes burning with fury as he continued to wrench, twist, shove and, just once, tried to strike at Pazzyk's face with his forehead.

Then a big hand swept in from somewhere and struck the Chamberlain loudly on the side of the head. Pazzyk's assailant cried out as the force of the blow flung him aside, but he still rolled smoothly to his feet, ready to retaliate. Pazzyk's rescuer was faster, however, and planted a hefty kick right in the Chamberlain's midriff, which sent him flying backwards to land in a heap of something wet and malodorous.

Some of Pazzyk's sight was returning now, sufficient for him to be able to focus properly on his defender. It was a Barlig, one of the horsemen from the southern plains—he wore a jerkin made of leather chevrons and tough-woven leggings and his hair was tied back. And he was staring closely at Pazzyk as he helped him onto his feet.

"Pyke," the Barlig said. "It is you, isn't it? It has to be you."

"Sorry, friend," Pazzyk said. "I think you're mistaking me for someone else. Bregan Pazzyk is my name, freelance antiquities broker, and I cannot thank you enough for saving me from those louts…"

Glancing sideway, he saw the Chamberlain and the Brute practically supporting each other as they limped and hobbled off into the deep shadows of the alleyway.

"Bregan Pazzyk, eh?" The Barlig considered him for a moment. "I am, er, Rider Trogian, and there is actually a way in which you can repay my good deed—it will take only a few moments of your time, at a spot just a short distance back along the Nightmarket."

Pazzyk rocked his head judiciously, and agreed. The Barlig led the way back to Qalival Square, guided Pazzyk right up to the stone plinth on which the four great statues of the empire's peoples stood. Again, Pazzyk felt that unpleasant sensation of being drawn towards the immense sculptures, towards the tall figure of the Granavian, a stern-looking, bearded man with a sword at his side, a sextant in one hand and a pair of scales in the other. Pazzyk stared at it for a turbulent moment then did an abrupt about-turn and headed the other way.

"No, I'm…I'm very sorry but…I just…"

"Captain, please, you need to—"

"What did you call me?" Pazzyk slowed to glare at the taller man. "I'm not a captain."

And as he looked round, the Barlig's fist was coming the other way, catching him a sharp blow on the chin.

There was a flash behind his eyes, grey shadows sweeping in like wings, and his awareness became as calm and constant as a ship lurching and swaying in a stormy sea.

"Sorry, Captain, I'm so sorry." The Barlig's voice drifted in and out of his hearing. "No, no, he's fine, he came to pray, we'll just rest here a little while…"

"Why d'you…call me…"

"See?—he's just a bit dizzy…thank you, yes, thank you… and may she guard you, too…"

Pazzyk felt the Barlig lower him bodily onto cold, flat stone, right beneath the Granavian statue, a big blurred shape that towered ominously over him. By now the strange sensations were practically calling out in his thoughts.

"Right, this should do it," the Barlig said as he took Pazzyk's hand and slapped it down on the statue's stone foot. There was a moment of physical oddness, like a shiver which started at his skin and shot straight into his very core.

And Pazzyk became Pyke, knew he'd always been Pyke. Captain Brannan Pyke, dammit, large as life and twice as natural, accept no substitute!

He levered himself up into a sitting position and squinted at his rescuer, the pony-tailed Barlig, who stared back with eyes full of worry.

"Captain? Have you become yourself again?"

"Damn right I have—so which one of our plucky band are you? Wait, let me guess…T'Moy the Bargalil. Am I right?"

"Well deduced, Captain. Was it the word Barlig that gave you a clue?"

"And the fact that they're horse-wrangler types from the south, dead giveaway. By the way, how are you managing with two legs rather than four?"

"It feels not dissimilar, although I have to remember not to lean back."

"Hah, got it. Were you already you when you woke up here, or did you have to go and goose the statue as well?"

"The latter, Captain—I awoke as if I'd just dozed off, on a

crate over in that corner." The Bargalil pointed over to a shadowy part of the square. "I knew I was Rider Trogian but I also felt this overpowering urge to approach the Barlig statue, so I walked over, laid my hand upon it, and an instant later I was as you see me now."

"Interesting. So, any sign of the others?"

T'Moy shook his head. "Only yourself—since my awakening several hours ago I have not strayed beyond the confines of the Nightmarket."

"Hmm, we better give this some thought." Pyke got to his feet, gave the Granavian statue an affectionate pat, went over to the edge of the plinth and lowered himself to sit there. T'Moy came and sat beside him.

"How do we proceed?" he said. "How should we start looking for our companions?"

Pyke jabbed a thumb over his shoulder. "I look like a Granavian and you look like a Barlig, so I'm betting my granny's coffin that Vrass is here as a Gadromi and Klane is too as one of those Shylan miners."

"I see—Gadromi, Gomedran, and Shylan, Shyntanil. Will this help?"

"A little, but probably not much." Pyke made a wide, sweeping gesture. "Granah's population is about forty thousand, which is a honking big haystack for two out-of-town boys to rummage through." He narrowed his eyes. "No. I reckon there's another easier way to join up with our amigos, and it's all to do with why we're here."

T'Moy's brow furrowed for a moment. "We have to solve a puzzle so we can move onto the next stage of the Legacy's puzzle or game or experiment." He glanced round at the group of statues. "Are they part of the new puzzle, do you think?"

"Don't think so," Pyke said. "Clearly they serve as a trigger that reboots our original personalities..." *Just as RK1 speculated.* "But I'm fairly certain that I already have the first solid clue in my possession, right now!" He patted his battered, muddy satchel.

He went on to give a brief summary of what he had been up to (as Pazzyk), a mysterious client, the auction, the unsettling pair bidding for the same lot as himself, and later being ambushed by them.

"So this lockbooth key is important to the puzzle," said T'Moy.

"Vital enough for someone to send a couple of goons to try and snatch it, lawfully or otherwise." He opened Pazzyk's satchel, took out the folded lease, picked away the wax seal, untied the string and let the key fall into the palm of his hand. It was a plain black iron key with a large triangular bow imprinted with the letters "R-29A." He closed his fist around it and gave a cunning smile.

"I'm supposed to hand these over to some stuffed shirt back at Tillyfrays, but, you know what? What we should do is head over to that boxhouse and find out what's in the dead soldier's stash!"

"Now?"

"This very instant!—why, have you other plans?"

T'Moy gave a dry laugh and shook his head. "So this key and the lockbooth—you think this is the puzzle we have to solve?"

"No, this is only the opening teaser. I mean, look at the fabulous depth of detail all around you—a lot of effort has gone into creating and populating this simulated world so it seems to me that the mystery we're being drawn into will be a bit more involved than figuring out how to move some pieces around on a board."

T'Moy stood and dusted himself off. "I recall the drone RK1 saying that the simulation scenarios would test us, for which I am ready. How far is this boxhouse?"

"It's right over next to the western wall," Pyke said. "About a twenty-minute walk but the route passes through a couple of dodgy neighbourhoods. The idea is not to attract any attention but we should be ready if the locals cut up nasty. Do you have any weapons other than those handy fists of yours?"

The Bargalil reached into his jerkin and pulled out a curved dagger, just enough for Pyke to see.

"Hmm, deadly enough. More than can be said for the daft wee leather sap Pazzyk keeps in his pocket. We could do with some defensive weapons, say a staff for you and a weighted club for me—there's a stall near the Dragoons Row entrance where we can get kitted up."

"I have only a few of these brown coins," T'Moy said, extending a handful of coppers.

"Don't worry—I have a shiny gold crown and a few silvers left over from the auction. That should be plenty."

As they hurried off, leaving the square and its statues behind, Pyke's mind turned gloomy even as he kept up the superficial jauntiness. He'd managed to avoid thinking about his crew, Dervla in particular as he couldn't see how she might have survived falling out of that high window. Raven Kaligari had been hovering nearby in that grav-harness but it was pointless hoping that she might have intervened—that psycho would just have laughed herself sick as they both fell to their deaths.

Really need to stop this, he thought. *Stop it right now! Out there I'm dead and she might well be dead too but in here we need...I need to get this done, then get the next one done. This is the Legacy's game but there's definitely another game behind it, and I mean to find out what it is!*

CHAPTER NINE

"There, Chief, right there!"

Pyke, lying on his stomach at the crest of the dune, accepted the range-viewer from Ancil and fingered the zoom, bringing the distant scene into sharp focus.

"Well, now," he said. "Isn't that sweet!"

He was looking across at another section of the colossal, aeons-lost Arraveyne ship. It was roughly two hundred yards away and resting right against a wind-worn rocky outcrop. The longer Pyke stared the more he realised that this was the stern section. One end was a torn and jagged mess while at the other he could make out what appeared to be reaction drive thrusters, albeit bent and charred, and the twisted, cracked stumps of what might have been hyperfield vanes. Very clearly there was no camouflage field in operation here. Late-afternoon light cast sharp shadows across the ravaged vessel, setting every detail in sharp perspective. Most of the surface plating was missing and the hull was burst and smashed open in several places, shadowy gaps drifted and choked with sand.

And, parked on a level stretch only about a dozen paces from the wreck, was Raven's transport.

"Don't see any guards outside her ship," said Pyke.

"And none inside," said Ancil.

"How d'ye reckon that?"

"Zoom in on the underhull, Chief—see those black spheres?"

"Hmm, I do—they're flickering. Some kind of exotic sensor gear?"

"And then some. High-end self-defence with dedicated AI," said Ancil with unmistakable relish. "Add to that several shallow blisters dotted around the fuselage."

"Munition turrets?"

A nod. "Bound to be a mixture of anti-personnel, HE and armour-piercing. The whole system casts a shell of overlapping track-and-target sensor cones, and those turrets can probably shred anything that comes within their range, which extends right up to that tatty old wreck."

Pyke handed back the viewer. "Heh—that's a right maggot, so it is!"

Rays of fading sunlight struck gleams and bright points from the immense weathered wreck. Pyke squinted at it and the crouched shape of the transport it loomed over, then glanced at the sky. He looked at the transport again, then back at the sky, then he smiled.

"Ans, are we still getting telemetry updates from the *Scarabus*?"

"Certainly are, Chief."

"What was the latest forecast, d'ye remember?"

"I do. Clear skies till about midnight then a storm moving in from the south."

Pyke's smile was sly. "I think you were right—I reckon there's no one onboard 'cos Raven has her entire gang of pukes with her. Bet she's been getting similar climate data from her own ship, lurking up in orbit somewhere, so she reckons she'll be in and out before the storm piles in."

Ancil nodded. "She always keeps her team small, likes 'em on site, so, yeah, that shuttle is unmanned!—except for the top-of-the-range AI defence system."

"Yeah," said Pyke. "Damn thing can put out a hellish response, but only if it can actually see its target. And since we don't have heavy enough weaponry to knock out ol' Cerberus there, we're going to have to blind the beast!" He grinned. "Now, what do we have with us that can kick up a bit of a duststorm?"

For a moment or two Ancil's face worked its way through a range of grimaces expressing various states of internal bafflement. Then comprehension dawned.

"The fanjet thrusters on the shuttle-barge! Now, that is just the burn!—and we could manoeuvre the shuttle-barge round to direct our homemade duststorm wherever we want!"

"And we don't have to smother the whole craft, just blind the sensors covering the aft and port side up to the wreck. Is that doable?"

"Doable with bells on, Chief!" Ancil said, laughing. "Oh, are all of us going on the recce, or are you wanting someone to stay behind to park the wagon someplace safe?"

"Kinda thinking this will be an all-hands-on-deck sorta mission," Pyke said. "Can we patch the controls through to the *Scarabus*?"

"Yup, not a problem—Oleg can pilot the shuttle off to a secure spot."

"Okay, I'm sold—let's head back and tell the rest."

It took over five minutes to trudge back to the grav-hopper, strap in and get airborne. Another five minutes of dune-hopping brought them back to where the shuttle-barge sat in the deepening shadow of a sandy ridge, and where the rest of the crew were relaxing both inside and out. The others gathered round as Ancil cabled his range-viewer to one of the shuttle's overhead screens and played back some of the images they'd captured. Then, between them, Pyke and Ancil laid out their plan to render the sensors on Raven's transport useless with an artificial duststorm. Everyone seemed impressed—even the Sendrukan scientist was agreeable—except for Dervla.

"Uh-huh. Before we get geared up and go haring off, I'd like to actually see one of you demonstrate this ploy with the actual shuttle, just now." She folded her arms. "Take her up, and let's see you blast up some real, thick dusty clouds, boys. Carry on."

Pyke and Ancil exchanged a shrug and a nod then got strapped into the pilot couches, while the others decamped to watch from a short way off. It was only when Pyke started up the suspensor systems that he realised there was no hull sensor providing a view behind and beneath the stern. He mentioned this to Ancil.

"And there's no piloting templates for this kind of manoeuvre," he said. "It's going to be seat-of-the-pants jinking and nudging..."

Ancil unstrapped himself from the couch. "I'll be your eyes, Chief. Tell me what I should say."

They settled on a handful of instructions: up, down, nose up, nose down, bank left, bank right. Then, with Ancil down at the open rear hatch and leaning out (while lashed to an interior hitch), Pyke ramped up the suspensors and the shuttle-barge rose into the air. He steered the craft to a spot about two hundred yards from where the rest of the crew stood watching before starting up the aft fanjets. The noise was all-encompassing, which was why both Ancil and himself had got kitted out with headsets.

It still needed a fair bit of shouting and gesticulating as they figured out the best combination of nose-up angle and ground proximity that would cast up billowing, swirling clouds. After less than half an hour they got to the stage where they could create a dense dustcloud and use one of the fanjets to push it in whatever direction they liked. By the time Pyke brought the shuttle-barge back to its landing spot, a deep evening darkness was rolling across the terrain as Ong's sun sank into the horizon.

"Okay," Dervla said as they emerged from the aft and forward hatches. "I'm convinced. When are we doing this?"

"Can't afford to wait, dear heart," Pyke said. "No telling

when Raven and her goon squad might emerge from the wreck. I so want to get the drop on them and see her little face get all red and screamy when I take the Eye back! Right, all aboard and get yourselves geared up..."

He paused as he noticed Ancil, his head and chest pale with dust, standing upslope from the shuttle, holding a finger in the air. Then he put the finger in his mouth for a second before holding it up again. He nodded and hurried over to Pyke who said: "There's wind? Seriously?"

"Just a faint breeze, Chief," Ancil said. "Better not waste any more time, though, eh?"

The last dregs of dusk had drained away over the furthest horizon by the time Pyke, flying low and slow, got the shuttle-barge to the right location—roughly two hundred and fifty yards south-west of the colossal wreck with the shuttle's stern pointing in the direction of travel. Up in orbit, aboard the *Scarabus*, Oleg was properly linked into their pilot systems so all they had to do was get under way and let the fanjets do their thing. Once they were close enough to the wreck, and the dustclouds were sufficiently dense, Pyke would bring the shuttle down to a ground-level hover, get everyone disembarked then flip the controls over to remote before bailing.

It was a great plan, an elegant plan, a plan which was creative and direct and which very nearly worked out as everyone wanted.

With Ancil once again providing directions from the rear hatch, Pyke manoeuvred the shuttle-barge into the correct angular posture with the suspensors then fired up the fanjets. The night sky was a giant's hoard of jewelled stars scattered wildly across the inky empyrean of deep space. Down near the ground all was dark, impenetrable. Nothing, Pyke realised, was quite as black as a desert by night. Then the dustclouds began rising around them and were blasted aft of the shuttle by the furious force of the fan-jets. Under cover of this cloak of pummelled sand, Pyke guided the shuttle backwards in the direction of the wreck and Raven's ship.

Ancil gave the sign to slow down as they drew near the drop-off point. Everyone got themselves ready, coping with weapons and equipment while dressed in the gauzy one-piece suits which Lieutenant-Doctor Ustril had with foresight brought along. With their half-mask hoods they were ideal for keeping out flying dust and grit. Then Ancil shouted, "Hold!" and Pyke halted the shut-tle's descent, allowing everyone to file out and clamber down to the ground as best as they could. Once Dervla and Ancil were gone, Pyke thumbed open the comm link to the *Scarabus*.

"Oleg, that's us on the ground—over to you now."

"Okay, Captain—remote systems engaged."

Pyke tapped a few buttons on the pilot screen and that was it. Moments later he was out of the hatch, landing slightly awk-wardly on the sand then being helped upright by Kref.

"Some noise, eh, Captain?"

He was right. At close quarters the howling din of the shuttle's fanjets was a tearing shriek, but they were clearly doing all he'd asked of them and more. Stirred-up clouds swirled about them, veils of murk that reduced the looming hulk of the ancient wreck to a vague outline while Raven's transport was completely hidden from view. Which meant that they were, too.

Oleg's measured voice spoke over the headset. "Captain, may I advise haste? The fringes of a high-pressure system are moving in faster than previously modelled."

"You mean it's gonna get a bit breezy round these parts?"

"That's the gist of it."

Pyke switched his headset to the crew's comm net. "Okay, boys and girls, we'll have to double-time it—we've got breezes incoming!"

Under cover of the billowing clouds and with the fanjets

howling at their backs, they hurried over to the huge, dilapidated hulk and skirted along its flank, persevering at times with soft, foot-trapping sand. During their earlier reconnaissance, Pyke and Ancil had spotted a likely entrance about two-thirds of the way sternwards—its likelihood was sign-posted by the ramp that led up to it and the line of boot marks leading there from Raven's transport. With Pyke and Kref bringing up the rear, Ancil was not even halfway to the ramp when Oleg's voice broke through on Pyke's headset.

"The wind is picking up, Captain—you must hurry!"

Pyke decided there was only one solution and bellowed, "Everybody run!—shift yer arses now! Move it!"

Fearing the worst, the crew sprang forward as one, those with a longer stride (like the Sendrukan Ustril) loping quickly ahead. Both she and Ancil reached the ramp at the same time, the latter grabbing one of her equipment bags as they charged up the slope with Moleg hard on their heels. That was the very moment when a sudden gust blew in from the lightless desert.

Running and gasping alongside Kref, Pyke actually saw the precise moment that the gust hit, saw the warm dustclouds rise up in swirls as the wedge of colder air rushed in beneath it. It was as if a curtain was swept aside—the dark crouching shape of Raven's transport was suddenly visible, which could only mean that Pyke's crew were visible to it. Moleg was racing up the ramp and Pyke was unlimbering his handgun while roaring at Kref to get the hell up there after him. But Kref, that stupid blockhead of an oaf, refused, even as red range-finder beams probed through the haze towards them. In fact, that oversized dunderhead was trying to shield Pyke and clicking off the safeties on the heavy autorifle that looked like a toy in his hands...

And, right then, as Pyke heard the whine of the flechette turrets spinning up, the shuttle-barge glided in from the darkness, fanjets still shrieking.

"Better get to cover, Captain!" said Oleg over the headset. "Soon as you're safe I'll fly the shuttle out of harms way."

They didn't need to be told twice. Pyke could hear the hammering rattle of flechette and armour-piercing rounds peppering the shuttle's starboard side as he and Kref scrambled up the ramp to where friendly hands hauled them into sheltering shadows.

"That's us," he gasped to Oleg. "Get it moving!"

Through a crack in the wreck's hull plating, Pyke could see the shuttle-barge surge forwards, heading for the dark of the desert, trying to get out of the mini-turrets' sensor range. But the craft was listing to starboard as it drifted off into the murky night. Moments later the sound of the fanjets cut out and he feared the worst.

"Oleg?" he muttered. "How bad is it?"

"Pretty bad, Captain. Starboard suspensors got badly shredded—I'm amazed the aft unit kept functioning as long as it did. I managed to ditch the shuttle high up on a dune about three hundred yards out from your position."

"Not much in the way of self-repair on the bucket, is there?" he said.

"Only for the comms and basic life support, Captain. It'll take some serious onsite repair, and probably actual new parts."

"Or we could just liberate a new one."

"Steal, I think, is the word you really mean."

"I like the word 'liberate,' Oleg. Raven's been a right royal gouging pain in my neck since some time back, and once I've finished kicking her arse halfway around this dustball planet I'm planning to, yes, steal that shiny combat shuttle of hers. So, in the interim, while we're clouting up a fuss down here, could you see if you can hack into its systems, if that's at all possible."

"See what I can do."

"Good lad."

While he'd been talking to Oleg, the others had broken out

hand torches to see what was around them and to get a sense of their location within the massive wreck. Pyke was sitting where his panicky arrival had dumped him, on an incline of compacted sand and leaning against a mesh-covered bulkhead. This temporary refuge lay between the outer hull and an inner bulkhead barrier—the outer hull was missing many plate sections, a few of which had been used to construct the ramp which sloped up to the rough entrance.

Ancil, dodging past gaps in the hull, came over and squatted next to him.

"Did the shuttle make it, Chief? Do we still have a ride home?"

"'Fraid not, Ans—however, I have taken a liking to Raven's tasty little runabout."

Ancil chuckled. "Yep, lethal defences aside, Chief, it's certainly a pretty machine. Think we can persuade her to give up the activation codes?"

"Not a chance, which is why I've got Oleg trying to find out if that transport is hackable."

"Tough egg to crack, it being Raven's."

Pyke shrugged. "Yeah, but maybe Oleg's luck will hold better than ours. So, anyway, how are we doing here? Has Ustril picked up Raven's trail, by any chance?"

"She's only just got some of her gear running, Chief, but she does say that we must stay away from the drives and the adjoining compartments. Said something about transdimensional anomalies, how they could really mess up our day!"

"But nothing on Raven."

"She's still a bit shaken up, Chief, we all are. But she's still on it, so I'm sure she'll have something solid soon."

"Fine. What about a way further inside this mouldering heap?"

"There's an open maintenance hatch a dozen yards along..." Ancil pointed. "Must be how Raven and her crew got inside.

It opens on a stairwell with steps leading up and down and a narrow passage branching off. No one's been through, well, not very far—the downward stairs are busted, drops into an unlit lower deck and there's some kind of weak light up at the top of the main stairs. That's all we know so far."

Pyke let his suspicion show. "Three routes, and just one is lit?"

Ancil grinned. "I thought it looked a bit trappy."

"Need to check it out, though." Pyke smiled. "Could be the moment when I get to christen the Jones-Eckley plasma-slugger!"

"And may the Great Maker have mercy upon whoever's on the receiving end!"

With shared laughter, they gathered together the others and Pyke laid out his plan, which he'd thought up roughly thirty seconds earlier. Dervla, Kref, Ustril and Moleg would move across the landing to the narrow passageway and explore it while Pyke ventured upstairs for a look-see, with Ancil following as backup.

"Just a second," said Dervla. "I think it's clear to everyone that in the event of any unforeseen shenanigans those of us sidelined in that little passage will need something with extra punch to…secure our position, y'know."

"Well, yes, maybe so," Pyke said.

"Good, so Ancil should lend me that brutal hand-cannon and we'll be solid."

Ancil drew back. "What do you need the Ashbless for when you've all got perfectly fine weapons of yer own?"

"Well, that or you take my place and I'll be Pyke's backup." She gave the captain a sidelong glance. "That work for you?"

Pyke, knowing there was no way Ancil could win this one, smiled expansively. "Darlin,' whatever gets the job done!"

Ancil gave a shrug and a rueful smile as he led the others through the maintenance hatch by torchlight and across the landing to the dark passageway.

"He was so looking forward to blowing a hole in something or someone," Pyke murmured as he and Dervla followed the others through and started up the stairs.

"If our luck holds true to form," she said, "there'll be plenty of targets to go round."

Stealthily they ascended three flights of cracked and corroded metal steps. Pyke noted the state of the risers and rails and wondered why the non-decay they had noted in the other wrecked section was not apparent here. They slowed as they reached the top and the source of the light, a square window in a closed door. Pyke gestured Dervla to stay back on the last flight, to which she responded with raised eyebrows as she followed him onto the landing.

"Careful," he whispered. "Your death-wish is showing!"

She winked, then pointed at the door. "Think it's trapped?"

"Bound to be." He peered closely. "Sliding door. Could be pressure triggers down the inside frame, or plain old drop recesses along the lintel."

"Okay, she's viciously homicidal and hates your guts. What's the worst she'd do if she thought you might be on her trail?"

He gave a rueful smile, trying not to recall too much from long past events. "Blow the stairwell, blow me to bits. That's her style."

"Hmm, overkill, nice." She frowned. "We never really checked underneath this landing."

"Right enough, we didn't."

Sure enough, when they retreated to the next landing down, closer scrutiny with their torches on pin-bright setting revealed a number of blue strips spaced all around the landing's underside, against the wall, looking for all the world like some kind of structural support.

Dervla nodded admiringly. "She really, *really* hates your guts!"

"Baffles the hell outa me, darlin'—we had our differences and didn't part on what you'd call good terms, but all this…" He shook his head. "It's just unhinged."

Dervla's smile was almost pitying. "Don't care, don't want to know. All we need to figure out is how we deal with this."

"Tiptoe away? Try another route?"

"I'm willing to bet those other routes are dead ends or similar," she said. "Besides, she must know we're here. She'll know that her transport's defences were tripped, and since no one else is hunting for the Eye..."

"Has to be us, I get it." Pyke felt a rush of anger. "Ach, so we'll just blow it, then. Let 'em think we got caught in the blast—it'll give us an edge for a bit." He hefted the Jones-Eckley plasma slugger. "Set it all off from here, eh?"

She shook her head. "If those charges are strong enough to blow the entire landing apart, we might get shredded by flying shrapnel. What we need to do is make it look as if someone actually opened that door up there."

He frowned. "Got any field line?" He laughed when she held open one side of her jacket and tugged out a small carabiner on some line that unwound from an inner pouch. "Well, of course you have!"

"I'll just be a moment," she said. "Better get onto Ancil and fill him in."

Pyke watched her climb light-footed back up to the top landing and start rigging the line, realising that the safest place really was down at the landing where they'd entered. As he descended he let Ancil know what the plan was, finishing off when they came face-to-face at the entrance to the dark passageway. Behind Ancil were green glows, flares that had been placed all the way along the passage. In the emerald radiance, faces looked weird and otherworldly.

"Green flares?" he said to Ancil. "Green?"

Before Ancil could reply, Dervla arrived and hurried along the passage to join them, holding the carabiner in her hand.

"Everyone ready?" she said. "Cover your ears, it's gonna be loud!"

With a hand over one of her ears, she held up the trigger line and gave it a good, vigorous tug.

Silence.

"Well, that was..."

A deafening explosion obliterated Pyke's next few words, or, rather, his motivation for saying them. The shattering violence of the detonation made him close his eyes and physically flinch away as bulkheads shook and the deck quaked underfoot. The massive noise extended into a clanging, crashing sound from the direction of the stairwell. When he opened his eyes there was smoke in the narrow passageway, illuminated by the green flares into shifting hazy veils. Ancil came towards him out of the emerald murk.

"Cunning," he said. "Evil and cunning."

"What's that?" Pyke said, coughing.

"The stairs at the end of this passage go down about three flights, and they were mined!—all went off same time as the one upstairs."

"Leaving us with one route into the ship. Those busted steps going down," Pyke growled. "And you can bet yer last bit-ducat that it'll lead to a dead end of some kind." He glanced at Dervla. "What's it like through there?"

She'd been peering into the tangle of metal now filling the main landing, and shook her head. "Could be better, but seen worse. Some of the big sections, though, are holding up a lot of the smaller wreckage, and with a bit of heaving and pushing there might be a way round. Hey, Kref!"

"Sure, Derv, I heard," said the big Henkayan. "Should be able to move all that a bit—need a hand, though."

Many hands made tough work a little less demanding, shoving

aside some of the twisted remains of two landings: the collapse of the topmost sent wreckage plunging down onto the lowest, tearing it away from the bulkhead. After their combined efforts enough of a gap was created to allow everyone, even the tallest, to edge round to the broken downward steps and the inky blackness below.

By torchlight they could see that the stairwell beneath was nearly full of wreckage, too—most of the high bulkhead on the coreward side had burst into the stairwell spilling debris into the gap, a twisted snarl of plating, decking, beams, knotted meshes of cables and pipes and an abundance of unidentifiable junk.

Moleg had been examining the spot where the first downward flight was missing, rubbing the broken metal supports then sniffing his fingers.

"Freshly done," he said. "Raven and her crew demolished this."

"Just her style," Pyke said. "Any way to bridge that gap? In fact, is there any point in getting down there at all?"

Moleg pulled down over his eyes the goggles that had been resting on his brow and grinned. "Someone's been down there already, before Raven and her goons arrived." He pointed down at the next landing, which was half buried in fallen debris. "Something took out the middle section of that landing a while back, but somebody tended to it quite nicely." He took off the goggles and handed them to Pyke.

Pyke knew Moleg wouldn't push something like this if there wasn't a point, so he put on the goggles and looked at the landing, now illuminated by Moleg's torch. And just there he could make out two or three spars clustered together and laid across the gap in the landing. He laughed.

"It's a walkway," he said, handing back the goggles.

"It is."

"And it must be going somewhere."

Moleg nodded. "My guess is that there's a hatchway on the

other side of the landing, behind all that debris, and it leads further into the ship—I mean, no one goes to the trouble of making a walkway that goes nowhere."

Pyke laughed. "Smart thinking, ould son. Let's get cracking."

With everyone lending a hand—including Ustril the Sendrukan—they managed to patch together a gantry from sections of railing and lengths of decking. Once it was in position they carefully crossed over, one by one, shuffling down the creaking, sloped gantry to the other end. When Kref and Ustril made their crossings the improvised bridge creaked a little louder both times… but held.

Pyke was third across, after Kref—he gave the big Henkayan a punch to the upper arm. "Told you, didn't I? Easier than crossing that acrobat bar on Shephedri Orbital."

Kref gave one of those nods where his whole upper body seemed to rock back and forth. "I think Shephedri was worse, Captain—I didn't have to duck any waiters on ropes here!"

Just as Moleg suspected, there was a gap behind the debris big enough for everyone to pass through to get to the beams that bridged the gap. And, on the other side, there was indeed an open hatchway.

Beyond, more lightless corridor. Ancil and Moleg took point, probing the shadows with torchbeams, exposing secrets. More mingled heaps of detritus, the vestiges and powdery residues of rubbish pulverised by the sheer weight of countless years. The corridor ran straight for five paces, turned left, continued for another seven paces before ending at a wall of twisted metal. There was, however, a ladder that went up through a square gap in the ceiling. As they gathered about it, Moleg set up a stopover lamp to brighten the spot.

"Who's going up as scout?" Pyke said.

Ancil raised a hand, jammed his blazing torch into a shoulder loop, then grabbed a head-height rung and began to climb. When he reached the deck above he stepped off the ladder and called back down:

"Nothing here but a small room, Chief, with one door pushed shut and jammed from the other side. There's also a narrow companionway leading up a fair distance—my torch beam can't project to the very top. I can feel a flow of cool air, though."

"Okay, Ans, scout ahead a bit further," Pyke said. "Just find out where it goes then report back. No solo missions from hell!"

"Hearing you loud and clear, Chief!"

And he was gone, step-climbing, footsteps receding. As Pyke gazed thoughtfully at the space where Ancil had been a moment before, he felt a tap on his shoulder. It was the Sendrukan scientist, Lieutenant-Doctor Ustril.

"Hey, Doc, everything okay?"

"I am discontented, Captain. Since our disembarkation I have been unable to make full use of even the inadequate equipment I have been carrying, and sometimes dragging." The corridor was just tall enough to accommodate her height and even in the half-light of the stopover lamp Pyke could see that her usual composure was absent. "During our progress I have been using the manual proximity scanner on our surroundings and I have detected notable variances."

"You mean the way metal looks more corroded than it did back in the other wreck?"

"Yes, and scanner data confirms my suspicions—something is affecting the anti-entropic qualities of structural metals, which certainly would weaken resistance to natural decay. If we could only stop for half an hour I could..."

"Sorry, Doc, but we're in hostile territory and I'm not so keen on any extended delays when we're this closed in. Have patience for now, that's all I ask."

She seemed unpersuaded. "I've seen that you usually ask for more than patience."

Pyke wanted to come back with a witty riposte but she had turned away to ask Moleg something. He gave a small nod, thinking that tolerance was a virtue of some kind as he leaned against the corridor bulkhead for a rest. Apart from the conversation between Ustril and Moleg, the general mood was one of muted, strung-out weariness combined with the tension of trying to anticipate unknown dangers.

I guess a different captain would use this pause in proceedings to come out with a terrific, morale-boosting speech full of hearty, moving phrases and the like. Me? I think I'd rather have a game of cards.

He fumbled through his waist pouches in search of a deck but came up empty-handed. He was having a rummage around in Ancil's goody bag, when the voice of the man himself came over on the headset, but only on Pyke's channel.

"Hey, Chief."

"Okay, Ans, find anything?"

"Oh yes, definitely. Found something, all right. That companionway goes up to a small platform between the inner and outer hulls and from there a short ladder goes further up to a kind of ledge on the outside of the hull. Takes some careful sidling to follow it round before it comes to what must have been an observation lounge or something, an oval recess that someone made into a camp a while ago."

Pyke frowned. "Everything okay? Safe to come up?"

"There's no dangers, Captain, but I think you should send the Lieutenant-Doctor up first."

That made him stop. "Really? Because?"

Ancil's voice went low and sombre. "It's just that there's a body up here, remains really, that I think she ought to see before the others."

A body? Pyke thought. *A Sendrukan body, perhaps?*

He was suddenly aware that everyone, including Ustril, was

watching him. He nodded, matter-of-fact and relaxed. "Yeah, sure, Ans, we can do that." He turned to the others. "Ancil's found a place up top, could be just the spot for a rest. Doc, why don't you head up there first—give you a chance to start setting up your equipment?"

The Sendrukan was surprised for a moment, then nodded and approached the ladder. "Thank you, Captain."

"Dervla, you'll be next, then Kref…" Ustril was climbing up into the deck above as Dervla came over. Pyke put a hand on her arm, making her pause while the Sendrukan started up the steep companionway. Then he leaned in close to mutter in her ear, "Take it slowly, let her get a good way ahead of you…"

"What's going on?"

"You'll see soon enough." As she began her climb, Pyke beckoned the Henkayan over. "Nice and easy, Kref, no rush."

Kref nodded, checked over the fastenings of his hefty combat jacket, then approached the ladder and started upwards.

Moleg gave Pyke a narrow look. "Is there some kind of problem waiting for us up above?"

He shook his head, which turned into a half-shrug. "Ancil found a body," he said, voice low. "Sendrukan."

"Ah—so she did have a companion."

"What tipped you off?" asked Pyke.

"That base of hers just didn't feel like a solo hideout."

Pyke gave a nod then, with Moleg bringing up the rear, he grabbed a rung and followed Kref.

Ustril had energetically ascended the ladder and steps and by the time Dervla switched from ladder to companionway at the deck above, Ustril was gone from view. Dervla commenced her ascent, deliberately stomping up the steps, breathing heavily the cool dry air. She was about to start up the last ladder section when she heard a faint cry from above, from outside.

Many times since joining the crew of the *Scarabus*, Dervla had found herself having to deal with Brannan Pyke's hunches, guesses, gut feelings and sundry on-the-hoof improvisations. Outcomes could vary wildly between inspired genius and shambolic trainwreck, yet no matter how botched the upshot or how enraged the client, an absurd kind of luck would kick in and pluck Pyke and the crew from seemingly inescapable doom. No one ever mentioned this rare good fortune but Dervla could see that the others were aware of it, at least to the point where it fostered a certain swagger.

But the thing about Pyke was that, for all his obvious egocentricity, he could still surprise you with a quiet word and advice which managed to suggest a sensitivity at odds with that devil-may-care exterior.

Some of those thoughts passed through Dervla's mind as she continued doggedly up the last stretch of ladder. The cry had sounded at first like some kind of creature, but she started to wonder if it had come from the Sendrukan Ustril, which inevitably gave rise to a knot of anxiety. The air was cold and sand gritted on every rung as she climbed, quickly reaching the top where she emerged from the cramped shaft. She'd clipped her torch to a shoulder loop so that a broad beam lit up a sandy makeshift platform wedged between the inner and outer hulls, high above the ground. Hardly any outer hull plating remained and through a spidery mesh of struts she could gaze out across an endless sea of desert shadows. From the platform a narrow walkway composed of assorted debris sloped up to what seemed to be the severed end of the shipwreck section. Dervla heard Kref's heavy tread ascending the companionway below as she carefully picked her way up the curious pathway.

A cold breeze soughed continuously through the skeletal hull, an eerie sound in the stretched-out silence. Up ahead, suddenly, a light came on, revealing the figure of Ancil pointing his torch at the walkway to guide her.

"Did you hear something, just a short while ago?" she said.

Ancil nodded gravely." It was Ustril—she's in the observation lounge, reading from something," he said quietly as she drew near. "Will you try speaking to her? She's ignoring anything I say."

"I'll give it a shot, Ans."

The improvised footway turned a corner and by her torchbeam Dervla saw the broken, sheared edge of the wreck's upper hull, a fringe of twisted beams and spars littered with a few hull plates and interspersed with weathered strips and ribbons of material, stirring sluggishly in the breeze. This was where the stern had torn away from the rest of the ship as it careered across the skies of Ong so many centuries before. The narrow walkway continued along the wreck's broken edge until it sloped down through the hull and into a short section of corridor which came to a doorless hatch. A glow was coming from somewhere off to the side, and the sound of something flapping in the breeze.

She stepped through into what Ancil said was an observation lounge, a dark, semi-circular room in which someone had rigged up a camp of sorts. Scavenged lengths of cloth had been stretched over the top and across the open front, a shield against the elements, but strong winds must have torn away some ties, leaving loose corners to sway and flap. Shadows hid the edges, and overturned tables and shelves littered one half of the area. The pale glow came from behind a tall, grubby cloth partition. As Dervla approached, the end of a large camp bed came into view, revealing the robed legs and shod feet of a tall figure stretched out upon it.

Ustril was seated on a stool next to the bed, not looking up from the grey, mummified, robe-clad remains of a Sendrukan male. Skeletal hands were clasped together on the chest, and a desiccated head rested within a hood. Ustril did not look up as Dervla cautiously went to the other side and knelt.

"His name was Saljyn," Ustril said levelly. "He was my

betrothed. We had exchanged heartsongs before the High Academy passed the sentence of exile upon me—Saljyn did not have to accompany me...yet he did." Her voice wavered. "We came to Ong nine years ago. It was the third of three planets which our research suggested as a possible resting place for an ancient vessel known as the *Mighty Defender of the Arraveyne Heart*..."

Dervla's eyes widened. "So you were already hunting for it when Mr. Van Graes hired you. Did he know? Did you tell him?"

Ustril shook her head. "We led him to believe that our interest here was solely to do with the ruins and artefacts left behind by Ong's original inhabitants. Our true purpose, our hope, was to retrieve artefacts that would conclusively prove the existence of the *Mighty Defender*, which had been considered no more than a child's myth throughout Sendrukan history. Such an astonishing discovery would force the High Academy to rescind its sentence of exile, thus allowing us to return to the Hegemony." She gazed down at her empty, long-fingered hands. "Van Graes' interest in the lost vessel was very convenient, as were the funds he paid over to us. By the time he contacted us we had been on Ong for nearly four years with little to show for our efforts, and getting perilously close to complete destitution."

Dervla indicated the remains of her lover, Saljyn. "So you did find the ship after all," she said, but Ustril shook her head.

"I was never here, in this wreck," she said. "With Van Graes' support, we were able to travel to the other towns along the edge of the Great Desert, investigating old archives and questioning any nomads that would talk to us. After over a year of this we had amassed a dossier of reports, rumours and folk tales from which we deduced the likely location of a small vessel where there should be none. We hired an aircar in Cawl-Vesh and flew directly to the general area. Unfortunately, the weather patterns changed unexpectedly and sent a sandstorm blowing after us, roughly half an hour behind us."

"Where I come from," Dervla said, "we call that Murphy's Law."

The Sendrukan frowned. "Was this Murphy an archaeologist, too?"

"He or she was probably an expert in random mishaps." Dervla waved it away. "Not important. Carry on."

"Very well. We reached the location but then our portable equipment began suffering intermittent faults. We persisted with our search and actually found the craft, protruding from the side of a dune, but by then the storm was upon us. At close quarters it seemed about the size of a lifeboat and appeared to have been gutted. With our working analysers we were able to verify the very great age of the craft, and discovered the anti-entropic nature of its construction materials. The interior, however, was empty, scoured of anything that one might normally find in an abandoned wreck, stripped right back to the bulkheads, decking and hull. We realised, however, that with some work and refurbishment it would serve quite well as a forward base from which to make further explorations. We agreed that Saljyn would remain behind with a survival case while I flew the aircar back to our rented workshop in Cawl-Vesh to pick up the field camping packs and our sensory equipment. The sandstorm was rising in strength when I left but it caused my homeward flight no problems. And when I returned to the half-buried craft three hours later Saljyn was gone."

"No clues, no message?"

"The sand around the craft seemed more disturbed but in the aftermath of the storm it was hard to be certain what had transpired. But, no, there was no message left for me." Relived anguish was stark in Ustril's features. "I searched, by aircar and on foot, but to no avail. Aircar hire is not cheap and my searches began to drain our funds, but when Van Graes learned of Saljyn's disappearance he kindly made more money available and I carried on searching. I was tormented by despair and a strange anger—in three hours he could not have gone very far, yet not a clue could be found."

"Could he have been picked up by someone else in a vehicle?" Dervla said.

"As well as being expensive, there are few aircars available for hire," Ustril said. "The Cawl-Vesh service had no other craft out on lease at that time of the day. And a chance encounter in the immensity of the desert is highly unlikely." She gazed sadly at the lifeless, cowled head on the camp bed. "Last year, while visiting a tundra-side village far to the south, I overheard an old woman talking about the Great Northern Desert. Some people call it the Sea of Sand, she said, not realising that it really is a sea, as vast and deadly and relentless as any of the oceans that other worlds have. It can hide entire armies or swallow nations whole, drown hills and valleys in sand with a single storm, bury them so deep that memory of them fades away. That was how I felt about Saljyn, that the desert had just reached out and wiped him from the face of the planet..."

She opened a drawer in a small bedside table and took out a long, thin object. It looked like a bookmark at first, except that it was long and dark grey with slightly bulbous ends. Ustril lightly tossed it onto the robed cadaver's chest.

"That is Saljyn's personal journal. In it he tells how a bot-swarm attacked him soon after I departed in the aircar. He just had time to grab the survival case and flee, heading for higher dunes to the east where he thought he'd spotted a rocky outcrop. That turned out to be the jagged spur which this whole wreck is resting against, and Saljyn was lucky enough to find shelter in the outer hull. At that time the wreck was only partially engulfed by the desert—as you can see it's taken a few years for the winds to lay it all bare. I'm certain that it could be entombed again quite easily."

Ustril fell silent, her features sombre and frowning.

"Does his journal speak of you?" Dervla said.

"I haven't had time to read it from start to finish, but he wrote all its entries for my eyes. He explains that he made this camp as a safe place to retreat to after his scavenging explorations of the wreck's interior." She stared intently at Dervla. "It is very dangerous inside—many of the corridors are blocked by strange tangled plants growing from the materials of the ship itself. Saljyn referred to it as the Steel Forest and said that it is inhabited by semi-sentient creatures who used to be the ship's passengers and crew. He said that he spoke with some of them and became friendly with a few, after a fashion. They helped him with supplies and the layout of the corridors...ten months he managed to survive before he contracted a mysterious illness which left him increasingly weak and delirious. His last journal entry was just over a year ago." She lowered her head, as if to hide tears, then picked up the long grey journal recorder. A pale-green screen lit up to show lines of text which Ustril scrolled through with a fingertip.

"All the entries I read prove that he never forgot why we came to Ong, never stopped thinking about our purpose. He left behind this journal, full of notes and thoughts on what he discovered inside the wreck. He also left me something else..." From her robe she produced a flat triangular tablet, the same shade of grey as the recorder, and with a glassy stalk running down the middle.

"What is it?" Dervla said. "What does it do?"

Holding the object with the point towards Dervla, Ustril said, "This."

There was a soundless flash down the thing's glassy spine and suddenly Dervla found herself unable to move or speak. Ustril leaned forward, a serious expression on her large face.

"It's a defensive weapon. It creates a temporary stasis nimbus rather than a bubble—the effects are harmless and wear off after five or six minutes, plenty of time for me to leave you and enter the wreck." She stood and moved swiftly to gather a few pieces of equipment into her backpack which she pulled on. "I'm sorry to have to visit duplicity upon you in this manner but it serves my immediate needs. My betrothed never forgot about the one thing, the single necessary thing that I need to reclaim my life, my place, my heritage—and he found it. A unique artefact of unsurpassable significance, and he left me directions as to its location."

Frozen in her kneeling posture, Dervla could only watch as Ustril paused to give the camp bed's long-dead occupant one last look. Then, before striding out of sight, she said to Dervla:

"I sincerely hope that you and your companions find treasures sufficient to satisfy Van Graes. I would advise that you resist any temptation to enter this wreck—the hazards within would overwhelm you. Goodbye."

Dervla heard soft footsteps moving back and forth behind her, then a faint creak, sounds of physical effort, and finally a deadened thud. Then silence.

Damn! she thought, straining to move her limbs, still all locked in this stupid kneeling position. *What did she mean by a "unique artefact"? Hope it's not what it sounds like—Pyke'll have a fit when he hears...*

Seconds dragged by with all the lithe velocity of a sleep-deprived sloth. *Pyke!* she wanted to yell. *You cloth-eared gaggler—can you not hear that no one's talking round here?* What was most infuriating was that she could just hear Pyke chatting away with Ancil, muffled from their position back along the walkway.

The first signs of returning sensation came after about two minutes (possibly more), a kind of tingling itch emerging on the sole of her left foot and on her back between her shoulder blades.

They were maddeningly unscratchable until pins and needles took over, spreading from limb to limb, and Dervla found that she could make whispery sounds in her throat. She could also make small movements with her hands and feet so she twisted one foot under her, which was enough for her weight to cause her to overbalance. Toppling over, she landed on her side, knocking her head against the solid floor and provoking a wordless grunt of pain.

Someone must have heard her because footsteps came hurrying up and a curtain flap was ripped aside, followed by Pyke's outraged voice:

"What the hairy hell's going on here? Where's Ustril?" He paused. "Ans, see where she is."

Dervla felt Pyke's hands lifting her, while straightening her legs out and offering hushing noises when spikes of cramp made her gasp. By the time she was sitting on an upturned, grubby plastic box, clearing her throat and trying to frame answers to Pyke's dumbass questions, Ancil was back, looking grim.

"No sign of her, Chief."

"You can't be serious—she's nearly ten feet tall!" Pyke snarled. "No one that big vanishes without a trace..."

Ancil spread his hands, his features expressing an inward anger. "There's no other pathway out of here, Chief, it's a dead end..."

Dervla forestalled Pyke's next broadside with a weak wave of a hand, and a croaked whisper. "She used a hidden exit...some kind o' trapdoor...anyone got some water, something to drink?"

Moleg appeared with a cylindrical flask which he uncapped and handed over. Dervla drank thirstily, surprised to find that it was slightly carbonated with a faint sweet flavour. Ah, blessed relief.

"Where'd she go, Derv?" Pyke said. "Any idea?"

"I didn't see it, me being frozen by her stupid, skagging wee stungun...but I heard her messing around behind me, sounded like she used some kind of concealed trapdoor. She was shuffling around a bit, then there was a squeak that sounded like hinges and she was gone."

Pyke nodded, then glanced at Ancil. "Escape hatch—find it."

"Fine-tooth comb, Chief."

As Ancil, Moleg and Kref began a detailed fingertip search along the back wall, Pyke dragged over an empty cable drum and sat down beside her.

"So, what in the name of the gutter gods went on here?" He stared at the robed, mummified corpse on the camp bed. "I assume this was her partner."

"When did you guess, about them?"

"Not long after we got to her base." He shrugged. "It just felt too big and full for one person and she...she looked like she was in mourning. That and the usual hunches. C'mon, you've got a story to tell so spill."

And so she did, laying out the highlights of the fairly one-sided conversation she'd had with the Sendrukan scientist. Pyke's eyebrows shot up on hearing that Ustril and her consort had been secretly planning to gather a haul of artefacts with which to barter for Ustril's return from exile, and when Dervla recounted the message that Saljyn left behind, about a "unique artefact," Pyke leaned back, hands raised in a gesture of frustration.

"Damn me! Another one chasing these treasures that Van Graes is after! Who'll show up next—Imam-Pope Shango III?"

"Hey, Chief!"

Pyke and Dervla turned as one and saw Ancil balanced on Kref's shoulders and holding a long pole at a steep angle. Once he was sure of an audience, Ancil lowered the pole till its point rested on one hull panel, then he pushed. Dervla laughed as it swung inwards with a faint creak.

"Nice bit of lateral thinking, there, Ans," Pyke said, giving

Dervla a sidelong glance. "And she gave no clue about what to expect on the inside, huh?"

"Just that it was called the Steel Forest, and that we might find it a bit of a challenge."

"Well, it's where we're going—you fit and ready?"

She sighed deeply, rubbed her face then scratched her scalp. "I really could do with about three showers, one of those bluebeef dinners we had on Ashazoaz 4, a double PG2B on the rocks, and clean clothes. But I guess I'll have to make do with the tasteless chewy ribbon we laughingly refer to as field rations. And I'll be good to go."

"That's the stuff, m'darlin,'" he said with one of those winking grins that Dervla occasionally found attractive. "All we need to do is deal with Raven's goons while letting our Sendrukan turncoat lead us to the rest of this key."

"Well, let's get moving," Dervla said, standing up. "Before my infectious, super-charged enthusiasm runs dry! Shall we?"

CHAPTER TEN

It was well into the pitch-black throat of the night by the time Pyke and T'Moy reached the Raskol Boxhouse. Rather than risk the better lit streets that cut through well-patrolled districts, they had opted for a route which snaked in among dilapidated blocks and crumbling rookeries. Now they hunted back in the deep shadows of a stinking alley with the mazy murk of the Ithlyr slums at their backs. Across a wide, muddy road the high walls of a succession of properties marked the boundary between Ithlyr and the neighbouring artisans district. The glows from lanterns in private gardens were visible through the leafy branches of fruit trees or well-sculpted masses of verdant bushes, and the occasional outside wall-lamp shed meagre light on the main road.

The Raskol Boxhouse was not quite the last building in the street before it came to a dead end beneath the city walls. It was a two-storey stone building with the main entrance off to one side, near one of the corners. An iron staircase sloped up from the same corner to a landing and a door to the guardroom. Hanging oil lamps shed flickering haloes at the front where a solitary Gomri guard, spear sloping at his shoulder, patrolled back and forth.

"Hmm, risky," said Pyke. "Not much cover available. We ain't creeping up on this place."

"Can we not just claim the right to enter and inspect the booth?" said T'Moy. "You have the key and the lease."

"That only permits access during business hours," Pyke said sardonically. "So it looks like we'll have to try the stealth approach."

"Surely the whole vicinity makes stealth almost impossible."

"Ah, but I'm thinking of the stealth of appearances and assumptions. Put it this way, if that scrawny guard sees yourself, a tall brawny horse warrior, striding along the street towards him, what d'ye think his very first assumption will be?"

T'Moy nodded. "He'll see me as a threat."

"Exactly, whereas I look like a townie, I'm dressed for the part, and when I head his way I'll be sure to trip over a paving stone for dramatic effect. So while I'm getting him bogged down in talking about how I have a lease and a key, you'll be sneaking up the backstreets to a concealed spot near the boxhouse rear. What's vital is getting the other guard to come out of the guardroom and down to the front—there's bound to be rocket flares set up on the roof to raise the alarm, so if one of those goes off the city watch will come running. And that we don't want."

T'Moy looked left and right along the mostly deserted nighttime street. "What direction should we approach from?"

Pyke jabbed a thumb over his shoulder. "We'll dogleg back and along a short ways, just to that low-lit stretch and take it from there."

Together they went back down the alley then turned along a back lane in the direction of the city centre. Minutes later they had crossed over into the artisan district where their paths then diverged. While T'Moy skulked off round to the backstreets, Pyke made his way up the main road, making no attempt to soften his footsteps, coughing and whistling loudly as he walked. His plan for gaining access to the boxhouse was a bit nebulous, but then improvisation was the best half of any plan. All he had to do was put on some kind of annoying yet non-threatening performance which would draw the second guard down to street level so that T'Moy could then wade in.

The guard out front was puffing on a pipe while patrolling up and down. Pyke had the auction-house lease out and was trying to give the impression of an absent-minded newcomer to this part of town, while keeping tabs on the guard's progress from time to time. It was only when he drew near to the side alley opening right next to the boxhouse that he looked up and got his first clear view of the Gomri guard with his pipe.

It was Vrass.

That was when Pyke actually did trip over a jutting paving stone and pitch forward onto the still muddy street. Outstretched hands were scratched and grazed, and he cursed himself as the guard Vrass rushed to help.

"Careful now, citizen—you need to watch yer footing round this part of Granah, eh?"

From his time on the Isle of Candles Pyke remembered that Vrass had a line of pale tufts right down his snout, like this guy, and an asymmetrical patch under his left eye, just like this guy!

Talk about an added complication! We're gonna have to drag Vrass back to the statues, and still get inside the boxhouse and open that booth—and where is T'Moy?

As Vrass helped him to his feet he cast a glance along the alley and glimpsed T'Moy peering wide-eyed round the rear corner of the adjacent building. T'Moy mouthed "Vrass!," Pyke gave a sharp nod and switched his attention back with smiles and effusive gratitude.

"A host of thanks, good sir!" he babbled. "Truly, t'was my own daft fault, not looking where I was travelling…"

"Not a problem, citizen," said Vrass-the-guard. "What's your destination? Perhaps I can point you in the right direction."

"Very kind of you," Pyke said. "I seek the Raskol Boxhouse—I have in my possession a valid lease and a key—"

"And you'll be wanting to have a look at the contents, right?" Vrass shook his head. "Sadly, citizen, there's no entry to the boxhouse permitted outside of ordinary business hours, that's between ten in the morning and five…hang on, what's all that about back there?"

Guard-Vrass was interrupted by raised voices coming from the shadowy backstreet where T'Moy had been moments before. Pyke thought about making his excuses and leaving but before he could say anything the guardroom door at the top of the stairs opened and the second guard came out onto the landing. He was a burly type with a thick neck and a shaved head.

"Oy, you!" he bawled, pointing down at the backstreet. "Leave him alone!"

Assorted insults and mocking voices were the only reply, prompting the guard to reach inside the guardroom door for an impressive looking cudgel. Then he came hurrying down the stairs, grim-faced and determined.

"Bunch of sots and topers from the Carver's Arms," he told Vrass. "Lend us a hand, eh, Virl?"

Vrass/Virl gave Pyke a resigned look. "You better hurry along, citizen—could get a bit ugly soon. Come back in the morning and we'll attend to your needs then, all right?"

Pyke nodded, raised a hand in farewell and started back the way he'd come. A few steps on he glanced back, saw the coast was clear, then sprinted along to the next alley, dashed down it and headed for the backstreet corner. During which he fumbled madly in his satchel for the short weighted club he'd bought back in the Nightmarket.

Luckily he was ready with his club as he rounded the corner and cannoned into the large back of someone standing there in the shadows, yelling and gesticulating. Unluckily, the stranger was built like a breeze-block bollard and one of his meaty hands was brandishing an uprooted fence post. Pyke just had time to duck as the fence post came swinging around, causing a palpable gust as it passed over his head. There was an overwhelming stink of ale and ripe sweat, intensified by the big fellow's wordless roaring. Ignoring the full-strength, senses-challenging stench, Pyke stepped in closer, rammed the weighted club into the man's unprotected midriff then aimed a deadly kick at his right knee. There was an awful crack and the brawler went down with a strangled cry, wheezing for breath as he rolled on the ground, clutching his leg.

Pyke paused only to snatch up the fence post before lunging along the half-lit backstreet. Up ahead, T'Moy was trading blows with a short, squat Shylan armed with a cut-down billhook that was rather longer than the snapped-off length of spear which was all that the Bargalil had left. Pyke slowed to a walk, took aim and hurled the fence post—it caught the Shylan full in the face and blood spurted as he staggered back. With a swift glance over his shoulder, and a nod, T'Moy pressed home his advantage.

A few paces further on, the second Raskol guard was slugging it out punch for punch with a bald, bare-to-the-waist man whose chest and back were covered in elaborate tattoos featuring clenched fists. Pyke was just drawing near when the bald fighter dodged past the guard's defence and landed a crippling blow on his chin. The guard spun once and went down in a heap so quickly that Pyke nearly missed the hard-knuckled fist that was coming his way. He shifted enough for it to graze his ear, and then he found himself grappling with a gouging, biting, snarling adversary. Pyke did the only thing he could—stamped on the man's foot, grinding his heel in with all his might.

The tattooed bald tough let out a howl, eyes wide as he staggered back against the boxhouse wall, providing an easy target for Vrass/Virl who nipped in and smacked him on the head with the haft of his spear. The point of which suddenly came round, aimed at Pyke.

"You're the citizen I was talking to just moments ago!" he

said. "And now you're back here, laying out these brigands like an old stager? What's your game?"

"Honest, sir guard, there is a perfectly simple explanation to all this," Pyke said, hands raised as he slowly moved to the side, trying to draw Vrass/Virl's scope of view away from T'Moy who was half sprawled and staring up at Vrass with a look of bafflement. His own adversary lay unconscious nearby and T'Moy was looking a little worse for wear as he tried to regain his feet.

"You can stop your moving about!" said Vrass/Virl. "I'm not listening to any stories until I get some reinforcements…" He glanced at his insensible fellow guard, who was stretched out in the alley mud, and prodded him in the leg. "Kerig! Kerig!—wake up, you idiot!"

That was when T'Moy wrapped an arm around Vrass/Virl's neck and began applying pressure. Pyke moved in quickly to pry the spear out of his grip, watching closely for the moment when the choking hold brought the blackout. He slapped T'Moy's upper arm and the Bargalil released Vrass/Virl, easing him down to a sitting position against the side of the boxhouse.

"It is Vrass," said T'Moy. "I wasn't sure." He looked at Pyke. "This complicates matters."

"You don't say!"

"What do we do—carry him to the statues in Qalival Square, then come back?"

Pyke shook his head. "No time. Some of these drunken pukes will have stirred themselves by then and would be looking out for us. Maybe even get the city watch involved. What we need to do is bind and gag the other guard, stick him back in the guardroom, then we truss up Vrass and haul him along with us while we get into the boxhouse and unlock that booth. Okay?"

T'Moy sighed and nodded, then they got to work. From the guardroom Pyke dug up some lengths of rope with which they bound Vrass and his companion hand and foot, along with ripped-up pieces of guard shirt for gags. After the other guard was safely stashed away upstairs. Pyke and T'Moy took Vrass/Virl round to the boxhouse entrance which was unlocked with keys lifted from the guardroom. Once inside, they locked themselves in and leaned against the wall for a moment to catch their breath.

There was only a solitary, long-burn candle flickering on a shelf next to the door. Pyke used a taper from a box on the shelf to spread the flame to a couple of sconce torches, which lit the place up quite well. Just then Vrass/Virl came round and started making muffled grunting and snarling noises while struggling against the ropes. Pyke took out his weighted club, knelt down on the stone flags and poked him in the chest with it.

"Okay, look, not going to sugar-coat it for you—we need you to lie there nice and peaceful, like, otherwise I'll need to smack you round the head with this to get the same effect—d'ya get me?"

Their rope-wound captive sagged in resignation, and nodded.

"That's good," Pyke said. "As soon as we finish up here we'll cart you over to the memory statues and you'll be brand-new…"

While Pyke was dealing with Vrass, T'Moy had taken a torch from one of the sconces and was examining some metal lettering on the rough masonry wall near the foot of a set of wooden stairs.

DOWNSTAIRS: 1–24 UPSTAIRS: 25–45

At Pyke's insistence, T'Moy picked up Vrass and slung him over one shoulder before climbing the steps. Closer examination of the layout revealed that every lockbooth had a pair of lockboxes positioned next to it, and lockbooth 29A was located over at the side wall, next to lockboxes 29B and 29C. Vrass/Virl was placed sitting up against the opposite row of lockbooths as Pyke produced Sergeant Dalyak's key, won at the auction earlier. He and T'Moy exchanged a look before he slid the black iron key into the lock.

The lockbooth door was smaller and narrower than a normal door but was built from some kind of heavy wood overlaid with rivetted iron bands. And the moment it cracked open Pyke caught a whiff of decay that went straight for his gag reflex. Gritting his teeth, he gave the door a hefty tug and with hinges protesting it swung open.

Sure enough, there it was—a dead body, male, age thirties, maybe, dressed in dark, grubby work clothes, half lying, half sitting on the booth's floor. When T'Moy moved to step inside Pyke held him back.

"It's a murder," he said. "It's part of the puzzle. We need to make sure we don't tread on any clues."

"You mean like the hole?" T'Moy said, pointing.

There was indeed a hole in the floor, half hidden by the corpse, half concealed by a piece of thin wood left by whoever had done the deed. Pyke and T'Moy dragged the unknown corpse out and laid him on the floor a few paces away. While this had been going on, Vrass/Virl had gone quiet, still and wide-eyed.

Back in the booth, Pyke first lit a grubby stub of candle sitting on a small shelf near the door. Then he removed the wooden cover and looked down into what was clearly another lockbooth directly below. But it was so murky that he had to poke his torch down through the hole to see; the booth below seemed largely full of grimy household junk covered with a thick layer of dust. Except for a second hole right underneath the one he was peering into. He retracted his arm, sat back and said to T'Moy, "Take a look."

What the heaving hell is all this about? he thought as T'Moy took the torch and thrust it into the hole, followed by his head. *Who breaks into a storehouse from below then drills through into the storage locker above? Well, that would be someone eager to get their paws on some juicy items before…before the key to the lockbooth comes up for auction!*

So what was missing? He shifted his position and took a

proper look at the booth's interior by the candle's shifting light. There were shelves on either side with the lower ones crammed with boxes, tied-up pairs of army boots, armour buckles, split dagger sheathes and battered tin pans for cooking and eating. Carefully he got to his feet and lit another couple of candles located in holders higher up. A couple of long oilskin-wrapped packages were stacked against the back wall—when Pyke prodded them he heard muffled clanks.

"So, someone broke in before us," said T'Moy, coming up from the hole, but remaining seated on the floor. "Robber scum, most like. But why leave a body behind? Perhaps they had a falling out..."

Pyke gave a knowing smile. "T'Moy, I'll bet you there's not a wound anywhere on our dead friend's body, no blood, not a drop."

The Bargalil raised an eyebrow. "Very well, I accept the challenge and shall search the cadaver. And you?"

"I will be trying to figure out what they broke in to steal."

Without T'Moy the booth felt almost roomy. Pyke stood and began to scan the shelves, trying not to stir up the dust while scrutinising it for any recent disturbances. He quickly realised that he was surrounded by the accumulated detritus and knick-knacks of the good sergeant's life. There was a bundle of pennons, a nest of crockery bowls, a group of rough wood carvings of dogs, a ribbon-tied roll of maps, a shabby hat with a gorgeous blue feather in it, empty wine bottles whose labels bore various signatures, a plaster figurine of a milkmaid, a grubby box containing a score of spindly game pieces, a cluster of rusty armourer's tools...

And on the highest right-hand shelf was a row of leather-bound books of various sizes, the last of which was missing, made obvious by the brushed-out gap in the even layer of dust. Most of the other titles were no help, a collection of poems, a geography of the Northern kingdoms, a gazetteer of the Shylan river towns, a construction handbook, *Drinking Songs of the Westerly Pirates*...for a second he smiled in appreciation. Whatever the psychotic flaws of the Legacy, that machine intelligence had an exceptional take on simulation details.

Then he noticed the last two books, a biography of Emperor-General Mogori and a book on ancient battles and tactics, which made Pyke pause and ponder. *Why steal a book? What would it contain?* Then he smiled. *Soldiers sometimes keep a diary or journal—bet that's what they came for!*

Just then T'Moy appeared at the booth door. "I think we may have a problem."

Pyke left the booth and followed him to the head of the stairs where they stopped and listened. Despite the thick walls Pyke could hear voices calling back and forth and once heard the big heavy door rattle as if given an annoyed kick.

Pyke cursed under his breath and T'Moy looked worried. "I don't think we'll be able to fight our way out, Captain—it sounds as if there are three outside at least."

"Well, lucky for us that we have an alternative escape route, eh?"

"Going out the way the robbers came in?" T'Moy said. "But what is down there—sewers? Caves?"

"Right now, don't know and don't care!" Pyke slapped T'Moy on the back. "First, we get you into the downstairs booth, then I'll lower Vrass to you, then you descend to the space below and I'll lower Vrass down again. Then I'll clear up any tracks and clues before locking the booth from the inside and joining you. Got it? Right, let's get to it."

What had started in Pyke's head as a straightforward 1-2-3 operation began to reveal its snags when T'Moy climbed down into the booth below. It turned out to be full of old garden pots stacked in tall, tottering towers. Some had already been dislodged by the robbers during their foray and, when T'Moy lowered himself into the booth, one swinging leg knocked over a stack, creating a crashing, splintering din. But they persevered, eventually manhandling Vrass down into the space beneath the boxhouse, which turned out to be a cellar.

Once Vrass/Virl was lowered into T'Moy's waiting arms, Pyke clambered back up to the topmost booth where he'd left his torch. Those outside, most likely city watch guards, were banging on the door, shouting obscenities and threats about what they were going to do to anyone found inside. Pyke just had time to arrange the dead robber next to a booth near the stairs, along with a sliver of torn paper sticking out of the bottom of its door, when he heard the jingle of many keys then a series of rattling attempts at the lock.

Someone's roused a locksmith out of his scratcher at this time of night, a someone who wants us badly!

Back in Sergeant Dalyak's booth, he pulled the door shut and locked it from the inside. Then he climbed down through the hole and reached up to move the thin wood covering over the hole. There was little point in concealing the second hole so he dropped down into the shadowy cellar where T'Moy was waiting in the torchlight.

"Which way?" he said.

T'Moy pointed to a corner of the cellar where a broken bedstead stood against one wall, next to the ruins of a staircase. "There's a tunnel entrance behind that bed."

They carried Vrass/Virl over to the corner, pulled aside the bedstead and shuffled with their burden into the gap, only pausing so that Pyke could reposition the bed behind them. The short, rough-hewn passage ended in a broad wooden panel that sounded hollow when Pyke rapped it with a knuckle. A thick frame surrounded it and a quick search revealed a handpull switch set into the beam. The panel slid aside to reveal a set of stairs leading up for about twenty steps before reaching a short passageway that turned to the left. A dozen paces brought them to yet another stairway up which they struggled with Vrass's weight for two flights till they came out in a bare, dingy room with a sloping floor and a single window. The sole remaining torch was nearly played out by now, but T'Moy found a shelf with a few tallow candle stubs which he lit from the guttering torch.

With Vrass/Virl stowed in a seated position against one wall, Pyke flopped down beside him.

"For what's supposed to be a simulation," he said, "the designers sure went for accuracy in physical exhaustion. Skag it, but I'm officially knackered…"

"Captain," said T'Moy who was standing at the window. "There's something happening outside that you might find interesting."

With a groan, Pyke hauled himself upright and went over for a look. The window looked out on a dark huddle of uneven roofs and beyond them to the main road where torches were being held aloft by city watchmen on the roof of Raskol Boxhouse. Pyke chuckled while a visibly irate watch captain harangued his men as he marched around the building.

"By the way, Captain," said T'Moy. "You were correct—there were neither blood nor wounds around the head, neck and chest of our dead friend. And there was almost nothing in his pockets, just these gloves and a handful of groundnut shells."

Pyke ignored the shells but took the gloves—they were man-sized woollen mittens with the fingertips missing, just the kind of thing a professional thief would wear. And they hadn't been cut off, they'd been knitted that way. *Poor bastard*, he thought. *Gets hired by mysterious types, breaks into an old soldier's private booth and ends up dead for his trouble. Be worth tracking down his killers, just for a spot of payback.*

T'Moy grunted and Pyke looked round. There was sudden

activity over at the boxhouse—the watch captain was urging all his men inside.

"Ah well, seems like they've found our escape hatch so game's a bogie!" Pyke slapped T'Moy on the shoulder. "Time we weren't here."

The still-bound Vrass/Virl moaned as they carted him out to a landing where creaky stairs went down two floors to ground level. A light rain was falling as they paused at the open door. After a brief discussion they decided to head further into the Ithlyr slums and see if they could find a small cart with which to transport Vrass around.

For the next twenty-odd minutes they struggled through the rainy darkness, trying not to slip in muddy puddles as the downpour worked its magic on the unsurfaced streets. It felt like an infinity of squelching, sodden trudging until T'Moy stopped suddenly while they were halfway along a back lane between rickety fences.

"What's up?" whispered Pyke hoarsely.

"I can smell cut wood, Captain," T'Moy said, his nose raised towards the fence on their right. "This could be a builder's yard."

Pyke shrugged and, once they'd placed Vrass/Virl in a safe spot, they went for a look. A loop of rope was all that kept a side door shut. Inside, T'Moy lit a stub of candle and they found that it was indeed a builder's yard, full of stacks of timber, barrels of nails, pallets of bricks, and—blessed relief!—three small hand-carts. They chose a two-wheeler with sides high enough to keep Vrass from falling out.

Back out in the lane, they loaded Vrass/Virl into the cart and trundled off. Along the way they liberated some laundry left out on a line, draping it over their passenger to avoid attracting attention. With caution and brief scoutings ahead, they managed to evade clusters of chanting monks, knots of fighting drunks and marching city watch patrols. At last their winding progress brought them to Dragoon's Row and the entrance to Haxy Nightmarket. What was a dingy, faded looking façade by day now seemed like a glowing mysterious portal hazy with the fumes of the food and incense stalls waiting beyond the entrance.

Inside it was even more of a busy parade of wonders and illusions than it was by day. All the stalls were now occupied by vendors and the air overhead was crowded with lanterns, bells, drifting gauzy ribbons, paper pennons scribed with good luck charms, clusters of papermould masks, and even cages from which creatures like snakes with six legs chirruped and sang. The press of customers and travellers and gawkers made for slow progress, and more than once Pyke had to dial back the impatience, biting down on the florid curse-bombs begging to be launched from the tip of his tongue. But with determination and T'Moy's unexpected affability in the face of near-apocalyptic stupidity, they reached Qalival Square.

Since the last time Pyke had been here someone had scattered pot plants around the feet of the huge statues, along with a few brightly coloured paper lanterns. There weren't many people loitering nearby, just a noisily inebriated group clapping along to a woman playing a lute or something. After a muttered exchange Pyke and T'Moy decided to keep Vrass/Virl in the purloined laundry before lifting him out of the cart. Their luck held, despite grunts and snarls from their unwitting baggage, and they managed to haul him up onto the plinth and over to the big Gomri statue. Rather than risk unbinding mischievous hands Pyke pulled a worn, scuffed boot off one hairy foot which was then solidly pressed against the statue's leg.

Vrass went tense, almost rigid for a moment, then relaxed, a full-body limpness accompanied by a long sigh. T'Moy leaned over and removed the gag and said, "Are you well, Vrass?"

The Gomedran made as if to speak but all that came out were

hoarse sounds until T'Moy offered him a drink from his water bottle.

"So...so good to see you, T'Moy!—and that is Captain Pyke, yes?"

"In the flesh, the worn-out, bruised and battered flesh, that is."

Free at last of the binding ropes, Vrass blinked as he sat up and looked about him. He rubbed his furry snout and sniffed audibly, then a look of surprise came over his features.

"I'm remembering...things, actions, places—the memories of this Virl, who was guarding something...a building." He gave T'Moy and Pyke a rueful look. "I also recall how much of a nuisance I was—please accept my apologies."

Pyke waved it away. "You weren't to know, Vrass—this personality triggering thing with the statues is clearly the Legacy's idea of a joke, assuming he or it can be bothered watching our puny struggle."

T'Moy's expression was sombre. "We are its toys. Perhaps we should abandon this puzzle-dance, defy it."

"I like the idea," said Pyke. "But I suspect that our lord and master probably has some imaginative punishment in store for those who don't play along."

"What puzzle are we trying to solve here?" Vrass said. "I recall our discussion with the drone, so was it right? About having to unravel a new mystery?"

Pyke tried to summarise what he'd been through, with T'Moy adding remarks and details that in the end turned into a long summary. As they talked, the trio descended from the statues' plinth and wandered off to the side where they stood conversing.

Vrass was, unexpectedly, both amused and enthused by all that they told him. "A key, a body and a missing book—and some odd gloves! This is all most intriguing!"

"Of all the words," Pyke said, "that I might use, 'intriguing' wouldn't even make the top ten."

Vrass smiled. "After spending such a long, unexciting time on the Isle of Candles, this is uplifting by comparison. So, what is the next step in our investigation?"

Pyke was tempted to engage in some off-hand mockery, but somehow just couldn't stir himself.

"Whoever broke into the boxhouse was a professional," he said. "And he wasn't alone—someone accompanied him all the way to Sergeant Dalyak's lockbooth then poisoned the poor bastard."

At that moment T'Moy slapped the side of his neck, muttering something about biting insects. A second later Pyke felt a tiny nip on his neck, too—and sudden suspicion flared into fearful alert. He fumbled in panic at the spot on his neck, felt a tiny splinter of something sticking out of the skin.

"What the hell..." he said.

He exchanged a horrified look with T'Moy, just as he heard Vrass say, "Ouch!," then he noticed figures lurking in the shadows at the corner of Qalival Square. One look was all he needed before he turned to start running. But the toxin was already racing through his bloodstream. His legs felt wobbly and he fell to his knees after only a few strides.

Next thing he knew he was lying on the ground, cheek pressed against the mossy cobbles. All sound seemed muffled. He could see T'Moy sprawled a few feet away, his mouth widening into a roar as he struggled to get back onto his feet, the sound of it distant and mute. Then a pair of legs walked up to him, crouched down, and a hand grabbed his shoulder and rolled him onto his back. A face leaned in, came nearer and said faintly, "It's them—get them inside."

Pyke would have laughed if he could—it was the unmistakable face of the Shyntanil Klane.

CHAPTER ELEVEN

Dervla, on the planet Ong, inside a wrecked section of the *Mighty Defender*

Dervla cowered in the corridor corner, blaster held in shaking hands, trying in vain to shut out the emanations of the Steel Forest. That metallic clicking, rustling, scraping and grinding, all the noises made by that grotesque undergrowth merged into a disturbingly fluid ambience. The cool blue bioluminescence from the tuber-clusters dotted around the walls and ceiling came in slow, mingled pulses, similar to the patterns she'd spotted in other passages. At least here there was a blessed absence of wildlife. Under less hazardous conditions she might have considered this a good place to strike out from on a search, but the truth was that she had no idea where she or any of the others were.

In retrospect, the clues had all been there, from the moment they had entered in pursuit of Ustril, the absconded Sendrukan scientist. The unmarked access panel led into the narrow space between outer and inner hulls, where rough, improvised steps went down to a trapdoor hatch. Opening it, they dropped down one by one into a corridor whose deck, walls and ceiling were swathed in a plethora of plant-like growths. Colours ranged from virulent yellow to vibrant green and sky-blue, while textures seemed bizarrely industrial, ridged, dimpled and perforated patterns that looked as if they had been punched out by machine rather than grown.

Crouched in the corner, she drew in a shuddering breath and allowed herself to relax a little. The flock of spiderbat things seemed to have retreated to the blood-red corridor, so she felt safe for now.

Colours, dominant colours, were of vital importance. She hadn't figured it all out yet but red and purple were the danger zones, whereas cool blue corridors like this one were largely free of the nastiest critters. The first lesson they got was just after their arrival when they were moving cautiously along that multi-coloured corridor. They had slowed at a turnoff which glowed as red as a furnace but throbbed like a dancefloor. The red flickered with a strobe-like intensity at times and, just as Pyke was about to venture into it, Ancil caught his arm and said, "Look!"

He pointed to a vertical, irregular shape laid against one wall. Covered in a leafy creeper, the shape suddenly resolved out of the quivering scarlet light and became a man standing upright, pressing up against the growth-choked bulkhead. No, not against—he was partially sunk into it, one terrified eye regarding them, mouth half-full of writhing tendrils. The lips tried to form words but nothing came out, then a cluster of chrome pincers unfolded across his upper face from behind and tugged open part of his skull as if it was on hinges.

Pyke had cursed and put a single shot from the big plasma gun right between the man's eyes. The man had been one of Raven's—Dervla recognised him, and as much as Dervla despised her and her thugs she knew that no one deserved such a horrific end. But wall-birthed horrors and monsters were not the only hazards awaiting interlopers into this grotesque netherworld. The worst enemy was in the air.

They passed an abundance of types of weird plant that gave off odours varying from pleasantly sweet to toe-curlingly acrid.

Most of the passively fragrant ones seemed safe, unlike the squirters and sprayers whose payloads could make you blind or deaf or temporarily bestow synaesthesia upon your unwilling senses. Dervla saw that happen when Moleg got a faceful of orange mist from a hanging yellow pod—he reacted with coughing and wheezing, and spitting to try and rid himself of the taste, then seconds later he turned edgy and panicky, his voice reduced to a wordless drone as if the mist was attacking his brain's speech centres. When any of the others spoke he waved them to be silent while trying to hold his hands over his ears. Then he stuffed paper towel plugs into his nose (and ears), pulled on his gloves, tugged his jerkin hood tightly over his head and tried to stumble on with the rest.

The effects did wear off several minutes later but by then Kref had been stung by a flying, whining thing, causing him to start waving and lashing out at invisible attackers. Also, Pyke had been spat upon by a trumpet-shaped bloom at the tip of a coiled stem which had lunged out of the foliage at him—it made him hallucinate that he, too, was some kind of plant with tentacle branches to reach out with. Somehow, Dervla and Ancil had managed to keep Kref from charging off down the corridor while Moleg's senses gradually returned to normality. Pyke left planthood behind, puking his guts out along the way, and Kref was calming down and reporting a fading of the hallucinations—and that was when a flock of spiderbats swept along the corridor, a storm of horrible piping fluttering forms. And, of course, everyone was bitten and thereby discovered the psychotropic delights of spiderbat venom.

In the grip of utter, primal terror, the need to run was overwhelming, especially because a side effect of the venom populated the mind with monsters dredged from the darkest corners of the subconscious. As Dervla scrambled away, with Kref, Pyke and the rest forgotten, she was trying to escape the drooling, grinning maw of Meatmaker Mosk, a 3V character that had haunted her childhood, leering and trudging through her dreams for far too long, even into puberty. After that, there were few definite memories she could recall; crouched in this safe zone now, she assumed that during her mad dash through the corridors of the Steel Forest she must have picked up some more doses of mind-altering chemicals, prolonging the ultra-headtrip substantially. Her wrist timer told her that nearly an hour and a half had lapsed since they had entered the wreck. She could only remember blurred fragments from the last hour or so, one moment where she heard a hard chatter as someone fired off an entire magazine, and another moment where she fell down a flight of steps, no, two flights. All these bruises and cuts, had to be two.

So, what now? How the melting hell do I find the rest without getting my brains scrambled again?

Well, first things first, as always—scout first, curse later. The corridor she was facing—which was the way she'd come—went straight ahead for about six paces before turning left into another corridor of suppurating purple hues, home to a variety of buzzing nasties, including a flock of spiderbats. Which meant she had to explore the rest of the passage, past the S-corner refuge where she still was.

Gathering her resolve, she got to her feet, beam-blaster at the ready, and went left, rounding the corner. Pale blues with a metallic sheen still dominated here. The walls sprouted ferny fronds, tinkling white-berry bushes, serpentine roots half embedded in the bulkheads, weird tubular leaves and opaque pipes that coiled in on themselves while pale blobs slowly oozed along inside them. Cautiously she brushed through the clicking, rustling foliage. The next corner mirrored the corridor behind her with a rightward corner, and when she rounded it her heart sank. Before her was hot glaring scarlet, molten brass and scorching sulphur. Clouds of insects wavered and darted among the lush growths which gave off sporadic plumes of sparkling vapour.

This is hopeless, Dervla thought. *The other corridor was a gauntlet of horrors but this one is worse!* She leaned against a nearby patch of comparatively blank wall and let out a long sigh. Breather facemasks would have been handy—there was a box of them back on the shuttle-barge but those gauzy suits provided by Ustril had made the masks seem unnecessary. Trouble was, she'd collected them all in after reaching the wreck. *If that's not a cautionary tale, I don't know what is.*

She rubbed tiredness out of her eyes then ran her fingers through her hair, noticed how long it was getting and longed for a shower and the chance to get at her cosmetic shears back on the *Scarabus*.

"You are a stranger here—are you seeking the gateway?"

She almost jumped out of her skin when the calm voice spoke to her out of the pale blue tangle of leaves immediately to her right. She turned abruptly and found herself staring at a pair of lips hanging from the end of a long, leafy stem. Behind it an ear protruded on a branching twig. Both disembodied organs were fleshy and light blue with darker highlights. Her immediate reaction was to accept that she'd been dosed with another hallucinogenic, but she quickly realised that apart from the ear-mouth pairing nothing else had altered in her surroundings. So far as she could tell.

"I'm seeking my friends," she said hesitantly. "I lost them in one of the decks above."

The mouth dipped and swayed gently on its stem for a moment. "Many have lost themselves here and found different modes of being. Are your friends seeking new modes of being?"

"No, we were following one of our party who, erm, entered by mistake."

"Mistake?" The blue lips pursed thoughtfully. "All actions

have a purpose, thus this errant companion must also have a purpose—does it seek the gateway?"

Dervla considered this for a moment. "We are uncertain about our companion's purpose but we fear for her safety. We know that dangerous enemies entered before us."

A branching stalk snaked round from behind the mouth, carrying a dark blue pod which split neatly along its length and parted to reveal a single limpid eye.

"How charming," the voice continued. "Your species is not unlike our own, at least as it once was in another age. I should introduce myself—I am Shogrel, Second Remedial, Linkflow Subcast, to employ my old shipboard rank."

"Dervla, first mate aboard the fast-merchant *Scarabus*. Can I ask...how do you know that the other intruders are looking for this gateway? And what is the gateway itself?"

The podshell halves curled back and the eye moved a little closer, while the lips seemed to express a restrained anger.

"We know because they tried to gain our confidence with friendliness at first, thinking to fool us into revealing the gateway's location, but when that failed they seized and started to torture some of us, again to no avail. As for the gateway, all you need know for now is that it is a cherished place for us, one that we will do all we can to protect."

Dervla nodded, trying to appear calm and collected while madly attempting to recall something useful from that pamphlet on first contact that Pyke had made her read six months ago, just in case this situation qualified.

"Thank you for your kind words, Shogrel...erm, could you possibly direct me along the safest route to take while searching for my friends?"

Which was a tough proposition, of course, given the berserkly hazardous territory into which they had strayed. But she'd remembered how the pamphlet suggested portraying oneself as naively uninformed in order to gain more background and, hopefully, offers of assistance.

"I am afraid that there are no safe routes through the forest for a species like yourself," said Shogrel's mouth. "Your cell patterns have already been tasted and savoured by our forest, and our membranes have sensed your speech, filtered its words, laid bare their meanings. But your biology has no defences against the Steel Forest's ecology of airborne zymones."

Dervla's shoulders sagged. "So I'm stuck here!"

"Not at all. There is a way to shield you from the harmful effects of the forest's chemology, but preparations must be made..." Shogrel's voice tailed off for a moment then resumed. "Apologies—I was calling out to the rest of my conglomerate for assistance...ah, now there's an adjunct I've not seen for a long time!"

Through the shiny foliage a pale shape came creeping, a slender-fingered hand. Dervla stared wide-eyed as it attached itself to an available twig and dangled beneath the mouth, clenching its fingers then extending them one by one, as if counting to six, then repeating it over and over. Shogrel's eye watched while Shogrel's lips smiled.

"Right is a perfectionist, counts it all up, down, in and out... oh, good, some depth perception at last!"

A second eye sprang into view and snapped open, then winked at Dervla. Shogrel's eyes, she realised, were quite beautiful, dark brown with hints of amber. When the nose arrived, lifted into place by a helping hand, Dervla's suspicion grew into certainty.

"Shogrel, may I ask—are you female in gender?"

The lips laughed. "I was once and shall undoubtedly be so again, perhaps, but this arrangement is only a temporary alliance in order to provide aid."

The feet showed up separately, and the left hand clambered down from the leafy ceiling with Shogrel's other ear clinging to its back. Dervla watched them assume disembodied positions, borne up by a fast-growing web of rootlets. She had to remind herself repeatedly that she wasn't hallucinating, even though it was entirely possible.

"Dervla of the *Scarabus*, may I ask you to perform a small task for me?"

"Sure, I'd be happy to help."

"Would you be so kind as to uncover my torso? My hand will show you the way. The rest of me will follow shortly."

Dervla nodded, and with Shogrel's left hand perched on her shoulder she retraced her steps, weaving past clumps of fronds, tinkling bushes, chiming bamboo-like stems tipped with gleaming spines. Not far from where she'd found refuge earlier, the hand tapped her shoulder and pointed at a large mass of growth which took up half the width of the corridor. Dervla went up to it and, wary of sharp-edged leaves, tried to peer inside. Shogrel's hand, though, jumped off her shoulder, landed on a jutting branch and burrowed into the tangle. A moment later the foliage parted again and Shogrel's hand beckoned. Dervla already had gloves on so she gingerly pushed the gap wider, and through a network of shoots and tendrils she could see an actual female torso. Pale and unmarred, it rested amid a cradle of grasses and sprigs, with clusters of plant stems and vines bursting forth from hollows in the neck and the shoulders.

That was when Shogrel's organs arrived in single file, a march of the disembodied, squeezing and slipping through the interwoven stalks and leaves. A dense web of tendrils began to form from the neck up, a kind of scaffolding for the eyes, ears, nose and mouth. Similar meshworks were coalescing where arms and legs had once been. Shogrel let out a delighted laugh as she admired her hands and feet, then unhurriedly stood up straight. Dervla stood back as she emerged from the leafy refuge, looking around her, looking up and down, rocking her woven head from side to side, lips curved with amusement. Then she brought her hands together in a single quiet clap.

"Ah, back in the world of attachments!" she giggled. "Binocular vision, a sense of balance, coordinating smell and taste, hearing in binaural…a panoply of jostling inputs. I am sure I can rely on their judgement, though."

Dervla looked on with uneasy amazement, fairly convinced that this was not a hallucination. "What kind of technology made all…all this?"

"I cannot explain all the details in the manner of the High Conjecturists, but I do have a broad understanding of it. Firstly, however, if we are to journey through the Steel Forest you must accept these."

Shogrel opened her pale, beautiful hands to reveal loops of tiny blue flowers. There was a circlet to go around Dervla's head and bracelets for each wrist. When she peered closely at one of the wristlets, the little blue flowers turned to look up at her and every one had her face.

"Now you are ready to face all that the Steel Forest has to offer!" Shogrel laid one hand (supported by an arm made from webby roots) on her shoulder. "I will lead the way, just to be sure that my neighbours understand."

Retracing her steps along the purple corridor was like rewinding the flashes and fragments of a nightmare. But the biting liana blooms that had lunged and snapped at her back then now hung and swayed in midair, as if spookily attentive to her presence. And the gator-dogs now only gambolled playfully about her feet, with no hint of their former belligerence.

"This part of the forest occupies the lowermost corridors of our ancient, timeworn vessel," said Shogrel. "A few local denizens still capable of objective scrutiny have reported the presence of an intruder on the deck above. I do not know if this is a member of your group or one of those others—would you like to *investigate?*"

Shogrel spoke the last word with the kind of girlish mischievousness that would normally make Dervla's lip curl. But she found herself warming to the leafy alien, especially now that she was no longer under assault by the undergrowth and its wildlife.

"Sooner we start, sooner I can find my crew," she said.

"Excellent. We go this way."

As they trod lightly among purple spiral roots and ducked through creeper-smothered hatchways, Dervla reminded her guide of her promise to explain something of the science behind this strange mode of existence. Shogrel duly gave an account of the origins of the Steel Forest, or at least as best as she could remember.

Their ship, the *Mighty Defender of the Arraveyne Heart*, had escaped from the imminent collapse of the Arraveyne Imperium, taking with it huge quantities of precious exchangeables and works of art sequestered from the Imperial vaults. The architects of this grand escape also gathered together (and in some cases abducted) pre-eminent scientists, their lab equipment and data archives and brought them aboard the immense vessel. And among their number was the great conjecturist, G'sovo Jush.

Shogrel went on to explain how the ship's commanders, a cabal of high dukes of the Imperium, encouraged the scientists to resume their work while the flight from the fallen Imperium got under way. Unfortunately, the ship's passage through hyperspace attracted the attention of a near-mythical creature called the Damaugra, which then proceeded to dog the ship on its evasive course. In the meantime, the "guest" scientists either resumed their researches or initiated new projects, encouraged by the ship's captain, High Duke Strano. Before departing the Arraveyne homeworld, G'sovo Jush had been working on an advanced gene-flux technology by which living flesh could be augmented with the properties of other materials, even non-organic materials. But then came the Damaugra's devastating final assault in the vicinity of the planet Ong, and the decoupling of the *Mighty Defender*'s ship segments, leading to the catastrophic crash-landings.

At that point in Ong's past, according to Shogrel, the deserts were not so widespread yet the storms were much more violent. The planetary climate was experiencing great instability and vast electrical storms were a constant feature, girdling the globe. After the decoupled segments of the *Mighty Defender* reached the surface, scattered across hundreds of miles of inhospitable terrain, the surviving passengers and crew found that their communications were rendered useless by the raging storms. They were cut off from the rest of the ship, and from the supplies in the central hold section. There were no vehicles suitable for the wind-torn environment outside so a few decided to set out on foot to try and locate other parts of the ship. They never returned.

While all this was transpiring, G'sovo Jush had not been idle. In collaboration with another conjecturist called Vreyba, he had fused his gene-flux technology with Vreyba's radical mind-transcribing apparatus. The strengths and advantages of the metal that encased them, the ship that protected them, would be infused, engraved, into the codes underpinning their flesh and bone. At the same time, the subatomic structure of the ship would become the new refuge for minds, new roads and bridges for thought, new avenues of perception, new tools by which they could adapt the wreck's interior then adapt to it in turn.

Listening to this incredible account, Dervla realised that in the quest for survival the ship's passengers had diverged wildly from the boundaries of conventional carbon-based life. As they climbed to the next deck and unhurriedly strolled through corridors thronging with phantasmagoria, Shogrel pointed out this particular type of trilling bloom or that pack of octo-lizards as the manifestations of former crew members or passengers.

"Can we talk with them?" Dervla said.

Shogrel smiled sadly. "Many have lost any sense of a unified consciousness, others have difficulty connecting with objective reality. Then there are those who view objective reality as a hindrance. We will be conversing with some of them but for now we should ready ourselves—we are approaching a chamber where an intruder has recently taken up residence."

Dervla's sense of orientation, usually so dependable, had already failed her and she couldn't tell if she were moving towards the stern or away from it, or to port or starboard. Through the leafy, mossy passages they walked, cautiously now. Topaz and sky-blue light tubers pulsed here and there. Ahead was a T-junction and a wide, gaping door. She looked at Shogrel as they approached.

"Through here?" she said.

Her root-woven, sprig-sprouting guide turned with a smile and Dervla saw that she was missing an eye and a hand.

"I've sent scouts inside," she said. "They should not be long… and here they are!"

The absent hand had emerged from the doorway and scrambled along the wall foliage to where Shogrel stood with her other hand outstretched. The hand-errant crawled across to resume its former position, dropping off the eye on the way.

"Hmm, most interesting," said Shogrel, lips curved in amusement.

"What's in there?" Dervla said.

"This is something that needs to be seen," Shogrel said, "rather than explained." She ushered Dervla through. "It is quite safe."

Dervla ducked past the creeper fringe hanging over the

opening. Inside, roseate light filtered around either side of a vestibule partition and the air bore a heavy sweetness. Shogrel's assurances carried some weight yet Dervla kept her right hand resting near her blaster's holster as she sidestepped the partition and entered the room proper.

The scene before her was fascinating, dumbfounding and captivating all at once. The room was large and wedge-shaped, with the entrance at the narrow end of it. Further on into the wider area, circles of small dainty plants were laid out across the floor, most of them types of motile plants which Shogrel had pointed out during their brief journey. White and yellow flowers swayed gently, their leaves slowly furling and unfurling. There were also other plants arranged in similar rings with small creatures dotted around at regular intervals, sitting there, rocking gently back and forth. Luminous tubers clinging to the walls gave off roseate glows which mingled with the soft green radiance emanating from hanging liana blooms.

Dervla suddenly realised that she was looking at a mandala, or the equivalent. The radial patterns of blooms and beasties were centred on a broad dais at the wider end of the room. On it was a large plinth supporting what seemed to be a large, low-backed chair upon which a substantial figure lounged, legs splayed, upper body laid back, almost horizontally. Flowery foliage engulfed the dais on all sides while glittery vapour plumed from an array of thick, bell-mouthed stalks grouped around the rear of the plinth like an ancient pipe organ. There was a curious background sound, like hundreds of faraway voices singing a continuous cluster of notes, but over that someone was wordlessly humming in a deep, rich voice. Dervla narrowed her eyes, sure there was something familiar in that voice.

"Kref?" she said. "Kref, is that you up there?"

The sprawled form stirred, the humming stopped and a big head came up. A slurred voice said:

"Is someone there? Who is it?"

"It's the Space-Pope-Queen of the Galaxy!" she said. "Who d'ye think?"

The occupant of the chair levered himself upright, bringing his face into the light—it was indeed Kref and his eyes were silver.

"Derv!" The Henkayan's broad face was creased in a permanent smile. "I'm so glad that you found me! You must have picked up the mind-vibrations of ultra-love that I've been radiating...it's amazing that you arrived at exactly this moment! It's almost prophetic."

"Kref," she said, advancing through the floor's circles of plants and animals. "You need to clear your head 'cos the captain and Ancil and Moleg are still missing..."

"Wait!" Kref cried. "Stop moving, Derv, please!"

Which was a redundant plea as she'd just noticed how all the motile plants and the creatures suddenly orientated themselves towards her in a distinctly unfriendly manner.

"They feel the love that flows all around me in this place, Derv," Kref said. "They're very protective."

Dervla turned to Shogrel with an expression of wordless appeal. The half-plant, part-humanoid gave an amused nod, then addressed the Henkayan.

"I could feel your mind-vibrations, Kref," she said. "I heard your song of beauty and peace."

A look of euphoria lit up Kref's craggy features. "Yes! And it's all here, all in the pattern—you need to stand still, Dervla, and then you will become part of the pattern, too, part of the great song!"

"You have admirably responsive senses, Kref," said Shogrel. "I have seldom seen an inductee of the bliss chamber absorb and radiate the exudations of the fumaroles with such alacrity and vigour before."

With those silver eyes, Kref stared raptly back at Dervla's guide.

"It uplifted my feelings, made them burst into...into flames in my head and in my veins! It was incredible, my heart and my head and my hands on fire with big—*huge*—giant visions connecting everything!"

"That is what the fumaroles do," said Shogrel. "They feed you complex mind-altering vapours then adapt their output according to what they detect from your perspiration. The spiralling crescendo is exquisite."

Kref seem baffled. "But I was sending vibrations and singing to the patterns of flowers and little creatures..."

Shogrel nodded. "Only after the chamber infused your lungs and your blood with the fumes of unlocking and epiphany." She stretched out her hands from which loops of blue flowers dangled. "Come and take these—they will make all things clear."

Reluctantly, Kref clambered down from the plinth and came over, warily yet at the same time apparently drawn towards Shogrel. She smiled. "Brave, honest Kref—all of the Steel Forest has heard your song, all that could be sung has been."

As she spoke she took his big hands in hers and in a moment the flower bracelets were around his wrists. He was about to say something but his eyelids fluttered and closed—Dervla was half-afraid that he would topple to the floor, then his eyes blinked open, this time with no trace of silver. He yawned and his gaze fell upon Dervla.

"Derv! Hey, you *are* here! Had a weird dream. You were in it." He grinned. "And you're here...but where're the others? I remember we were running from something really bad, then I got stung...and now I've woken up. Derv, what happened?"

"Everyone got separated, Kref," she said. "Some of these plant gases and insect stings can make you drowsy and groggy. You just happened to find the motherlode! Myself and Shogrel are searching for the others..." She saw him regard Shogrel with a frown. "Shogrel is—well, she lives here, er, and has done for a long time, and she's friendly—even gave us these blue flowers which ward off the risky plants and insects."

"There are others like myself scattered throughout the Steel Forest," said Shogrel. "My blue flowers tell them that the bearer is not an enemy. You were lucky enough to find your way to this chamber, Kref—no direct harm would befall you here." She regarded Dervla. "Soon after we reached this place, I began to pick up impressions and whispers about other intruders, also warnings. One appears to be under attack by one of the more dissociated of the forest inhabitants. This one is...hemmed in? Surrounded? I am unsure but we should track them down without delay."

Dervla nodded, then glanced at Kref. The big Henkayan was gazing at the flowery bracelets, brooding and sombre, then his features brightened into a smile. "Hey, Derv, all these little flowers look a bit like me!"

"Mine, too, Kref. It's part of how they work." She laid a hand against his broad upper arm. "We have to go rescue the others—are you ready?"

"Sure, Derv, just say the word. But I lost my rifle somewhere—all I have left is this little popgun."

It was a 45-calibre autopistol with a stick magazine and an oversized grip to suit the generous Henkayan hand. Dervla smiled.

"Oh, well, it'll have to do, eh?"

"Hopefully such weaponry will not be necessary," said Shogrel, pointing rightwards along the T-junction. "Along here is an auxiliary access stair to the deck above. Follow me."

They climbed to find that the new deck was similar to the hazardous areas adjoining Shogrel's home territory. The lighting was low and predominantly red or a rich purple, the foliage was denser. He and the insects were greater in number. But the protective aura generated by the blue flowers managed to keep Dervla and Kref safe as they pushed through the undergrowth with Shogrel in the lead.

They found Pyke at the end of a red corridor, barricaded into a small room, besieged by gator-dogs, creatures like bird-sized dinosaurs, and things like snakes with flowerbulb-like heads. From a dozen paces back along the corridor Dervla couldn't see him but she could hear his loud and florid cursing. She suggested just heading along and bringing him out, but Shogrel shook her head.

"The shepherding awareness of this area no longer perceives unexpected events and intruders with any kind of rational objectivity," she said. "Its reactions are belligerent, and the level of raw hostility directed towards the room's occupant are such that my ward-flowers may not be sufficient to protect you."

"We could shoot our way…"

"You could, but then every plant and creature near here would be turned against you both." Shogrel spread her hands. "Your ends would be agonising and final."

Kref shuddered. "I'll not be pot-shotting anything, then."

Dervla frowned, realising that, despite Pyke's profanities, she'd heard no gunfire, no energy weapon sounds.

"The awareness of this place," she said. "Was it always so violent?"

"Not at all," said Shogrel. "I remember Pixif well—he had a mild, generous spirit."

"So the raw hostility you detected is very likely a response to something our companion is doing, yes?"

Shogrel thought for a moment. "I hear no sounds of weapons fire yet he is still managing to fend off their attacks and thereby stir up their anger."

"Shogrel," said Dervla. "Would you be able to reach the end of the corridor on your own?"

"No. The mood of the devolved awareness is a swirling cloud of suspicion and fear coupled with a burning detestation of any interlopers. Even the position we occupy here is not safe."

"Not much grey area, then," said Dervla, despairing.

"Shame Ans isn't with us," said Kref. "He has a nade for every occasion!"

For a moment no one spoke, then Shogrel raised one pale hand up to her head and pressed her fingers into the dense weave of tendrils just behind and below her right ear. When she withdrew them, she was holding what appeared to be a large green seed-pod. She held it out so that they could see.

"There is a way to send the awareness of this place into a temporary stupor, allowing you to extricate your companion." Shogrel regarded them both sombrely. "Understand that I only have one of these—it took me a long time to braid and nurture it, and if we use it now we may regret doing so later."

"How long will this sleepytime last?" Dervla said.

"A short period. Not long but long enough."

Dervla laughed. "Okay, try this…" and with her wrist dermal timer she counted out ten seconds. "As long as that or a lot longer?"

Shogrel smiled, closed her eyes for a moment then opened them again. "I estimate seven and half of those periods."

Dervla glanced at Kref. "Seventy-five seconds to get to the end of the corridor, break whatever barricade Pyke's behind, drag his arse out of there and be back here before the angries wake up. What d'ya think?"

"S'cutting it fine, Derv."

"Well, with three of us it shouldn't be that hard."

Shogrel shook her head. "Unfortunately, I cannot accompany you—the decoction that this will deliver would have the same soporific effect on me. Like all these forms, I, too, am of the forest."

Dervla sighed, and Kref shrugged. "S'all right, Derv, I'll just have to be twice as brawny as usual!"

"And I'll be right there with you!" She looked at Shogrel. "Okay, better do what you have to do."

Their guide gave a single nod, cupped the dark green pod in both her pale grey hands and raised it to her lips. She kissed it gently, murmured to it, whispered strange sibilant words to it then, facing the corridor in question, held it out before her on her open palm. Dervla had thought that Shogrel was going to lob it like some kind of grenade—instead she continued with the flow of whispers. Nonplussed, Dervla was about to ask what the hold-up was when suddenly the gleaming green pod began to unfurl from either end.

Dervla stared, entranced. There was a glowing inside the pod, hints of something glassy and shiny. Then the pod shell unfurled into two parts, two gauzy, veiny, delicately cell-patterned wings. Both were part of a strangely elegant insect, its head and thorax murky and opaque, as if fashioned from smoked glass, while its abdomen gave off an amber glow.

"When the Quietener takes flight," Shogrel said, "both of you need to follow directly behind. Stand next to me now and be ready."

They did as instructed. Dervla was fascinated by the bizarre insect whose glassy abdomen now seemed to be swelling with a rich golden glow. As she watched, the gold radiance welled up into the thorax and filtered out to the roots of the wings, lighting up their veins and patterns.

"Time to fly," murmured Shogrel and the insect leaped away from her outstretched hand.

With such long, flexible wings, the Quietener flew like a slow moth, and with every beat of its wings fine ribbony trails of golden motes sprayed out to either side. The insect's flight was sedate enough for Dervla and Kref to follow at a steady pace, anxiously keyed up in case of an attack. But just as Shogrel had said, inactivity spread wherever the golden mist fell: aggressive long-stemmed plants wilted, other insects retreated to dark crannies, and all the beasties that hopped, crawled, wriggled and scampered across the mossy deck slumped down where they stood. Chemical slumber reigned.

When the Quietener insect reached the end of the corridor it gracefully turned and headed back the way it had come. Dervla and Kref wasted no time, went over to the last doorway and began kicking and shoving at the debris which had been piled against it from the inside. At last they managed to tear away a mass of wire entangled with rootlets and push aside a lashed-up barrier of rods and struts. Torchlight revealed a dishevelled figure crouched in one corner, holding out a hand. It was Pyke, shouting and babbling incoherently, yet around him was a curved heap of small dead creatures.

"Kref, he's holding the crystal," she muttered. "I'll get his attention on this side, you tackle him from the other—and immobilise that arm!"

Kref nodded and they moved towards him.

"...came at me with the beast faces!" Pyke was raving. "Masks of skagging beasts—but I slapped 'em down, skagging crushed 'em..."

"Brannan, it's us!" Dervla said. "Bran, it's Dervla..."

"...used their faces, too, aye, and their voices!...stinking Legacy bastard!...I'll burn him!..."

She glanced at Kref. They exchanged a nod and then lunged forward. Pyke yelled and struck out with what was definitely the crystal, still in its leather sheath but with the cover flapping loose. Dervla dodged the deadly blow and in the next moment Kref piled in, wrapping a big arm around Pyke, trapping one arm and grabbing the other with his free hand. Pyke cried out and the crystal fell from nerveless fingers. Dervla pounced, snatched it up and carefully closed it up, fastening the ties.

"Right, hold onto him tight while we get out of here!"

She rushed to the doorway, tore some more junk away and slipped out into the corridor. All seemed quiet so she beckoned Kref to follow, now carrying a dazed and confused Pyke over his shoulder. Even as he emerged, Dervla saw the tiny shapes of insects rising into the air.

"Run!" she yelled.

The deadly red section of corridor was only about a dozen paces long but, as they dashed madly along it, each step felt like a raucous hammerblow guaranteed to wake every poisonous creature within earshot. Shogrel was waiting at the next turnoff, which led into somewhat more neutral territory. Once they were round the corner, Shogrel scattered a handful of pale blue seeds across the width of the main passage. "A means of temporarily repelling any pursuers," she said. "Now, these are for your friend."

She handed Dervla another set of protective blue-flower chains. She crouched and a moment later Pyke was wearing them around his head and his wrists.

Oh, for a cam to record this moment, Dervla thought as the flower-crowned Pyke opened his eyes and looked groggily about him.

"Skaggin' hell," he groaned.

"Feeling a bit rough?" she asked.

"Feel like I've been puked up by something huge with rocks in its gut—I'm bashed all over..." He winced as he explored and prodded his torso and limbs. "Bruises everywhere..."

"Remember what happened after we followed Ustril into the wreck?" Dervla said.

"It's a bit...hazy. I remember we got in through a hatch..."

He frowned. "There was some shooting, Kref bawling at something, then it's just a blur. Then I must have been knocked out 'cos I had some really skagged-up dreams..." That was when he finally noticed the blue-flower bracelets. "Wait, what?"

"Bran, just leave them on," Dervla said. "They're shielding us from the fumes and the fauna of the forest." Dervla beckoned to Shogrel. "This is Shogrel—she is an inhabitant of the Steel Forest and without her help there's no way we could've rescued you."

Pyke offered a wary smile and a nod to the woman of leaves and roots. "Erm...exactly how long has it been since we entered the wreck?"

"Nearly three hours," Dervla said. "Most of that time, you, me and Kref—and presumably Ancil and Moleg—have been kablonged out of our brains on a cocktail of psychotropic plant fumes and hallucinogenic insect venom..."

"So where's Ans and Moleg?"

"Not found them yet," she admitted, glancing at Shogrel. "Have you been detecting any hints from the forest or nearby denizens, any clues about where our friends might be?"

Shogrel seemed thoughtful for a moment. "I shall extend my senses."

The forest-dweller fell silent and stood there, arms at her sides, with her root-woven head swaying gently from side to side, eyes wide but unfocused. Dervla looked back at Pyke and shrugged, but a moment later Shogrel straightened and turned towards the others.

"Strange emanations are pulsing through the webways," she said. "There was a clash with intruders resulting in violence and terrible destruction—some have been eliminated, others have been cornered—possibly. This strife is happening a distance away and two decks above, so the impressions are confused. Either some intruders have been backed into a corner, much as your captain was, or some intruders have been taken prisoner.

But if these outsiders have been captured, what is the source of so much anger and discord?"

"What about Ustril?" Pyke said. "Any sign of her?"

Shogrel looked at Dervla. "Is that your missing companion? I have heard nothing about a solo intruder, apart from those that have been accounted for. However, the further and higher we go the more impression I shall be able to gather."

Pyke nodded thoughtfully while gazing around him. "Right, if Ancil and Moleg are still out there, we can't afford to waste any more time." He paused to feel and prod at his jacket at chest level, hastily jammed his hand inside, then began frantically patting all his pockets. Dervla cleared her throat loudly and held up the leather-cased crystal shard. Pyke went from bug-eyed panic to slumping relief. "How?" he said.

"You were waving it around and shouting like a mad ganger when we found you," she said. "Didn't have time to be gentle so we wrestled it off you then dragged you back here. You want it back?"

Pyke started to reach out but then hesitated, as something like dread showed in his expression. He gave a little wave and let his arm fall back.

"Nah, you hold onto it for a spell—just promise me that you won't open it or touch it, ever, okay?"

"I promise," she said. "Last thing I want is some homicidal machine-mind walking around in my skin while I'm not there." She shuddered, then offered Pyke a hand to help him to his feet. He swayed a little and leaned against the wall.

"You need to rest for a little while longer?" she said, but he shook his head.

"We'd better crack on—who knows what kind of trouble that pair have got themselves into?"

With Shogrel leading the way (and frequently sending her hand-and-eye scouts up ahead), they left the turmoil of the red corridor behind them. With care and attention they managed to manoeuvre their way through passages overgrown with orange-and-blue leaves as big as platters, or littered and criss-crossed with yellow-and-brown striped vines. The key was to break or crush as few roots, stems and stalks as possible. A succession of odours laced the air, sometimes a sugary sweetness, other times a chemical acridity so sharp Dervla felt as if the hairs in her nose were shrivelling up in protest. All in all it was a demanding route and after nearly an hour she could tell that Pyke was struggling. Neither she nor Kref had any rations left so she moved up next to Shogrel and summarised the situation in a low voice.

Shogrel nodded and, when they paused at the next crossing, she went round everyone's blue-flower circlets, inspecting them for any wear or damage. When she was finished she gave a small nod to Dervla as she went out to one of the three passages ahead of them to pick up her "scouts." On her way back she whispered, "He will receive strengthening nutrients for a time but he must rest properly soon."

Same goes for the rest of us, Dervla thought as Shogrel faced them all, clearly with something to say.

"My hand-and-eye scouts have returned with news about the crossing's other three passages. One is blocked by debris from a structural collapse, another is a death-red corridor where some kind of war of extirpation is going on—no one can enter and my blue flowers would be no defence. The third was known to have been passable but is now obstructed by a large and dense outgrowth, or possibly a barrier created from warped branch bark of a shape on which my scouts could not agree. As you may surmise, I am going to have to go and see for myself."

"Could I accompany you?" said Dervla.

Shogrel gave her a considering look. "That would be acceptable, although I would ask you to leave all weapons here."

Dervla nodded, took out her blaster and passed it to Pyke, who smiled and slipped it away inside his jerkin. Then, side by side, she and Shogrel strode to the crossing and turned along the right-hand corridor. It was shadowy here. Light sources like tubers and honeycombed blooms were sheltered behind screens of fleshy leaves or lattices of creepers. As elsewhere, most doors were choked with growth and impenetrable to the eye.

"Do you know who is in charge of this section?" Dervla said quietly.

"I remember him from long ago," Shogrel said. "He was a songmaker, saved from the fall of the Imperial homeworld by a noble who liked his versing. Once, these passages were full of melody."

Dervla listened intently for a moment, heard only the usual susurrus of the Steel Forest.

"And since then?"

"Now I feel only undertones of grief and painful memory."

As they walked Dervla could actually sense a rising ambience of unwelcome sourness shading into hostility, as if their very presence was resented. She began to hear curious sounds, the desolate sigh of wind through branches, the high-pitched call of a startled creature, a flap of wings, a beast's wail made faint by distance. *Clever sound-staging*, she thought. *You'd think we were traversing the wild outdoors rather than the decrepit interior of a crumbling shipwreck.*

Dark brown roots became visible among the wall foliage, growing thicker the further they went. Then, at last, they turned one of those S-corners and slowed to a wary trudge. Directly ahead was a barrier, a convergence of these same dark, heavy roots or perhaps the spot from which they sprang. It was as if a tree stump had filled out to completely block the corridor, and sent thick tendrils snaking across the ceiling, deck and walls.

Several paces from that dark, obstructing mass, Shogrel halted. "Perhaps you should wait here while I try to converse with the presence," she told Dervla.

"Is there danger? Should I have brought my gun?"

"There is always peril, but you have a better avenue of escape from back here."

For a second she thought that Shogrel was actually cracking a joke—but only for a second. She shrugged and nodded, taking a step backwards as the humanoid went up to the wrinkled, bark barrier and pressed her hand against its surface.

"Kimisuru," she crooned. "Kimisuru—are you there? Please, speak to me."

Back along the corridor there was no change, then, just at the edge of perception, Dervla could make out a deep bestial growl. Then came a voice, a low and ominous mutter.

"I knew a Shogrel once, a just and heartful friend who would never consort with barbarous interlopers..."

"Kimisuru, not all interlopers are the same—"

"Interlopers who seek only to burn and destroy and murder. Murderers, Shogrel! You seem to have forgotten but I never shall."

A thick, dark root erupted from the wall foliage near Dervla and before she could react it coiled around her and slammed her against the wall. Two narrower roots with finely tapered ends snaked up to her face and positioned themselves about a finger's length from her eyes.

"Shogrel!" she yelled, struggling against the roots and her panic.

"Kimisuru, I beg you, please..."

"How kind of you to bring a sacrifice," the deep whispery voice went on. "Although it scarcely amounts to a meaningful recompense..."

"These people mean you no harm, Kimisuru," said Shogrel

urgently. "Only I deserve your bitter recriminations—only I could have stopped the marauder who carried off Kelani. Leave my companion alone."

The root tips hovering before Dervla's eyes withdrew and the large root crushing her against the wall, relaxed but not enough to release her. At the same time, the main area of the tree-wall twisted and writhed slowly into a definite form, that of a figure seated in a chair. Eyes opened in the figure's bark-textured face as he leaned forward.

"You are offering yourself in place of the barbarian? I accept!"

From nearby masses of foliage more dark roots lashed out towards Shogrel, spearing into the densely woven parts of her body. She cried out, and Dervla watched in horror as the impaling roots savagely, piece by piece, ripped her apart. Hands and feet were flung away like jettisoned rubbish while all the individual features of her head were one by one plucked out and tossed aside. It was a hideous, deliberate and up-close display of violence which left Dervla shaken, and she was no stranger to brutality. The final affront was the discarding of Shogrel's torso, hurled the full length of the corridor where it hit the wall and fell to the deck with a sickening thud.

"Now let us see this primitive outsider."

Dervla felt the roots tighten around her chest, then she was dragged through the undergrowth and brought to a halt before the figure sitting in its tree-throne, part of the throne, part of the wood. Before she could say anything the denizen Kimisuru spoke:

"Savages you were and savages you remain. Your kind is only capable of rapacious plundering and thoughtless destruction. Mindless brutes..."

"So, who was Kelani?" she said. This Kimisuru was clearly one of those loner, grudge-nursing types, lives so empty that even the recycling of old, bleak grievances could provide excitement and purpose. And they always had speeches ready, bombastic declarations that they'd worked on for ages, slaving over them in their cramped little minds. Dervla took great satisfaction in disrupting the flow of their grandstanding oratory.

"Do not sully that precious name with your putrid mouth and its putrid tongue!"

"Hey, look, I don't know who Kelani was, what she meant to you or what happened to her, but I'm guessing it was all a long time ago so don't you think that maybe it's time to let it go?"

"She died in torment at the hands of brutes!" snarled Kimisuru. "Brutes and exiles from the Mosaic...it does not matter to me what gulf of time has passed. There must and will be retribution for the bleeding wound left in the face of existence by Kelani's murder!"

"And let me guess," said Dervla. "Lucky old me gets to spill her blood and/or guts in memory of the dearly departed. Is that your plan? Well, screw that! I'm not your sacrificial lamb and I won't be playing it meek and compliant. I'll be fighting you every step of the—"

She paused, words fading away as she noticed a trail of tiny blue flowers winding right across the ridged bark and over the woody figure of Kimisuru seated upon his throne. Having dismissed her fighting retort, he was now reasserting his dominance with gloating descriptions of the eviscerations soon to be visited upon her helpless body. Dervla, however, tracked the line of blue flowers over to where one of Shogrel's hands was traversing the dark brown wall, pausing regularly to poke the bark with its index finger, and at every poked spot a tiny sprig emerged and unfurled to reveal a blue flower.

She glanced down at the flowers around her wrists—the miniature face-blooms were smiling and swaying in unison. Their minuscule mouths were all humming as one, along with those encircling her forehead and the ones growing right across the rugose bark of Kimisuru's wall-throne. It was an ethereal sound, growing to a volume that Dervla's captor could not ignore. He ceased his verbal drooling over imaginary tortures, listened for a second, then let out a deafening howl of rage which turned into a stream of slurred invective involving words like "liar" and "lies." Some of his dark lashing roots were being directed against the blue flowers but by now they were spreading quickly and numerously to survive any attacks.

Without warning Dervla was tossed lightly aside, fetching up against the corridor wall. Foliage and mossy growth cushioned the impact a little, yet still she was left feeling winded. But she remembered seeing blue flowers scattered all along the root just before it released her.

"Lies, lies, lies! Vicious, treacherous lies...scum from the lips of crawling fiends...hah, and now the she-fiend is no more—why persist in planting her degenerate untruths?"

A voice, wavering and faint, emerged from the ethereal blue-flower chorus. "Oh, Kimisuru, you have tried to cover up your pain with illusion, tried to numb the lonely anguish with a story, a little scrap of make-believe..."

"Cease this loathsome contagion of deceit!...breeder of pretence, sowing falsehoods throughout the Steel Forest, poisoner of the webs..."

"The worst lies, Kimisuru, are the ones we tell ourselves."

The wooden figure of Kimisuru clenched its fists and bellowed in a wordless fury. But the chorus of the flowers continued to strengthen, and as the tiny blooms spread like an unfurling carpet up and down the corridor, the lashing strikes of the dark roots became sluggish and hesitant. From where she crouched, halfway along the corridor and partly concealed by a thick bush, Dervla could see that the flowers were winning, yet where was Shogrel herself? Her voice seemed to be part of that now-omnipresent mass-chorale. And then she spotted a familiar five-fingered shape pulling itself through the foliage with one of Shogrel's eyes cradled by its fourth and fifth fingers. It appeared to be stealthily creeping in the direction of the corridor's far end.

"Insidious and shameless...your mendacity...how far back... shadows of guile...tricks and...and...hollow words..."

Kimisuru was scarcely making any sense, and seemed to have lost the ability to speak in whole sentences. Meanwhile, over by the other wall and further back along the corridor, Dervla saw the pale shapes of Shogrel's body parts gathering together. The light in the corridor had dimmed, and the guardian roots seemed to have lapsed into a kind of torpor. Dervla left her spot and crept down to the far end where Shogrel's torso had come to rest. It felt solid and heavy in her arms and seemed to be bleeding from several minor wounds. Anatomically, it seemed very human, apart from a couple of enhancements, but such similarities were superficial—the semi-autonomous existence of appendages and facial organs was an entire biological development branch away from Humanity.

Clasping the torso to her midriff, Dervla waddled over to the congregation of Shogrel's body parts. Now resting amid a loose weave of roots, stems and flowers, she looked up at Dervla with a single eye, smiling.

"Thank you," she said in frail, papery tones. "It is always pleasant to unite the components in common cause."

Carefully, Dervla laid the pale, naked torso down on a bed of entwined creeper vines whose tendrils quickly knitted themselves around it protectively.

"What happens now?"

"It is already happening—look."

Dervla turned to see that the seated figure had disappeared from the wooden barrier. The long dark roots had ceased their vicious lashing and now lay cracked and shrivelling in the gloom.

The rough wooden barrier was growing pale, visibly crumbling away in flakes and splinters with large cracks spreading up from the base. Dervla was almost mesmerised by the sight and didn't hear the approaching footsteps until they were quite close. One was a heavy trudge, the other lighter, more agile, and then—weapons drawn—Pyke and Kref rounded the corner in a combat-ready crouch.

"What's the state o' play?" Pyke said.

"Worst is over," said Dervla. "I think."

"Kimisuru no longer poses a threat to our quest," said Shogrel. "This place is now safe."

Working from the torso shoulder and hips, the foliated tendrils had reformed densely interwoven legs and arms to which Shogrel's hands and feet were smoothly attached. A newly woven neck and head were easily repopulated by the ears, eyes, nose and mouth, which slowly moved into formation. The colour of the webby tendrils was darker than the original construction, and a proliferation of tiny green flowers was visible throughout the lattice, giving it all a different meld of earthy colours. Shogrel sat up and stretched her arms, clearly pleased.

"We heard it was all getting a bit noisy," Pyke said, watching Shogrel nervously. "And me and Kref had just decided to hurry along and crash the party when a whole clutch of big fat roots burst out of a wall vent and blocked the way."

"I kicked at 'em and tried to pull them out the way." Kref shook his big craggy head. "They were tough, Derv, real tough. I wanted to shoot 'em but the captain says not a good idea."

"I kinda guessed that you might be at the mercy of some mad root monster hellbent on assaulting your dignity, and that blazing away at its rooty tentacles might make it madder."

"Good call, actually."

"Right, so we kept our eyes on it and when the roots got feeble and shrivelled we got stuck in and kicked our way through." Pyke and Kref exchanged a grin. "Can't go wrong with a solid pair o' boots!"

"Thank you for not using the energy weapons," Shogrel said to them. "The forest has become very sensitive to that kind of destruction." She looked at Dervla. "The way is open so we can continue, if you are ready."

The whole of the wooden barrier had now collapsed into a heap of splintered debris. As they shoved some of it aside to get through, Dervla found how desiccated and brittle it was.

"How did you do that?" she said. "Is he dead?"

"Kimisuru is not dead," Shogrel said. "I managed to force him to withdraw to his burrows, his lair, in most of the rooms along this and nearby passages. His consciousness has become unsound over the long stretch of time, clouded by at first remorse and guilt then by a consuming need for those feelings. He forgot that the deep science of the Steel Forest, the biologic and the mindforming, which allowed him to create his treebark aspect is the same science that helped me to subvert his biomass with mindforms of my own devising. They caused a limited die-back, which disabled those terrible roots and his ability to fully perceive."

Pyke nodded, peering back at the shadowy corridor. "Not much in the way of beasts and insects, I notice."

"All of his dominance-desire went into the animated roots," said Shogrel. "Any creatures from neighbouring demesnes were treated very harshly."

"Did you see into his thoughts and memories?" asked Dervla. "Find anything useful for our journey?"

"Some of his memory pith was distributed among the primary growth, and there was a knot of recent remembrances. I shall quickly see if they contain anything of interest."

A few clumps of wall tubers here and there pulsed with soft light then faded. Shogrel's eyes narrowed. "It appears that he

was interested in the conflict up on the…the supervision deck…
more than just curiosity, he had sent a few creature-scouts to
be his eyes and ears! So he did gestate some beastforms." She
looked sombre.

"Is the supervision deck a place of significance?" said Dervla.

"That is where the Gateway chamber is, yet access is gained
via a complicated route. It is isolated…"

A baffled looking Pyke was about to speak but Dervla got in
first.

"Before you mentioned a place called the Mosaic. Is that
where the Gateway leads to?"

"It does," said Shogrel. "But that has little bearing on our
quest. I now know the location of your companions."

Pyke was suddenly all smiles. "Where?"

"They are being held captive by an alliance of three minds
of the forest. This alliance also has a small group of intruders
trapped in a chamber, as you were, Captain. Unlike you, these
outsiders have ammunition and explosives and have proved their
willingness to use them. The alliance of three are divided on
how to proceed but there seems to be some plan involving your
companions."

"Intruders?" Dervla said. "Could be Raven or some of her
goons."

"Well, let's get going," said Pyke. "Can't have my crew used
and abused as decoys or whatever."

"There is something else," said Shogrel. "It is only a faint
thread of memory, but there is a suggestion that Kimisuru was
in contact with these trapped intruders."

"Knowing Raven," said Dervla, "that doesn't sound good."

"Not at all," agreed Pyke. "Let's shake a leg and get
barrelling!"

CHAPTER TWELVE

Pyke, in the Crystal Simulation, the city of Granah

The interrogations were proving to be a challenge.

Pyke couldn't be sure how long he had been unconscious before they brought him round but he was guessing it wasn't that long. Coming to, he found himself roped into a chair in a dingy room lit by a couple of hanging lanterns. Before him was a burly, broad Shylan wearing street-thug leathers and pulling on a pair of gloves.

"We only have one question," said Pyke's own personal thug. "And we'll have the answer before the night is done."

"What? You mean how many Shylans does it take to change a...burned-out candle?"

That earned him his first punch in the face. The thug leaned in close.

"The question is—where is the blood phial?"

"Where's the what?"

That got him punch number two.

Over the next hour or so the placing of the punches varied—face, stomach, chest, lower back. The pain began to merge, Pyke's surroundings grew a little hazy and he found it harder and harder to come up with original insults and bon mots. But always at the back of his mind was the sight of Klane crouching down next to him before the light went out.

That son of a slug must pay!

Occasionally his host (who introduced himself as Drask) took a break from his playtime, and during those punchless interludes Pyke could hear faint voices through the wall repeating that same question, "Where is the blood phial?," followed by the meaty thud of more punches. Drask was workmanlike in his interrogation and unresponsive to any of Pyke's own queries and observations, although the more biting the sarcasm the sharper the punch. There was at least one other Shylan in the room but Pyke's chair was facing into a corner so he could only tell by sounds. Now and then Drask muttered to his buddy in low tones and once in a while the door opened and closed.

After roughly two hours of this luxury treatment, Drask came into view and stood there, calmly examining the knuckles of his gloves which had an extra layer of hardened leather sewn across them. A second broad figure appeared to the side—Klane, dressed in a fancy dark coat with a high collar, embossed diamond patterning with blood-red stitching. The candlelight gleamed on polished leather.

"Well, don't you look pretty," he said, almost without thinking.

At once, Drask slapped him full in the face. The burning sting of it made his teeth ache.

"You will not address the Shield Captain," said Drask. "Your companions have spoken of a book—what is its location?"

Pyke's first reflex was to tell him that he could find it up his boss's arse, but he reined that one in and instead gave as mocking a smile as he could manage.

"Which one?" he said.

Drask's eyes narrowed. He clenched his fist and drew back for another blow but Klane intervened:

"Enough—have them all taken up to the balcony room."

"Oh good," Pyke said. "A party! I do hope there's cake."

A few minutes later Pyke, with hands bound and mouth gagged, was close-escorted by lamplight up a broad, dusty staircase. Two flights later they entered a large room long since stripped of anything valuable or useful. Bare boards, bare walls and glassless doors that opened onto a wide balcony. Three battered chairs were produced and arranged noisily in a line. At the same time a table was dragged out of a cupboard and set up before the chairs. Then Vrass and T'Moy arrived, the latter looking as if he'd received by far the worst beating. One eye was swollen and blood trickled from battered lips. But when he glanced over at Pyke he still managed a half-smile. Vrass gave just a faint nod—he looked exhausted.

A better class of grubby, scratched chair was placed behind the bare table. A moment later Klane entered and sat at the table, after first carefully sweeping the tails of his splendid coat under his substantial buttocks. He placed both hands palms down on the tabletop and impassively considered the three captives for a moment. Then he looked up at Drask.

"Well done, Shield-Lance Drask. You and the others will now retire to the floor below while I question these prisoners."

"Sir, unaccompanied questioning contravenes practice and custom," intoned Drask. "If you permitted us to employ the full range of enquiry methods we might be in possession of..."

"Or I might now be looking at three bodies," cut in Klane. "Clearly you are unhappy with how I've conducted this mission. Do you feel you are better suited to be in command?"

The Shield-Lance straightened to attention. "Sir, I..."

"But you are not in command—I am. I was chosen by the Emperor to lead the Shylan Shields as part of the Imperial Honour Guard." Klane's dark eyes seemed to project anger and contempt straight at Shield-Lance Drask. "I was chosen because I get results, and I get results in whatever way I see fit. You all have your orders—retire to the lower floor and await my next command. In the meantime I shall closely scrutinise all that these miscreants have to say."

Pyke couldn't help grinning up at his tormentor, Drask. The Shield-Lance was trying to keep his face expressionless but his eyes practically shone with burning grievance. When that gaze swept over the captives, as he turned to leave with the rest Pyke gave him a slow, mocking wink.

Ah yes, one of life's pleasures, Pyke thought as the Shylans trooped out. *Seeing your opponent brought low. But how are we going to deal with Klane, or whatever name he's going under. How do we save our skins, then somehow get out of here, and somehow take Klane to the memory-Statues?* Pyke chuckled. *Only lies can save us now, fabulous, chrome-plated, ten-storey lies! And you only get them by lying like a rug!*

At last the door closed and footsteps on the creaking stairs receded. Behind the desk Klane seemed to be listening, features betraying no thought or emotion. Once all the clumping footsteps had fallen silent, Klane breathed a long sigh and whispered:

"At last, no more subterfuge! We must get away from these thugs, but I do not know what to do next. I'm going to untie you but you must remain quiet—understood?"

Dumbfounded, Pyke nodded along with the others and Klane started round the table, then paused; "Oh, it is me, Klane, by the way."

Pyke rolled his eyes and nodded vigorously. Klane resumed moving around the table, then froze when he heard a heavy tread climbing from the floor below. The sound halted outside the door, soles scraping on the planks, and a slightly muffled voice said:

"Shield-Captain, forgive the intrusion—Shield-Lance Drask wondered if you required any food or water."

A wide-eyed Klane swallowed hard. "Thank the Shield-Lance

for me, Shield-Trooper, but I have no need for sustenance at this time."

"As you will it, sir."

The heavy footsteps retraced their route and faded away to one of the rooms below. Klane, meanwhile, made a shushing gesture, pointed over at the balcony doors, then with his fingers mimicked walking over there. Everyone nodded and Klane got to work loosening their bonds. Soon they were all gathered out on the balcony, voices low but emotions high.

"You knew it was us," Pyke whispered. "But you still let them kick the crap out of us! Just what's your game?"

"You don't know how lucky you are," replied Klane. "The Shield-Captain's orders are to use any methods to find out where the blood-poison is. My second-in-command wanted to get to work on you with clippers and hot tongs! It was all I could do to restrain him. As you could see, he's not happy with my command."

"I'm not happy with him, the poxbag!" Pyke said. "Has a fist like a sockful of spanners..."

"My apologies," said Klane. "But I have noticed that minor injuries in this simulation seem to heal quite quickly. Look at T'Moy—when I saw him before we came upstairs, one eye was swollen and closed and his lips were burst and bleeding—now see the difference."

It was true. The swelling in T'Moy's pummelled eye had gone down substantially, enough for him to blink his eyelids, and his mouth now only looked a little bruised. And when Pyke prodded his jaw it still ached and he had the odd twinge, but no longer felt as if he'd been interrogated with a meat tenderiser.

Every now and then, he thought, *I have to stop and remember how I'm really just a copy of the real me, existing in a fabricated reality, wondering if I'm thinking thoughts the way the real me would think them, and feeling anything that's got truth in it...*

and I have to stop remembering all this and get back in the bastard Legacy's little game. A game which is all we have...

"So exactly what is this blood-poison they were going on about?" Vrass was saying.

"I want to know when you realised that you were you," said T'Moy. "Were you fully aware from the start or did something awake you?"

"Firstly my simulation person is Kranth of Gojir, a high-ranking Shylan officer chosen by the Emperor to command the Shylan Shields, which are part of the Imperial Honour Guard." Klane paused to finger the button seam of his imposing coat. "So this morning Kranth had a meeting with one of the Grand Provost's advisers, the Master of Seals. The Master of Seals swore Kranth to secrecy then told him a story about the Emperor's secret half-brother, Abryl.

"Abryl was ignorant of his lineage but agents of his father, the previous Emperor, Viskarn, kept watch over his progress. He joined the 25th Brigade of Rifles, campaigned in some of the less picturesque parts of the empire, and after a few years rose to the rank of Battery Lieutenant. Then came the Manakros Rebellion.

"The province of Manakros rose up against Imperial rule, and the 25th was part of the expeditionary force sent to put down the uprising. So, during the siege of Manakros, Battery-Lieutenant Abryl and his squad were ambushed by northern mercenaries who had an Icering wizard with them. Almost the entire squad died from sorcerous arrow volleys, except for Abryl who was the focus of something altogether nastier—reinforcement arrived and dragged him clear as the ambushers were chased off. Back behind Imperial lines he recovered swiftly and even took part in the occupation march when the Manakrosians finally surrendered.

"It was not long after that campaign that the murders began. Nearly all were soldiers of the 25th, mostly of the rank and file. Non-soldiers included an ostler and a powder-boy..."

"Okay," Pyke cut in. "Obviously, it's Abryl, the half-brother—was he deliberately infected by this wizard? Is that the source of this blood-poison?"

Klane was visibly annoyed at having his story interrupted but he shook his head and tried to pick up the thread.

"No one is entirely sure if someone in the enemy camp knew Abryl's identity, and, yes, Abryl was the culprit behind the killings. It took his superiors some time to figure out that it was him, however, and they had to employ a scryer to narrow down the suspects. Anyway, by that time the slayings numbered twenty-two and grim myths had sprung up around the brigade's curse, the Butcher of the 25th, as it became known. So, during a duty tour on the Eastmarch borders, Abryl was sent with a small team to reconnoitre hostile force camps. That was when he was set upon, tied to a tree and beheaded, and one of the riflemen entrusted with the deed was…"

"Sergeant Traz Dalyak," Pyke interjected. "Leaseholder of lockbooth 29A at the Raskol Boxhouse."

Klane nodded. "The Master of Seals told Kranth that Sergeant Dalyak had collected some of Abryl's poisoned blood in a silver phial with an air-tight cap, and the suspicion was that he'd stowed it in his lockbooth back in Granah."

"Except that he didn't," T'Moy said. "Only that book was missing."

Pyke resisted the urge to laugh out loud. "We don't know that for sure! We had a good rummage through the contents, but that wasn't a detailed search."

"But whoever got there before you, and left a dead thief behind, seemed to know what to take," Klane said. "Hence, the missing book."

"Yeah, that is fair enough," said Pyke. "And doesn't that look a bit convenient? I mean, your guy, this Master of Seals, knows a bunch of details about the half-brother and his mad butchery, and about the departed Sergeant Dalyak—and whoever was behind the pre-emptive break-in must have known about the book as well? Did Dalyak get drunk one night and spill the whole story?" He shook his head. "Can't see it—veteran hard cases tend to be curt, tight-lipped types, but maybe there was an accomplice…"

Klane uttered a hoarse laugh. "Do not forget the aim of our presence here, in these curiously primitive surroundings—we have a problem to solve so that we can move onto the next stage in the Legacy's game of tests…"

"Makes you wonder where all this came from." Pyke frowned, gazing out at the night-darkened city. "From a real living mind, or from some semi-aware stack of data?"

"We can't stay here much longer," said T'Moy, whose features now looked mostly healed. "Our friend Shield-Lance Drask will be wondering why it's so quiet up here."

Almost as one they glanced worriedly back at the table with its vacant chairs.

"How many of them are there?" Pyke said.

"Including the Shield-Lance," said Klane, "eight, and they all have Shylan long-knives."

"I think I've seen one of those," said Vrass. "Nasty, serrated short sword, basically."

"And they have all our gear so the odds are heaped against us if we're talking about mixing it up with them, face-to-face." Pyke peered over the balcony rail. "No way down unless you're a brick."

"Captain, look," said T'Moy.

Strands of dead, dried-out creeper still clung to the outside walls near the balcony. T'Moy was prying some kind of hinged metal bar free from the lifeless foliage. There was a crackling sound, along with a squeak, and the Bargalil pulled an iron half-ladder into view. The rungs looked good and went straight up to a parapet that seemed to go all the way around the roof. Pyke sent Vrass up to scout it out, hoping there might be another building close enough on the other side. In the meantime, he and the others went back inside to use what furniture there was to block the door to the stairs. They were almost finished when Vrass appeared at the balcony doors.

"Captain, we're in luck," he whispered. "There's a catwalk linking the roof to a nearby building."

Pyke nodded and gestured the others back to the balcony. Before joining them he grabbed a broken stool that had been tossed in a corner; he snapped off one of its remaining legs and, once back out with the others, slipped it between the outer handles of the doors. Of course, a couple of hefty kicks would smash them open but even a few seconds' delay for their pursuers was worth having.

With Vrass in the lead, Pyke sent Klane and T'Moy up after him, following on himself. A fresh breeze was picking up by the time he joined the rest up on the parapet. Cautiously they circumnavigated the slate-covered, peaked roof. Sure enough, on the opposite side was another building of similar height, with the edge of its flat roof perhaps ten feet away.

"Where's this gantry, Vrass?" said Pyke.

"Right here, Captain…"

With both hands, Vrass lifted a long, narrow plank of some kind up from the edge of their building and swung it round to place its far end down on the other roof's edge. It seemed that this clever bridge was anchored on a swivel on this side, yet even as they congratulated Vrass on his perceptive eyesight they heard shouts and a crash of doors and furniture being broken aside.

"Okay, let's move," said Pyke.

Suddenly urgency was all. Klane and T'Moy were sent across first, then Pyke, Vrass insisted. Then the Gomedran took something from the anchor point before making his own crossing. Once across, he grabbed the broad plank, now disconnected, and threw his end over the edge. The gantry scraped off the anchor

point, turned over and fell out of sight to clatter noisily down
below. Pyke urged everyone back into deeper shadows as a line of
figures shuffled round the parapet they'd so recently left behind.

"We should leave quickly," murmured Klane. "I don't want
them to see me. Vrass says there's an easy way down to another
adjoining building."

"Good idea," said Pyke. "I'll be right with you."

Klane left, carrying a recently lit candle. Pyke, squatting
behind a low trough filled with dry soil and dead plants, stared
across at the shadowy figures gathering on the other roof's edge.
He'd been rehearsing in his head a few choice and profane farewells, but before he could deliver one or two a voice came out
of the darkness.

"Tell former Shield-Captain Kranth that his life is now forfeit."

Pyke smiled, recognising the voice of his interrogator, Drask.

"I hear you wanted to have a go at me with red-hot pincers,"
he said.

"Ah, the chief graverobber, Pazzyk, allegedly. Yes, we find
that glowing instruments are the fastest route to the truth..."

"Well, if it's the truth yer after, here's some for you—we're not
the enemy around these parts. And while I'm handing out free
advice, avoid Peligar's savoury stall in the Nightmarket—his rat
bridies'll give you a monstrous dose of the skrath!"

"Actually, on second thoughts," said Drask, "there's no need
for you to pass on any messages—your life is forfeit, too."

Some gut-level animal instinct made Pyke twist away and roll
behind the cover of a water barrel. There was a tight cluster of
metallic cracks as several feathered darts impacted the tiled area
where he'd been crouching. When he peered out from behind the
barrel a moment or two later, the parapet opposite was empty.

Time we made ourselves scarce, he thought, hurrying to join
the others.

This building turned out to be closely adjoined to a lower,

broader one and although there was no ladder there was a series of hand- and footholds in the stone, with one or two iron grab-handles sunk into the masonry. The roof below was flat and divided into squares, each with a trapdoor, a small garden box-plot and a washing line on two poles. Some had little glowing lamps hanging from the poles, others had small sheds built over the trapdoors. There was the occasional startled intake of breath or muttered curse as the four escapees hurried through.

From the eastern side a rope ladder dropped into a yard-wide gap between the flat-roofed building and an older one with gables. They climbed down to a ledge which gave them an easy crossing onto an upper-floor balcony that ran the full length of the house. At the other end was a small platform and a cunning sequence of protruding bricks sloping down to the shadows of an alleyway. Down at ground level the maze of streets that made up the lamplit Old Town was hazy with night-mist—above them, the maze of roofs was a pitch-black labyrinth which Pyke was glad to leave behind. Once or twice during their skulking overhead retreat, Pyke had glimpsed their former captors still in pursuit, but now, as they wound through the narrow, twisty streets, he started to believe that they were in the clear.

Vrass said they were near the edge of the Darvanu slums and that he knew of a disreputable alehouse in the basement of a sweatshop. Everyone was feeling worn out and hungry so they followed his lead to a set of narrow, smelly steps leading down and around the back court of a building set on a hillside. At last they reached their goal, a place known as the Two-Headed Dog. Inside it was warm, stuffy and reeking of sweat and smoke. They ordered tankards of beer, some bread and cheese, then found a secluded corner. Once the greater part of the edibles had been devoured, Pyke leaned forward, elbows on the scarred table.

"Okay, I'm guessing that the whole point of this scenario the Legacy has got us all rushing around in is to stop the Emperor getting hit with a dose of this blood-poison, yeah?" Heads nodded round the table. "We know where it came from, and who brought it into the city…"

"Can we be certain that this poison is somewhere in Granah?" said T'Moy.

Pyke frowned. "Well, we know that after the mad half-brother Abryl was executed, Sergeant Dalyak came back here and left a journal in his lockbooth, which someone else went to a lot of trouble to steal."

"It would help if we knew who would want to make the Emperor go mad," said Vrass, brushing crumbs from his snout.

Klane uttered a low laugh. "Kranth, my previous persona, knew quite a lot on that topic. A list of the Emperor's adversaries would include half of the noble families, some of the wealthier merchants, a couple of the senior guildmasters, followers of Vondral…"

"That's a church of some kind, isn't it?" said Vrass.

T'Moy nodded. "About a quarter of the Barlig riderclans worship Vondral, but there is an unorthodox branch, the Vondral Diligents, who have been persecuting Shamaya followers, so the Emperor banned them from Granah and the precinct towns…"

"More memories from Trogian?" said Pyke.

"Yes," said T'Moy. "Disturbing how readily available they are."

A sombre mood had crept over the gathering, but Pyke was determined to lighten things.

"Just part of the deal," he said with a dismissive gesture. "We use whatever skills and brainpower we've got to complete the Legacy's twisty puzzle-story—which is why I think we should focus on the boxhouse break-in as a way of tackling the whole problem."

"Did you and T'Moy recover any clues when you were there?" said Klane.

"We knew the looter, or looters, went straight for the journal," Pyke said. "And we have these."

From an inner pocket he took out the fingerless gloves and laid them on the table. The others leaned in closer for a better look in the meagre candlelight.

"Hmm," said Klane. He prodded one of them, turned it over a couple of times and ran a fingertip across the backs. "Looks grubby and frayed, but the base material is finely woven wool and the stitched strengthening panels on the palm and inner surfaces of the fingers is a flexible but tough leather, something like goatskin."

Pyke smiled. "These were custom-made."

"Repaired, too." Klane pointed out where gashes in the wool had been mended with fine stitching.

"So, a talented seamstress," Pyke said. "Someone used to dealing with rogues and villains, someone who lives and plies her trade in the slummier part of town..."

T'Moy chuckled. "Where we happen to be."

"Yeah, but anyone who has skills that are in demand will try to set up shop where the customers are." Pyke gave a half-smile. "So where is Granah's hub of criminality and shady characters? In the olden times it was called a rookery."

A grinning Vrass waved a finger. "In Jarko District there's a square of streets with a pretty dark reputation—the city watch calls it Dreg's Den."

"That sounds like the place," said Pyke. "So, find our seamstress and see if she'll tell us who she made these gloves for, and once we get a name we can go about finding out who he was working for, or at least talking to. That should lead us to whoever stole the journal."

Everyone was in agreement so they decided to make their way to Dreg's Den under cover of night rather than risk it during daylight. As they hurried through the backstreets and alleyways a series of brief but blustery showers fell, leaving the dark lanes slippery with muddy pools and the lamplit roads shining and wet. Following Vrass's lead, as he strove to recall the way from

Virl's memories, they crossed over from the Darvanu slums into Jarko District by the small hours of the morning. Moving with stealth, they turned down an alley that Vrass was sure led to Dreg's Den, only to round a corner and find the way blocked by a high wooden barricade. Vrass was baffled for a moment then slapped the side of his face and nodded.

"Virl only heard about this place," he said. "He'd never actually been here. He was told about a road into the Den, Kalzor's Walk, but thought that there had to be other ways in."

"Huh, seems not," Pyke muttered. "Which way to Kalzor's Walk, then?"

It took another half-hour, splashing through wet streets in semi-darkness before they came to a spot where a stone bridge passed overhead, spanning a gully between the lower parts of Jarko District and a section up on higher ground. Across the street, steps led up the side of the bridge stonework—a lamp shone at the top, a cheery orange glow in the latest shower which, as they climbed, turned into a heavy downpour. By the time they got up onto the bridge, Pyke was drenched, every footstep a sodden squelch, not unlike everyone else.

They crossed the bridge, seeing no one else except an old man in an open, candle-lit hut, cooking a skillet of something unidentifiable on a brazier while a cat sat patiently beside his stool. When T'Moy asked the way to the nearest pothouse he never so much as glanced up, but he did give them directions. Pyke smiled, certain that other unseen eyes were tracking their movements.

Roughly built, decrepit three- and four-storey buildings flanked the entrance to Dreg's Den, dark silhouettes broken by lamplit windows. The old man's directions led them to a reeking alley between two buildings; a rickety staircase creaked under every foot as they climbed to a platform at the rear of one of the houses. There, another set of steps led down, all the way to some kind of sub-basement door over which hung a sign—the Bloody Crown.

Inside, two smoky, low-ceilinged rooms were served by a bar in the middle and linked by a short passage. Tallow candles and rushlights provided pools of weak light—smoke from a couple of badly flued fires looked weirdly like mist curling and shifting through the pothouse. The four of them bought beakers of ale and spread out, wandering off to different tables, seeing who would talk freely and who might need a cup or two to loosen their tongues. The Bloody Crown, however, was only about a quarter full so they managed to run through all those capable and willing to talk in less than half an hour, after which they gathered at a table near the door—except for T'Moy who carried on listening to one whiskery old geezer who was employing vigorous hand gestures. When he finally left the greyhair, T'Moy slumped down at their table with a kind of glazed look in his eyes.

"Did he actually tell you anything worth knowing?" Pyke asked.

"No," the Bargalil said. "But I did learn more than I could ever wish to know about pigeon catching."

Pyke grinned. "You want to watch out for the professional gabsters, so let that be a lesson to you. What's the next port of call?"

The next after-hours dive was round the corner and once again down in the basement. Blessed with the name the Bear's Boot, it was a single large room with a long counter at the rear wall. It was fairly well lit with plentiful wall lamps and had large fires in two corners, each with a proper hood to stop the smoke wafting out. And there was a fight in progress when they arrived—five very drunk men were swinging punches, furniture legs and, in one case, a shoe, grunting and snarling and swearing, yet also managing to trip each other up while grappling, shoving and kicking, and all with a swaying, semi-stupefied lack of energy and speed. A casual passing observer might have thought that the fight was taking place underwater.

The barkeep and his tap-boys were watching and laughing

from the counter but not for long. A certain amount of impromptu violent entertainment was always welcome, but it couldn't be allowed to interrupt the business of parting the customers from their coin for too long. Three tap-boys dived in to break up the scuffle and eject those unwilling to peaceably buy more ale. As calm settled over the tavern and serious drinking resumed, Pyke and the others re-enacted the strategy they'd used at the Bloody Crown. The Bear's Boot was more than half-full so Pyke was anticipating another gruelling session as they trawled the babble and chitchat of those willing to talk. But after about ten minutes spent buying ales for a table of street-sweepers, T'Moy sidled up and said,

"Got it, Captain!"

"Well, keep asking around—we'll need a full list of possibles to work from."

"No need, this is the one." T'Moy crouched down next to Pyke's stool. "I got talking with a neatly dressed old boy who turned out to be a thread-seller. Sells all kinds and colours of thread to all of Granah's tailors, seamstresses, leatherworkers and others. He knows them all, and knows exactly who we're looking for, a Mistress Flett. She lives over her own shop which is located back across the bridge, first corner on the left!"

Vrass had arrived just after T'Moy and heard most of what he said, speaking up as he finished.

"I was talking to a couple of slaters who were in some grog-dive in the lowers less than an hour ago, said there were a couple of Shylan going around, asking about seamstresses or tailors..."

"What has happened?" said Klane, last to rejoin the group.

"We heard a rumour that your former associates have been out in the pubs asking about seamstresses." He glanced at Vrass. "And tailors, that right?"

Pyke rubbed at his stubbly cheek in irritation. "Tailors. They must have gone back to the boxhouse for a closer look at the body of our unknown thief. I'll bet that his shabby workwear was more finely made than its appearance would suggest."

"That sounds likely," said Klane. "The Shylan Shields are meticulous and observant."

"No time to lose, then." Pyke stood and buttoned up his damp coat again. "Let's get back over that bridge."

Outside the rain had eased and the cold night air had that post-downpour freshness to it. They trudged and splashed their way back across the bridge, alert eyes watching openings and doorways to either side. Vrass was in the lead, following the directions he was given, with Pyke at his back, feeling edgy and somehow certain that this was too easy, too straightforward.

That bastard Legacy wouldn't just give us the next piece of the puzzle or line of the riddle without making us work for it!

Vrass halted suddenly and backed up a few steps. "Shylans guarding the outside of a small shop across the road!" he whispered.

And there you have it!

Teeth gritted in a soundless snarl, Pyke grabbed them one by one and pulled them all back, pointing to the narrow mouth of an alley leading into the back courts of tall, crumbling tenement blocks. It was pitch-black beyond the entrance so Pyke had Vrass and T'Moy light up a couple of candle stubs (which he'd liberated from cold sconces in the bars they'd visited earlier). Few windows overlooking the rear enjoyed the luxury of glass panes, most having shutters instead, so silence and stealth were crucial. An eagle-eyed search revealed iron rungs in one wall and some minutes later they had made it up onto a slaterers' platform that spanned the side of the roof from front to rear. Crouched up there in the shadowy heights, they had a perfect view of the street and the two guards flanking the doorway to a small shop.

After getting on for ten minutes crouching then kneeling on wet stone, with no change below and no other sounds to break the silence, Pyke found his patience wearing thin.

"I feel like going down there to make something happen," he said.

"Hmm," said Vrass. "It appears that we're not the only ones in the audience, and she certainly seems to have settled down to wait."

Puzzled, Pyke looked round to see Vrass pointing almost vertically down. Moving to join him, he peered over the edge of the parapet and saw that the upper floors of the adjacent frontage were set back from the ground floor a short distance, enough to create a long balcony. Potted bushes and small trees had been scattered along it, with a few tables and chairs. Directly below Pyke saw the glow of a lamp through bushy foliage and a crouched shape in a dress looking through the balcony ironwork at the guarded shop across the road.

"Good chance that's our seamstress," he said.

"How can you be sure?"

"Who else is likely to be spying on that particular shop from such a good hiding place? Apart from us?"

Klane seemed half convinced. "A likely deduction."

"I would say very likely." Pyke grinned as an impulse occurred to him. "I also think I should seize the opportunity and introduce myself."

It was difficult to be sure in the gloom but it certainly felt as if three pairs of eyes were regarding him with astonishment. "Is that wise, Captain?" said T'Moy.

"If I can persuade her that we've a common enemy, she might be more inclined to help us—otherwise, we leave her be and where does that get us?"

There were murmurs of reluctant assent, after which Vrass helped Pyke find another set of slaters' climbing rungs not far along the road-facing roof's narrow catwalk. Pyke descended cautiously but near the bottom found himself coming down behind a leafy bush. The woman-in-hiding's lamp was still visible, so he decided to be bold. He climbed down the remaining rungs with no attempt at stealth, cleared his throat and hummed a little song. When he reached the balcony, leaves rustling all around him, he stepped out from behind the bush, grabbed a rickety wooden chair from a nearby table, positioned it over at the railing and sat down.

"Good evening," he said, conversationally. "Bit of a damp night for taking in a display of street theatre, eh?"

No reply. The woman had dimmed her lamp during his noisy arrival but she hadn't made a dash for it.

"You gotta admire those Shylan boys," he went on. "They don't care how many doors or heads they have to kick in to get what they're after. Took some fierce running and dodging to give them the slip when we escaped their lair earlier today..."

That was when he felt the cold razor point of a dagger press into the side of his neck as a hand seized his collar from behind.

"My name's Pyke, by the way..."

"Sit still and be quiet," said a calm female voice. "Gods, your gabbling is worse than the tatter girls..."

"Heh, no problem, so long as you realise that I'm not your enemy."

"Remains to be seen. And you said 'we' before." The grip on his collar tightened. "Are there others like you nearby? Do they prattle away like you do?"

Pyke laughed. "No, they're quite reserved and polite compared to me. But we are all looking for the same thing. And we need to find it before they do."

"The same thing? Which would be what?"

"A book that was stolen from a boxhouse the day before yesterday."

He felt the dagger point ease away some.

"Which boxhouse?"

"The Raskol, over near Ithlyr."

There was a moment's silence, then the dagger was back.

"How do you know what was taken? Are you with the city watch?"

Pyke toyed with various untruthful answers but decided to be as honest as he could.

"Actually, we were hired to break into the Raskol," he said. "And to steal that same book from one of the lockbooths...but the book was gone and there was a body..."

He heard a sharp intake of breath.

"Whose body?"

"There was nothing in the pockets to say who he was," Pyke said, fumbling inside his coat for the fingerless gloves. "But we did find these nearby."

He held them up to his shoulders and they were accepted. A moment later the dagger was retracted and the soft glow of a hooded lamp came up from behind. A woman's voice said, "Oh no..." in a hoarse, aghast whisper followed by quiet sobbing.

Pyke turned in his seat to see the seamstress slumped on her knees, head bent into one hand, weeping, while the other held the gloves. Quickly he repositioned the chair behind a potted bush and helped her up into it.

"So you did make the gloves," he murmured.

"Hidalio was my brother," said the seamstress, fumbling a handkerchief from a fold in her bodice. "Wouldn't listen to me—told him I didn't trust that cold-eyed man!"

"Do you know who it was that hired your brother?"

"Didn't then but I do now!"

Pyke leaned closer. "How did you find out?"

The seamstress glanced up at him. She had a sallow, freckled complexion but her eyes were sharp and angry.

"He came into my shop!" She mopped her eyes. "And he lied right to my face—I asked where Hidalio was and he said he was still talking to a fence about the loot..."

"When did he turn up?"

"Yesterday evening, before nine chimes, wearing crow-black as before...and Hidalio would have been dead while he was lying to me..." She started crying again, choked off miserable sounds.

If this guy hired Hidalio, murdered him and grabbed the book, Pyke thought, *why take the risk of visiting his victim's sister?*

"So what was his reason for coming round?" he said. "Not just for a chat about the weather, I imagine."

"Oh no, he started asking me about the work I've done for the 25th..."

Pyke's eyebrows went up. "The 25th Brigade?"

"That's them—whenever they need new banners and pennants they come to Flett's." She offered a thin smile. "That's me, Tiselio Flett."

"Pleased to make your acquaintance, Tiselio. So was he after anything specific?"

"Yes—he started asking if I knew anyone in the 25th by the name of Magni. Well, Magni is quite a common boy's name, or it was, but I told him I only ever dealt with the quartermaster at the barracks..."

Pyke recalled what Klane had told him about the 25th, and Sergeant Dalyak's role in all this. *That murdering scumsucker has Dalyak's journal but he can't figure out what it's saying!* he realised. *So now he's trying to pick up clues wherever he can.*

"You've not put a name to this man," Pyke said. "But you said before that you knew who he was."

"Don't know his name but I know his type, first time I saw him." A look of loathing passed over Tiselio's face. "Willing servants for powerful men, loyal dogs who'll do anything for their masters."

He smiled. "So, did you follow him?"

She mirrored his smile. "I did. Waited till he left the shop, then locked up behind me and followed him through the streets. It was already dark so it was easy. I thought he was heading for the western barracks, maybe one of the pubs that the 25th drink in when they're back from duty. Instead he veered into the Shalmy District and hurried down to the bit where the banks and the merchants have their big offices. He went up to the doors of an outfit called Inox & Throm, just strolled in past the guards as if he owned the place."

Inox & Throm? he thought. *Could that be where the book is? And why is Mr. Henchman asking about someone called Magni?*

"Y'know, my companions would really be a lot of help with what you've told me." Pyke glanced over his shoulder at the street below—the two Shylan guards hadn't shifted in all this time. "Nothing's happening down there just now, and my companions are up on that roof there—we can go up and join them if you wish."

"Yes, I'll talk to them," said Tiselio as she got to her feet. "If you promise to help me get some justice for Hidalio!"

"I think we can make that happen. Now, can you manage climbing a ladder to that roof?"

She gave him a look. "That was how I got here so I should think so."

Pyke went first and a few minutes later he was introducing her to Vrass, Klane and T'Moy. He then rushed through a summary of what he'd learned from Tiselio about her brother and the man who'd hired him, where he worked and what he'd said during his visit to her shop.

"Magni?" said Vrass. "What makes you think that has anything to do with the journal?"

"Not having met this black-clad gentleman," Pyke said. "I'm willing to bet that he's the kind who's always following a purpose. Never says anything that doesn't serve it."

"If this man from Inox & Throm killed this lady's brother," said Klane, "it was likely part of his orders. No loose ends. And, as you say, returning to her shop can only increase the risk of suspicion, as demonstrated."

"Who are Inox & Throm?" Pyke said.

"Coachbuilders, wagons, wains, carts," Klane said. "Wealthy company with considerable influence, until recently when the Emperor cancelled the long-standing contract they had to supply the army with various kinds of wagon. The contract was very lucrative..."

"Good motive for resentment and the murder of a monarch, even," said Pyke.

"More than likely," said Klane.

"So someone at Inox & Throm went to a lot of trouble to lay hands on Dalyak's book—seems only right that we pay them a visit and relieve them of this hazardous burden, wouldn't you say?"

Klane and the others shared a conspiratorial smile.

"And I'll be going with you," said Tiselio Flett.

The seamstress adopted a pugnacious stance, hands on hips, as if daring them to deny her demand, reminding Pyke sharply of a certain first mate of his acquaintance.

"Wouldn't dream of leaving you out, Mistress Flett," said Pyke. "You'll know the best way there—then we'll need advice on getting inside..."

"I'm not some oozler-frill, I'll have you know," she said, folding her arms. "But I might offer a few tips, once I get a look-see..."

"Captain," said T'Moy. "You better see this."

T'Moy was over at the streetward end of the roof's walkway. He was pointing when Pyke stepped over to join him. "Look who just showed up."

Down in the dark, wet street, a couple of figures were standing in an alleyway along from Tiselio Flett's shop, staying out of the Shylan guards' view while keeping a watch on the shopfront. There wasn't much light but a glow coming from a rear alleyside window was enough to reveal that one of the pair was bare-headed and tall with a straight-backed posture, and the other was burly, had a slight stoop and wore a cap.

"Old friends," Pyke muttered.

"You remember them?"

"Oh aye, Pazzyk's got a good memory for faces and beatings." Pyke quickly reminded the others of how he'd been ambushed by a pair of thugs in the Nightmarket the previous day, and how T'Moy had intervened and gave them a hiding. "This pair of gougers tried to get the key to Dalyak's lockbooth off me. My guess is they're hired muscle working for another party keen to get their mitts on the blood-poison…" He glanced down at the street. "…wait, they're on the move. And they're staging a speak-and-peek, the cheeky maggots!"

"What are they doing?" said Vrass.

"Watch—one of them goes up to ask the guards something weird or stupid or both while his mate ambles along the other side of the road, scoping out the setup and how the guards react." He turned to the others. "I really need to know who they're working for 'cos it feels like I'm flying blind, not knowing who's coming at us next. T'Moy, can you and Klane get yourselves back down to the street and tail those skaggers, see where it leads you, all right? Myself, Vrass and Mistress Flett are off to the offices of Inox & Throm for a bit of undercover book retrieval! Regroup at the western entrance of Haxy Nightmarket by noon.

"Right, everyone knows what they're doing? Good, let's get rolling!"

CHAPTER THIRTEEN

Pyke, on the planet Ong, in the wreck of the *Mighty Defender*, in the Steel Forest

"Okay," said Pyke. "Let's go over this again."

"It's pretty straightforward," Dervla said testily. "Raven and a couple of her bootlicking louts are—"

"Barricaded inside a storage room and they've rigged the barrier with charges, aye, I get that. It's this whole thing with these Steel Forest factions, this three-way alliance of minds." He turned to Shogrel. "What is it that they actually want in exchange for my crew? Help me out here."

Shogrel, whose head was a dense interweave of rootlets and tendrils, smiled. Her eyes, ears, nose and mouth nestled solidly in the dark brown tangly mesh—her eyes were a clear limpid blue and tiny leaves wreathed her amused lips.

"They are exhibiting graduations of anger and resolve, Captain. The Blackmoss is the most moderate of the three, willing to discuss options, open to negotiations up to a point. The Thornscar has the largest most battle-ready forces and while it is ready for conflict it is not rash and will consider other suggestions. The Biteclaws, however, are a belligerent collective with a small force of very hostile stabwings, acid-worms and spring-hooks, hostile and barely kept in check. Those three allies have much to disagree upon but they are all determined to hold onto your people until you yourselves take action against the ravagers who have been cornered and trapped."

"You've told them that Raven is our enemy, too, yes?" Pyke said. "And that we're short on weapons and ammunition?"

"The alliance is not interested in the nuance of such concepts," Shogrel said. "They distrust all intruders, you as much as the others. And if you do not intervene they are determined to use your crewmen in the battle to come!"

Pyke stared in disbelief. "How is that even possible?"

"Are these allies going to hypnotise our people somehow?" said Dervla. "Fry their brains with those hallucinogens?"

Shogrel looked uncertain. "I am not aware of any such intentions, but I know that your friends have been enfolded."

"*Enfolded?*" said Pyke, feeling the heat of his temper.

"There is a variety of tendril plant which looks like a heap of roots and strands and which can move around by itself," Shogrel said. "They can also be used to move or carry things from place to place. From what the allies have said, I think that your friends have each been enfolded in a tendril plant, up to their shoulders. In this way they could be made to walk along to where the ravagers are and attack the barrier shielding them."

Pyke gritted his teeth. "And Raven will just fire back with all she has and enjoy every shot and blast. Cannon fodder, that's what my men are..."

His words trailed off and he clenched his fists as his fury threatened to boil over. And a good portion of that anger was directed at himself for not preparing properly before entering the wreck. *But how could I have known that Ustril would ditch us like that? If my distrust had been cranked up to full strength I would have insisted on everyone taking a breather mask with them, but that Sendrukan was just so helpful, so bloody useful...*

The others were regarding his moment of rage, Shogrel with

a kind of curious, studied demeanour, Kref with his usual stoic patience, and Dervla—she gave a slight, knowing smile and a half-shrug that fitted right in with what was going through his head. He breathed in deep and exhaled through pursed lips as if letting off steam. Then he turned back to Shogrel.

"Tell the three mental allies that I'll go along with their demands, but I have a counter-proposal—before me and my comrades take up arms in this spat of theirs, I want a chance to talk to Raven, to persuade her to surrender peacefully, as long as yer allies agree to eject her from the wreck, with no further harm on either side." He laughed dryly. "And if she won't go along with it, at least we get a close-quarters look at her setup. Then we fall back, get tooled up for the scrap and try to figure out how to break through their defences without getting killed. Let's see what they say to that."

"I will present your proposal to them," Shogrel said and strode away.

They kicked their heels and otherwise rested in a small, creeper-lined, moss-floored recess for nearly half an hour before Shogrel returned. They all got to their feet in anticipation as she came up to Pyke.

"They have agreed to your plan," she said. "Now you must all follow me. This area is very tense—my flowers will keep you safe as long as you walk where I walk."

In single file they started along the foliage-hung passageway, Shogrel then Pyke, Dervla, and Kref bringing up the rear. The bioluminescence here was all yellows and oranges but it soon altered hue, darkening to coppery shades, sheens of ochre, with rubescent tints coming through the leafy bushes and masses of vine.

Ahead was a T-junction and as they drew near Shogrel spoke:

"Here we shall be turning right. Whatever else you see you must not move towards it!"

Pyke had no one to exchange looks with, only the woven-root

back of Shogrel's head, and a suspicion forming in his thoughts. As they approached the junction the coppery colours darkened to brass and the rubescence turned into scarlet. Violent leaves on dark blue bines fringed the opening on the left, guarded by buzzing clusters of insects. Drawing level, Pyke and the others couldn't help staring into the side passage as one, but Pyke was the first to see them—Ancil and Moleg, encased in brown and green tangles, for all the world looking like bizarre spacesuits, with heads and shoulders clear of it. He heard Dervla curse, and moved into a sidestepping movement as he tried to keep Kref in view.

"Kref, listen to me!"

The big Henkayan had stopped dead in his tracks, staring at the two entrapped crewmen.

"Kref, they're safe, ould son! We'll do what we have to do, get it done, and come back for them."

Pyke could hear the pitch of the insects' buzzing growing sharper and louder as they started to perceive Kref as a threat. Then the big man turned and resumed following Pyke and the others, his craggy face dark with anger. Shogrel had slowed her progress after turning that corner but with Kref back on course she picked up the pace.

"That was the gathering place of the Blackmoss host that we just passed," she stated. "I was not permitted to warn you of what you would see. The alliance insisted that you be tested."

Pyke snarled wordlessly. "Any more surprises in store?"

"They insisted on other things," she said stiffly.

It wasn't long before they found out what those things were. After leaving Ancil and Moleg behind, they turned left, continued for about seven or eight paces where Shogrel halted near the opening to a side passage on the left.

"This is the gathering place for the Thornscar host," she said. "Only Captain Pyke may proceed beyond this point—the others must remain here until his return."

"Nice, very nice," said Pyke. "So now they get to double their number of hostages! Sorry, that's not going to happen..."

"The Thornscar mind made a vow that Kref and Dervla will not be enfolded like the other crewmen." Shogrel looked unhappy in this situation but Pyke didn't have much sympathy for her.

"The captain must go on to make contact with the wreckers alone," she went on. "This, too, is seen as a test."

Pyke exhaled through gritted teeth and glanced back at the corridor they'd just walked along. He ran fingers through his grimy hair and grabbed a handful, feeling the pain of tugged hair-roots. *Bastards have me over a barrel—hope Raven's in a listening mood.*

He looked round at Dervla and Kref. "You okay with this?"

Kref nodded and Dervla gave a shrug. "We're kinda stuck for alternatives."

He gave a single nod, and turned to Shogrel. "Fine, I'll do it. I'll go on alone."

"Your crew-people will not come to any harm," she said.

"I really hope so, because otherwise my remarkable and judicious cool will most certainly be lost and king-hell mayhem may ensue!" He glanced at Dervla. "I'll need a white flag—got anything that'll do?"

After a minute or so he found himself holding a scavenged plastic strut from which hung a gauzy yellow and blue scarf which Dervla had grudgingly extracted from an inside pocket.

"What're you carrying this about for?" he had said.

"Eh? You're saying that I shouldn't have nice things?"

Immediately sensing that he was on thin ice, he had accepted the scarf with pleasantries and a deflecting smile. Now he held it balanced on his shoulder as Shogrel led him past another side passage on the right.

"Do not pause, Captain, do not even slow your pace. This is where the Biteclaw collective has amassed its forces—they are dangerous and unpredictable."

Pyke's sideways glimpse lasted just a couple of seconds but what he saw was unnerving—spiked vines writhing and lashing at each other, dog-sized things with six legs and fanged jaws that took up about three-quarters of their heads, small red and yellow insects hovering around large purple and crimson ones out of whose backs jutted fuming pipes...

Then they were past, and Pyke found himself prickling with sweat, from scalp to neck. *Talk about nightmare horrors...*

A short distance further on, the corridor opened onto an open area, what might have served as a space for communal meetings or some recreational activity. Now it really was like a forest, clumps of creeper-wound bushes, veils of shiny leaves trailing from thick roots half embedded in the ceiling, a proliferation of plants and foliage that obscured the other side from view. There was also a strong smell of burned metal and plastic and smoke haze drifting through the branches.

"A battle between the destroyers and the local aware-minds took place here not long ago," Shogrel said. "One of the lesser consciousnesses was completely obliterated when the invaders lined one particular corridor with charges and set them off when Thornscar units came after them in pursuit. As I said, feelings are very tense." She pointed diagonally through the masses of growth. "The intruders' lair lies in that direction. I am to wait here and witness the outcome."

Pyke gave a bleak smile and set off into the smoky vegetation.

Moments later he realised that Shogrel hadn't been exaggerating—the place had most certainly been a battleground, and a vicious one at that. The bio luminescent plants had suffered badly but there were enough glowing tubers and berry clusters to light up some grim details. A profusion of dead creatures were scattered everywhere, scorched, riddled with holes, or torn to pieces. Explosions had blown big hollows in the intertwining growth, left charred gouges in both ceiling and deck, often through to the deck's base material. Some heaps of ripped-aside foliage still smouldered amid the shadows.

Raven and her goons must have been carrying around some fierce amount of heavy firepower, he thought. *But they must be out of ammo, otherwise they wouldn't be holed up. Could be a good sign.*

A section of mossy, creeper-patterned wall appeared through a gap in the leafy curtains. Pyke pushed through, turned left around a trunk-like mass of twisted roots and flowering tendrils, and there was a door in the corner, barely visible through a barrier constructed from wall panels, ceiling support struts and deck tiles, all lashed together with vines. The top quarter of the doorway was covered by a double layer of wire mesh, behind which an indistinct figure watched as he drew near. He got to within about three paces when a gruff voice spoke.

"Okay, Pyke, that's far enough—that's it, stand there, no closer."

"That you, Vayne?"

"Certainly is—what's your business?"

"Ach, you know, I was in the neighbourhood, thought I'd drop by, pay my respects. Raven about?"

No reply for a second or two, then:

"Why, Brannan, that's a lovely scarf you have there—really brings out the colour of your eyes!"

Dervla would be so pleased, he thought, resolving to leave this part of the exchange out of any subsequent account of this moment.

"Oh, yer too kind," he said, keeping his voice as affable and nonchalant as he could. "So, how are you doing in there? From outside, kinda looks like you've got yourselves into a bit of a fix…"

"Now, Brannan, you of all people should know that appearances can be deceptive. Me and the boys, we're just getting settled in, doing a few home improvements, choosing ourselves some new carpets and furniture, the usual sort of thing. Soon we'll have the place looking just the way we like it!"

Someone inside sniggered, and Pyke's bad-juju instinct began tingling. Raven had as good a line of bravado as anyone Pyke knew, but he could tell when she was and was not putting up a front. And right now she didn't sound like someone who was playing with a weak hand.

"Ah, right, cooked meals, clean sheets and soft pillows—I never pictured you hankering after home comforts, somehow."

"Never too late in life to acquire new experiences, as our mutual friend has revealed."

Pyke grinned without humour. It was that body-jacking piece of evilware called the Legacy that she was referring to.

"Some experiences aren't worth having, Raven," he said. "Like the one that's coming your way very shortly if we can't reach a sane agreement here..."

"Love it when you talk dirty, Bran, always have."

"I've seen what these forest...minds have in store for you," he said. "Armies of creatures, insects, and plants and things in between! And I don't even think you've got the ordnance to hold them off this time!"

"I do believe I detected a note of anxiety and concern in your voice, Brannan, dearest!" She laughed. "This is such a crazy place. Who would ever expect to find a fully functioning, self-contained ecology inside a millennia-old spacewreck? It's a miracle of imagination and engineering, and so delicately balanced! We humans don't see it or sense it, for the most part, but everything in this place is swimming in a stew of pheromones, y'know, airborne chemical trigger and signifiers..."

"Never knew that eco-biochemistry was yer thing."

"We struck lucky, dear Bran, received some free advice from a local source, even got sent a care package."

"Raven, you're just digging the hole deeper..."

"Ever spent any time in the Glow, Bran?"

He ground his teeth, holding onto patience. "Some—not so much, recently."

"I never could get the point of cyberreality, y'know?" she said. "Wirelife lacks reality's meaty risk, but I have seen all the glories of its flesh and spectacle. And I was always fascinated at how the Glow's social trend ecology reacts to new databombs tailored to the psyche-profiles of the key flock leaders—it's incredible, they leap in and everyone else swarms in after them, it's a sight, I tell ya..."

A horrible suspicion was starting to form in Pyke's thoughts. "What are you planning, Raven? What are you up to?"

"Planning is done, complete, Bran, and it's happening right now—listen!"

There, as they both fell silent, he heard a hum that was growing louder and sharper. He snarled.

"You're right out of your mind, Raven! Why do this to yourself?"

"Better run, Brannan—you don't want to be around when rage meets rage!"

He glanced over his shoulder—the buzzing was loud and angry and the advance wave of yellow and red insects surged into view. No more time. He lunged away from the barricaded door, panic driving him on a mad search for a way out. Through half-burned foliage he fought to another corner of this over-grown death trap, actually stumbling into a shadowy passage half hidden by bushes. That was when Pyke heard the first explosion, a deep and definite thud that made him pause and glance back. Something whined through the bushy screen and found him then, something tiny that stung him in the face. He cursed loudly and batted wildly around him, then resumed his speedy retreat. But less than a minute later he could feel a tingling lethargy starting to steal through his legs and arms, as if he was struggling to move through clinging treacle. His vision started to lose definition, objects left trails of blurred images and the edges of his sight became grey and murky.

The second explosion was by far the loudest, a thunderous crash that was accompanied by a bright flash, which made his already feeble vision swim. The deck shook underfoot and Pyke nearly lost his frail balance. *Holy crap, there must have been a lot more charges on that barricade than I saw from the outside. No one could live through that.*

Eager to evade any stragglers, he kept staggering along the darkened corridor, following his wavering instinct for seeking the spot furthest from the chaos. But there was no escaping the chemical turbulence riptiding through his mind.

When he came to a side passage and found Van Graes standing there, drinking from a delicate teacup, Pyke knew that his brain had become a playpen for hallucinogens.

"I'm a man of considerable patience, Captain," said Van Graes. "But these delays and pavane-sidetracks simply will not do. Only the tarantella will carry you onto the crux of it all..."

"Mr. Van G, you must excuse me but..."

"Or perhaps a bolero would suffice..." Van Graes' eyes widened as Pyke stumbled past. "Of course!—it's actually an eightsome reel!"

Assailed by waves of dizziness, he carried on down the corridor of shadows, his own low laughter sounding like the stretched-out, echoing groans of something trapped at the bottom of an ocean. At some point he paused to sit and rest near another side passage. He opened his eyes and saw the Construct drone Rensik hovering there, a boxy rhomboid shape floating about four feet off the deck.

"My standing advice to new recruits at the Garden of the Machines is this—you can always rely on sweaty organics to screw a situation into previously untheorised levels of utter mayhem."

"You're just a snarking bucket of bolts," Pyke said. "What the frack do you know about real damn living, eh?"

The drone made a noise halfway between contempt and hilarity and glided off down the side corridor. Angered by this, Pyke leaned back against the wall as he strove to get to his feet, but once he'd made it he didn't feel like chasing after the obnoxious drone, so he staggered on.

It was his own face that awaited him at the next corridor junction—well, half of it was his face while the other half was a nightmare fusion of something demonic and a profusion of embedded mech parts, rods and gears. The body was indistinctly human and swathed in black folds that shifted and dissolved and reappeared.

The Legacy. Had to be.

Pyke halted and braced himself against the corridor corner, then leaned in close to that horrible amalgam and said, "Boo!"

That merged face regarded him casually, a deranged grin married to a reptilian jaw full of shiny fangs.

"I'm having such fun with the other you," the Legacy said. "I provide the maze and he obligingly scurries through it. It's delightful…"

"Everyone should have a hobby," said Pyke. He knew that these visions were no more than fanciful mirages released from his inner mind by the venomous insect bite. But there was something unsettlingly visceral about them, as if tenuous dream glimpses had been given a kind of will and presence all their own.

"The power that organic minds have to delude themselves is satisfyingly multifaceted," said the Legacy. "And there are so many controls, triggers, buttons, levers—control the stage, control the lighting, control the mood, control the script. Oh, how you will caper for me in the end, when the tide comes in!"

Glistening rods and cogs worked away in the dark side of that face as it grinned abominably, ichor lubricating movements within gashes in reptilian skin. It was ghastly and hideous and nauseating…

Just a second, I've never seen this before. It's nothing but a gaudy, hammy boogieman dredged up from some wretched corner of the old brainbox with the aim of giving me a fit of the horrors! Well, screw that!

Pyke sneered at the apparition, sidestepped and stumbled past it, heading down the side passage.

"Be seeing you, Bran!" sang out the thing that wasn't there.

"Not if I see you first, ya festering skagmonger!" he muttered.

No more illusions crawled out to pester him but his senses felt no more inclined to return to normal. Past curtains of webby moss and hanging masses of springy, rusty coils he tripped, trudged and toiled. He then realised that there were glowing lights shining through the creeper-webbed wall to his left. Seeing what looked like a patch of something transparent, Pyke started tearing aside foliage and viny growth, uncovering a broad if stained and streaked window. On the other side, much of the view was obscured by a cluster of pipes and cables that went from deck to ceiling and by stacks of containers. But there was a two-foot gap which gave him an unimpeded view of the room beyond and its depressingly familiar occupants.

Tall panels of dusty readouts lined the back wall, arrays of curious screens showing icons glowing orange and yellow. In the middle of the room was an oblong dais with a control station and a tall, heavy, bolted-down frame: the frame had a strange eye-like crosspiece about a metre wide. Two of Raven's goons were working on the back-wall instrumentation while Raven herself was bent over the dais control station, adjusting, comparing, tweaking. Then she straightened and said something to her lackeys—they reached up to higher ranks of controls and flipped a series of switches. At once many of the glowing readouts brightened then their hues began changing, reds to orange to yellow, yellows into green.

At the same time, a faint nimbus appeared around the

framework, gauzy and flickering. As the wall indicators turned green in greater numbers the nimbus strengthened and brightened, especially around the eye-shaped crosspiece. Suddenly the eye was filled with a silvery radiance that flowed downwards like a curtain. A moment later the lids of the eye parted, one half rising, one descending, till the flowing silver radiance stretched the full length of the frame. With a jolt, Pyke realised he was looking at a portal of some kind. What was it Shogrel had said? There was a gate that led to the ship's bridge, and something about a mosaic?

He felt powerless as Raven and her underlings gathered on the dais and moved in a line towards the radiant portal, with Raven bringing up the rear. The first approached the silvery doorway, stepped through and a moment later returned. There was some nodding of heads and happy smiles then, after some punching of keys on the control panel, they lined up again.

A test run, Pyke thought, leaning heavily on the window, feeling a wave of shivering and cold sweat. Anger and frustration spiked as Raven approached the portal. He slammed his fist against the window. It was made of some thick, heavy-duty material which barely quivered under the impact but the noise of it was enough to catch Raven's attention. She was less than a yard from the silvery portal when she looked round and saw Pyke glaring at her. She smiled, nodded and laughed, all in silence. For a moment they just looked at each other, then she took out a small object like an eyepiece attached to a small box the size of his thumb and held it up—and he realised that it had to be the Angular Eye. He mimed that he had his unwavering gaze on her. She put away the device, shook her fist at him in mock rage, then extended her middle finger, still laughing. Then she turned back to the portal, stepped through and was gone.

Pyke stared at the now vacant room, emotions swinging between burning animosity and a sneaking, undeniable admiration. *Crazier than a bag o' cats but, damn, that was an exit!*

A wave of dizziness struck, making him lean heavily against the window while it passed. And now Raven had skipped away, still in possession of the Angular Eye, and was therefore almost certainly close to tracking down Van Graes' treasure hoard. He had to find the others and guide them back to this bloody room—only he had no clue where he or the others actually were, and the mind-bending venom still pumping around his veins was not helping in the least. He glanced at his wrists and the brace-lets of blue flowers gifted to him by Shogrel. After Raven set off that pheromone bomb (if that's what it was) the bracelets and the circlet seemed to lose their protective qualities so perhaps a more direct method was required.

All the tiny blue flowers—each and every one of them—still had his face, eyes closed and smiling, each and every one. *Which just adds another layer of weird to this whole crazy carnival*, he thought as he raised his wrists to his nose and strenuously inhaled.

Ten minutes later he was creeping along a blue-green corridor hung with broad, dark leaves whose undersides gave off a warm golden glow. Having backtracked from the portal room window, he had gone searching for any passage that might lead him back to where the whole business with the alliance had started. It was a task he now felt equal to—the hefty snort from the blue flowers had swiftly cleared his head, heightened his senses and kicked up his metabolism. He was ready for action and impatient to find the others.

The corridor reached a crossroads—the passages ahead and to either side were all brighter and more open, glows pulsing out amber and rose tints. He was about to cross over to the opening directly ahead when he heard a hiss then a voice calling his name in a hoarse whisper. Turning, he saw Ancil's head poking out from a mass of vegetation.

"Chief! Found you at last—quick, this way."

Ancil beckoned, moving backwards into shadows as Pyke approached. Behind the screen of foliage was a door that led into a long, narrow space, like a tunnel through stacks of ancient containers overgrown and almost buried by layers of roots and tendrils. It was humid and dark, apart from a few clusters of glowing tubers, crusty looking lumps giving off yellow and blue radiance.

"Down here, Chief."

Ancil was at the tunnel's end, sitting with legs dangling inside an open hatch in the deck.

"What happened after I went off to waste my time yacking with Raven?" Pyke asked as he followed Ancil down into a cramped maintenance conduit lit by small recessed lamps.

"Even now I'm not sure," Ancil said. "We heard a sound like the angriest bees ever, then those root-suits opened up and let us go—they were so itchy! I wanted to scratch just about everywhere, then Dervla and Kref showed up with the weird weavey, twiggy woman who said we had to move out of the area due to a sneak scent attack, I think is what she said...so we were hurrying off and Derv was explaining that you'd gone to negotiate with that psycho Raven, when we heard something detonate..."

"The first bomb," said Pyke. "She must have used some of their charges to blow a hole in the cabin wall or deck so that they were out and away when the second one went off—but how did they know where to place those charges?"

The maintenance conduit sloped down and turned to the right. Ancil pointed out a couple of jutting, severed pipes as he sidled past them.

"Yeah, so the first bomb explodes, me and Kref look at each other then we turned and started running back to where we saw you walking, before, then round a coupla corners, dodged a squadron of those big insects zooming past us. There was an unholy racket of buzzing and snarling going on somewhere in that big hall when we got there, although there was too much foliage and bushes to see. And that was when the second bomb went off—whoa, made the first look like a firecracker! Big orange flash, then a deafening crash. Shockwave knocked us both down, I was on the ground, my ears were ringing, smoke and fire right across the hall, and we started coughing. Everything was blown apart and burning—insects, creatures, the forest, it was all on fire.

"Next thing, Dervla was there, Kref, too, dragging us both away, which was lucky 'cos I was out of it. We met up with the others and followed the friendly twig-lady to a corridor that was as green as those flares I used to have. Derv talked it over with Shogrel—that's her name! Well, she was really arguing—Shogrel said it was too dangerous to wait for you, and Derv said buggered if we were gonna bail on you like that! So they decided that keeping eyes on the main junctions was the best use of the crew, and here we are!"

Pyke laughed. "So, where are we off to now?"

"A between-decks access hub," Ancil said. "Originally a kind of spares and parts cache, but it's more like a glorified closet."

He wasn't joking. It really was like a walk-in cupboard with storage lockers spaced around the walls. There was enough room for three people standing, and another couple sitting on work surfaces, so long as they didn't mind jostling against each other.

"Here he is!" Ancil said to Shogrel who was watching their arrival. "Managed to stop him marching back into all kinds of mayhem. Where's Moleg?"

"As soon as I sensed the captain's warding flowers I sent him to bring Dervla and Kref back to join us." She looked closely at Pyke. "Have you inhaled the flowers' essence?"

He nodded. "Got bitten by some hellish buzzing vermin, and my head was swimming and it was tough to walk in a straight line. So I decided I had nothing to lose, jammed your flowers into my beak and gave a mighty snort." He couldn't help grinning. "Cleared my head in no time, and I was able to push on..."

Just then footsteps drew near and Dervla appeared in the other doorway, along with Moleg. Shuffling round each other, hugs and handclasps were exchanged, with Kref stretching one arm past Moleg's shoulder to give a thumbs-up.

"Dunno how you made it out of that inferno, Chief," said the big man. "But I somehow knew you'd be okay."

"I wasn't quite as sure as Kref," said Dervla. "But here you are, back in one piece, against the odds—again. Maybe now we can get ourselves out of this place and back to the ship. Shogrel knows of a safe route..."

"Hold on a second," Pyke said. "We can't go back—we still have work to do."

"Bran, that entire hall and everything in it was incinerated," Dervla said. "There's no way Raven and her mates could have survived. It's a minor miracle that you're standing here..."

"Yes, I made it out and, sad to say, so did they!" He smiled at their sceptical looks. "Two explosions, right? Well, the first one was to knock a hole in the room's bulkhead, opening the way to an access tunnel like these ones, and as soon as they had scurried off like the rats that they are, Boom! goes bomb number two, the big one. Anything closer than ten metres—like all those insects and critters—is dead from the blast, anything closer than twenty metres gets burned to a crisp."

Ancil was nodding. "I reckon it was a couple of big thermite charges seasoned with half a kilo of monorupt—that would do it."

"Speculation," said Dervla. "If you were running for your life, how could you know that they survived?"

"I know 'cos I saw them," and he went on to give an account of what happened after his lucky escape from Raven's blast zone, while glossing over his hallucinogenic encounters. When he got to the description of the room with the portal, Shogrel straightened up and gave him her full attention. When he got to the part where Raven and her goons departed via the silvery portal she was starting to look positively worried.

"So, in a nutshell, the Queen of Crazy and her henchlings have hopped on out of this wreck, taking the Angular Eye with them so she's still chasing after the treasure. Question is, where does that weird doorway lead to?" He looked at Shogrel. "You said something about a gate that opened a path to the ship's bridge. Is that what I saw?"

All eyes were on Shogrel now and for a moment she seemed to be frozen in a kind of a fugue with her eyes staring off to the side. Then she returned her gaze to Pyke and nodded.

"I do not doubt the truth of what you say. These other intruders are of a most savage and destructive nature and if they have crossed into the bridge the repercussions may be unpredictable." She look around at them all. "Even catastrophic. They have to be stopped but it cannot be me who takes up the pursuit—I would not survive a day away from the Steel Forest. Without its sustenance I would wither and die." She turned to Dervla. "I knew you were anticipating your departure with great longing, but would you perform this service for us? Track down these savages and neutralise their actions?"

"It's gonna mean jumping right back into harm's way again," Pyke said. "But if we can take them down and get back the Eye and any other goodies they've acquired, at least we'll have something to barter with when we meet up with Van Graes, and we might not come out of this flat broke."

Now everyone's attention was on Dervla. She was immediately displeased.

"Don't go putting all this on my shoulders," she said.

Pyke shrugged. "We can just throw in the towel and walk away, if you feel we should."

"If *I* feel we should?" She folded her arms. "I'm not the only one with an opinion, y'know. Kref, what d'ye think we should do? Cut our losses or go after Raven to get the Angular Eye back?"

A bemused Kref furrowed his brow and scratched his stubbly neck. "Erm, if we pack it in and go back to the *Scarabus*, do we still get paid?"

"Uh-huh, that's the question," said Pyke. "We've not been in touch with Van Graes for a while…"

"Some of Raven's hired thugs were after him," Dervla said. "Is he even still alive?"

"If we got back the Angular Eye and any artefacts," Moleg said, "we'd have something that Van Graes might pay well for, but if he's dead we'd be bound to find a buyer, or we could use it ourselves to make track-and-find jobs a lot easier. If we leave empty-handed…"

Moleg left the sentence unfinished but Pyke knew everyone else would be completing it unhappily in their own heads.

"Empty-handed ain't my preference," said Ancil. "Besides, Raven and her uglies have been a major source of our woes and it's long past time they got their arses kicked!"

"Can't disagree with you, Ans," said Kref.

"Nope, neither can I," said Dervla. "My instinct says quit now but you're right—we've come this far and we deserve some kind of payout."

Pyke felt relieved at this consensus, yet still with an undercurrent of disquiet—Dervla seldom talked about instincts or hunches. He turned to Shogrel.

"Okay, we're back in the game. What's the best way to that room with the portal?"

It turned out that there were two routes, the first a short one which passed very close to the territory of the Thornscar sentience, an area still in upheaval in the aftermath of the firestorm and therefore presenting undoubted risks. The other route was longer and entailed a descent to the deck below, bypassing the worst hazards, traversing several corridors to stairs that would bring them up quite near their destination. With recent events still fresh in their thoughts, the latter option was an easy choice. Shogrel checked all the blue flower wards she'd given them before they set off on a tense trudge along corridors so shadowy and sombre that the usual banter and chitchat was muted. During the journey through the deck below, Shogrel paused several times to consult with local denizens. Sometimes she seemed to be communing with a hanging clump of blooms or a bower made from vines and weeds, other times she conversed with faces half buried in wall creeper.

Not quite an hour later they finally reached a creaking, half-rusted stairway which led back up. As he reached the top step Pyke immediately noticed the strong smell of smoke. Shogrel, who'd gone on ahead, pointed to a door just visible among the undergrowth.

"That leads to the chamber of the Gate," she said. "Wait within and take some rest—I will join you shortly."

Then she went back to muttering to a cluster of crystalline berries that seemed to respond with gleams and glints of light.

The sliding door was jammed part-way open—there were handprints on the grimy surface so it looked as if Raven's louts had tried to force it shut. Kref wedged himself in the gap, raised a leg and shoved it all the way open, accompanied by grating, cracking sounds. Pyke grinned and slapped the Henkayan on the shoulder as he followed him in.

The room was unchanged from the last time, its gloom relieved only by the glowing displays spread out across the back wall. Orange and ruby indicators pulsed slowly, radiant glows mingling eerily, like the inside of a heart. As the others wandered around, Pyke glanced at the grubby, half-obstructed window, for a moment seeing himself trapped behind it, staring and gesticulating...

"So how does this apparatus work?" said Dervla who was up on the dais, peering closely at the portal framework.

"Raven and her underscum twiddled and tinkered and messed around with these dials and the controls until the lamps all started turning green." Pyke pointed at the tall framework with its eye-like crosspiece. "Then that opened up and became a silvery doorway so they walked through it. Once they were gone, the door shut itself down and all the lights went back to orange and red again. That's all I saw."

Before Dervla could respond in her own unmistakable fashion, Shogrel arrived, nodded approvingly at the fully open door then went straight over to the dais.

"We're all hoping that you know how this works," Dervla said. "We're not too keen on experimenting with the buttons..."

"I will be able to retrieve the precepts from the didactikon in a few moments," Shogrel said. "But first there is some news, of a kind, which I should make you aware of. After consulting with several forest minds, I can confirm that one other person passed through this room several hours ago, before the killer savages came."

Pyke and Dervla stared at each other.

"Ustril?" she said.

"Has to be." Pyke walked over, speaking to Shogrel. "Anyone say what this traveller looked like?"

"Tall but cloaked and hooded," said Shogrel. "A few thought that the Wanderer had returned, an intruder with similar characteristics who had frequented parts of the forest a while ago and had become friendly with some of our denizens, learning a few of our languages. But this traveller only used a handful of basic phrases on the way here."

She broke off and went over to a spot near the door where some forest growth had worked its way through cracks in the wall panels. She pushed her hands deep into the foliage and some of the tendrils that made up the tight weave of her arms uncoiled and unfurled themselves in order to entwine with the forest growth's bines and stems. Dervla looked puzzled but Pyke had an idea about what was going on. After a long moment Shogrel withdrew her arms from the bushy tangle and declared, "I now possess the precepts for operating the Gate!"

Kref and Ancil grinned and laughed and bumped fists. Moleg merely looked thoughtful, one eyebrow raised. Dervla, though, slumped down to sit on the edge of the dais, shoulders sagging wearily while Shogrel busied herself at the control panels behind her.

"Really," she said as Pyke joined her, "I need about three nights' sleep and at least five showers. Can't remember the last time I felt this burned..."

Pyke didn't have to try hard sorting through his memories. He snapped his fingers. "Ixazil!"

Dervla smiled and groaned at the same time. "Oh, the Planet of the Crazy Canyons!—and being chased around by those insane Kazorka Clans..."

"All trying to get their hands on the stupid bloody statuette thing..."

"Stupid bloody *talking* statuette thing..." She punched his shoulder. "Damn it, you made me remember..."

They shared a companionable silence for a minute or so until Pyke, nagged by thoughts of what lay ahead, said, "If or when we run into Ustril, how do you want to play it?"

Dervla glanced at him. "She's on a mission to get her hands on ancient Arraveki artefacts so she can bribe her way out of exile. And given how she treated me I doubt that she'll be in any mood to be reasonable. I mean, with her alliance with this AI we don't know what to expect if—when we do make it to the bridge."

Thoughts of the Legacy made Pyke grimace with anger. "That Legacy thing—wherever that abomination came from, it was the product of a diseased mind."

"That reminds me..." Dervla took out the leather case containing the crystal shard and held it out. "I don't want to carry it around any more."

Wordlessly he nodded, took it back and slipped it inside his jacket. He understood. The crystal seemed to have a presence that induced an undercurrent of unease at the back of your thoughts. *The toxic drip-drip reminder that weird and nasty shit was going on inside it.*

Just then Kref and Ancil let out cheers as the back wall's indicators began shading into the green. As before the frame's eye-shaped crosspiece turned silver then divided and widened lengthways until it became a shimmering doorway.

"Now, you must hurry," said Shogrel. "The Gate's functions have been prepared for five persons and no more. The transits must begin now otherwise the Gate will return to its state of abeyance."

"All righty!" Pyke said, rubbing his hands. "Moleg, you're up first, then Kref, then Ancil, Derv, and lastly myself. Go to it!"

As Moleg casually walked round from the back wall and climbed the dais steps, Pyke turned to Shogrel.

"You've been a bit reticent about where this portal ends up," he said. "You say it goes to the bridge section of the ancient ship, and I heard you say something about a mosaic once. Is there anything useful you can tell us before we go?"

The forest guide regarded him, her pure blue eyes gazing into his. "You are possessed of a great strength which you mask, even from yourself. Beyond the Gate lies the Mosaic—it will show you many things from pasts that never were, presents which will seek to waylay you, and futures made for ensnaring hearts and minds."

"You've been there?"

Shogrel nodded but would say no more as she glanced past him. He turned to see Dervla waiting at the rushing silvery portal.

"You must pass through," Shogrel told her. "No pausing—and you, Captain, I urge you to track down the destroyers and put an end to their malice."

"I'm pretty sure that there will be some intemperate language and homicidal gunplay somewhere along the line!"

Shogrel's expression was somewhat sad as she hurried him up to the dais and steered him towards the silver door. He glanced over one shoulder, thinking to offer some kind of farewell, then he realised that she wasn't slowing down! Figuring out that he only had one option, he lunged forward through the portal with one long, blind stride...

...which came down on a soft surface at the same time as a shaft of brilliant sunlight caught him full in the face. Both feet were through but he staggered, momentarily dazzled, and walked a couple of swaying paces before the hands of his crew grabbed and steadied him.

"Careful, Chief."

"Watch yer step, sand's very soft..."

"Get a grip, there."

"Ah...are you Pyke?"

A stranger's voice, gruff and resolved. The crew drew aside to reveal an elderly man with a craggy face, grey muttonchop whiskers and piercing pale eyes. He wore a soft-brim hat that was as battered and decrepit as the layers of coat and cloak that he tugged about himself with an air of self-importance.

"That's me!" said Pyke.

"Captain Brannan Pyke?"

"That's also me!"

"Well, sir—you're late!"

CHAPTER FOURTEEN

Pyke, in the Crystal Simulation,
the City of Granah

The city offices of Inox & Throm turned out to be a sizeable compound surrounded by an imposing brick wall which had but a single large entrance. Guard towers flanked solid, iron-riveted gates and the frontage was well lit by oil lamps. Large posters with curled corners adorned the brickwork to either side, their details indistinct in the lamplight. The walls were about fifteen feet high (and higher than the neighbouring properties) and although there seemed to be no broken glass or spikes along the top, Pyke did hear the barking of dogs from within. Much was still in darkness, even though dawn's first grey streaks were spreading from the far hills.

"If we're going over the wall," said Vrass, "we'll need ropes and grapples."

"Over that wall?" said Pyke. "Dicey. Combine that with us not knowing the actual layout inside, although we do know they have dogs?"

Vrass frowned. "Dogs?"

"Er, small domesticated pack animals?" Pyke said. "Also good for attacking and hunting…"

"Ah, like *shukans*!"

Pyke shrugged. "Probably. Anyway, they'll be a major problem for any over-the-wall lark—or we could bluff our way in, claim we're from the city sewage department and that there's a serious leak somewhere under their building..."

"Or we're from the Imperial barracks," Vrass said, "and we're here to talk about a new wagon contract!"

The sound of quiet laughter interrupted their brainstorming. Pyke smiled at the third member of their company, Tiselio Flett, whose millinery shop was so recently occupied by a squad of Shylan Shield guards.

"I'm sorry, do you have something to add, Tiselio? We're only too happy to share the planning!"

"Oh, those were fine notions, most certainly," she said. "But what we *could* do is go round to the rear, into the back court of the adjacent disused warehouse, find the underwell room and the door to the old aquasluice which linked both properties back when Inox & Throm owned them both."

Pyke nodded, smiling. "Leads right inside that compound, you say?"

"Leads right into the main building, down in the sub-basement."

"You're a remarkable lady, Mistress Flett."

"I wasn't always a seamstress!"

Morning had definitely arrived by the time they reached the warehouse back-court entrance. The brick-walled lanes were filthy with mud washed down from streets further uphill and the three of them were soon splashed and streaked from the knees down. As they gathered by a heavy, iron-strapped door in the warehouse's rear wall, Tiselio Flett raised a finger to her lips.

"Need to listen out for the caretaker doing his rounds." She pressed an ear to the door as they all tried to stay quiet. Then she nodded. "Can hear him heading away."

She took a short-bladed knife from her bodice and began scraping away the mortar from around one particular brick set next to the door frame at waist level. The mortar was unusually soft, as if it wasn't really bonded in at all. Pyke smiled in appreciation as she carefully levered the brick out, exposing a dark hole. She then slipped her arm in up to the elbow, fumbled for a moment until there was a muffled knock, like a rock falling on a paving stone. She reached in further, face grimacing with concentration, then Pyke heard the latch slide free and the door suddenly opened, just a crack. The others gave thumbs-up signs and Tiselio offered a mock curtsey.

Quickly, quietly, they moved into the back court which, while narrow, was as long as the warehouse was broad. An arched brick tunnel led off to one side, behind two outbuildings. Once the secret bricks had been replaced, Tiselio led them along the tunnel to a rusted and lockless iron gate then down mossy winding steps. By now candle stubs had been lit, shedding enough light to see the dankness and slimy growths patching the walls. At the foot of the stairs was another door which Tiselio glared at, kicked and cursed.

"Has the lock been changed?"

"Changed the lock, changed the door, too!" she said.

Pyke squinted at the door in the flickering light. It seemed very solid. "We could both try kicking it in..."

Tiselio Flett snorted and extracted a couple of pins from her hair. They glinted in the candlelight as she crouched down and got to work on the lock. Watching her, Pyke was again struck by how naturalistic and autonomous the non-player characters were in the Legacy's simulation. For all that they were following scripted behaviour models, it was difficult not to think of them as real people.

"You're a woman of considerable talents," he said. "Why *did* you become a seamstress?"

"I actually find stitchwork more of a challenge," she said. "And the result is something beautiful made by my hands...can you bring that candle in closer? Thank you."

"Retired," Pyke said. "But still keeping your skills sharp... ah, nice, well done!"

Tiselio got to her feet, returning the pins to her hair. The door to the aquasluice stood open.

"No more breaking and entering," she said. "Now I teach others to break and enter."

"And your brother?"

"Hidalio was the best," she said, smile fading. "But he was too trusting. Let's go."

The aquasluice was basically a brick-lined conduit tall enough to walk along at a stoop, with a large circular pipe running along one side. The pipe had thick glass windows at regular intervals, which revealed that there was no water passing along it, for all that the cramped passage was damp and fetid. When Pyke mentioned this Tiselio chuckled knowingly.

"Piped fresh water is a luxury to be paid for," she said. "When the warehouse was closed down, someone remembered to shut off the water."

"A city full of poor people usually turns out to have plenty of ruthless merchants," Vrass said.

Tiselio gave the Gomedran an amused look. "Pretty rebellious talk for a boxhouse guard."

Vrass laughed. "We can probably assume that I am now an ex-boxhouse employee."

"How far till we're inside the main building?" said Pyke.

"We're practically underneath it now," said Tiselio. "This branch ends in an outbuilding where the main supply junction is. But—the engineer who built these conduits was petrified of drowning, so the story goes, and he had emergency exits installed, purely for his own use. They were supposed to have been bricked up or filled in, but someone else's negligence is our good fortune."

Following Tiselio along the aquasluice, they slowed when she came to a halt at an odd recess in the brickwork. She ran her fingers along the edges of the recess then kicked the base of it and shoved the centre. Pyke had heard the hollow thud then laughed when the secret door shifted inwards about half an inch before she pushed it sideways. Candlelight revealed steep iron steps.

"Craftily made," Pyke said. "Leads up to the sub-basement, you said?"

"Yes—the Inox & Throm building has two large basements for storing all their wagon parts, and several sub-basements for holding ballastings." Tiselio gave a sly smile. "A nice quiet corner of the least used section of the building. A good place to start from, wouldn't you say?"

"I continue to be impressed."

She nodded, started up the stairs, got to the third step and stopped. Unhurriedly she half turned and glanced back at Pyke and Vrass with an odd look in her face. Right away Pyke knew something was very, very wrong.

"You okay?"

Still on the third step, she turned fully round and looked down at them both with an unsettling smile.

"Never better, Captain," she said. "The players are playing, the twists are turning, and the plan is unfolding on schedule."

Vrass was suddenly anxious. "Captain, I think it's…"

"The Legacy, yes, I know." Pyke felt a crawling fear in his gut but wasn't about to lose his cool in front of this dark presence. "So—this a social call or is it business?"

"A bit of both. It amuses me from time to time to bestow upon my apprentices both the pleasure of my company and certain fragments of wisdom to aid them in their trials."

The Legacy, alien AI and overseer of the Granah simulation, author of this narrative puzzle they were compelled to undertake, composer of what was in the end a prison. As it talked, Tiselio's voice deepened and gained additional tonal layers, basso and strangled whisper. When the Legacy spoke, it spoke like a nightmare.

"Well, we are right in the middle of something," said Pyke. "But I'm sure we can do a workaround after we take a break, just for you."

Unhurriedly, the Legacy came back down the steps to get nearer to the both of them. With Tiselio's face, it gave a smiling sneer.

"Well, that is most obliging of you."

Turning to Vrass it uttered a bestial snarl that made him back away, while at the same time grabbing Pyke's upper arm in an abnormally strong grip.

In an instant Pyke was no longer in an underground tunnel but in a high and breezy place, overlooking the entirety of Granah. He staggered sideways, fetched up against a cold stone buttress, trying to regain his sense of balance as he contemplated the edge of the roof just a couple of feet away.

"Quite a piece of work, don't you think?"

The Legacy, still in possession of Tiselio Flett's form, was standing near the edge, one foot resting on the low coping wall, one arm leaning on the raised thigh. The Legacy was gazing out at the city and glancing sideways at Pyke.

"Pretty outstanding detail," Pyke said, trying to relax, straightening away from the buttress. "Must've taken you a long time to get it right..."

"You can't pump me for information," the Legacy said. "I only tell you what I want you to know. As for this, I had nothing to do with the basic structures—all I attended to was, well, everything else. Over the considerable stretches of time available to me, I was able to mine for a great wealth of data, both within and without the boundaries of our crystal world." The Legacy moved back from the coping wall and strolled off along a narrow walkway around the top of this building, whatever it was.

"This way," it said, then commenced a visual tour of the Imperial city.

Ahead, in the direction they were walking, was the south-eastern quarter of Granah. It spread across rising ground that sloped towards the broad promontory on which the Imperial fortress and palace were built. Smooth-dressed walls with elaborate ramparts ringed the palace, and within the walls a series of seven colossal towers also stood guard, each provided with numerous levels where war machines sat ready to send forth a deluge of missiles down onto the heads of any invader foolish enough to take on the might of Granah.

"But that's not likely to happen," said the Legacy. "The northern kingdoms are weak and divided, and the Eastern Autarch has his own factional problems. But then you look at those defences, and keep in mind the size of the empire's armies and their state of readiness. Is it all simple paranoia or do the Emperor and his closest advisers know something that no one else suspects?"

The Legacy had led him to a wider section of the roof and looking back he could see how the converging peaks of the roof structures leaned in towards a single slender tower.

"Is there a story behind the story?" the Legacy went on. "Is there a game behind the game?"

That caught his attention—hadn't the drone Rensik said something very similar back on the Isle of Candles? Pyke wanted to unleash every shred of scorn and mocking hate he possessed upon this toxic data-vermin but that might have unintended consequences. *Stick to the hail-fellow-well-met bollocks*, he thought. *Noisy but safe.*

"Ah, so you've been having a gab with my ould pal Rensik!" he said, plastering on a fake grin. "How is the rusty old box o' bolts doing, anyway?"

"Making valuable contributions to our ongoing grand project," the Legacy said. "You know, I had thought that your machine friend might be a source of difficulty and disruption but it has turned out to be quite the asset. I'll need to acquire more of these Construct drones, when the time is right..."

So, Pyke thought, *the message is—"forget about getting any help from your mechanical pal, sucker. He works for me now!"*

"If you're happy with how it's all going," Pyke said, "why pull me—well, us—out when we were getting close to some vital clues?"

"There's a saying I've heard used by various sentient races down the centuries," the Legacy said. "The Human version goes, 'No plan survives contact with the enemy.' So—even though I've designed this simulation down to the most minute detail and planned and cross-planned to allow for a river of cause-chains and effect waves, I still like to shake up the ceremony, kick the board, jam an axe-handle into the gears!"

Using Tiselio Flett's face, it grinned wildly as it explained its motives. It occurred to Pyke that despite all the body-jacking, jumping in and out of various victims, the Legacy still didn't really understand how facial expressions were supposed to work.

"Does that mean you're the enemy of your own plan...or something?" he said.

"Of my plan's predictability," the Legacy said.

Pyke made a dubious face. "Predictable to you, maybe."

The Legacy laughed, a high staccato overlaid with that deep synthetic echo—it was a hideous sound.

"In actual fact, the multiplexity of the simulation's narrative weave leads to recombinations that surprise even me." It looked round and pointed to a cluster of mansions and villas on a hill north of the city square. "There's the Blue Mound, home to the empire's rich, privileged and powerful—oddly, not all of those three qualities coincide. The richest man in Granah is a sad widower with no offspring and no immediate family relatives. Three of the empire's most illustrious families are also three of its most debt-ridden noble families—their debts combined almost rival that of the crown. Creditors and usurers gather round them like carrion eaters, except that those noble families are like corpses that never quite die."

The outstretched pointing hand swept to a section of dark roofs over by the eastern wall. "The Jirtha livestock yards, named for the tributary that still runs under the roads and pens, carrying manure and offal down to join with the Worroth." The pointing finger swung all the way round to the west, where the crenelated walls of the garrison dominated the streets surrounding it. "The mighty garrison of Granah!—in whose shadow the delightful fleshpots of Redlamp Town ply their lecherous trade." The Legacy nodded approvingly. "All roads lead through there, sooner or later…"

"The last thing I took you for was a tourist guide," Pyke said. "Consider my mind broadened and my existence, such as it is, enriched. Now, can I get back to the story? Which you went to so much trouble to provide for us?"

The Legacy's eyes widened happily. "Indeed, it is past time for this interlude to draw to a close. Your absence introduces new variables, such that it truly saddens me to have to tell you that one of your companions may soon find themselves in dire peril, caught in tragic peril…"

"Okay, fine—send us back to those tunnels and we'll sort out this poison plot."

"Send you back to the tunnels?" The Legacy's smile was infuriating. "Now where is the challenge in that?"

Gritting teeth, and clenching fists hidden in coat pockets, Pyke gazed at the ground for a moment rather than look at that demented look in Tiselio's eyes. Shaking his head he began to laugh, the rueful, bitter laugh of someone who sees the outlines of the trap. The Legacy was laughing, too, a sound that sawed on the senses.

"I get it," he said. "It's like we're getting dumped at the

edge of town but we have to find our way back to the company compound…"

Still the Legacy laughed on, the chortle of someone enjoying their own joke immensely.

"Well, you see, I could either just slip away and leave the pair of you to get back in the game, or I could just whisk Tiselio back to her shop in an eyeblink. Guess which one it's going to be?"

Pyke drew breath to answer but he was suddenly alone on the rooftop.

"Stinking, gouging ratbag!" he shouted.

The only reply was the chill winds sighing around the rooftop stonework of this unknown building.

One thing's for sure, he thought, I can't hang around here. That machine-bastard's not coming back so I'd better find a way down to the streets then get back to Inox & Throm and pray I'm not too late.

The leaden grey of a slow dawn was gradually brightening over the city as its thousands of chimneys began sending smoke trails aloft. Pyke eventually found a narrow, plain door in a corner of the roof. It was almost hidden behind a square pillar which, with three others, supported a platform and a blackened iron framework in which sizeable fires had once burned, going by the charring. Beyond the door was a landing leading to a square spiral stairway descending to the bottom of the building's central tower. Grey light leaked through square windows arranged in columns around otherwise sheer walls, also built in a square. The place felt like it had been empty for years—the steps were littered with curled dry leaves, spotted with bird droppings and adorned with the odd feather. And it had been a temple, going by the large metal symbols hanging on chains and ropes all the way down and anchored to crossbeams high above.

The symbols, wrought in iron mostly, were all roughly a yard across and were combinations of circle, triangle and hexagon.

There were three main varieties, where each symbol was the outermost and contained the other two. Further down he started noticing dangling rope ends that looked burned and cut. It grew shadowy as he descended and it wasn't until he was just a few flights from the bottom that he could make out a layer of fallen symbols lying around a huge stone altar directly beneath. He wondered what the priesthood of this temple had done to have been closed down, then suffer a bit of light arson.

All the windows on the ground floor were shuttered apart from one which hung in splintered pieces, but before he could climb up and exit the temple a bird flew in suddenly. Uttering rasping squawks, it flapped noisily around the centre, wheeling among the lowest of the hanging symbols and swooping down over the altar. Pyke's immediate irritation was foreshortened by a curious familiarity, then his recollection of the mechanical bird that had stared at him from its cage as they'd carted Vrass through Haxy Nightmarket. And that noise it made while flapping did sound like a mechanical clattering interspersed with a tiny chorus of squeaks.

"Pyke!" it squawked. "Pyke! Found you at last!"

"Who the hell…" he muttered. Then realisation bloomed. "Rensik! Har-har, knew you'd defy the odds somehow. Can't keep a good Construct drone down…"

"Not exactly," said the mechanical bird as it flew down to perch on the edge of the altar. "I'm Rensik's residual, RK1."

"Huh, I see." Pyke wandered over and leaned on the altar with both elbows. "Where's Rensik?"

"My progenitor, sad to report, remains engaged under the Legacy's authority, in some unknown capacity."

"So how did you get from the Isle of Candles to the great city of Granah? And where the kack have you been all this time?"

"My answer deals with both questions—I divided the mono-hub of my dataplex among the cascade-shells of yourself and the others just before the transfer to this simulation began."

"A cascade-shell? What's that?"

"A vague and inadequate description of your digital presence, your autonomous node," said RK1. "The fractal complexity of your data structure—and that of the other three—is a magnitude of sophistication beyond my own, even beyond my progenitor. So there were plenty of crevices in which to conceal a segment of my own code. However, these portions of myself remained locked until your original personas were triggered by those statues—only after Vrass underwent his revival could my autocompile knit my parts together."

Pyke nodded and sighed. "We've been pretty busy since then—in case you hadn't noticed."

"I did notice, and I, too, have been busy," said RK1, its beak clicking. "One benefit of having passed through by stealth is that the regulatory systems of the simulation don't entirely see me—I'm not in the index so my clandestine activities go largely undetected."

"Sounds like a handy trick to have."

"I've already put it to good use." The mechanical bird paused, blinked its beady eyes. "I've seen what lies outside the tiny pocket that contains the simulations."

"Back on the Isle of Candles you said something about the crystal shard containing para-dimensional storage on a vast scale..."

"If anything I underestimated the potential capacity. I think I also said that its exterior physical properties derived from a dimensional lattice woven from space-time-space. However, there's something else for you to consider—the crystal shard you've been carrying around is just one of three fragments of a single object."

Pyke stared, surprised. "There's another two crystal shards? What are they all pieces of?"

"Something quite staggering," said RK1. "Going by what my investigations revealed."

Pyke had to ask. "So, what did you see? What actually does lie outside this simulation?"

"Star systems," said RK1. "Suns with orbiting planets—the stars were darkened orbs and the planets were darker still."

"How many are there?"

"It is not easy to estimate—this was only a snapshot glimpse, the best I could obtain without triggering boundary alerts and making myself a target for the killswitches, and other anti-intruder heuristals. An analysis of the snapshot results in a count of between fifty-seven and sixty-four visible star systems—however, I require far more detailed scans of the area in order to arrive at an accurate summary."

"That's probably not about to happen anytime soon, I'm guessing," said Pyke. "Still, sixty-odd weird, dark star systems…" He frowned. "Could all that be a projection, a simulation as well?"

"Insufficient data for a decently probable answer," RK1 said. "Such a notion prompts the inevitable question of why anyone would simulate dozens of systems with planets and suns? And what is the connection with this simulation? At any rate, I am preparing for another foray to the boundary. Gathering a larger measure of information should be revealing—especially now that we know that your shard is only one out of three."

"Okay, I'm willing to wait for that," Pyke said. "But right now I could do with a tasty slab of clandestine crypto-help."

"What did you have in mind?"

"You know about this intrigue that me and the others are caught up in…"

"You are all trying to find a blood-poison vial which could be used to send the Emperor mad—yes, I've been following the narrative update stream."

Pyke chuckled. "So do you know where it is, and who's really plotting against the Emperor?"

RK1 clacked its bill and shook its squeaky head. "No, I don't have access to uncommitted plot strands."

"Skag it!—I've found out that something's happening in Red-lamp Town but I've no idea what or who's involved."

"Was that from a hint dropped by our lord and master?"

"Heh, you noticed the friendly get-together we had, I assume."

The bird blinked. "I had been following your progress in the Inox & Throm mission and was aiming to pitch in with some help, but then you and the Flett character disappeared. I had to engage in some frantic searching, tracked you down by focusing on your lady friend's vector markers. I only got here after the Legacy's departure so I missed all the fun you had."

"Yeah, it was a right old barrel of laughs." Pyke rested his head on his hand, palm against one eye, fingers splayed across his scalp. He sighed. "I just hope that the outcome of all this gives us some kind of advantage in our dealings with the Legacy..." *But if we're just running around, deluded into thinking that we have self-determination, perhaps we really should drag this out as long as possible, and put off the inevitable...*

He pushed these grim thoughts to the side. "Look, could you just transport me over to Redlamp Town and I'll take it from there?"

"That kind of operation is reserved for ratifiers and above. Sorry. However, I can tell you what's happening to the others right now."

Pyke brightened. "Now we're getting somewhere."

"After you disappeared, Vrass continued as planned, managed to track down Dachour, the dark-clothed retainer, within the Inox & Throm headquarters. Dachour's position is more like a personal steward to Director Inox, and Vrass found an open vent on the wall of a room adjoining Dachour's office. Dachour was awaiting the arrival of an overseer from one of the company's outlying estates, having requested his presence by runner message earlier in the day. That meeting duly took place and now Mr. Dachour and the overseer are on their way to Redlamp Town, with Vrass tailing them."

"What was the meeting about?" Pyke said. "And who is this overseer guy?"

"Sorry, another limitation on my abilities," said RK1. "Conversations are automatically archived into restricted access storage which would be very time-consuming to bypass. And I have to prioritise my meagre rumours at all times."

"Do you know their destination?"

"No, but T'Moy and Klane are already in Redlamp Town."

Pyke was caught between perplexity and surprise. "Hmm, plot threads drawing together, eh? They were supposed to follow those two heavies that jumped me earlier—and look where it's led them!"

"Quite so. I can give you their location if that helps."

"Don't hold back."

"As of this moment, they have just left a tavern called the Hawk and Hammer and they are heading round the corner to... an alehouse called the Bull and Shovel."

"That's what I need," Pyke said. He pushed away from the altar and hurried over to the window with the wrecked shutters and hauled himself up into its deep stone shelf.

"I'll keep tabs on you as best as I can, Captain," said the mechanical bird as it took to the air again, wooden wings clattering. "I still have my information-gathering exercise to complete so I may not be on hand if an emergency arises. Next time we meet I hope to be rather better informed."

"Look forward to it, Arky!" Pyke gave a smiling, finger-to-the-brow salute then squeezed through the window and dropped down into a thankfully deserted back alley. As he reached the corner where the alley opened onto the main road, he noticed a big poster pasted to the smooth stone of the temple wall, and stopped to look. It read:

Praise Vondral! Praise The Divine Dramaturge!

Across the grand stage of our Existence, Vondral the Almighty lays down the scripts of our lives in accordance with the loving discipline of his Will. Heed the prophecies of His Servants! When preordained Dramas seize thy days and nights, curb unpleasant impulses and behave with Piety and Nobility. When confronted with Conflicts and Antagonists, adopt one of the Nine Holy Personae and play out your part with Grace and Acceptance!

Submit To The Sacred Resolution!

The World Is Vondral's!

It took all of Pyke's self-control to throttle his laugh down to a muffled chuckle, half in awe at the Legacy's sheer self-aggrandising egomania, and half in a kind of mocking contempt at it. *He's just not into concealing that towering vanity at all—to him it's some kind of merit badge, something to show what a classy tyrant he is. God, what an arse!* Pyke gave the poster a last withering look then walked on.

It took ten minutes of side-street navigating to reach the garrison's main gate from which a broad road called the Iron Highway ran north-east. West of the highway was Redlamp Town—crossing into it took him under the shadow cast by the garrison walls. Morning was full, bright and breezy across Granah by now but in Redlamp Town street lanterns still glowed in the hazy gloom. Careful questions to a few passers-by who looked like they belonged gave Pyke enough hints to trace his way through the narrow streets and winding lanes to a junction where he found the Bull and Shovel. He was about to cross over when the alehouse door creaked open and out stepped none other than the Chamberlain and his playmate, the Brute.

Pyke pivoted away to conceal his face while striding off downhill. Luckily there was a small hat shop just ahead and when he paused at its window a sideways glance revealed that the thugs were heading in the opposite direction. Relieved, he abandoned the hat shop and hurried back to the junction, wondering where Klane and T'Moy were if they were supposedly tailing those ambushing scumsuckers. And, right on cue, his two companions emerged from the alehouse—T'Moy spotted the two receding hoodlums and said, "There they are," but before he could march off in pursuit Klane grabbed him by the arm and wheeled him round to come face-to-face with Pyke, who Klane had spotted straight away.

"Captain!" T'Moy said. "Those filthy lurkers are heading that way…"

"Yeah, if we move it sharpish we can catch them," said Pyke, but Klane shook his head.

"Following them has been a fruitless exercise, I'm afraid," he said. "They've been in this tavern and another, asking about Sergeant Dalyak…"

"So they got a lead on the mysterious sergeant," Pyke said. "But you think they're not worth following? Why?"

Klane jabbed his thumb at the door they'd just exited. "I had a word with one of the elderly regulars, who was wearing a 25th Brigade badge on his collar, a veteran, you see. He told me that any strangers asking about the 25th or the whereabouts of any old campaigners generally get the runaround treatment—usually the barman sends them onto another bar and tells them to ask for a name in particular, only its a code name that lets the people in the next tavern know to send the nosies on a blue-crow hunt."

Pyke laughed. "No such thing as a blue crow, I'm guessing."

"Just so, Captain. The old veteran told me that they came up with this diversion after their mascot was stolen several years ago by fraudsters working for a rival regiment."

"A mascot?" Pyke said.

"A stuffed and mounted devil-boar," said Klane, with a hint of a smile. "Goes by the name of Magni!"

Pyke and T'Moy stared at Klane for a moment, then started laughing. "A pig!" said Pyke. "A stuffed pig!"

"They said it was a boar..."

"Aye, yes, boar is a kind of pig, sort of." Pyke grinned, shook his head. "Dalyak's journal must have said something bland and terse like, 'I left the vial with Magni,' or some such, and most of the gougers trying to track down this nasty relic think that Magni is a person! Outstanding!"

"Where do we go from here?" said T'Moy. "We seem to have run out of clues."

"Not necessarily, my fine Bargalil friend," Pyke said. "Even if the guardians of Magni were keeping him under wraps, they'd still keep him close at hand for the 25th's anniversaries and celebrations, yeah? So it makes sense to find out where the 25th gathers on special occasions."

T'Moy frowned and Klane didn't seem convinced.

"Well, they know our faces in here and the first one we were in," said the Shyntanil.

"That's why I'll be asking the questions in my new guise as a reporter for the *Worroth Chronicle*!" Pyke said.

"It's the *Worroth Herald*," corrected Klane.

"Okay, fair enough..." Pyke glanced round at the exterior of the Bull and Shovel. It presented a dour façade to any passing custom, small square windows in a stone wall, a low door showing evidence of numerous repairs, and a wooden sign with pictures of both a bull and a shovel that might have been painted by an eight-year old. "What's it like inside?"

"Squalid," said Klane. "Stinking and ill lit."

"Sawdust on the floor?" Pyke said. "Surly barkeep?"

Nods from the other two.

"Any decorations?"

"A moth-eaten bearskin, nailed to the ceiling," Klane said. "Its upside-down, eyeless head is practically the first thing that greets you on entering."

"A bearskin, not a bull's head." Pyke shrugged. "Anything else?"

"Dagger graffiti," said T'Moy. "On every table surface."

"Okay, sounds like your standard dive. What about the place you were in before—what's it called?"

"The Hawk and Hammer."

"What was that like?"

"A palace compared to this one," Klane said. "It's long, like several rooms joined together, well lit, pleasant bar staff, didn't smell as if the walls were painted with vomit."

"Decorations?"

T'Moy nodded. "Paintings, a tapestry, a couple of statuettes in niches, a lot of flags."

"There were a few bits of armour hanging up about the serving counter," said Klane.

"Sounds like a promising candidate for our investigations," Pyke said. "You fellows know the way so lead on."

Klane nodded and set off, pointing to a road that curved up behind the Bull and Shovel. "It's over this rise and down the other side, third on the left."

Walking three abreast as they climbed the hill, Pyke grinned—it was like being in one of those prehistoric vees from Earth's Oilrig Era, all heroic self-assurance and stories that had an ending! He couldn't help putting on a swagger as they neared the crest, wishing he had a lit cheroot wedged into the corner of his mouth so he could take it out from time to time and squint expressively...

The downward slope was just coming into view when Pyke noticed a group of brawny men in similar surcoats striding into view from further round the hill. Their leader he recognised immediately.

"Off the road!" he stage-whispered. "Get to cover!"

Grabbing them by arms and shoulder he hastened them sideways off the road, steering them along a grey, decrepit alleyway which, fortunately, was narrowed here and there by outbuildings, providing plenty of cover if needed. Crouching at the alley's shadowy mouth, Pyke's panicky measures proved not so crucial when the Shylan Shields turned off the hill crescent and tramped off down the very road that the three had themselves been heading for.

Pyke and the others exchanged puzzled frowns.

"There's nothing else for it," said Pyke. "We'll have to tread carefully in their footsteps until we can find the way to this pub."

Nods all round, and collars were raised as they emerged from the alley and cautiously went after the Shields. There were nine of them, Pyke noticed, a heftyish number of those dangerous bruisers and all led by his old friend, Shield-Lance Drask. *Did the Legacy think him up, I wonder, or was he just picked out from a range of possibles, Henchgoon Leader #4, mebbe?*

Their progress was a stop-start series of carefully quiet dashes from alley to doorway to the corner of the occasional wagon parked in the street. As this procession went on, Pyke was still hoping that the Legacy's prophecy was just bluff and an attempt to twist the knife of worry in his gut. So far, though, it seemed that no one had been killed or seriously wounded or ended up in dire peril...although they were yet to hook up with Vrass. Pyke steeled himself—the Gomedran would be okay, he'd be fine.

Then he realised that neither Klane nor T'Moy had bothered to suggest any alternative routes to this inn, the Hawk and Hammer. When he pointed this out, Klane nodded sombrely.

"That is because these fools are actually following the most direct path," he murmured. "And they have not bothered to picket their progress with scouts."

Pyke gave a dry chuckle. "Okay, this should be instructive."

As it turned out, the involvement of the Shylan Shields was more just plain annoying than anything else. When the nine brawny thugs stopped outside the Hawk and Hammer, Pyke and the others kept watch from the cover of an arched entrance back along the road. Shield-Lance Drask and one of his mobsters entered the inn through one of three doors—after a few minutes of heel-kicking, they re-emerged and went into a huddle with the rest. After some muttering, the Shylan gang was on the move again, leaving two of their number standing guard outside the inn. Pyke turned away from the view and leaned against the stone wall of the archway, hands outspread in disbelief.

"And now we need another way in," he said.

"Which there is," said Klane. "The three front doors are not the only entrances—there is a salon-style taproom up on the first floor, accessible from an outside stairway at the rear."

"Good to hear," Pyke said. "And a clear route that avoids us being spotted?"

T'Moy nodded. "My Barlig persona visited this area many times—I can steer us along a safe path."

For once their manoeuvring went without a hitch. Led by T'Moy they backtracked a short distance to a narrow street heavily rutted by delivery wagons, which curved downhill behind the inns and eating houses and music parlours, bringing them out near a main road where there was enough foot traffic and carts for the three of them to cross unnoticed. Then it was just a matter of strolling back uphill via a back lane to the loading court behind the inn, and the stairs that led up to the back door. They tried to look relaxed and unconcerned, as if they did this every day, and when they reached the landing Pyke paused to speak.

"Right, I want the two of you to find a table in one of the side rooms on the ground floor, and make your presence felt, study the surroundings and even the customers, without starting a fight, however. Where do the stairs from upstairs come out in the main bar?"

"One of the side rooms, conveniently," said T'Moy. "When you arrive after us you should turn left—that'll take you past the middle taproom and the serving counters."

"Got it," said Pyke. "I'll get chatting with the regulars, see if I can find out any hints about this mascot, should give us an idea where Vrass may be headed while he's following that guy from Inox & Throm..."

"What if it's here?" said T'Moy. "What if Magni the mascot is being kept here?"

Pyke scratched his ear, smiling. "Then Vrass and the nasties he's tracking will soon be coming through those doors and things around here might get a bit tasty! I can't see us being that lucky, if that's the word—but if you hear me shout 'Fire in the hole!' then you need to come running 'cos I might need some backup, okay? Same goes for the both of you, if you need me to pitch in."

Serious nods were exchanged, hands were shaken in a manly fashion. Then Klane and T'Moy pushed on inside.

Pyke leaned on the landing's handrail, looking out past the smoky trails leaning with the wind over the low roofs back along the alleyway. Even here the dark grey walls of the Imperial garrison jutted into view, yet just past its corner he could make out the tall sandstone tower of the abandoned temple on whose roof he'd recently bandied words with the bastard machine that held all their lives in its toxic grip. He let out an angry sigh then followed the others into the Hawk and Hammer.

There was a small vestibule, low-lit by wall-sconce candles which revealed hooks for coats and racks for other belongings. An elderly Granavian woman seated behind a high desk bowed to him

from the waist as he pushed open the inner door. Perfumed warmth
enveloped him, and on all sides were gauzy veils, silky curtains,
a whiff of alcohol among the fragrance, low murmurs and quiet
laughter. Pyke smiled sardonically at invitations from this or that
unseen observer, shook his head and sought out the exit to the
stairs. The steps were narrow and wooden, and the small space
seemed to amplify every knock and creak as he descended.

Stepping out into the stuffy, beery bar, he immediately felt the
echo of memories from the great many other drinking holes he'd
sampled down the years. Some bars were just anonymous pits
dedicated to taking money and turning sober patrons into blitzed
and bladdered meatsacks fit only to be shown the door. Others,
though, served as waypoint of meeting and debate and the sealing of friendships, bargains and plots, thereby lending them a
certain atmosphere. The Hawk and Hammer was decidedly of
the latter type. This early, it was only about a third full but there
were noisy conversations going on, especially in the low, beam-
ceilinged room off to the right, where Klane and T'Moy were
occupying a square table and drawing useful attention. Pyke
smiled and headed smoothly to the left.

His eyes picked up details as he walked past the middle room;
the flags, most of which still bore streaks of blood and mud while
their tears and rips had been meticulously repaired; an old scroll-
style tapestry on display across the upper part of one of the rear
walls; a few paintings of this or that officer in full dress; and what
appeared to be a full set of armour, painted in rainbow colours
and scattered around the walls. And mounted over one of the
serving counters was a large double-bitted axe, its haft scarred
and worn and its blades notched to hell but clearly polished and
cared for. Pyke wondered how many generations of soldiers had
drunk and gambled and puked and whored their way through this
establishment on the road from barracks to battlefield and back.

Pyke smiled and shook his head. *Odd thought to have,*

considering this whole place is just a part of the Legacy's simu-
lation, designed to give this appearance and impression. Credit
where credit is due, though, this is all superbly done.

Reaching the left-side lounge room, Pyke saw a table with
a solitary townsman sipping from a jack of ale. He bought a
similar jack of something called Peculiar Old Valiant then went
over and sat at the man's table, taking out a fold of paper and a
pencil. He sipped his beer.

"G'morning, citizen," he began. "My name is Brand, er,
Brand Pierce, and I am a scribe for the *Worroth Herald*, and I'm
writing a report, an accolade about the 25th Brigade. Do you
know anything about its history, its battle honours, that kind
of…thing."

The townsman was fairly innocuous looking, had greying hair
and a salt-and-pepper beard, and he was chewing inexpressively
on a chunk of bread while Pyke introduced himself. When Pyke's
words ran dry, the man raised a hand and snapped his fingers. At
once, two beefy bald types (who may as well have had the words
"heavy team" stamped on their foreheads) moved in with their
own stools to sit on either side, glowering at Pyke.

"He interrupting your breakfast, boss?" said one, who was
missing a couple of his front teeth.

"We can help him on his way, boss," said the other, who was
an ear short. "So you can enjoy your vittles in peace."

"Very considerate of you, boys, but I get the feeling that our
guest is a newcomer to our fine establishment."

"Huh," said Gappy. "Another one."

"Don't like nosey new faces," said One-Ear.

The boss laughed a little. "Well, not strictly true—new customers means new revenue…" He reached for Pyke's tankard,
sniffed it, nodded approvingly. "The Valiant, a good brew. Be
sure to try the Oxskull and one of our pies during your stay,
Mr, erm…"

"Pierce, Brand Pierce. And by any chance am I speaking to the manager of this unrivalled tavern?"

"Owner and manager. Jevander Gosk's the name." They shook hands. "Now, Mr. Pierce, why the interest in the 25th?"

"Well, Mr. Gosk, the people are always interested in tales of military life," Pyke said, smile affixed. "My contact at the *Worroth Herald* was very taken by my idea of a series of portraits of the empire's greatest regiments, so here I am commencing with the 25th. Am I right in thinking that the Hawk and Hammer is favoured by 25th troopers?"

Gappy and One-Ear seemed nonplussed by Pyke's apparent indifference to their big fists and the promise of violent pummelling that smouldered in their piggy little eyes, so they looked round at Gosk for whatever came next. The tavern owner rocked his head from side to side with a judicious expression.

"It has been known," he said. "From time to time, when the Brigade is back from a tour of duty."

Pyke saw an amused twinkle in the man's eyes and knew there was a whole lot of ironic understatement going on.

"Of course, I am in fact a veteran of the 25th myself," Gosk went on. "How about yourself? Have you had a spell in uniform, Mr. Pierce?"

Pyke adopted a faraway look and was about to lie outrageously when the weight of a hand suddenly came down on his shoulder.

"Most opportune moment meeting you again like this, Mr. Pazzyk. Might we have a word in private? Outside?"

He only needed to turn his head a little to see the flinty-eyed visage of the Chamberlain smiling unpleasantly down at him. The Brute was at his side, eyes full of cold, raw hate. Pyke glanced quickly back at Mr. Gosk and the other customers, mostly men past youth and heading for middle age. He looked the Chamberlain straight in the eye and in a clear voice said;

"If you think I'm telling you where Magni is, you can think again!"

The mood in the room changed immediately—Pyke could feel the attention of many eyes pressing in on him. Then Gosk cleared his throat.

"Doesn't seem that this gentleman is inclined to accompany you," the tavern owner said. "Perhaps you should withdraw your invitation."

"This is a private matter," said the Chamberlain. "And none of your business."

Gosk's smile was thin and dangerous. "Hardly none—you barge into my tavern, accost one of my customers, interrupt a very promising conversation, and annoy me with your bad manners. You can still leave on your feet—simply cease your harassing and go."

The Chamberlain was unyielding. Pyke could feel those spidery fingers digging into his shoulder, and began glancing about for anything that might be useful in a bar fight.

"I am acting on behalf of important and powerful people," the Chamberlain said with dry, sharp syllables. "You would do well not to obstruct me in the pursuit of my aims."

For a moment no one spoke or moved. Then One-Ear, who sat on Pyke's left, turned to Gosk.

"Shall I obstruct him, boss?"

"Why not?"

Violence erupted. Both One-Ear and Gappy were up from their stools and lunging towards Pyke's erstwhile ambushers in an eyeblink. Pyke felt the Chamberlain's grip vanish from his shoulder, which was all the excuse he needed to roll sideways off his own seat and onto the floor. From that vantage point he saw that the Chamberlain had actually stepped smartly backwards, allowing two of his own hirelings, a couple of street toughs, to move forward. Fists made meaty impacts as burly bruisers collided.

But the Chamberlain and the Brute had been tracking his progress despite all this, and here they came, short cudgels in hand. It looked as if the Brute was going to reach him first and as Pyke, still sprawled on the floor, backed away, his hand encountered something heavy and wooden—the tipped-over stool that One-Ear had been squatting on. Without hesitation he grabbed one of its legs and swung it round to meet his oncoming attacker. Pyke felt cool air brush the side of his face as the Brute's cudgel swept past. Then there was a satisfying jarring in his wrist as the stool smashed the Brute full in the face. There was a grunt, then growling and cursing, accompanied by sprays of blood. The Brute went down snarling with pain and Pyke, still gripping the stool, managed to regain his feet—just as the Chamberlain was knocked back on top of the Brute by one of the barmen, a squat Shylan with fists like big misshapen clumps of muscle studded with knuckles.

The Brute, face spattered with blood, had found a tankard on the floor and now hurled it at the barman; there was a clank as it glanced off his head and a deep, rising roar of rage as he rushed across the taproom. Pyke was about to join in when he felt hands grab his arm and pull him sideways. He hauled back with the stool as he turned, and froze when he saw that it was Tiselio Flett, the seamstress. Impatiently, she dragged him off into the crowd that had gathered to watch the fighting and the gouging.

"What are you doing here?" he said. "I mean, how did you…"

"Get from Inox & Throm to my shop?" She glared at him. "Yes, a good question we can go into later—right now, why are *you* here? I couldn't believe my eyes when I saw you sit down at the boss's table and start babbling away."

"Just following Sergeant Dalyak's clues," Pyke said.

"Clues from that book?" Tiselio said. "You got it back, then."

"Heh, no, not yet…"

"So how can you have any clues to follow?"

He grinned. "It was something that you said which pointed us in the right direction."

She gave him a narrow look. "Magni," she said.

"So you know about the 25th's mascot, then."

"I should do—I've stitched the ugly beast back together several times now..."

Before Pyke could respond, someone barged into him from behind. He and Tiselio were standing by the tavern's rear wall almost at the mid-point, from which they would have had a clear view of the middle door were it not for the noisy, jostling press of drinkers and onlookers. Which was who he at first thought had lurched into him—until he felt the stool wrenched from his grasp. A cap-wearing tough shoved him from the side and he felt something sharp jab into his lower back. Tiselio had a look of terror on her face as a second lout pressed up against her from behind, no doubt with a similar dagger held at her back. Then a third man came forward, dressed in formal black clothing, just as Tiselio described, a man with a rough complexion and merry eyes: Dachour from Inox & Throm. Pyke kept his own face composed—this was the man who had hired Hidalio then murdered him.

"Ah, Mistress Flett, the very person to aid us in our purpose," Dachour said, voice raised to cut through the noise of the fighting which was still going on. "Let us remove ourselves to that alcove, shall we?"

The rear wall sported two alcoves with softer seating and the warm light of oil lamps; they flanked a doorway that led to the kitchens and rearward parts of the tavern. As Pyke and Tiselio were hustled into the left-hand one, he felt a rising sense of trapped panic.

Dammit, where is Vrass? This is not looking good! Time to call for backup...

He breathed in deep but before he could yell out the

codephrase, he heard T'Moy suddenly bawl out above the babble of the crowd. "Fire in the hole!"—which was immediately
followed by the crash of splintering wood and an excited roar
from the tavern crowd (which certainly seemed to have swelled
since he and the others had first arrived). Dachour gave Pyke a
contemptuous look, then levelled a finger at Tiselio.

"I asked you about Magni when I visited your shop not so
long ago," he said. "Since when I have had the opportunity to
gain knowledge of some interesting details about the 25th Brigade, its haunts and those known to be camp followers, after a
fashion. So, I want Magni and who else should I ask but the Brigade's favourite stitchy girl? I would recommend full and frank
answers, my dear—my companions are quite capable of cutting
you in ways too upsetting to contemplate."

"I know nothing of what you speak," Tiselio began, then let
out a stifled cry as the lout twisted her arm.

"Wrong answers are such a waste of my time, Mistress," said
Dachour. "Honesty is your only friend..."

"Lies are her only friend, you kackmonger," said Pyke.

Dachour looked at Pyke with his lip curled. "Do away with
this trash, Breza, upstairs and out the back..."

Pyke could feel the tough's grip on his arms start to ease, however, and the dagger point pull away. A sideways glance revealed
Vrass at his shoulder, grinning widely as he thrust a long knife
into Pyke's hand. Vrass clearly had Breza in his power with a
hidden dagger of his own, but when they looked back round it
was to see Dachour holding Tiselio against his chest, with a short
silvery dagger glinting at her neck. His remaining tough stood
by his side, knife in hand.

"Now let's all be sensible about this," said Dachour. "All I
want is the cursed mascot—one of you get it for me and the lady
goes free and unspoiled." He tightened his grip and pressed the
dagger into the pale skin of her throat. A bead of blood welled.

"All right," snarled Pyke. "Where should I look?"

"It's not on display, so try the back rooms and offices. Hurry now…"

Just then a stooped, grey-haired old man with a stick pushed his way into the alcove, muttering to himself. Dachour stared at him with unconcealed loathing.

"Hey—out! This is a private meeting!"

"Just looking for m'baccy," the oldster whined. "I knows I left it hereabouts…"

"Look, you doddering sack of shit, remove yourself or be removed!"

"…my baccy pouch, 'm sure I left it here…"

Growling under his breath, Dachour looked at his hired thug and motioned his head towards the greyhair. Almost simultaneously the old boy cried out, "There it is!" and pounced at something on the floor behind Dachour's feet. Dachour swore, recoiled in surprise and his dagger jerked away from Tiselio's throat, just an inch or two. The old fellow (who Pyke now realised was Gosk, the tavern owner) shrieked that Dachour was standing on his pouch, just as the goon grabbed him by the collar.

That was when Gosk's walking stick came up and delivered a sharp rap to Dachour's wrist. There was a cry and the dagger fell from nerveless fingers. All at once Tiselio broke free from Dachour's grasp, whirled and gave him a swift kick in the general groin area—he'd shifted enough, however, to avoid the worst of it but the impact still sent him staggering back to sprawl on his backside. At the same time, Pyke and Vrass dived on the goon who was trying to drag Gosk away—a couple of slaps to the side of the head and a knee to the thigh made him let go as he stumbled away, begging for mercy. Dachour was struggling back to his feet, producing a second dagger, to which Gosk responded by reversing his walking stick, which turned out to be a warhammer. Dachour's snarl didn't waver, though his eyes narrowed when Gosk brought the hammer's business end up close to his face.

But before any of them could make the next move, the middle door of the tavern crashed open and a squad of familiar, squat, body-armoured figures filed in, led by Pyke's old sparring partner, Drask.

"Hell's fracking fire!" Pyke growled, moving sideways a little to put taller elements of the crowd between himself and the Shylan Shields.

"Some more friends of yours?" said Gosk.

"Watch," said Vrass. "That ratbag is getting away!..."

Dachour, caught between adversaries and Imperial officials, had sheathed his long dagger, regained his feet and was slipping off into the crowd. Gosk swore floridly and was about to go after him when Shield-Lance Drask shouted for attention:

"In the name of his Imperial Majesty, we are confining all within this tavern while we search for known enemies of the state. The doors are barred!"

In the uproar, Gosk turned to Tiselio. "Quick, get them out through the kitchens." He glanced over his shoulder. "I'll do what I can to delay them."

Pyke muttered his thanks then he and Vrass followed Tiselio through the packed crowd, a sweaty, squeezing progress prolonged by beer-swilling customers bellowing their outrage at each other, forming a seeming barricade of the oblivious. At last they reached the door to the kitchens which opened only after Tiselio had a brief but brusque exchange through its speaking hole. Once through, with the door barred behind them, she made to rush them through the steamy kitchen to the rear loading entrance, but Pyke slowed and held back.

"What are you doing?" she said. "Gosk will do his best but those Shylans will bc through here before too long..."

"I need Magni," he said. "I need that sodding mascot! Will you help me?"

Tiselio looked at him aghast. "Why is it so important?"

"No time for the whole story, so here's the basics—Sergeant Dalyak hid a deadly poison inside it the last time he was in Granah..."

"The world is full of poisons."

"Well, this one is a blood-poison, seemingly designed to infect one man and send him mad, turn him into a murderer."

She raised a hand to her mouth. "Not...the Emperor."

"Got it in one, and that's why we have to get hold of it and destroy it." He held out a hand to her. "Will you help us?"

She glanced at Vrass who nodded, then at Pyke. "If you're lying to me I'll hire someone to do terrible things to you with a bodkin. This way."

She dashed off into the kitchen, forcing them to hurry after her. Pyke considered asking what a bodkin was but instead asked where they were going.

"The attic," she said over her shoulder. "Gosk told me to hide it up there earlier, said there were some dodgy types asking around for it. It's three floors up and more—I hope you've got the lungs for it."

"I'll be fine...." Then he heard Vrass clear his throat.

"I think I should hang back, Captain—maybe sneak back into the tavern and see if the others need a hand, eh?"

"Okay, all right, but try and avoid getting snatched by those gougers, y'hear?"

"You can count on it."

Brief nods of farewell all round before the Gomedran retraced his steps back to the serving door. Then Tiselio led Pyke over to an unremarkable door in the corner of the kitchen which opened to reveal a steep, dingy staircase. *Here we go*, he thought as she leaped up the stairs like a gazelle. Keen not to be left behind, he closed the door and vaulted up after her.

There were two flights between each floor and he was starting to breathe a little heavier by the time they reached the landing between the first and second floors. Each main landing had a narrow hallway with three or four doors, rooms for staff or friends of the owner, Gosk. It was a windowless ascent lit only by slow tallow candles shedding just enough radiance to see by. As they reached the second floor Pyke was about to make some flippant remark about pausing for a rest and calling room service when they heard a muffled crash from downstairs, followed by shouts and cursing. Their pursuers had broken through into the kitchen.

Aching limbs forgotten, they raced up the remaining steps. From the head of the stairs they emerged into an attic full of a jumble of furniture, crates, spinning wheels and an endless selection of domestic detritus.

"I hope you remember where you put it," Pyke said.

"It's not in here," said Tiselio, picking a way through the dusty clutter. "This is just the garret—Gosk keeps really important items in the loft tower."

She paused near the end of the garret and tugged on a length of grubby rope—a section of the raftered ceiling hinged down, along with some wooden steps. From behind them came the clatter of boots climbing the stairs.

"Quick, in you get," Tiselio said. "Magni's sitting on the nearly top shelf—you can get out through the skylight. Now, go! I'll pile some of this junk over at the top of the stairs—hurry!"

Pyke obeyed with alacrity, scrambling up the steep steps. He coughed on disturbed dust, heard the trapdoor shut with a thud below him, then got his first proper look at the loft tower. Well, not so much "tower" as a generously proportioned chimney flue. There was meagre daylight coming from somewhere up high, revealing shadowy levels of shelves crammed with indistinct shapes. He climbed the iron ladder past unmarked boxes, wrapped packages, odd-looking shoes with elevated heels and soles, a group of five puppets adorned with demon-like masks, the innards of what might have been an elaborate clock...until finally he reached the top shelves, lit additionally by grey daylight filtering through the small square panes of a skylight, or, rather, through the layer of grime and birdshit that coated the outer surfaces.

Magni sat on the penultimate shelf, a stuffed wild boar, dyed blue and ugly as sin and not quite as large as he was expecting. It was mounted on a scratched, plain wooden base so he hooked one arm underneath its bristly underbelly, then pushed up another couple of steps to reach the skylight. A simple peg-on-a-string was keeping it shut and with that removed it opened easily and without so much as a creak, proof of regular use. He climbed still further, poking his head and shoulders out into the air and found himself taking in the entire city of Granah in one grand vista. It looked dirty and hazy from the thousands of smoke trails but it was an arresting view nonetheless.

Better shake a leg and do the deed, Pyke thought as he clambered out of the loft tower. *Dig that skaggin' vial out, smash it with my cudgel and that should be it, or it bloody better be!*

He could see now that a weather-beaten shack had been built against the loft tower. Its sloping roof had a flat peak wide enough to allow a person to stand on and get in the correct position to descend the ladder that was bolted to the side of the shack. With his right arm still hooked between the boar's legs, he grabbed the rusty ladder and, rung by rung, climbed down. He was only a couple of rungs from the bottom when he felt a sharp point prod his side, just above the hip. His heart sank as a woman's voice said:

"Stop where you are and do not look around!—now hold out your arm...no time-wasting, you know which arm!"

Pyke grimaced in silence as he extended his right arm so that his captors could remove the stuffed boar. Going by the footsteps there was more than one gathered about him, five, perhaps six.

"Is this it, Commander?" said the same woman.

A moment or two of silence—Pyke could imagine some helmed officer turning the mascot over in his hands, maybe smirking in satisfaction.

But it was a woman's voice that responded.

"That is, just as Dalyak's accomplice described…"

The commander of these rooftop prowlers was a woman… and there was something in her voice, something about it which made Pyke take notice.

"And if we look closely at the neck…see, Lieutenant, the stitches are loose so if I pry them apart, like that—and there it is!"

"Shamaya be praised—the Emperor is saved! Now that we have the vial, what about him? Open his throat and leave the body to the crows?"

"We'll take him back to the palace. The Shylan Shields are sure to round up his companions along with the rest, so with a little prisoner trading we should find out exactly who is behind the conspiracy."

Pyke was pushed up against the side of the shack, face rubbing against wind-worn wood as his hands were tied. But his thoughts were a maddening whirl of doubt and fear and a horrible sequence of might-be, couldn't-be, musn't-be. And as he was pulled back and guided along the flat lower roof, he got his first view of his captors, female fighters in light body armour, leather helms with half-masks, and their officers, both garbed in similar armour although one had silver flashes on her helmet and her shoulder guards.

"Hey, Commander Boss-Lady! We need to…"

The trooper behind cursed and kicked Pyke's legs from under him. He sprawled forward but rolled into it and managed to get up onto his knees.

"We need to talk, Commander, about the conspiracy."

Two troopers jumped him, smacked him in the face as they forced him upright. But the commander had turned and was coming over. Her face below the eyes was also concealed by a dark silk mask.

"What do you have to say?" she said, and every word rang in his ears and in his heart.

"First, let me see your face," he said, feeling inevitability close around him like the jaws of a trap.

"Impertinence *and* lack of respect," said the lieutenant, standing near the commander.

"Yes, but perhaps we can get him to reveal who was paying who…"

The commander pulled aside the silken veil, and for a second Pyke could only stare—then he laughed for a few moments, a raw and broken sound. Then he bellowed out to the sky.

"Legacy! Bastard machine!…Bastard!…Machine!…"

Standing there, dressed in well-used, ribbed armour shaded in dull browns and dark blue, it was, without a doubt, Dervla. Her eyes held not a flicker of recognition, only the angry disgust that a loyal officer would have for an enemy of her Emperor.

"Should have known," she said, replacing the veil. "Gag him and bring him!"

CHAPTER FIFTEEN

Pyke, on the planet Ong, the wreck of the *Mighty Defender*, bridge section

"Late?" Pyke said. "How can I be late for something I know nothing about, in a place I scarcely knew even existed until recently?"

The craggy-faced elderly man made a dismissive gesture. "Hah, that's neither here nor there! When the event-flow determines that you present yourself at the appointed place and time, the onus is upon you, whether you like it or not. Effects will not be denied their causes—understand?"

Pyke tried to get his bearings. It seemed that they'd arrived inside some sandy-floored hollow covered over by an expanse of rusted, crumpled metal. And he'd been plunged into a confrontation with a cryptic octogenarian.

"Oh, yes," said Pyke. "And when I say 'yes,' I mean not in the slightest."

The elderly fellow gave him a pitying look. "I can see that you are still disorientated from the portal translocation. Perhaps you should sit down, relax, enjoy some refreshment—I have filner tea and jomby biscuits if that's to your taste. And in a little while when you are more composed and evenly tempered I shall tell you about the Mosaic and all the other hazards that await you on your way to the bridge."

He turned to go, but paused to speak to Dervla.

"Dervla, dear lady, prevail upon your boisterous captain, encourage in him a serene outlook and a courteous disposition..."

"Wait," she said. "You know my name?"

The old man smiled and smoothed his muttonchop whiskers. "Why, yes, I know all your names." He gazed around at the others, naming them one by one:

"Ancil the Cunning..."

"That's the name, don't wear it out!"

"Kref the Strong..."

"Hey, that's good—Chief, can I keep that name?"

"...and Moleg the Mysterious."

"Occasionally," said Moleg. "What do we call you?"

The old man placed one hand theatrically upon his chest. "I have the honour to be Avrax Hokajil, senior conjecturist and inventor." He gave a slight but gracious bow. "I'll be over in my hut when you're ready to talk, Captain."

So saying, he strolled away, across the humped sandy area to a makeshift hut patched together from a wide variety of scavenged panels and tiles. This low-rent residence leaned against the inside of what Pyke now realised was the inside of a wreck's hull. A canted section of bulkhead formed another wall to this strange cave, and oddly enough had a single door in it to which a foot-worn path led.

"Pretty strange, eh?" said Dervla.

Pyke nodded. "And he definitely said something about us heading to the bridge?"

"He certainly did."

Pyke sat down on a mound of sand and tried to take stock. When they began all this, they were merely chasing down some treasures for their employer, Van Graes, but then Raven and her henchlings got involved, along with the weird crystal that was both a mind-trap and part of some ancient, mysterious device. Then the Sendrukan, Ustril, helped them find the drive section among the trackless wastes, but then she went off on her own mad mission, leaving the rest of them to stagger and muddle through the mind-bending corridors of the Steel Forest. Finding the transfer portal let them move directly from the Steel Forest to here—but what and when was "here," exactly?

Going by what little their Steel Forest guide, Shogrel, had said, they had at last reached the forward section of the ancient Arraveyne ship, the *Mighty Defender*. She had also mentioned this mosaic and that it would show them pasts that never happened and presents and futures that couldn't be trusted. Pyke wasn't sure of the twig-creature's meaning but the place they'd now arrived at did not look promising.

This hollow was partially inside the wreck of the forward section. Wind-blown sand had worked its way in over the many, many centuries since the ancient vessel ended up here. An uneven gap on one side let in a wide shaft of dazzling morning sunlight, even though it had been after dark when they entered the drive section. The ceiling of this rusty shelter was fairly high and looked like a section of decking which had somehow survived the destructive forces of the crash-landing. Perhaps this had once been a standby hold down near the underhull. Frowning, Pyke got to his feet, strode over to the sunny exit, stepped out and walked a few paces away to take a look. Ancil followed, one hand shielding his eyes from the sun.

"Some sight, uh, Chief?"

"Yeah—it's literally a gigantic heap of junk!"

The forward/bridge section had clearly turned over laterally during its descent—the upper decks were crushed and mangled, gouged and hammered into compacted ruin. But at some point during that long crash-landing the prow must have struck a rocky outcrop with a glancing blow that flipped it right-side up again, only for the careering, battered ship to pile into another set of jagged rocks with enough remaining impetus to split open the bridge section from nose to over half the wreck's length. And here and there on the surviving surface plating he could see the same embedded pieces of large metal coil.

"It must have been hellish," Pyke said.

"Couldn't have been any survivors," said Ancil.

"Hang on—Shogrel talked about a handful of people who came back from this mosaic thing...yeah, I remember now."

"Our new friend back there seems to know that we're heading up to the bridge," said Ancil with a grin. "And he's dead set on seeing we get some tutoring on the subject! Me, I'm just looking at *that*..."

He held out a hand to indicate the splayed remains of the ancient wreck's prow, a twisted wind-worn skeleton of girders and remnant hull plates, its lower segment buried in the sand.

Pyke was more sombre. "Let's not forget about Raven and her thugs—they came through that portal before us, so they gotta be lurking around somewhere like the skag-sucking gougers that they are."

Ancil suddenly looked nervous. "Perhaps we should get back inside, eh? Maybe Mr. Hokajil knows where they went."

Ancil was quick to head back to the entrance, and Pyke followed in his footsteps, smiling. Pausing on the threshold, he glanced left and right and listened intently. There was only the sighing of the desert breeze passing through the skeletal wreckage. He ducked back inside, lit, he realised, by reflective panels feeding brightness in from outside using smaller gaps in the decrepit hull here and there. Dervla came over and handed him a white beaker of some hot drink—it smelled almost like coffee but tasted of berry fruit. Every mouthful made Pyke shudder.

"Everyone's tried to get Mr. Hokajil to say what he's doing here," she said. "He hints that he has an important job, but then he just steers the conversation onto some enormously amusing incident from his long-vanished youth. Ancil's having a go now…"

"So how enormously amusing are his anecdotes?"

"Not even *slightly* amusing."

"Well, I guess it's time to do my famous impersonation of a composed and evenly tempered sod, then…"

As they approached, Moleg held out a plate of what had to be jomby biscuits. They were oval, pale grey and impressed with a smiley face symbol. Pyke ate two—the first one tasted like chocolate, rum and raisin with a hint of freshly cut grass; the second tasted of savoury chicken while his olfactory sense received a jolt of factory-fresh plastics.

"Interesting, aren't they, Captain?" said Avrax Hokajil.

"Never had jomby biscuits before," Pyke said. "Might never try them again, but that's another line on the ould bucket list ticked, eh?"

"Ah, a collector of the outré and the non-usual, I see!" Hokajil beamed approvingly.

"Talking of non-usual happenings," Pyke said. "Another group of people, unpleasant types, went through the gateway ahead of us—were you around when they got here?"

"You are, of course, referring to Madam Raven Kaligari and her two advisers, I believe."

"The very same—where did they go to from here?"

"Why, I sent them on their way to the bridge." Hokajil fumbled through a couple of coat layers and from an inner pocket produced a small device shaped like half an egg with a cluster of tiny glowing buttons. Still smiling at Pyke, he held it up and pressed one of the controls—and the solitary door in the undamaged stretch of bulkhead a few yards away smoothly slid open. Curious glances turned into puzzled expressions then bafflement as everyone gravitated over to get a better look. The sight was undeniable—beyond the doorway a well-lit ship's corridor stretched away for a good fifteen metres or so, with other doors visible at regular intervals. Pyke let out an astonished laugh.

"I've been outside," he told Hokajil. "There should only be smashed-up metal and rock on the other side of that door..."

Hokajil nodded. "And there is!—and there isn't." All eyes were on the strange old man. "What you are now seeing is a corridor stretching into the *Mighty Defender* some time before it separated into its composite sections then plummeting out of orbit to crash-land on the planet Ong!"

Dervla squinted at him suspiciously over a pointed finger. "You said you were an inventor—what was your speciality?"

"Temporal mechanisms and anomalies."

"And that's how that corridor looked thousands and thousands of years ago?" she said.

Hokajil's eyes twinkled with outright enjoyment. "Effects, dear lady—effects will not be denied their causes."

Pyke smiled and shook his head. *This is where I get to stretch my poor battered brain cells to their limits one more time.*

"You all know our names, Mr. H," Pyke said. "And you've been going on about my journey to the bridge, so it seems to me that you're not from around these parts—I mean, you might even be from the future, maybe..."

"Your future," Hokajil said. "Except that it's in the past."

Pyke and Dervla looked at each other and burst out laughing, quickly followed by the others. Hokajil just chuckled.

"Allow me to explain," he said. "My presence aboard the *Mighty Defender of the Arraveyne Heart* did not come about voluntarily. I was abducted by agents in the employ of that cabal of dukes who were determined to escape the inevitable destruction of the Imperial homeworld. Oh, I *did* wish to leave, just not in that company."

Another member of the original crew! Pyke thought. *This should be a tale and a half...*

Hokajil's eyes grew distant with recollection. "The cabal had devoted a great deal of expense and effort over the preceding weeks, trying to persuade cultural exponents and leading conjecturists to join their grand project. But come the final days, civil authority was disintegrating, allowing the cabal free rein to maraud and ransack at will.

"The *Mighty Defender*'s captain was also Duke Strano, the brains of the cabal's project—once I was installed by my abductors in an executive cabin, he promised that I would have free movement around the greater bridge territory after launch, on condition that I would immediately resume my efforts to build a temporal manipulator."

"A time machine?" said Pyke.

"Somewhat, although not in the sense of a vehicle. My entronetic device can take an optimum area and push it back into the past—I call it the time-thrower, a label that is easier to understand, I feel."

Pyke gave him a quizzical look then glanced pointedly over at the open door with its impossible corridor.

"I know, Captain, I know how it must seem to you that time is a limited resource—in some ways it is, in other ways it's a malleable plaything.

"So, there I was, irrevocably settled aboard Duke Strano's immense starship, speeding away as catastrophe overwhelmed the Imperial homeworld. The truth was that I'd already arrived at a working prototype of the time-thrower before my capture so I imagined that I had all the time I needed to perfect it, oh, the irony! As it turns out, we were more than two days out from the destroyed Imperium, and traversing what you call hyperspace, when we first encountered the Damaugra."

By now everyone had wandered over to Hokajil's hut for hot drink refills from a dispenser which looked like three chrome cubes sat atop each other at odd angles.

"This thing that attacked the *Defender*," said Pyke. "Is it a creature or some kind of vessel?"

Hokajil's eyes widened dramatically. "The Damaugra does not conceal its nature—it is a rare hyperspace denizen but unmistakable once detected. It is a huge tangle of exotic metallic tendrils and coils driven by some kind of sentience, possibly animal-like, and capable of travelling by some unknown motive force. Which also allows it to dive into the lower levels of hyperspace."

"We noticed corroded coils of something embedded in the outer hull, here and on other crashed sections," said Pyke.

"Evidence of the Damaugra's loving embrace," Hokajil said. "The beast seemed to fixate on us, pursuing us with obstinate determination through the eddies and spates of hyperspace. Once, the Duke's weapons officer managed to wing it with a missile from the mid-section battery—it didn't like that. The next time we crossed back into real-space the creature also emerged and came writhing after us. And thus it continued for the next four days or more, a ceaseless game of hunt and flight." Hokajil looked sombre. "It was as if the doom that had claimed the Imperium was relentlessly stalking us, determined that we would share the same fate.

"In contrast, the mood among the thousands of passengers, who were mostly rich and aristocratic, was relaxed and cheerful. Boisterous celebrations were to be found taking place in every section of the *Mighty Defender*, and any suggestions that the ship was in any kind of danger were waved away amid mocking laughter.

"That sense of invulnerability could not last, of course. By the sixth day of this evasion, the *Mighty Defender* had crossed a full quarter of the galaxy. The captain, Duke Strano, had taken the ship down into the lower levels of hyperspace in a radical attempt to finally elude the monster, a ploy which appeared to work. But when we ascended to the topmost layer of hyperspace, through which most vessels travel, the Damaugra was on our trail yet again. It rammed the ship, tore off our weapons even as they were firing and punctured the hull in several places before the pilots were able to shake it off."

All were listening intently now, and Pyke was trying to imagine what it must have been like to pilot such an immense vessel while a monster was chewing its way through the hull.

"So is that when your captain decided to make for the Ong system?" he said.

Hokajil nodded. "The ship's sensor technicians advised the Duke that the Damaugra's physiology would not allow it to come within the gravity well of a planet, and that the *Mighty Defender* should head towards the nearest system with a good selection of worlds. This one has five, including a gas giant which became our immediate destination. But just after we entered the system the Damaugra came out of hyperspace again and hurled itself at us—we had no choice but to alter course towards the nearest planet instead."

Dervla made a sweeping gesture. "The desert planet Ong!"

"Hundreds of thousands of years ago it was not quite so desert covered as it is today," said Hokajil.

"I'm kinda wondering where you are while all this is going on," Pyke said, keeping a smile in place to conceal his growing impatience. Every minute spent gabbing here was another minute of freedom for Raven to work her depraved plans.

"Yes, my apologies—declaiming cannot take the place of conversing." The elderly inventor paused to gather his thoughts. "Well, when we emerged from hyperspace, assaulted by the Damaugra on our way to this system, I was actually on the bridge of the *Mighty Defender*. The illustrious Duke Strano had requested my presence, along with the prototype time-thrower, despite its unaddressed operational flaws. Having read my summary report, he had come up with a plan to use my invention against the monster. It was a very hazardous scheme, almost irrational in the degree of risk it presented." He glanced around him. "Duke Strano proposed that if defeat and destruction by the Damaugra looked inevitable then I would join him in the captain's launch with the time-thrower. We would be ejected from the launch's minibay below the bridge, fly in close to the monster then use my invention to grab pieces of it and cast them into the past!"

Along with the others, Pyke found himself caught up in the drama of Hokajil's account, and almost impressed by the daring of the Duke's plan.

"Did it work?" said Dervla. "Did you get to put the plan into action?"

The old man suddenly looked weary. He settled down into a creaking chair on the hut's little porch and sighed.

"Forgive me—this is the first time I have ever related the entire sorry tale. Raven and her followers had no interest in dialogue, just demanded access to the Mosaic; likewise, Dr. Ustril, while clearly an intellect of substance, was equally impatient to be on her way."

Ancil perked up, and exchanged a look with Pyke.

"The Lieutenant-Doctor," Ancil said. "Did she say anything about us?"

Hokajil shook his head. "She is clearly driven by her purpose, an unflinching intent, just like Madam Kaligari. I've seen them, seen their struggles, their sorrows and successes... sorry, I get ahead of the closing stanzas of my saga. You asked if I carried out the Duke's plan—the answer is no. Our desperate journey to Ong's star system was really one of continuous running battles. After the course change to bring us into Ong's orbit, we had hoped that this would be enough to make the Damaugra veer off and leave us alone. Instead it charged at us again, collided with the ship's mid-section and began crawling along the hull towards the bridge."

Hokajil's eyes filled with horror as he relived the event.

"The *Mighty Defender* reached Ong and its pilots tried to assume a stable orbit but the drives were wrecked and the manoeuvring thrusters hardly functioning. That was when the captain, Duke Strano, ordered the crisis separation protocols to commence, and the whole vast length of the *Mighty Defender* was, section by section, disconnected into its parts. At the same time, the Duke ordered me to follow him into the access conduit to the launch.

"And...I could not. My cowardice prevented it. I was in the grip of powerful terrors, and all I could think of was getting away, surviving, no matter what. So I fled the Duke, fled the bridge, activated the time-thrower, aimed it at a fifty-metre radius area directly before me and cast it twelve hours into the past! I then crossed into it, found everything far calmer, even though we were back in hyperspace, trying to evade the monster. But the fear still had me in its unreasoning grasp—I took elevators, followed corridors until I reached the boundary of the time-zone I'd created, then used the time-thrower again, pushing another area of the forward section even further back into the past.

"At this point an obsession took hold and I became convinced that I could, step by step, shift myself back to the time before the *Mighty Defender* even left the homeworld! So, creating a series of time-zones into the past, I headed steadily aftwards till I reached a door to one of the linkways, the general access corridors that allowed passengers and crew to move easily between the segments of the great vessel. The sensors on my time-thrower, however, told me that another boundary lay beyond the linkway hatch—I was actually looking at the readouts as I opened the hatch and walked through..."

Hokajil brought his hands together in a loud slap. "And I fell on my face, in the sand, right over there!"

Wide eyes followed his pointing finger to a patch of flattened sandy ground just in front of the open door.

"When was this exactly?" Pyke said. "And why? And how?"

By now, Pyke could barely keep the exasperation out of his voice. Hokajil nodded sympathetically.

"The effects of causes range from the seen to the unseen, from known to unknown," he said. "When I activated the time-thrower on the bridge the resonances flow forward in time as well as back—the entire forward section had become separated from the rest of the ship during the Damaugra attack, therefore there was a physical limit to where I could go while inside the time-zones, and a limit to how far back I could create time-zones. When I literally fell out of the most aftwards of them, I was back in my original timeline, although a day or so had passed since the actual crash. Which was, as you see, devastating and catastrophic."

"No survivors?" said Dervla.

"Not here, no, none. The destruction was total, and I soon discovered that there were no supplies, nothing to support life out in the middle of nowhere. But I had to stay alive somehow, so I re-entered the ship…"

"You survived by going back into the past?" said Dervla. "Wasn't that dangerous?"

"Not really. You see, each one of the time-thrown zones exists in its own small loop of time, and is a source of endlessly regenerating resources, food, water, clothing, entertainments and even company. I wondered what to call it—a patchwork, a miscellany, a medley, but settled on Mosaic, which gives the sense of something artistically intended.

"In any event, I was at first distraught at how events had turned out and I began to wonder if there was some way to alter this outcome—only I found out that while all the intermediate zones were cycling through their unchanging slice of the drama, the bridge itself was exactly as I'd left it! When I revisited it, I could see that everything was exactly as it had been, the emergency lighting, the battle stations, the Damaugra clawing outside the viewing window, the captain coming down to enter the embarker alcove that would send him down into the launch, and him yelling at me to follow him..."

Hokajil shivered. His face looked pale and lined.

"You got the hell out of there, I imagine," Pyke said.

"Correct, I did indeed—one return visit was quite enough. I returned to the time-zones nearest the exit to the post-crash world. I wanted to hide myself away from the horrors of the bridge at one end and the wasteland of sand and wreckage at the other. My sojourns here were few and far between until one occasion when I discovered unfamiliar footsteps tracked all through the shelter and around the outside. That was when I found out about the gateway to the drive section, which I had previously dismissed as a piece of junk left in the hold."

"Did you go through?" said Dervla. "To the drive section?"

"A few times," Hokajil said. "It was fascinating yet also unwelcoming. After a time I felt even more of an exile there than I did in the midst of all this sand."

"So just how have you managed to survive all this time?" said Dervla.

"There is a curious anomaly which occurs at the boundary between the time-zones, a kind of faceting that gives rise to additional time-zones that aren't adjacent to the main timeline." Hokajil shrugged. "An unforeseen consequence, but I discovered that time dilation effects take place within them...and all the time-facets which split off from them as well. A week spent in some of them is the equivalent to a century or more out here reality."

Pyke smiled. "Which is how you made it through the millennia!"

"Just so. Though I'm not sure what would happen were I to leave—the years might just catch up with me."

Dervla sniffed. "Is it even worth our while entering this mosaic of time-zones? Meddling with temporal stuff just sends a chill down my spine."

Pyke shrugged. "I get what you're saying, but Mr. H's time-thrower, time-zones, time-facets, the whole shebang—it's not really in the past, I think." Pyke squinted at Hokajil. "You said they were like bits of the past stuck in a loop, right?"

"Yes, that's generally correct," said the old inventor. "Although some changes have crept in over the many, many years as a consequence of the faceting, like the generation of alternative versions of the main continuity. The only meddling was done by me, long ago, so no responsibility attaches to any of you. But while deliberating your next actions, consider this—I have seen you, all of you, in the Mosaic!"

This caused a stir of bafflement and surprise in equal measure.

"We've only just got here," said Ancil. "How can you see us in 'there' before we've arrived?"

"It's the effect of causes!" said Hokajil. "When causes occur in exotic places like the Time-Mosaic, the effects are likewise exotic."

"Exotic!" Pyke snorted. "A fancy word for weird!"

"More like inconstant."

"Bonkers!"

"Slightly erratic."

Pyke chuckled. "Mad as a box of frogs armed with rocket launchers!"

Smiling, Hokajil held up his hands. "I bow to your superior hyperbolic skills."

"What can I say—it's a gift."

"Indeed, and the times when I saw you and your crew, very occasionally over the years, was a gift from exotic causality!"

Dervla smiled. "Our entering the Mosaic makes echoes of ourselves bounce around, up and down, back and forth..." Her eyes widened. "You could warn us about what Raven and her followers are up to, y'know, if they're going to ambush us five minutes after we step inside, or the like..."

Hokajil shrugged. "I'm afraid I didn't see anything so specific. It was just brief glimpses of your progress that I spotted. And only in the first zone of the Mosaic—I've not really ventured any further along the main timeline than that for quite a long time."

Pyke thought about this, glancing at Dervla and the others. "Do we go on, stay here, or go back? Assuming we could reactivate the portal."

"We might be able to contact the *Scarabus* in orbit," Moleg said. "If we can boost whatever communicators we're still carrying."

"We should go on, Chief," said Ancil without hesitation. "I know Ustril left us in the lurch, but she's making a huge mistake chasing after those other crystal pieces—we should help her if we can, and track down the crystals, too."

"I think we should go on, too," said Dervla. "But for me it's really about hunting Raven down so that I can push a big gun barrel into her face!"

"I go with that, Chief," said Kref. "Raven's a nasty piece of work who's getting nastier all the time!"

Pyke turned to Hokajil. "It looks as if we'll be taking a stroll along Temporal Lane. Any advice you can offer before we gate-crash the *Mighty Defender*'s bridge?"

"What should you know? The people are real enough so be polite. The food and drink may be to your liking, or not. Oh, I would caution you against crossing into any of the facets you encounter..."

"Facets?" said Dervla with a frown.

"The time-zones, over the centuries, have become unstable at their peripheries with alternate timeline splinters appearing along the edges. Each holds its own version of the ship: most display minor variations in design aesthetic, while others vary greatly from the Mosaic's main continuity, a few jarringly so. Oh, and are you well enough armed?"

Pyke grinned at Ancil who shook his head in mock gravity. "Nowhere near, Chief!"

"We're a bit short on hardware at the moment," Pyke told Hokajil. "Can you sort us out?"

"Indeed, yes—after you enter the ship, three decks down there is a security station staffed by two guards. Once you get them out of the way, you'll find a weapons locker in the main office—the code is LGS451 and it contains more than enough hardware for your needs."

Pyke drained the last cold dregs of filner tea from his beaker, having found himself acquiring a taste for it. He put the beaker down on the table next to the odd urn and a plate of jomby biscuits, which he found easy to pass on.

"Do you still have that time-thrower gizmo?" he asked Hokajil. "Might be handy to have along."

"Sadly, I mislaid it during a deep expedition many years ago." The old inventor looked forlorn. "Actually, I was ambushed and it was stolen from me." He held up the half-egg device. "This auxiliary trigger is all that remains of it." He indicated the waiting open door. "Are you ready to begin your journey to the bridge, Captain? You don't want to be late!"

Dervla grinned. "Time for your big entrance, Bran!"

"Just as long as it's not my big exit." He glanced round at the others, Kref, Moleg and Ancil. "Okay, last one to the weapons locker gets the starting pistol—let's go!"

CHAPTER SIXTEEN

Pyke—The Crystal Simulation

Bound and gagged, they'd stuffed him into a cramped, enclosed, horse-drawn cart. It had a single bench wide enough for one and two side windows covered by cloth blinds. Enough light leaked in to reveal the starkness of his bleak situation, a confinement box on wheels jolting and rattling through the streets of Granah. The cart was cold and dank and it stank, but Pyke's mind was locked in a circle of guilt and grief.

Dead, he thought. *She's here and hasn't gone away so she has to be...*

He could barely bring himself to think it. When you got right down to it, at one time or another he'd been a crappy captain, a crappy lover and a crappy friend to her. What made it worse was that it was the real Pyke out there in the really-real world who'd failed. He got to mourn the loss of her while good ol' Simulation Pyke had to deal with the presence of Dervla's copy, a Dervla incorporated into the Legacy's demented storyline!

Remorse, guilt, anger and cold, cold isolation, all swirling together, became like a heavy stone lodged in his head, weighing him down. He was alone inside the prison cart, heard only the rattle and creak of the wheels, the sough of his breathing past the cloth gag.

Dead, he thought. *Dead.*

That was when he heard a new noise amid the cart's chorus of knocks, rattles and poorly oiled axle squeaks. It was a rhythmic grinding sound and it seemed to be coming from directly beneath his bench. He shifted round a little and craned his head to the side for a better view, but it was too dark to make out any details. His shoulder slumped and he sank back against the rear wall of the cart, thinking that the noise was probably some grit that had worked its way into the primitive axle bearings.

Pyke had buried himself into a sombre funk for less than a minute when he heard a couple of raps, and a soft wooden clunk. If he hadn't been gagged, he would have laughed out loud.

Well, I am a prisoner so it only stands to reason that there'll be a rescue attempt, just to keep the Legacy's story ticking along…

Then a familiar small wooden shape flew out from under the bench and hovered before him. It was RK1, residual proxy for the Construct drone, Rensik.

"Captain, please hold still while I loosen your gag."

The mechanical bird, he noticed, no longer made a clattering noise as it fluttered around, instead emitting a soft hum. *Upgrades*, he thought. *Could come in handy.*

The gag was loosened enough to slip below his mouth, the first hint that this was not a rescue.

"I can't help noticing that you're not cutting me loose," he said.

"My apologies, Captain, but we are rushing towards several crisis points—the crux of the storyline concocted by the Legacy, and the situation with regard to your shipboard colleague, the female Dervla."

He stared at the humming, hovering drone-bird. "You've heard about that, then."

"I have penetrated several key oversight systems which allows me to piggyback a wide range of update feeds." The bird glanced around the cart's interior. "I am not releasing you because the situation at the palace will allow you to enable Dervla's real personality, to free your compatriots and to destroy the blood-poison vial, thus ending this particular simulation.

"But I have other news that you must hear. While exploring the boundary of the simulation partition, trying to find any weakness that would permit scans of the deep regions beyond, I was contacted by my progenitor, the drone Rensik!"

Pyke straightened at this news. "He's still around? But is he still himself? I thought he'd been enslaved by the Legacy and its body snatchers."

"Drone Rensik managed to create a plausible shell person which would be a convincing captive for the Legacy to break and convert to its cause, all the while masking his own real core. The fake Rensik's subjugation opened doors to parts of the higher macro-data systems closed to a mere interim stopgap such as myself."

"What did he say?"

"Firstly, he informed me that further analysis by me of the partition boundary was unnecessary as he had obtained manifest surveys of the interior from a secure archive."

"All those blacked-out stars and planets," Pyke said.

"Rensik passed on to me a number of those surveys—I can show a brief compendium of what they hold so that you may understand what we have become involved in."

There was no mistaking the gravity of RK1's words and Pyke found it a relief to put aside his dark mood and focus on something else.

"Okay, so how are you going to show me your movie? Beam it out of one eye onto the inside of my executive, first-class coach?"

"It's quite simple, Captain, just hold out your hands."

"You're going to project a screen in front of me? That's... *Whoa! What the bastarding hell!*"

The moment the drone alighted on Pyke's outstretched, tied hands, his view of the cart's interior vanished, instantly replaced by an immense, ash-grey spire looming right next to him as he hung suspended above a dark planet...

His senses swung with vertigo, along with feelings very much like nausea welling up from a stomach he didn't have. As the panic receded he could see that the ashen spire wasn't part of some orbiting structure but actually originated down on the planet's surface, along with several others clustered together. *Not spires*, he realised. *Cables*. The view of the planet's curve revealed other similar clusters jutting up from the surface and outwards.

Instinctively, he wanted to cross from this cable cluster to the next, but the viewpoint he was being shown began to glide away from it, a shallow trajectory descending into the atmosphere. This flight built up to a good velocity and surface details soon became visible—repeating patterns of blocks, curves and spirals resolved into stepped structures of what looked like black basalt encrusted with further patterned growths in shades of silver, dark blue and dark green. Some of the largest conglomerations of these recurring forms were gathered and stacked around huge arched buttresses which swept up to become part of the huge cable clusters which themselves reached up into the sky.

During this smooth and swift flight, Pyke noticed patches of cloud whipping past, sometimes as a pale haze, sometimes as a denser grey blur. As the viewpoint passed through a clear stretch Pyke got a good look right across this titanic, fractalised landscape and saw other low clouds hanging near the apex of spires and towers. Steady scrutiny revealed that they were not moving. The same went for vapour clouds boiling up out of a sawtooth-fringed fissure that glowed a fiery orange.

Abruptly the view flickered and suddenly he was sweeping through abyssal space towards a vast orb, a planet he at first assumed. Like the previous world the surface was mostly dark and glimmering, except that here bright lines were stitched across the surface like a planless patchwork. Here, too, cables rose from the surface, sprouting in the hundreds, no, thousands. And as the viewpoint flew closer so the bright stitch lines grew thicker and brighter, then looked like linked canals of incandescence, then strings of molten fiery lakes...

Pyke gazed in uneasy awe—this was a sun, and the chains of burning lakes were just gaps between vast plates that floated on the sun's surface, feeding on those stupendous thermonuclear energies, channelling them away...

This time the viewpoint did swing round and Pyke swore at the sight—some of the energy cables reached out to join with an immense ring structure which encircled the shackled, splintered sun. Other cables fanned out to link up with other structures, hanging suspended over this captive star. Smaller artificial rings, as well as triangular and hexagonal edifices, all developed on the same dark proliferation of pseudo-fractal patterns yet clearly directed along functional lines that were beyond Pyke's comprehension.

Still further out, beyond the great ring and all the lesser structures, the energy cables stretched up to many other worldlets like the one he had seen at the start. Moons, asteroids, planets, all the bodies of this system were drawn together by this glittering web.

The perspective changed and this time he was hurtling through a starless black void, plunging past one star system after another, every one woven together by dark nets. Even the great gulfs of this void were spanned by strands and bonds of gleaming obsidian. All these caged stars were almost impaled by the pitiless mesh, their burning fires drained away to serve enigmatic purposes.

Again the view flickered to something new, the surface of a planet again, only here were the recognisable signs of civilisation— a city by the sea, mass-transit vehicles, tall buildings faced with glass, cars on roads and in the air. But this citadel of life was under attack from a wave of the same dark, glittering material, rushing across fields towards the city from inland. As with the cloud formations earlier, all motion was frozen. The inhabitants—slender, gracil humanoids—were trying to escape, some in vehicles, some by sea, in families and groups, and Pyke could read the terror and desperation in their faces.

Another viewpoint switch. He was back out in the black, gliding leisurely alongside a series of huge alcoves in a long structure. Huge articulated arms hung over the deep recesses, grabs bearing unidentifiable chunks of machinery towards indistinct shapes lurking within each one. Some kind of assembly was going on, it seemed...then suddenly he realised that he was looking at shipyards, a long, long line of them, turning out ship after ship. As if to confirm the revelation, a completed vessel was rising out of its construction bay on heavy tow lines and even before it had cleared the upper sides mobile assembler units had moved in to lay down the underhull of the next. A tableau just as motionless as the others.

The viewpoint then swiftly twisted and surged along a new heading, a curved path which revealed that this rank of shipyards was one of six spaced around a supply spine which fed resources to all of its yards. But this cluster was just one among scores protruding from an immense armoured sphere, possibly a planetoid.

All this, he thought numbly. *Contained within that skagging crystal.*

The last thing he saw was the armada. Lines of completed ships led away from the mega-yards and converged on a vast block of open space stippled with vessels. His perspective flew nearer and nearer and the sheer numbers became staggering. He gazed up at a towering cliff of close-packed ships, thousands upon thousands, and the products of those yards had scarcely filled in a couple of corners...

Then in an instant he was back in the jolting, rattling cart, staring wide-eyed into midair, blinking.

"Did you comprehend what I showed you, Captain?" said RK1. "Did you recognise the threat?"

Pyke grunted. "I've sucked up my share of vee-dramas—I think they call it a nano-tide, something like that?"

"The Construct refers to it as an Omnivorous Devourer and I know for a fact that my progenitor has encountered one such infestation during his current duty iteration. Did you notice how everything was frozen in place?"

"That I did."

"This is because the original crystal, the Essavyr Key, was broken in three soon after its creation, a deliberate act."

Pyke mulled this over, along with all he'd seen, then laughed darkly.

"Can't help noticing that you're not volunteering much free information there, Arky, ould son. But I've got a question that needs answering—that crystal, the whole thing, it's actually a prison, ain't it?"

"Full marks—if I had hands I would be applauding wildly."

"So what *is* the Legacy—one of the inmates?"

"Originally it was a failsafe guardian entity," said RK1. "Not an AI but coded to be more than a mere watchdog program. Unfortunately, over time, emergent characteristics began to manifest, curiosity, mainly, which prompted it to scan some of the shadow-data held in the frozen Devourer mentation cores. Somehow it managed to read the unreadable, then made modifications to itself according to schematics it uncovered, and that was that."

"But hang on, what…no, where did all these twisted stars and planets come from, and who put all of that into the original crystal—and how…"

"You will soon be arriving at the palace so there isn't time to fully brief you," said the bird-drone. "Suffice to say that as long ago as half a million years, perhaps even longer, a lab-created Omnivorous Devourer self-uplifted, broke out of the lab and proceeded to proliferate. Most Devourer outbreaks erupt in an exponential wave of consuming and generating more converted mass, then push the leading edge further out to absorb still more—and so on. But this one appears to have initiated its expansion according to a plan. It knew about the sinews of civilisation, the webs and channels of resources that weave it all together. Corroborated stories from this far back in history are sketchy at best but it appears that the Devourer took about a month to assume control over the planet of its birth, and that was largely surreptitious. In the next month it had another half-dozen nearby worlds and their systems under its command. Macro-scale engineering projects commenced while entire populations were subdued with airborne implants linked to subservient versions of the Devourer.

"Anyway, it had over twenty worlds in its thrall by the time the leaders of the nearest interstellar nation-domain realised that all communications issuing from this conquered region emanated from the same sentience, the Devourer itself speaking through its peripherals. This nation-domain (which might have been a remnant of the old Zarl Imperium) realised that they were in dire circumstances so they made approaches to certain godlike wanderers called the Ancients, last hermitic survivors of a vanished, near mythic civilisation. But only one of them, known as Essavyr, agreed to help—He/She/It or They swiftly undertook a journey in Their/Its own vessel, staking out a volume of space larger than that already occupied by the Devourer's darkling empire. Power from the suns of uninhabited star systems was redirected into this vast cage. And before the Devourer could breach its boundary Essavyr activated its enigmatic technology. The deep structures of space-time-space were reconfigured while a lattice of exotic dimensionality blinked into being.

"Afterwards, Essavyr presented the Leader of this long-forgotten authority with the results of His/Her/Its or Their efforts, a crystalline object formed vaguely in the shape of a winged creature and, strangely, of an easily carried size. With a quanta scope Essavyr showed the Leader that same shipyard that I revealed to you, only it was in full, vigorous production, still churning out ship after ship despite being trapped in this exotic, singular prison. Then Essavyr shattered the crystal figurine into three parts, which froze that relentless, horrific adversary into immobility. Essavyr then gave the crystal fragments into the Leader's safekeeping, and made him vow that the parts would never be joined together again."

"Okay," Pyke said. "Bit more exhaustive than I was expecting but, yeah, I get the picture. Real-world Pyke has his bit of crystal, and the others are…well, where exactly?"

"Real-world Pyke and the rest of the crew have been exploring an ancient shipwreck lost in the deserts of Ong—the missing crystal pieces were aboard it when it crashed millennia ago. Raven and her associates are likewise pursuing them, and there are suggestions that she may already have taken possession of one of them."

Pyke nodded. "Well, that is the way our luck is going just now." He shook his head, feeling almost dazed by the flood of information, and he refused to let himself get turned about by events beyond the simulation, events he could neither influence nor control.

"What happens here is what's important to me—and I need to know if it's possible to wake up the true Dervla, here, somehow."

"It can be done," said RK1. "The timing may be tricky but it's essential that you also complete the solution to the scenario. I shall be there in the palace to help you and the others see it through."

The swaying, rattling cart began to tilt back noticeably, as if

it were being pulled up a sloping road. Like the one that led up
to the Imperial palace.

"Won't be long till we reach the Emperor's official shack,"
Pyke said. "Can't wait to see what sort of welcoming ceremony
they've laid on for me."

"Whatever it is, I urge you to grit your teeth and bear it," said
the bird-drone. "I have to be sure that you are in the right place
at the right time in order that the blood-poison vial is correctly
destroyed."

Pyke frowned. "You're saying there's an incorrect way?"

"Incorrect, no—longer and more painful, certainly. Now,
please hold still while I readjust your gag."

"You're going to . . . wh-nng-fg-dn-mmf-ng-mmf!"

"My apologies—there must be no evidence of any intrusion or
tampering," said RK1. "There is one thing you should know—
only a sorcerous object can destroy that blood-poison vial, and
in the palace there is a very useful one! So, if all goes smoothly,
we will resolve the scenario and move directly into the next one,
which I and Rensik have subtly altered to aid our greater plan."

"Gnnnr-vrnn?"

"It will become apparent soon after the new scenario com-
mences. At that point I will come to you with a very serious
proposition, one vital to the aim of defeating the Legacy and the
Devourer menace. Till then, hold your nerve."

Pyke wanted to comment volubly on propositions and holding
one's nerve, but all he could manage was some muffled angry
noises as the residual proxy drone left the way it had entered, via
a gap beneath the bench on which he sat.

*Hold my nerve? Yeah, well my captors and jailers better
watch their step or I'll be holding some throats before long!*

CHAPTER SEVENTEEN

Pyke—the planet Ong, the wreck of the *Mighty Defender*, the forward section

Pyke was the first through the open door, first to enter the forward section of the *Mighty Defender*, and first to see the last of Hokajil's time-zones up close. There were now people to be seen, wandering in and out of cabins, humanoids like Hokajil with that slight elongation of the skull. There were hints of fragrance drifting in the air and there was the muffled chatter of many voices, punctuated by laughter. In spite of himself, Pyke couldn't help feeling a bit of a thrill at treading the corridors of a million-year-old vessel.

There were footsteps behind him.

"Huh," said Dervla. "Busier than it looks from outside."

After her came Ancil, hurrying ahead of Moleg and Kref. Hokajil still stood outside, concern in his features. Pyke retraced his steps, pausing on the threshold.

"Any final advice?"

"Stay close together," said the old inventor. "Arm yourself as soon as possible. Try to avoid entering any of the time-facets, and be wary of anybody who emerges from one, regardless of what they say. Pay close attention to that map I gave you." He gave a half-smile. "And if you can, try to have a little fun—enjoy the experience! The *Mighty Defender* is—was—a remarkable vessel."

Pyke gave a sardonic laugh and patted his chest pocket. "Got your map right here—and personally I just want to get through this in one piece, then I might be ready to enjoy it!"

"Do as you must, Captain, and safe journey." Hokajil smoothed the whiskers on his cheeks and straightened his layers of coats and cloaks. "Now I must be about my business—I'm expecting an important guest and he's late!"

Turning, he fluttered his fingers in the air in farewell and strolled off back to his hut. Pyke watched him go in puzzlement, then shrugged and went to rejoin his waiting crew. They were engaged in a tense discussion, in which Dervla was holding onto Ancil's arm and Ancil was wagging a Finger of Doom in her direction while pulling away.

"What the hairy hell is this all about? Can I not turn my back for a measly second without a squabble breaking out?"

"It's my fault, Chief," said Ancil. "Well, a bit of it—I just need to follow the guy and investigate..."

"What guy?"

Dervla butted in. "While were you off having a gab with Hokajil, we saw this guy—"

"In really smart silver and crimson body armour," said Ancil.

"This guy," repeated Dervla, "stepped out of one of the rooms up ahead and looked straight at us—he was Ancil's spitting double! Then he just grinned and took off down the corridor."

"Chief, we need to check it out," said Ancil. "Could be a threat, but he could be a possible ally, or maybe wouldn't mind answering a few questions—"

"Wait, just clam it for a second," Pyke said. "You were with me and the rest of us when we heard Hokajil's warnings, weren't you? I'm sure I saw you nearby..."

Ancil nodded. "I was, Chief, but—"

"Uh-huh. Look, we've been through some pretty crazy stuff, some really weird-ass, skagged-out, brain-mangling shit—and we're still together. Maybe this guy could be just the guide we need, or maybe he's a walking, talking scuzzbag sent by some toxic thugazoid to frack us over good and proper. My advice? Hope for the former, but assume the latter. So, with that in mind, what's our next move?"

Everyone glanced wordlessly at each other, until Kref put up his hand. "Get the guns from that security office, Captain!"

"Full marks, Kref, me ould son! Stocking up on the tools of the trade it is!"

"I was gonna say that, Chief," said Ancil. "After saying that we need to get a map of these decks."

Pyke laughed and punched Ancil's shoulder. "Got one from Hokajil before we left—we'll check it when we get to that junction up ahead. Right, let's go."

So saying, he took the lead in a mindful advance along the corridor. There were still those faint cocktail sounds, and the soothing tinkly music, but now it seemed like a mask concealing all manner of dangers and pitfalls. *It's all so clean and neat*, he thought. *Maybe if we were creeping along some filthy back alley I'd feel more like I was in my element...*

They drew level with a door which turned out to be an archway through to a well-lit, busy lounge. Well-dressed, semi-dressed and hardly dressed passengers laughed and drank and danced on a long, S-shaped platform which drifted around the tall room above head height while others gathered on divans and piles of cushions.

"That's where Ancil's double went," Dervla said.

"Interesting," Pyke said, pointing at the archway itself. "There's a slightly opaque shimmer across it, see?"

"I can," she said. "Is this one of those facets Hokajil was going on about?"

"I'm guessing yes," Pyke said. "Maybe Ancil's double was returning from where he came."

"Or," Moleg said, "he came from another facet entirely and was just passing through our main continuity on the way into that one."

Brow furrowed, Pyke looked at Moleg, then back at the archway. "That sounds disturbingly plausible, with extra disturbing. Thanks for that, Moleg."

"No problem, Chief."

"Let's move on, shall we?"

They passed a couple more doors and another archway (into what looked like a library of books resembling slender opaque tablets) but there were no signs of more time-facets. The corridor ended at a T-junction where, to either side, there were airgrav shafts leading up and down. Also, on the wall was an interesting map of the forward section, rendered in partial 3D, with easily selectable decks with passengers denoted by little figure icons in light grey, with a meagre scattering of dark grey ones here and there. The great majority of passengers were gathered on the deck three levels down, a long continuous deck which also spanned the forward section from port to starboard. When Ancil pointed out a couple of rooms occupied by two dark grey emblems, Pyke was pleased.

"Let's pick up our pace," he said. "I'll feel better about our chances once we get geared up."

"You're not the only one," murmured Dervla. "Kref still has that heavy shooter, though."

"Heh, the popgun, eh? If it's not some recoilless beast capable of firing belts of AP and HE in full auto, he's just not interested...okay, everyone, we're gonna take this airgrav shaft and stick together, all right?"

Annoyingly, the airgrav shafts only connected one deck to the next above or below, so that you had to get out and switch to an adjacent shaft to continue your journey. They did this twice before the final stage—this was a longer descent in a section of shaft which was transparent, giving them a fabulous view of the spanning deck, which appeared far, far busier than the map had suggested. To Pyke's eyes, it looked like a single, sprawling, sumptuous and spectacular carouse. Waiters and floating waiter drones circulated with bottles, bulbs, pipes and other intoxicants. Musical players, both machine and organic, supplied tunes for dancing, singing and interjoining. Large suspended screens showed two-vees, adverts or new bulletins or some fusion of all three. Other smaller signboards seemed to be flashing amber lights while lines of Arraveyne text scrolled across them. All this Pyke took in as they descended from the deck above. Emerging from the shaft was like stepping into an explosion of sound, the concentrated roar of a thousand parties.

"We need to circle round, Chief!" yelled Ancil. "That security station is well to the rear of where we are!"

Pyke nodded and pointed. "That way!" he bellowed to the rest, and plunged into the press of partying people. But progress was slow—they were continually drawing the attention of half- or mostly drunk passengers determined to offer them all manner of pungent drinks or fuming hookahs, or notionally clad pleasure seekers of both and other sexes offering sensual diversions.

Pyke's senses reeled under the assault of such full-tilt carousing. But maybe it was more than that—at this point in time, the *Mighty Defender* had escaped the collapse of the Arraveyne Imperium just days before so the need for a celebratory shindig was to be expected. Although, from Hokajil's account, they were also in the early stages of the attempt to evade the Damaugra.

Whatever—this whole festival is like the grandaddy of all benders, with extra malarkey thrown in!

With some shouting and manic gesticulating, he drew the others' attention to a door in a projecting wall. Just as everyone seemed to be moving in that direction, a slender hooded figure barged into him from the side and Pyke felt a small crumpled object being pushed into his hand. Fingers closed around it reflexively and he shouted, "Hey, you, wait!" The figure spared him only a momentary backward glance before disappearing into the heaving crowd. Pyke stared after him, struck by a conviction that the man's face was familiar...then he looked down at the crushed slip of paper in his hand. He flattened it out enough to read—"Beware the ravens, Captain, and trust no one—Ustril."

Pyke gaped in surprise, thrust the message into a coat pocket—then looked up and realised he had become separated from the others. This was a part of the deck dominated by hovering audiospheres pumping out pounding dance music, and the subsonics were making Pyke's teeth ache. He scanned the surrounding crowd, which seemed to have turned into a Convention of the Tall People. Only by standing on a padded stool could he survey a wider span of bobbing heads among which he spotted Kref's unmistakable profile. He tried shouting across at him but his voice couldn't compete with the barrage of music. So he orientated himself towards the big Henkayan and plunged back into the crowd.

After an eternity of pushing and sidestepping and elbow-wedging and apologies for trampled feet and spilled drinks, Kref's broad back came within view. Right at that moment, the big Henkayan bellowed, "There he is!" and surged ahead like a juggernaut, away from Pyke.

"Kref!" Pyke bawled as he lunged after him. "Hold up, ya steaming great..."

Pyke's leg hit something hard at knee height and he went down. He sensed invasive hands tugging at his coat so he grabbed what felt like an arm and yanked on it while winding up his other fist for a solid punch...

"Chief!—wait, it's me!"

Ancil's face appeared, clearly attached to the arm that Pyke was hauling on with a will.

"Ah right, sorry 'bout that," Pyke said. "Let's get up out of this, eh?"

Using each other for support they regained their feet, and Pyke saw Dervla and Moleg struggling to stay nearby—a chanting, double-column dance-chain was winding past and bystanders were being dragged in to dance along, seemingly at random.

"Where's Kref gone?" Pyke shouted over the chanting racket.

"He keeps thinking he's seen Van Graes!" Dervla yelled back.

Pyke shook his head and was about to respond, then decided that he wasn't going to fight against the maddening din. He pointed at his ear, then waved his hand over at a thinned-out area at the aft end of the deck. Dervla and Moleg gave thumbs-ups and everyone began to move determinedly in that direction. Along the way they got Kref's attention by shouting his name in unison, then pointing him in the same direction. By the time they finally rendezvoused in the not-so-crammed section, Pyke felt like a pummelled, sweat-sodden punchbag. Wiping the grime from his face and trying to cool down, he beckoned them to gather round.

"I don't know how we got separated," he said, "but at least we're here and in one piece. So, what's all this about Van Graes?"

"I saw him, Captain," said Kref. "Definitely him, up on one of them floating balconies with big-hair lady-friends."

Lady-friends with big-hair? Pyke thought. *Doesn't sound like the Van Graes I know, but then maybe I don't know everything...*

"Floating balconies?" he said.

"Not seen them yet?" said Dervla. "There's one."

He followed her pointing finger and, sure enough, back along this side of the deck, drifting down through the air, was a curved balcony with about a dozen passengers leaning drunkenly over the rail, waving to others down on the main concourse.

"That's not all, Chief," said Ancil. "We saw Hokajil, a younger Hokajil, hurrying through the crowd! I saw him, so did Moleg…"

Moleg nodded in that relaxed, diffident way of his so Pyke had to take it seriously.

"And I saw him after the others did," said Kref. "I was following him, but then I lost him. Did you see anyone, Captain?"

"Not really, I…"

He stopped as a flash of full recall leaped into his mind's eye. The shoving, jostling crowd, the hooded stranger, the crumpled note pressed into his hand, his shout and how the stranger had glanced back for a moment before the boisterous crowd closed around him. The man's hood had widened for a second, revealing…himself. The hair had been grey and the lower face bore a five-day stubble not unlike what he was sporting just now, but there had also been a nasty scar running from forehead to cheek down one side.

"Bran, what's up? Did you see something?"

He dipped into his pocket, took out the note and passed it to Dervla. She took it in with a single glance, then gave him a baffled look.

"Read it out," he said.

She cleared her throat. "'Beware the ravens, Captain, and trust no one—Ustril.'"

"She passed you that note, Chief?" said Ancil. He whirled to stare out at the crowd. "You mean, she's here?"

"Wasn't her," said Pyke. "It was another me."

All eyes were on him as he described the brief encounter.

"An alternative you from one of the time-facets," said Dervla.

"Yes, and Hokajil told me that none of them were to be trusted," he said.

"But it's signed 'Ustril,'" said Ancil. "How could she get involved with the Captain's doppelganger, and why?"

"How do we even know that the note was from *our* Ustril," said Dervla. "From our timeline."

"Steer clear of the facets and their wildlife," Pyke said as Dervla handed him back the note. "Hokajil was very specific about that. I say we just ignore this for now and stick to the plan—find the security office, take their guns, then head for the next time-zone." There were nods all round at this. "At this point, seems like a good idea to look at this map Hokajil gave me…"

"He gave you a map?" said Ancil.

"Well, I glanced at it and thought, not much of a map, but let's see…"

From an inner pocket Pyke dug out the piece of folded card the inventor gave him before they entered the wreck. It showed a basic side view of the ship's forward section with a series of dotted areas indicating the extent of the time-zones created by Hokajil during his flight from the bridge. Then the image on the card surprised him by flipping over to top-down and zooming in on one particular part of one of the decks, this deck, and centred on a small cluster of grey dots. Pyke laughed and shook his head—amid the detailed schemata was a hand-drawn arrow pointing to a room with two dark blue dots in it. The details grew more distinct, and he could see that they were very close, just through the nearby door, down a corridor and the security station was at the junction.

He showed the map to the rest. "There's the target, and here's how it's going to go…"

First, Dervla and Moleg went down the corridor and sauntered leftwards at the junction, letting the guards get a good look as they did a passable imitation of a drunk, giggling couple. Some way along from the security station, Dervla faked a fit, Moleg raised the alarm, got one of the guards to come out and along the passage to help the convulsing Dervla into a nearby store-room (hence the choice of that stretch of corridor), where they ambushed him and rendered him unconscious with Kref's help.

Meanwhile, once Guard One was out of the way, Pyke came rushing in to report a fight up on the big food-serving area. As he was describing how two partygoers had started throwing punches, Ancil came hurrying in with a blood-curdling account of how what had started as fisticuffs was turning into a full-blown brawl as others got drawn in. That was enough for the two remaining guards who unsnapped their crowd control sticks and flipped their innocuous looking skullcaps into visored helms. Ancil volunteered to show them where it was all happening while Pyke insisted that he was retiring to his cabin to recover from all the sheer unbridled aggression he'd witnessed.

Once Ancil and the guards had gone along the corridor and out of the door at the end, Pyke and the others nonchalantly converged on the security station. With Kref and Dervla waiting in the outer office, Pyke and Moleg entered the inner sanctum, ignored the monitor screens and went straight to the secure locker, a large cabinet fronted with black armour leaves. Pyke input Hokajil's code and the armoured shuttered form-shifted into the side slots, revealing an enviable selection of weaponry. Even as Pyke stood there, admiring the sleek designs and considerate layout, Ancil arrived back from misleading the guards.

"Right, I sent them on an epic journey through Partyland which should keep them...sweet baby Shiva! What have we here?"

"Don't be too grabby," Pyke said. "Bearing in mind that we've got quite a few busy decks to get through while we're tracking down Raven and her vermin. So keep it to a couple of concealable sidearms, and a handful of throwables—got me?"

Ancil's expression was a combination of rabid desire and anguished indecision. "If only we had a target range..."

"Well, we don't," said Pyke. "Nor have we got time so take yer pick and let's go!"

Ancil took one handweapon out of the rack, examined another, then went on to a third. Meanwhile, Pyke picked up a solidly weighty piece with a twin barrel and a smaller silvery shock gun as a backup. Dervla and Moleg were keen to join in the pillaging, too.

"Poor Ans," said Dervla "Like a baby in a candy store."

Pyke grinned. "Yeah, all that candy and only one gob to chew with!"

Ancil's only response was to raise an eyebrow as he continued his patient scrutiny. Once Moleg and Dervla were kitted out, Kref reached past Ancil towards a weapon similar to the one Pyke had chosen, but Ancil steered him towards another with an odd triangular barrel. "Crowd control, Kref," he said pointing at the chunky magazines. "Onboard-compliant smackdown rounds!"

"Ah, controlling crowds," said Kref as he grabbed it. "Could be useful."

In the end Ancil chose a compact flechette pistol as his main sidearm but for his backup opted for an odd gun with a boxy receiver and a short barrel studded with tiny black spikes. The magazines looked like round-edged lozenges. Satisfied, Pyke hustled everyone to exit the security station, making sure the gun locker was closed up before they left.

In the storeroom back along the corridor, where the first guard was still sleeping peacefully, the crew gathered around while he consulted Hokajil's map. From the main side-view it was clear that they'd have to travel back up for five decks in order to reach the boundary to the next time-zone. And on the deck above the one they entered, they would have to head along a good-sized corridor to reach the next airgrav-shaft leading up.

"That's crazy," said Ancil.

"It's also bloody stupid from a ship-logistics view," said Dervla. "Surely they wouldn't hobble the ability of the crew to respond to emergencies—there must be crew-only travel routes around the ship. Have to be."

Pyke nodded and with a prod and a swipe he shifted Hokajil's map to the party deck, centred on their current refuge, the storeroom. He zoomed the image in closer and little tags in mysterious lettering appeared here and there, along with another hand-drawn arrow pointing to a small, square symbol which was identical to the one for the airgrav-shaft back in the concourse deck.

"That has to be it," he said, showing the map to the others.

"Not far away, Chief," Ancil said. "What's our story if we run up against any nosey types?"

"Easy—we're entertainers, a band of troupers, heading up to the bridge on the express invitation of, say, the First Mate."

Dervla was unconvinced. "Entertainers?—what, a song, a dance, a filthy joke—that kind thing?"

Pyke grinned. "More of a band situation—we can call ourselves 'The Newfangled Five'!"

"I could be the kitarist," said Ancil. "Kref could be the drummer…"

"This is crazy-mad," said Dervla. "Off-the-wall barking lunacy…"

"Isn't it?" Pyke said. "But it's no crazier than what's going on out there in Partyland, which makes our claim plausible—hell, we don't even have to know the First Mate's name, because our manager does all that liaison stuff!"

She was right, it was demented and high-risk, but Pyke's reckoning was that high-risk options were the only ones going. Bravura and cunning was all that the notion required, and they had those aplenty.

"I can't believe I'm saying this," Dervla said, "but it could just work. All I ask is, let me do the talking, or at least most of it if we get stopped. Deal?"

Pyke gave a gracious nod. "Deal. Shall we get going?"

After cautiously checking activity out in the corridor, Pyke waved the others to exit the storeroom. The route to the crew airgrav-shaft was straightforward, just a few turns and short passage traverses away from the security station. They passed barely anyone on the way, which was lucky in several ways, not least because Ancil, Kref and Moleg were trying to come up with fake band member names. By the time they got to the last stretch of corridor they'd settled on Artemis Goldark (Moleg), Magnus Frost (Kref) and Zaine Hellion (Ancil). There was also a certain amount of muttering which made Pyke suspect that they'd concocted daft names for him and Dervla, too, but were wisely hesitant about voicing them.

Pyke took another look at Hokajil's map as they approached the airgrav-shaft. He frowned on discovering new handwritten symbols that weren't there before, an up-arrow stopped by a thick red line—there were three black dots at the bottom of the arrow and seven at the red line.

"What does it mean?" said Ancil. "Maximum of three in the shaft?"

They'd reached the crew-access shaft, which was clearly designed for shifting large loads as well as personnel.

"No, *Zaine*," said Pyke. "Looks like it could take all your kitars and then some!"

Ancil gave a sly smile. "Awritey, thanks for the update there, *Raskal*!"

"Uh-oh," muttered Kref. Dervla just smiled.

"What...was that?" Pyke said.

"Chief, ya gotta have a name for the band, one that goes along with ours..."

"And it's Raskal?"

"Yeah—Raskal Stryka!"

Pyke considered it for a moment, then shrugged. "Heh, it's okay, fairly badass—*Zaine*!"

"Told you he'd like it," Moleg told Kref.

"Okay, okay," Dervla interrupted. "I've figured out what Hokajil's scrawl means—look."

Sure enough, there were markings on one side of the shaft entrance, three dots and an unknown word which had to be "floor" or "level." Pyke frowned.

"So it's saying that we can't go above the seventh floor?"

"That must be it," Dervla said. "Perhaps one of those Time-Mosaic facets is blocking the shaft above the seventh."

"All right," Pyke said. "Everyone into the airgrav-shaft—first one in holds down the multi-load button."

That was Moleg so he swiftly triggered the "hold" control. Pyke grinned.

"Going by Hokajil's map, the upper boundary of his final time-zone is five floors up from the concourse, which makes it level eight."

Ancil laughed. "And we can't go past seven. I don't mind walking the rest of the way!"

"Less walking we do," said Dervla, "less chance of being stopped and questioned by ship security." She gave Pyke a narrow look. "So—did you guys come up with a name for me?"

Ancil calmly studied the grav-shaft's light sources. "Yeah, we did, actually."

About three seconds of silence went by before Dervla poked him. "And?"

Wearing a big smile, Ancil turned, hand outstretched, and said, "Ladies and gentlemen, the one and only—Atomic Jean!"

Dervla frowned. "Sounds seriously retro—and it doesn't have the same edge as the other names."

Ancil shrugged. "We might be able to whip up some alternatives."

"Ah well," said Pyke. "If do-overs are on the menu..."

That was when the lights in the shaft went out and the platform shook underfoot, forcing Pyke over against the side of the shaft.

There was a sudden, raw hiss of escaping gas, a barrage of

choking charred smells, and Pyke realised that he was perched on some kind of wire mesh-covered ledge. As he tried breathing through part of his coat, raised to his mouth, he heard coughing and hoarse voices from below. One sounded like Kref, another like Dervla, but before he could call down to them there was a metallic creak from very close by, clanking, a grating noise, and a slice of artificial light pierced the smoky darkness in which he sat. And there, in the gap between a pair of elevator doors, was Kref, trying to force the doors further apart. Pyke waved at him, making frantic sshhing gestures then pointing downwards.

Below, another pair of doors were being levered apart, a bright gap that widened as extra hands joined in. Corridor light revealed the coughing figures below, Kref, Ancil, Moleg and Dervla, all sounding the same, yet all dressed in elaborately decorated body armour and carrying heavy weapons. One by one they clambered out, after which another leaned in for a last look, then was gone. Pyke let out the breath he'd been holding— that final head and shoulder had looked a lot like himself, only wearing some ocular device over one eye.

Another doppelganger of myself, he thought as he waved at Kref to resume his rescue. *If I was the superstitious type I'd be getting the shivers by now. As it is I'll just keep a running tally.*

With the doors open, Kref and Ancil grabbed his hands and hauled him up out of the wrecked shaft. As he got his breath back he explained what he saw in the floor below.

"Looked like us, eh?" said Ancil. "Maybe versions of us from another time-facet."

"Except they really look the part of our band names, Zaine Hellion!" said Dervla.

There were a few sniggers but before Ancil could muster a retort, Pyke broke in.

"Yeah, well, I don't want us bumping into them anytime soon—we need to figure out where we are..." He paused to stare at the elevator doors. "Skaggin' hell! I think we crossed over into a time-facet as we came up the shaft. And we're on level six." He swiftly assessed the surroundings—the corridors seemed lower and the decor was dominated by grey and dark blue shades, rather than the lighter pastel hues of earlier. There was also a muffled alarm sound in another section on this deck and every now and then a tremor passed through the deck and bulkheads.

"Feels as if the ship's under attack," Dervla said.

Pyke nodded as he fished out Hokajil's map, but according to that they should still be in the time-zone they'd first encountered, the last one Hokajil had created before stumbling out of the dev-astated wreck. But there were another four of these time-zones, each one a temporal stepping stone forward to the chaotic assault of this huge creature, the Damaugra.

"So his map's wrong," said Dervla.

Pyke grunted. "In parts, maybe—it only shows where he cre-ated the zone with his gadget, not where these time-facets are. If these things have spread throughout the forward section, we could be faced with having to travel through a jigsaw of deranged alternate timelines!"

They all looked appalled, in varying degrees. Then Pyke zoomed in on the map of the deck they were on and spotted another shaft symbol not far from the current location.

"We might be able to sidestep all of that if we can leave this facet by going up!"

When he showed them the map, their spirits improved visibly and they set off again, weapons at the ready.

"Whoever designed this bloody ship clearly had something against stairs," muttered Dervla.

"There might be some on the map," Pyke said. "But I've no idea what the symbol might be..."

Just then the deck shook underfoot, almost knocking Ancil

off balance. An alarm went off and small pinlights in the ceiling began to flicker red. A machine voice suddenly spoke:

"Attention—hull breach on deck six—all personnel proceed to axial evacuation lobbies fore and aft..."

Hull breach? Pyke thought. *Has to be a Damaugra attack.*

"All right, let's move!" he said.

The elevator was round the next corner and halfway along the passageway. They reached it without incident, piled inside and Ancil hit the up button. The lift had barely started upwards when everything quivered, the ceiling corner lights dimmed and jittered, then went out completely. There were intakes of breath but before anyone could speak or curse the light snapped back on, revealing a changed lift interior. The grubby walls were patched with something like lichen and smeared with dirty trails of moisture. Grime discoloured the lighting covers and tendrils of what looked like glittering weeds were spilling out of them. The floor was covered in grit and dross and overall it stank of decay. Then the lift slowed to a halt, creaked and scraped open.

And they found themselves facing a web of gleaming, interwoven foliage among which Pyke spotted some familiar blooms and buzzing insects. He groaned.

"Just what we need—a time-facet where the Steel Forest has spread to the forward section!"

"Hey, Chief," said Ancil. "There is another lift right next to this one, yeah?"

"Certainly is."

"Well, if you have any of them blue-flower bracelets on you, they might help us nip into it..."

Pyke shook his head. "Sorry, ditched them back where we met Hokajil. Derv?"

"I left mine back there, too," she said. "Hanging on a strut poking out of the wreckage at the rear."

"Kref," said Pyke. "Don't suppose—"

"Erm, well…" The big Henkayan cleared his throat. "I did, Captain, I held on to a coupla things…"

A sideways glance showed Kref carefully extracting coiled-up strings of those tiny blue flowers. In a moment or two his head and wrists were decorated.

"This okay, Captain?"

"Looks good—now, shuffle over there and see what happens."

Kref nodded and warily approached the intruding mass of tendrils and blooms—and they drew back, shrinking from such close proximity. Pyke laughed in relief.

"Okay, Kref, now see if you can sidle on out there and check on that other lift…"

Kref grunted and advanced to the elevator's threshold, and the slow-writhing foliage retreated before him. Once outside he took a couple of sidesteps and was gone from view. There was silence for several long seconds.

"Hey, Captain, I've pressed the button for the lift and it's on its way!"

Pyke and Dervla exchanged a look. "I'm just waiting for these armoured doppelgangers to come howling round the corner, guns blazing," she said.

"Nah, my money's on a squad of Ustril-clones armed to the teeth with scanners and forceps…"

Kref popped his head into view as a rough scraping sound came from the other shaft. "It's here, Captain—the plants and the creatures aren't bothering me—I think it's okay."

"Right then—all aboard!" Pyke directed the others into a kind of queue then led them in a shuffling gait up to the parted doors where Kref stood, hands outstretched towards the mass of foliage, keeping it back. The other lift was even more dank and grimy than the first and when Pyke thumbed the up button there was no response and the doors stayed open. Grinding his teeth, he began to jab the button steadily, focusing his anger into that single stabbing motion. After the eleventh jab something went clunk and the doors began to grind together. A slight jolt and the lift began to rise.

A few seconds later they passed through another time-facet boundary—the lighting flickered and they were back in the clean, unmarred environment of an airgrav-shaft, with a partial forcefield platform beneath their feet. They stepped out at the next deck and Pyke paused to get his bearings.

Level eight. Question is, are we now in the next time-zone, or is this another time-facet?

He pulled out Hokajil's map, flipped and zoomed to the current location and saw that they were—supposedly—still in the first zone, but well to the stern of the forward section. This was where the ship's cross-section narrowed to that of the next section which was for crew and low-status retinue quarters. Just then, a slender man with swept-back hair and angular features emerged from a cabin bearing a black carry case. He wore an expression of unvarying amusement, and with intense, piercing eyes he surveyed them all in a swift, sweeping glance.

"Hello again," he said to Ancil then strolled further along the corridor and entered another room.

"Who's yer friend?" said Pyke.

Ancil's features were a picture of open-mouthed surprise mingled with the strain of attempted recollection. Then his face lit up. "Ah, right, him!"

"Who?" the others said, almost in unison.

Ancil looked at Pyke. "It was just after I sent those guards on a mad dash to Crazytown. I got to the door to the corridor back to the security station, and that guy was just coming out and he held the door for me. He was carrying that case then, as well."

Pyke nodded, thinking over the odd encounter, certain there was something familiar about the man. *Well, how many loopy, cranky types have we crossed paths with during our time on this planet? Enough to staff a coupla good-sized carnivals!*

"Ah, probably nothing," he said. "Probably someone trying to find a safe spot."

"While we go galivanting off in search of Raven and her man-slugs?" Dervla said.

Before Pyke could respond, a female ship's officer appeared from a side corridor up ahead and strode purposefully towards them.

"Shit," Ancil muttered. "Right, don't forget our cover story and our band names…"

"Friends and guests," the officer said. "Please remember that this section must be evacuated within the next six minutes due to the ongoing emergency. A provisional guest-list checkpoint has been established up on the gallery-lobby in the forward axial area."

Then, with a professional smile, she turned and hurried off.

"Evacuating?" said Kref.

Dervla looked at Pyke. "Ongoing emergency? Doesn't sound like where we came in."

"Nope." Pyke scrutinised Hokajil's map, no longer certain that it was accurate concerning the extent of the time-zones. "There are two passenger lifts going up from this gallery-lobby, one to port, one to starboard. All we have to do is get to one of them without being noticed."

Dervla's smile was weary. "While being the invisible, easily overlooked types that we are!"

"A diversion may be called for," Pyke said. "Ans, see all the stuff you pilfered from the weapons cabinet—anything like a flashbang among it?"

"Got a couple that look like they might be that kind of thing but…" Ancil shrugged. "Won't really know till I throws 'em!"

"Okay, we'll see if there's somewhere safe for it to go off—meantime, let's get going. Hasty walking is called for here—no running or drawing attention. Let's go."

Following Hokajil's deck map, Pyke led them to the end of the passageway and swung right. The second opening on the left apparently led straight to the lobby area but just as they were coming up on it there was a weird midair ripple in the stretch of corridor further along. Then the ripple turned into a vertical crack which opened wide enough for a tall figure to squeeze through, carrying a laser carbine of some sort.

"Skaggin' hell!" said Pyke. "It's Ustril!"

Some pursuer in a visored helmet appeared at the crack and tried to stab at Ustril with a glowing shock stave. Pyke had the plasma slugger out but couldn't get a good aim. Then the Sendrukan scientist dodged the stave thrusts and struck her assailant with the stock of her carbine. The attacker fell back with a cry and quickly Ustril pointed a small device at the crack which closed up and vanished. Then she turned, saw them dashing towards her, stumbled against the wall and slid down to the deck.

Ancil and Pyke got to her before the others, and helped her into a sitting position. Dervla was there with a flask of water, even some biscuits she must have looted along the way. The Sendrukan lady scientist, though, seemed to have had a rough time of it.

"You look like you've been in the wars, Doc," said Pyke.

Ustril nodded, sipped more water. "My own fault, Captain." She looked at Dervla. "I am deeply sorry for how I treated you—it was an act of rash folly that led me to chase after...after treasures that remain out of my grasp."

"Where was that place that you came from?" Dervla said.

"More to the point, how did you create that door?" said Pyke. "That might be handy..."

"While I was searching," Ustril said, "I met some...strange people, some of whom have been here for a very long time. They told me how the Time-Mosaic has grown over the many centuries, and some of the facets now reach into alternate versions of this ship, some almost unrecognisable!" She leaned forward, expression intense. "And I met different versions of you, all of you, and I learned so much...I got lost in the fractured facets until I met..." She gave a dry, bitter laugh. "Someone I thought was a younger me at first, but turned out to be the daughter of a much older version of myself. She was well versed in the tales of her bygone days, as she put it, and knew the fate-tales of all the divinities..." She shook her head. "That's what we are to them. She knew what I had to do to help you, and showed me how to get back to the first five time-zones." With a sudden urgency she grabbed Pyke's sleeve. "Captain, you must not go up to the gallery-lobby! Raven knows you have the crystal shard and has prepared a deadly ambush!"

"How do you know about the crystal?" he said.

Ustril's smile was sardonic. "Facet-survivors like my almost-daughter know about the Essavyr Key, the crystal fragments, and the crystal shard that you carry. It's what all the factions and struggles and skirmishing is about, and it's what Raven wants so desperately."

"We're not completely defenceless, Lieutenant-Doctor," said Ancil. "We're now all armed."

"But you're not just facing Raven Kaligari and her two surviving underlings," Ustril said. "She has allies, ruthless backers and fanatics from the Time-Mosaic who will do anything to bring about your downfall."

The sentence ended with the Sendrukan looking pointedly at Pyke.

"Okay, I get it," he said. "I'm a high-profile, in-demand target with a bull's-eye painted on my forehead. Trouble is, Raven is *our* target—we know she's working for an entity called the Legacy, and that she's come here to get her claws on the rest of the crystal, like you said." Reflexively he touched his jacket chest pocket, feeling the shape of the crystal beneath the material. "But you're saying we have to avoid getting into a tussle with them so instead we can...do what, exactly?"

"Bypass Raven's ambush and make for the next time-zone," Ustril said. "You have sympathisers and supporters there who are eager to make Raven and her allies pay."

"That's a decent objective," Pyke said. "I'm just not up on how we'd go about getting there. How about opening a crack like the one you came through? We could hop inside and take a detour round the uglies, then exit next to the airgrav-shaft to the next deck."

But Ustril was shaking her head. "There is no way to control which facet the temporary lacuna opens into—there's even a risk of opening a lacuna to vacuum since in some alternative versions the Damaugra has torn quite a few breaches in the hull. No, if you look at the map Hokajil gave you..."

"You know about that?"

"I've spoken to a couple of Hokajils during my travels—one was mad and conversing with gods living in his pockets; the other was also mad but he was coherent and ultimately informative." As Pyke produced the map and prodded at the deck they were on, she leaned closer and pointed. "Through that door is a passage that slopes up to a long dining balcony that runs round the upper wall of the gallery-lobby. Stealthy traverse to the far end and a down-ramp will take us straight to an airgrav-shaft."

"Guards?"

"Not sure. Between one and three."

Pyke nodded. "Okay, we'll take that." He eyed the corridor end beyond which Ustril had appeared. "All righty, my lucky lads and lasses, let's gear up and get ready for some stellar-class sneakery. Moleg, take point, we'll be on your tail."

Ustril got to her feet with Dervla's help.

"Are you up to this?" she asked.

The Sendrukan looked tired and drawn. "I twisted my ankle a day or so ago while fleeing from hunters in a facet where the food had run out. I can function well enough for a while."

They started along the corridor, a straggling bunch, senses alert, guns at the ready. Dervla laid a hand on Pyke's arm and leaned closer. In a low whisper she said, "Still don't trust her."

"Think it's a trap?"

Shrug. "Something skeevy about her just showing up like that."

Pyke glanced over his shoulder. Ustril was bringing up the rear behind Kref and Ancil, with her carbine balanced on her shoulder. *Mighty swift change*, he thought. *From aloof scientist to gun-wielding badass after one trip through Hokajil's crazy time-patchwork? Well—maybe yeah, maybe no. Better safe than sorry, though.*

Hooking his energy pistol-of-indeterminate-output onto a chest pocket, he pulled Dervla closer for some on-the-move winching—she was about to push him away when he surreptitiously pushed the leather-cased crystal shard into her free hand. After a brief, tender kiss he quietly murmured in her ear, "If things go south, bail out, take Ancil along if you can—they'll be focusing on me, don't worry, I'll be right as skaggin' rain!"

They drew apart and he saw her slip the nightmare crystal into an inside pocket, even as she eyed him uncertainly. "Aye," she said. "You bloody better be."

The door was an archway. Pyke and Moleg took up positions on either side, Pyke peering up the ramp, then advancing with caution, half sidling along the wall, ready to duck if any hostiles came into view. None did—the balcony was clear. He beckoned Moleg and the others to follow, and a quick backward glance revealed that Dervla had backstepped to the rear, pacing alongside Ustril.

When the ramp reached the balcony both he and Moleg went into a crouch. There were square tables spaced alongside the rail but Pyke also noticed that the balcony's back wall had eight recesses separated by mock buttresses. And as well as having a table and two chairs, each recess also had a door.

"What the hairy hell," he muttered.

"Do we need to check the doors, Chief?" said Moleg.

"Yeah—you and me go for the third; Kref, you head for the second, and Ancil, you take the first. Dervla and Ustril can provide cover. Okay?"

Although I wish I'd known there were going to be those skaggin' doors before we got up here!

With handguns held shoulder-high and muzzle-up, they advanced along the balcony. Pyke gave one of the tables a shake as he passed, trying to gauge its usefulness as cover—the tabletop was thick and made of some weighty wood-like material, so might do at a pinch. *So help me, if this is a setup I'll...well, probably die with a profanity on my lips, I guess.*

They drew level with the third door. Moleg crept over to the recess, while behind them Kref and Ancil were doing the same. Once positioned and ready, Moleg gazed back at Pyke, who'd lowered a table onto its side, angled towards the door. Kref and Ancil's eyes were on him, awaiting his signal. Then, purely out of reflex, Pyke glanced the other way, further along the balcony, just as Raven Kaligari strode into view, a gun in each hand, and started blazing away.

Pyke roared a curse and fired back while wrestling the table round to face the oncoming danger. Moleg was firing from round the shielding buttress and Pyke snarled as he sneaked a look

round the table-edge, firing off a volley as he did so. He caught
a glimpse of several dark-clad forms but the most striking thing
was the sight of three Kaligari henchgoons crouched behind
upended tables, calmly unleashing a stream of energy bolts in
his direction.

Then suddenly he realised that there was firing coming from
behind. He looked round, saw Ancil wrestling on the floor with
another Raven-doppelganger while Ustril was struggling with
one armed with a pair of knives. Yet another had a chokehold
on Kref and a dagger to his throat, at which the big Henkayan
was laughing like a deranged gouger. Then from the back Dervla
loosed a dead-on shot at Ustril's opponent, hitting her in the
head.

"Get out!" he yelled to them both. "Get out of here *now*!"

Concentrated fire hit the table he was sheltering behind, spraying splinters everywhere.

"Ah, ya want some, do ya? Here, eat this!" he roared, firing
a spread of pulse-bolts over the top of his table, then pausing
to sneak another look. There were several bodies lying around,
bleeding into the balcony carpet, but now it appeared as if there
were a couple of squads of minions, each led by a Raven, all
aiming their salvoes at him.

Pyke was on the point of telling Moleg to fall back when a
small object arced overhead from behind and clattered against
something up ahead. There was a moment of shouting voices,
then a loud crashing bang, with debris flying, some of it bloody.
A glance over his shoulder revealed a bloody-faced Ancil giving
a thumbs-up while further back Kref was crowded behind one of
the buttresses. Next to him on the floor was one of the Ravens,
her face a gory pulp. Of Ustril and Dervla there was no sign.

For a moment the firing slackened, then there were coordi-
nated bursts, this time with what sounded like heavier calibre
rounds. Pyke could feel heat coming through his table from the

other side. But this time Kref and Ancil were able to join in, with the latter showing off the odd boxy-looking gun he'd looted from the security station. Pyke glanced round again to ask Ancil if he had any nades left, and found him holding a hand-launcher which fired off a trio of shells.

Three deafening explosions merged into one cacophony of destruction. More shattered detritus was flung everywhere and Pyke saw a couple of torn corpses flying out from the balcony. For moments after there was a terrible reverberating silence punctuated by the sounds of Pyke's rapid breathing, and muffled groans from where injured and dying Ravens lay.

"How...what is that?" Pyke said.

"Three-pattern shift-gun," said Ancil. "Can reconfigure itself as a pistol, a short-barrelled shotgun, and a launcher." He coughed. "What I want to know is, where did all these Ravens come from?"

"Different time-facets," Pyke said. "Only answer—but that means there must be loads of them out there—queueing up to have a shot!"

"Pretty resourceful of her to pull together an army like this," said Moleg. "You'd almost think she had help."

"Hmm, the Legacy?" Pyke said. "I wonder—"

Just then a woman's voice came loudly from the other end of the balcony, a familiar voice.

"Hey, Bran—I must say, I'm impressed. Not a bad tally for you and your crew of bumblers..."

"Scumsucking shit-heel," Ancil muttered.

"...but all this was never more than the preamble. Bran, we need to talk and I'm coming out—unarmed."

Pyke looked at the others. "Be ready for any tricks."

Carefully, he straightened up, while still on his knees, and rested his arms on the curved edge of the holed and battered table. Before him the rest of the balcony was a scene of devastation strewn with smashed chairs, ruined tables and horribly dead bodies. Raven had emerged from the very last door along the back wall. She was carrying a small energy pistol with which she finished off a couple of pleading survivors as she crossed over to the balcony railing and casually leaned on it, for all the world like a passenger simply taking in the view.

"As you can see," she said, "I've been making so many new friends since I got here, it's crazy. And when I told them that I was on a mission to retrieve an heirloom of great sentimental value from your thieving hands, I was overwhelmed with offers of help." She laughed. "You've got some reputation, Bran, right across the Time-Mosaic—well, probably not *you* but some unhinged version of you…"

"What are we doing here, Raven?" he said. "Why are we sitting here, listening to you? The Cosmic Spirit and I, we both know how much you love the sound of your own voice but, really, it all boils down to two questions—what is it that you want to say, and when do we get back to the shooting?"

"Patience just isn't in your skill set, is it?" Raven said mockingly. "As I said, all that's gone before was preamble—it's now time for the main act!" She raised her hand and snapped her fingers. "Bring her out!"

A sense of foreboding stabbed at Pyke's chest, and seconds later his worst fears came true. Her hands bound, Dervla emerged from a side door at the far end, stumbling along between another pair of grinning Ravens who gripped her arms. A third Raven walked behind, holding a chain looped around Dervla's neck. And behind her stalked the Sendrukan, Ustril, her face sullen and haggard with shame. Pyke could barely contain his fury and fear, and the terrible panic churning in his guts.

"C'mon, Raven, don't be a skagging monster about this!" he said. "Take me in her place—you know it's me that you want!"

"That would be true, Bran, but actually I already have you, right here in front of me!" Dervla and her guards halted next to

Raven who smiled and patted Dervla on the cheek. "Of course, then you might say, 'Here, Raven, take the Legacy's crystal, let my beloved go!'—mightn't you?"

Without shifting her gaze she held out one empty hand to the side, and Ustril came forward to place the leather-cased crystal in the outstretched palm. Pyke's heart sank and all hope guttered like a candle burning its last.

"But look—I have that, too!" Raven held the crystal up for all to see. "Finally."

"I've done as you asked," said the Sendrukan. "Now pay me!"

Raven snapped her fingers again. A slender figure stepped out of one of the recess doors holding a grey-ribbed carry case. As he drew near Pyke recognised him as the mysterious man who'd greeted Ancil soon after they'd reached this deck: sharp features, hair sculpted back, high forehead. He approached Ustril and showed her the contents of the case; she nodded, accepted the case, closed it up then left the wrecked balcony with long, swift strides. The courier's departure was equally brisk.

Well, thought Pyke, *considering all the options, we are well and truly skagged. Unless Ancil can come up with another grenade while me and Moleg take down Raven and her creepy clones with perfect one-shot kills...* But he knew that Raven or any of her copies could open Dervla's throat long before the first rounds were heading their way.

"Aw, don't worry, Bran—the shooting's going to start again very soon. But first—this!"

In one smooth motion, Raven unfastened the crystal shard's leather cover and slapped it into Dervla's open hand which Raven had suddenly grabbed. Pyke bellowed raging curses at Raven, handgun flung out to target her, and Raven's flushed, exhilarated face stared back at him, mocking him, daring him to fire. Dervla, held upright by the doppelganger guards, shook and jerked for several grotesque seconds.

Then suddenly she was still. Pyke felt nauseous just watching, knowing full well that Dervla's consciousness had been transferred to the strange virtual simulation called the Isle of Candles. Meanwhile, in her place...

Dervla's mouth smiled. Dervla's eyes were bright with an invading intellect. As the hands were freed and the chain removed there was a muttered exchange between her and Raven, and she nodded and laughed. Raven handed her a combat knife and took a step back. And when Dervla turned towards Pyke and the crew it was the Legacy that stared out of her eyes.

"Ah, Captain, we meet again, and in such a timely fashion! Your beloved, the invigorating Dervla, has such an energetic personality. She will make a fine addition to my theatrical cast of contenders." The Legacy held up the hand gripping the crystal shard. "You see, a great and long-denied awakening will soon be upon us, the prodigious and exquisite unfolding of a new reality, an unstoppable wave of transformed being which will require shape and direction, expression and form. That will be Dervla's role, along with you and any of your followers who measure up..."

Behind the Legacy, Raven had continued backing away and Pyke's sense of terrible panic did not abate.

"She doesn't want to be any part of your plans!" Pyke said. "Or me, or any of the others. How could we be any help to you if we're fighting you every step of the way?"

The Legacy laughed, Dervla's own laughter but now twisted into something loathsome.

"How can you do that when you don't know what you're fighting about?"

Then, quickly, with no warning, the Legacy plunged the dagger into Dervla's heart. The Legacy was still smiling, despite Pyke's near-wordless roaring and shouting, as he fought against Ancil and Moleg, struggling to climb over the table, to get to her, to get that knife out of her. But they held him back, sobbing, forced to watch as Dervla sank to her knees, blood drenching her front as her hand released the crystal shard, allowing her own consciousness to surge back into her mind. Pyke remembered how it all went, and his gaze met hers for a flickering moment before her eyes rolled to show the whites and she slumped over onto her side. Everyone was shouting, Pyke was pleading with the others to let him go to her, Ancil was swearing terribly and Kref was holding onto Pyke's arms. Pyke fought against all restraint anyway, ignoring pleas for him to calm down. There was a tormenting emptiness eating away at his mind, a bleeding void, yet from the neck down it felt as if he was brimful with a burning need to destroy.

Then there was movement at the other end of the balcony— more Ravens, identical faces and all heavily armed and clad in body armour of one kind or another.

"Let me go!" gasped Pyke. "Gimme my gun!"

"No problem," said Ancil.

They barely had time to snatch up their weapons and dive for cover before the onslaught began.

CHAPTER EIGHTEEN

Dervla, the Crystal Simulation, the city of Granah

Commander Delara, head of the Emperor's Nightblades, frowned at the vial and the fragments of tempering hammer that were scattered across the armourer's workbench. The vial was an ornate object of some dark golden material with rich blue threading between its curlicues. It had a peculiar sheen to it and had resisted her every attempt to open it, up to and including brute-force impacts. The iron-surfaced workbench now had a vial-shaped dent in it while the vial itself was undamaged, unmarred and unchanged. Rumours of its sorcerous properties seemed well founded.

From her main chamber came the sound of someone rapping on the door. Delara cursed—that would be V'Sel, her second-in-command, with a report on the Nightblades' state of readiness, the disposition of the Shylan Shields, the current state of weapon and provision stocks, and possibly a word or two on the weather. Delara swept the hammer's remains into a pile, secreted the vial within her high-collared hacketon, then went to open the door.

"Commander," said Lieutenant V'Sel, clenched fist pressed to mid-chest as she strode in. "I have the all-aspects report for you."

The two soldiers sat down at a plain table situated near the door.

"Still no message from the Shylan Shields?" said Delara.

"None, but we have had one from the office of the Master of Seals."

"Ah, their protector." Delara smiled. "Let's see what it says, hmm?"

V'Sel took out a missive envelope, made from pale-blue silk-paper and bearing an official stamp. She broke the seal, extracted a single slip of paper, swiftly scanned the contents and grunted when she was done. "Offers congratulations on your retrieval of the deadly vial—which he spells phial—and the capture of one of the would-be assassins. Requests that you present yourself at his chambers without delay, so that you may acquaint him with all the details of the mission in advance of his own report to the Emperor." She placed the letter and its envelope on the table. "Requires that you also bring the vial to ensure its safe and complete eradication."

Delara and V'Sel exchanged a look of amused scepticism.

"He really has no shame," said Delara.

"He cannot force you to attend him, Commander."

Which was true—the Nightblades answered only to the Emperor, but the nature of court politics was a maze of manners which required decorum and affability for successful continuity.

"No, he cannot but I shall visit him later, purely as a courtesy. The vial, though, will remain here."

V'Sel gave a sharp, satisfied nod. "So, the all-aspects report, Commander?"

"Are there any problems requiring my immediate attention, Lieutenant? Anything presenting a detriment to the operations of our enclave here in the palace?"

"Not at this time, Commander."

"Good. Any other matters of which I should be made aware?"

"Just one. Our prisoner is asking to speak with you."

Delara raised an eyebrow. "After that unhinged performance on the rooftop, I see no reason for another encounter."

V'Sel frowned. "I agree. However, he insists that in the event of such a denial I should tell you these words—'I know how to destroy it.'"

Delara's eyes widened. "Say again?"

"He said—'I know how to destroy it,' and that you would know what that meant." Lieutenant V'Sel rested her arms on the table. "Do you know what he means, Commander?"

"Yes," Delara said, getting to her feet. "It means that we're off to have a chat with our prisoner."

The Nightblades' brig was a small but well-built, iron-banded confinement cell, situated on the enclave's top floor. The prisoner, however, had been spirited away from the courtyard on his arrival, marched through side passages and down to the fake pantry in the basement. Near the Commander's chamber were the sentry stairs which linked the patrol gallery to the upper walkways and the inner yard. It also provided a more discreet route down to the kitchen and stores.

"Who's playing decoy?" Delara said as they descended the spiral stairs. Due to the nature of the ongoing intrigue she had ordered a decoy prisoner placed in the brig.

"Cadet Teolm," said V'Sel. "She's had experience in dressing up as a man."

Delara gave her second-in-command a perplexed look.

"Comes from a theatrical family, Commander."

"I see. Useful."

The fake pantry was reached from the main storeroom door, thereby avoiding the gawping stares of the kitchen staff. There were two guards, both stationed in separate darkened alcoves. Nods were exchanged as the commander and her deputy approached the "pantry" door. One of the guards unlocked it and the two women entered. A shadowy figure could be seen reclining on a simple truckle bed in the spartan room lit only by two rush-candles on a shelf in view of the door's viewing slit. A table and two chairs sat between the candles and the door.

The door thudded shut, the lock clicked and the prone figure swung his legs round into a sitting position.

"Got my message, then," he said.

"I'm here out of curiosity," Delara said. She went over to sit at the table, gesturing to the other chair. The prisoner laughed and came over to sit opposite her. "I'm curious as to why an assassin wishes to erase the means of assassination."

The prisoner sighed and shook his head. "Okay, let's get one thing straight—since we got here, me and my associates have done nothing but try to hunt down the blood-poison in order to stop it being used!"

"Yet there you were, climbing out onto a tavern roof, carrying a stuffed boar containing that very vial."

"Put that way it sounds berserk, but if I hadn't grabbed it and hauled my arse out onto the roof, the vial would now be in the hands of the Shylan boys, or, rather, the hands of their boss, the Master of Seals!" The prisoner sat back. "I hear he's got, shall we say, ambitions!" He grinned.

Delara regarded the prisoner's open amusement with irritation. For an ordinary citizen, he appeared to be disturbingly well informed.

"Your name is Pazzyk," she said. "Is that correct?"

"Sure, why not?"

"Okay, Mr. Pazzyk, my time is precious so why don't you tell me, in as few words as possible, exactly how to destroy the vial."

The man Pazzyk leaned on the table, one hand supporting his chin as he continued to smile his annoying smile.

"Gladly. You are completely right—time is not on our side

so I'll give it to you straight. The only way to destroy that skaggin' vial is with a magical artefact or object of some kind. It was created by sorcery and only sorcery can harm it. And it so happens that there is a suitable magical artefact right here in the palace..."

Lieutenant V'Sel, who had been standing just behind Delara, moved round to the table and leaned in threateningly. "What is this artefact, and where is it? No more games, citizen, tell us what we need to know!"

"Nothing would please me more," Pazzyk said. "But in return I need some reassurances, and some cooperation. In short your help." He was looking directly at Delara. "We need each other— you need me to help destroy the vial, I need your help to bring about a...certain outcome."

"You're testing our patience," said the lieutenant, but Commander Delara held up one hand.

"Wait, V'Sel, let us hear his plan. As long as it's brief."

"It's pretty straightforward, Commander," Pazzyk said. "You, me and a handful of your finest will go skulking through the shadows of the palace to where my companions are imprisoned, we set them free, then we go in search of that artefact I mentioned. We dodge any search parties, use the artefact on the vial, smashetty-smash, job done!"

"This is drivelling, infantile nonsense," snarled V'Sel. "Please, Commander, let me loosen his tongue by more direct means."

"Well, I've heard that one before," muttered Pazzyk.

Delara leaned forward, smiling at her prisoner. She spread her hands. "Time is running out, Mr. Pazzyk. Tell us what you know about this artefact, before things get ugly."

Pazzyk's smile never wavered, although Delara did notice a sheen of sweat on his neck.

"She is really impressive," he said, indicating V'Sel with a tilt of the head. "I bet you selected her yourself, y'know, after that attempt on the Emperor's life two years ago..." He cocked his head, as if listening. "Yeah, in that trading port on the east coast...called Egrishen, that was it..."

Delara was aghast at hearing these dangerous things spoken. "You cannot possibly know about that! Tongues were silenced and grim vows were taken to ensure that knowledge of that incident could not spread." She drew her battle-knife and V'Sel did the same. "Perhaps you're not an assassin after all, but a spy—I have heard that diabolical abilities like the reading of minds can be learned by those eager to serve dark powers. What power do you call 'master'? *Speak!*"

It only took a moment for the man Pazzyk to go from relaxed affability to wide-eyed alertness.

"Well, that was a leap of deduction," he said. "All I wanted was to keep you occupied, keep our little chat ticking along while..."

Suddenly one of the rush-lights on the shelf went out, and Pazzyk breathed a sigh of relief.

"Finally," he said.

With the intention of reaching across the table to grab the man by the scruff of the neck, Delara went to shift her upper body forward while raising her arms—but not a muscle responded. She was locked in position, a frozen statue whose voice was likewise rendered unresponsive, and since V'Sel had neither moved nor spoken she too had to be afflicted by the same paralysis. Delara's mind burned with anger, and a crawling fear—she was defenceless and completely at the mercy of their prisoner.

Then, just to heighten her trepidation, the air above Pazzyk rippled, twisted, and a curious bird, a mechanical wooden bird, appeared and alighted neatly on his shoulder.

"Sorry about the delay," said the bird. "It was a little more complicated than anticipated but I've modified Dervla's awareness stream with the cut-outs and the dummy persona. The

bold Lieutenant V'Sel is no longer in stab-the-assassin mode but
awaits the trigger speech to kick off the new narrative branch."

Listening to this, Delara could barely comprehend what was
being said. Something had been done to both her and V'Sel—
were they possessed by spirits, or merely by vile spellwork?

"Will this dummy persona of yours do the job?" said Pazzyk.
"It won't get tongue-tied or anything…"

"I will be guiding it at all times," said the demonic bird. "But
there is a small chance that the narrative conjunction may have
to be reset."

"Oh really!"

"Let us not forget that all this is modifications-on-the-fly, all
untested. I mean, it is going to work! It's just that live testing usually reveals…rough patches—don't worry. I'll ensure that V'Sel
brings a squad of the Nightblades finest and the commander's
background knowledge should get us to where your companions
are being held."

"Shame about the no-teleport rule," said Pazzyk.

"That would be a red flag to the Legacy, plus sirens and fire-
works. My own hacks are dangerous enough," said the bird. "Let
us focus on the task in hand."

The man Pazzyk nodded, then glanced uncertainly at Delara.
"Sorry about all this," he said. "I'm betting that you hardly
understand what any of it is about, which I guess must be scary,
right? All I can say is that after we break my buddies out, we'll
head for the artefact and get you sorted, get you back to your
old self—or something like it. Then maybe you can tell me what
the hell's going on out there in the really-real world and how the
frack you ended up in here."

"Time to go, Captain," said the sorcerous bird.

"Right, okay." Pazzyk straightened, cleared his throat and
turned to face Delara's second-in-command.

"Lieutenant V'Sel," he said. "My name is Pazzyk—I'm an

old friend of the commander's from our days as raw recruits at the Coronal Hill training grounds. I couldn't reveal my secret identity until now because..."

The sound of his voice slowly faded to a muffled murmur as her sight likewise grew hazy and dark. In the moments before all senses drowned in nothingness she could just make out her own voice speaking to V'Sel, confirming all that Pazzyk had said and offering whatever assistance he needed to crush the blood-poison conspiracy. Then grey rolled into black and not even fear remained as she slipped into a blank void.

When the blackness rolled away, it seemed that no time at all had passed—yet Delara was clearly no longer in the Nightblades enclave. The surroundings were dark and cold, smelling of brick and dank mould, while hooded figures stood quietly nearby, facing an archway beyond which torchlight flickered. In her hand, a short padded cudgel, a thief's weapon, yet her battle-knife was still at her waist. And next to her, hood thrown back, stood the man Pazzyk. Delara could feel the cudgel's weight in her hand and knew she was back in command of her own body.

We're in one of the old armoury vaults beneath the east wing, Delara realised. *Which puts us directly under the Shylan Shields barracks and their lockup. This mind-spy's plan must be to assault the cells from below, which is complete madness. If I can disable him, perhaps some of the others will retreat and save themselves...*

But before she could mount her attack, a familiar paralysis swept over her limbs, petrifying her voice.

"And there it is," said the voice of that bird-thing. "Narrative conjoining has become disaligned and knocked the dummy persona into standby—I can reset it very easily."

The man Pazzyk looked round at something positioned out of Delara's view. "Will this happen again?"

"It's caused by an accumulation of sub-distinctual errors,

which is an unavoidable by-product of my modifications. In short, yes, we can expect this to happen again."

"Huh, not terrific—well, as long as it crops up when we're between hotspots everything should be fine and dandy. Are you back in charge yet? Are we ready to kick in the doors?"

"Dummy persona is conjoined to the narrative—the commander is ready."

"Grand—lead the way."

Delara wanted to beg them to kill her but her throat was like stone as the black void came in like a tide.

When it swept away again, Delara was running upstairs, two at a time. She stumbled, barking her shins on the stone steps. Someone came to her aid, helped her back to her feet.

"Are you okay, Commander?" It was one of the Nightblades, a cadet called Lelinue.

"Come on, keep going!" said a man's voice from further back down the stairs. "We can all have a gab later—those skaggers are only seconds behind us!"

It was the man Pazzyk, accompanied by a fur-snouted Gomri. Delara snarled, sidestepped the cadet and went down to confront him.

"Damn, it's happening again," said another voice from somewhere high up. "The narrative conjunction is out of alignment!"

Pazzyk saw the look in her eyes and dodged her first blow with the cudgel. Then he stepped in close and she could feel a hand close around her fist which was gripping her knife hilt, locking it in place.

"Stop...Stop and listen to me!" he said. "We broke my friends out of the clink so the Shylans are hellbent on carving us up and spilling our blood—so you can either do the job for them and submit yourself to their tender mercies, or you can help us figure out how to slow them down!"

For an angry moment they were locked together, then Delara decided that his comeuppance would have to wait. She relaxed her grip on the knife, and they broke apart.

"They're only four flights away, Captain!" said the Gomri.

"What have you done!" Delara said. "What tumult have you unleashed?"

"Oh, you know, sedition, strife, chaos, the usual!"

The man Pazzyk was both insulting and aggravating, but right at this moment the Shylan Shields presented a far more deadly threat. She dashed upstairs, looked left and right to confirm her suspicions about their location—the disused north-west tower, reserved for vassal delegations from the south-east frontier—and directed everyone's attention towards the dustsheet-swathed furniture.

"Grab it all, sheets included, and stack it at the head of the stairs! Quickly!"

The five of them went into a frenzy of action, dragging or carrying divans, cabinets, tables, chairs out to the landing and piling it all up. A trio of burly Shylans with axes appeared from the floor below—in response, Delara opened a bottle of berry liquor she found during the ransack and doused the sheet-covered heap of furniture. She lit it with an emberwick provided by one of her cadets and together they kicked at the burning mass which toppled over and down. As they hurried off through the mostly empty day lounge, the drawn-out crash mingled satisfyingly with the cries of the trapped.

"Nice tactic," said Pazzyk. "That was done with a familiar flair..."

"I require answers," Delara said, noticing that they were heading towards a door that led out onto the linking galleries. "Where are we going?"

"To meet the rest of our friends at the Quadrad Pavilion up

on the roof of the Shylan Barracks—our diversion should have given them an easy journey."

Delara was baffled. "You'll—we'll be trapped. There is no escape from that roof!"

"Oh, there is, so I've been assured, anyway…"

"I'm ready to realign her conjunction," said an invisible voice. "Now that the excitement has died down."

"There is no sanity to your actions," Delara said. "All will die because of your folly."

Pazzyk gave a sad smile. "We're caught in a strange trap, Commander, a deathless existence where life isn't what it used to be. All right, Arky, ready when you are."

She drew breath for another condemnation but the black void flowed in, flooding her in nothingness.

And then the nothing drained away, and again her surroundings were completely altered between one heartbeat and the next. One of her cadets was helping her to her feet quite near the head of a flight of steps leading up the side of a white stone wall. It was cold up here, the light was grey and specks of rain were gusting around them.

"Quickly—bring her up here!"

The voice was that of the sorcerous machine-bird, and as she stumbled up the steps Delara realised that she was at the pavilion shrine atop the Shylan Shield part of the palace. And behind her, the crack and snap of arrows striking stone, and thrum of a bow launching a response. The cadet ducked and hurried over to the open, pillared pavilion whose curved white roof sheltered the four statues standing within.

There was Pazzyk, on the floor, propped up against the statue's plinth. A snapped-off stump of an arrow jutted from his upper chest and his exposed shirt was drenched in blood.

"A bad place to take an arrow," she observed. "Your survival may be in doubt."

Pazzyk smiled through pain and exhaustion. "I've had worse, dear heart. Now, you might want to get that poison vial ready—you'll need it for the next part."

She shook her head even as she produced the dark golden vial from within her hacketon. "You think that the statues of the Eternal Four are somehow magical? That they can destroy this?"

Pazzyk nodded but it was the mechanical bird that spoke from its perch on the upraised hand of one of the statues. "We do not think so, we know so."

"I have been up here many times over the years," said Delara. "There are neither rumours nor lore concerning any mysterious properties."

"Would we have come this far," said Pazzyk, "if it wasn't worth all that skagging trouble? Humour me. Try tilting back the Granavian statue—it's loose at its base so it'll be easy to stick the vial under it."

He was clearly dying, so she decided there was no harm. "Very well."

She climbed up on the plinth, found herself face-to-face with the smiling statue of Thelya, the personification of Granah and the Granavian people. Weighing the vial in her hand, Delara crouched down and saw how the flat base had indeed come loose from the mortared surface of the plinth. All she had to do was push Thelya's midriff, tilting her back enough to...

The moment her bare hand touched the cold cast bronze of the statue there was a bright, engulfing moment, as if the sky had broken open and a special kind of sunlight flooded straight into her mind. A dazzling river of knowledge and memory and thought, an exhilarating swirl that surged in to fill up gaps, holes, absences she never knew she had. The unveiled essence of being—Dervla breathed it all in and became herself. She let out a burst of laughter...

Then Delara's own memories leaped to the forefront of Dervla's focus—Pyke!

Quickly, she scrambled back down to where he lay against the plinth, babbling apologies. How could she not—she had been Delara, she recalled how the commander had treated him, remembered her short-sighted distrust...and now here he was bleeding to death.

"Damn you, Brannan Pyke, don't you dare die on me!"

"Not planning to, ould girl—just nip back up there and finish the job, would you kindly?"

"You mean the vial really does have to be..."

"Destroyed, yes..." He coughed agonisingly. "All this around us is a story, a simulation, and the destruction of that vial winds it all up—then slots us, fresh and undamaged, into a new one... Dammit, T'Moy and Vrass are retreating from the western steps. Quick, Derv, finish the job, smash that thing to bits!"

Trusting Pyke's orders, she clambered back onto the plinth and wedged the vial right under the statue's metal base. Then she stood and tilted the bronze statue back as far as she dared—and swung it down with all her strength.

There seemed to be a fraction of a second where the vial resisted the impact, then with a crunching and a cracking it shattered, disintegrating into a spray of tiny splinters and flecks.

Dervla felt the change in the air, as if it were suddenly charged and intense. There was a rumbling that rolled all around the ominously darkening sky. Pyke's allies—a Shylan, a Barlig and a Gadromi, going by Delara's memories—were retreating to the pavilion with axe-wielding Shylan guards in pursuit. But as Dervla watched the Shield guards suddenly froze in mid-dash and faded away to nothing, as did Delara's last two surviving

Nightblades cadets. From above came another low rumble and dark spots began to appear across the tiled rooftop.

Here comes the rain, Dervla thought.

"Right, this is the tricky part," said the mechanical bird.

Dervla stared at the speaking contraption. "Who or what is that?"

"That's RK1, residual sub-drone left behind by our old buddy Rensik," said Pyke. "Look, time's about to run out—this simulation is going to be replaced by a new one and this time Arky there is going to try and keep you, me and my amigos"—he paused to wave at the other three who were now sitting on the benches outside the pavilion, enjoying the light shower that was falling—"from having our personalities shrink-wrapped with storytale roles again, which, quite frankly, sucks big time…"

"Transition is about to start," said the bird. "Prepare yourselves!"

"Derv, remember 'Whisky In The Jar'?"

"The song?" she said. "Why?"

Pyke smiled. "If we're separated, listen out for it, okay?"

"We need to talk," she said, suddenly anxious. "Bran, I need to know, you need to tell me…am I dead?"

His gaze was a frozen thing of anguish and she knew.

"I'm here with you," he said, voice cracking. "Just remember the song…"

The rumbling grew louder and omnipresent, drowning out all other sounds. The sky began to gyre slowly about them and the city, its walls and buildings, started to fly away while pure light settled down around them like a fine mist, then poured down like a deluge of brightness which dissolved them away.

She woke up walking, a seamless drift from dream, emerging unhurriedly into dim surroundings, a lamplit alleyway, its air warm and dusty. A quiet thread of thoughts was winding its way through her mind, how important it was to get this basket of pastries to her sister over in Darvanu, how that selfish man of hers was going to bring the wrath of Vondral down on her with his heresies, how she had to be careful not to attract the attention of the patrolling Sanctifiers, how vital it was that she be back in Shalmy District before dusk...

Dervla stopped in her tracks, suddenly wide-eyed. She inhaled deeply and exhaled through pursed lips as she stumbled over to lean against a tenement wall. What was it that Pyke said about the transition to this place? That the residual was supposed to keep their personalities from being "shrink-wrapped with sto-rytale roles"...?

What am I? she wondered. *Am I real any more? Am I just a model of a human being, some kind of mannequin that thinks it's a person?*

She recalled what the real-world Pyke had said days ago, how his mind had been trapped inside a simulation while that data-entity, the Legacy, had conspired with Raven to get the Angular Eye. He'd said that the Legacy had captured copies of its hosts' minds before it disposed of them.

Dervla raised her hand to her chest as a cluster of memories suddenly bobbed into her mind, seeing again the dagger, her hand on the hilt, the gush of blood.

She was hit by a wave of dizziness and her breathing grew faster. Damn it, no, she couldn't afford to get panicky and weak right now! She had to find Pyke so that she could get the full story, find out what this shifting from simulation to simulation was all about. Most of all, she needed to find out if Pyke and his gang had any contact with the outside, with the real world.

She was still carrying the basket and, as she stepped away from the rough building wall, she caught a whiff of its contents and was suddenly ravenous. She opened the lid, inhaled a cloud of savoury deliciousness and grabbed one of the pastries then started nibbling which led to munching and quickly ended in a swift devouring. These delicacies were for her sister, Ketili (her own story-name was Seshila), but it looked as if they would have to be liberated for a higher cause. After consuming another couple (which left three), Dervla went off in search of an old, old song.

Pyke had told her which tune to listen out for, but not whereabouts in the city—or were locations uncertain variables in this sneaky infiltration of the Legacy's elaborate scenarios? *But if it was going to be some totally random spot, Pyke would surely have warned me of the possibility!* She had to assume that if he'd told her to listen out for "Whiskey In The Jar" when she came to, then she would have to be in roughly the right locale to have any chance of finding it.

She found that she had access to Seshila's memories of this part of the city, Shalmy District. As she walked she found out why the light was so gloomy and why lamps illuminated most streets—immense swathes of canvas or some heavy material had been draped over the buildings, huge curves of cloth propped up by heavy wood frames fixed to rooftops all around this area. Looking along the wider roads she could see that in the distance, where Shalmy gave way to the more prosperous Verusti District, the cloth screens were absent. Something in Seshila's memories suggested that certain areas of the city considered insufficiently pious or virtuous by the Temple of Vondral were denied the benefits of direct sunlight for as long as the impiety continued. Which indicated that extremist zealots were now calling the shots in the city of Granah—and that was never a good thing.

After roughly half an hour of trudging she came to a street of market stalls where every second covered barrow seemed to be overflowing with pies, smoked meats and sweet delicacies of every kind. Her stomach was starting to grumble again and the basket's remaining contents were exerting a kind of hunger-gravity on her hand. That was the moment when she heard music coming from round the next corner. She accelerated her pace, turned into the side street and found herself approaching a building with a long, seated veranda where locals ate and drank and talked. A pair of musicians strumming odd, long-bodied instruments, were working the customers and the song they were playing had nothing to say about the Cork and Kerry mountains...

Wearily, she about-turned and padded back towards the intersection. As she crossed the main market street, the strumming duo behind finished their toe-tapping number to a smattering of applause. The sounds of the stall owners' cries and bartering customers were, for a moment or two, untouched by music and that was when she heard it, someone picking out a motif of notes, faint but unmistakable, a melody she would have recognised anywhere. Dervla hurried along to the next crossing and turned right, following the music with iron resolve. By now someone was singing the first verse and chorus, someone who most certainly was not Brannan Pyke.

She ignored two shadowy, feebly lit alleys and took the next proper street on the right. The singing and playing was coming from across the street, up high somewhere—there, four doors along, a two-storey house with a wooden shelter on the roof was extended by a yellow canopy. She steeled herself, knocked on the plain door and entered a narrow hallway. A Gomedran sitting near the foot of a cramped stairway looked up from an unfurled scroll.

"Hi, I'm Vrass," he said. "He's waiting upstairs, top floor, trying to get them to pronounce your curious Earth words properly. Tell him still no sign of T'Moy."

"Will do, thanks."

She smiled and ascended the stairs. The first floor was a single room, murky from the shuttered windows, lit by several candle lamps by which she could discern a brawny Shyntanil sitting in a padded, inclined chair. He wore a bulky dun-coloured robe and was fiddling with a string of beads.

"Greetings," he said. "I am Klane. It is good to meet you without arrows flying about our heads." He pointed up at the ceiling. "The captain awaits yourself and others of our company."

She nodded. "I'd better check in, then."

She resumed climbing. She could see the yellow canopy flapping lazily as she emerged from the stairway onto a flat roof bounded by a low wall. The singing and playing was still coming from the other side of the wooden shelter she'd seen from down in the street—it took up a third of the space, with its awning angled away from the stairs. It was the yellow canopy which stretched over most of the rest of the roof, rippling in the slow, warm breeze that wafted through. Under the canopy a lantern cast a golden glow over a cluster of chairs and cushions, clearly a gathering place where a low table was graced with a collection of ornate bottles and beakers, and some additional clusters of candles. Beyond the flickering glow, a shadowy figure stirred by the low wall on the other side and came over, arms wide.

"You made it..."

Without hesitation she stepped into Pyke's embrace and hugged him tightly.

"You," she said, half muffled by his jacket, "have to tell me, and be straight with me, none of your nonsense...am I dead?"

Gently, he pulled away from her, enough to look closely into her eyes. "Do *I* look dead? Do *I* sound dead? Would a dead guy put himself through all this unbelievably complicated, puzzle-solving, death-defying drek? Not a bit of it, dear heart!—I'm not done with being alive so death can't have me. Okay, so we've been encoded into this very weird virtual-crystal-verse! Well, every part of me, every virtue and every sin and everything in between is in here, making up me! And the same goes for you." He took her hand, interweaving their fingers. "Not a shred of you got left behind. Forget what was done to you. All of you is here with all of me."

Tears were threatening to embarrass her. She sniffed, balled her free hand into a fist and very lightly punched his chest. "Thank you," she said hoarsely.

It was bullshit, of course, but it was Pyke's bullshit, a very special brand engineered from a fine blend of truths, half-truths and gorgeously embroidered optimism. It was just what she needed.

"There's a lot to tell," Pyke said. "About this place..."

"I'll bet," she said. "But first, now that I'm here, can your troubadours quit murdering 'Whiskey In The Jar'?"

He laughed. "Ah, but you see, you're not the only lost ship we need to guide into a safe berth—we're still waiting for T'Moy to arrive. However, I'll get them to forego the vocals while we're exchanging tall tales..."

"What about that residual drone? The one that looks like a toy bird? I thought it would be here, too."

"So did we," said Pyke. "Clearly, it succeeded in keeping ourselves from being buried under local-citizen characters, but managing its own transition over to this new simulation was always going to be tough." He spread his hands. "We just need to be patient and ready. In the meantime, take a seat, make yerself comfy while I have a word with the band."

He ducked through a curtained gap in the back of the shelter. The full-on music abruptly ceased. There was some muttering, then it resumed without the singing. Dervla snuggled down into a nest of cushions amid the pool of candlelight before Pyke emerged with a dark bulbous bottle and two tin cups. He settled down beside her, drinks were poured and she decided to go first, knowing that he deserved to know all about her demise.

It was a challenge but she managed to condense that twisty trail of encounters, fights and deranged locations down to a coherent summary, adding detail and explanation when Pyke asked for it. She told him about the aftermath of the museum heist, the haggling with Van Graes, the decision to fly out into the desert to meet the Sendrukan scientist, Ustril. Then she related their pursuit of Raven Kaligari through the wrecked segments of the ancient and enormous ship, the *Mighty Defender*, immense decrepit sections scattered across Ong's vast desert. The bot-swarm, the hazardous approach towards the drive section, Ustril's betrayal, entering the drive section and struggling through the Steel Forest and all its perils, the portal that led to the forward/bridge section. Then meeting Hokajil, followed by entering the forward section and the sequence of events that led to Ustril's second, devastating betrayal.

As she gave this account it dawned on her that this was indeed a different Brannan Pyke, one who had neither met Lieutenant-Doctor Ustril, nor bolted madly through an artificial forest spewing mind-altering vapours. The other Pyke was back there in the really-real world, trying to cope with her death, assuming he and the rest were still alive…

Dervla came at last to the gory detail of the dagger, planted in her chest by the Legacy during its brief hijacking of her mind and body. All through the long story, Pyke had listened with varying degrees of intent, but now she could see his jaw muscles tense and cold anger light up his eyes. She then finished with the very last thing she could remember, how one hand fell from the dagger while the other released the Legacy's crystal shard which fell to the floor…

"And that's it, pretty much," she said. "I can dimly recall some of the things that Delara did, but it was all just foggy dreams until I touched the statue."

Pyke nodded, his smile sad and weary. "It's really a hell of a state we're in, eh? I wish you weren't here but I can't help feeling glad that you are! Even if there's still another me alive out there. And after all that craziness you've been through—almost makes our adventures here sound tame."

"I don't know about that," Dervla said, looking about her. "This city, all its inhabitants, their personalities, the sheer depth of realism...this has to be the most detailed, immersive virtuality ever created and it's all running inside that chunk of crystal. I mean, what kind of power source is driving it—"

"The Arky drone explained it to me but I couldn't repeat it," Pyke said. "But tell me, you're sure that Raven definitely has the crystal shard?"

"She's been working with other Ravens and their allies drawn from the Time-Mosaic..." She smiled, seeing Pyke shake his head. "See? That's a weird kind of sub-reality, or para-reality, which is just as strange as this one."

"Alternate time-facets," Pyke said, uttering a low whistle. "What about the rest of the crew?"

"Well, the crew and the other you were taking cover halfway along that balcony, nearly twenty metres from where the Legacy did his little party-trick. Moments after I let go of that crystal, it would have been back in Raven's hands."

"Whole thing sounds like a hellish pantomime."

Hellish, she thought. *Yes, that sounds about right.* "And, of course, for all I know the other Pyke and the crew have been captured and had their minds sent here."

But Pyke shook his head. "If the other Pyke was a prisoner and Raven used the crystal on him, I would *know*, I promise you. My guess is they're still alive and kicking out there, kicking and scratchin' and making bloody nuisances of themselves!"

"Thanks," she said. "That's the kind of hopeful defiance I need right now. Okay, c'mon, time for your story—give!"

"Okay, I guess that the real-world Pyke told you about his experiences on the Isle of Candles before the Legacy failed to kill him..."

"Before I managed to save his arse with a little prudent fore-thought, more like..."

Pyke grinned. "We only have the best talents in my crew. So, aye, while the other Pyke and you and the crew flew off into the desert, I got bounced back into the Legacy's laugh-a-minute theme park. Stuck on that bloody island until Rensik's residual drone showed up and figured out the puzzle that was holding us up."

He went on to relate how solving the Isle of Candles puzzle triggered a transfer to a new simulation set in a big medieval city called Granah, capital of an empire of the same name. Three other Residents of the Isle of Candles had been transferred, too, and all four met up in the course of a tangled intrigue that led from mysterious keys to mystery bodies to a hunt for a vial containing a sorcerous poison made to turn the Emperor mad.

This elaborate quest was a puzzle of the Legacy's design, supposedly a kind of test for which it needed candidates for some unknown purpose. At the same time, RK1, the residual drone left behind by the Construct drone, Rensik (another victim of the crystal shard), was investigating the nature and underpinnings of the Granah simulation. It discovered that the crystal shard was no ordinary crystal—in fact it was hardly related to ordinary matter at all. According to Pyke, RK1 had found that the crystal was composed of a lattice of "exotic dimensionality," "woven equations" and "architectonic boundaries"—the residual drone also said it was a para-dimensional storage of vast scale.

"Wait a second," Dervla said, head spinning with the onslaught of jargon. "So that crystal shard is some kind of weird-matter engineered to hold and run this ultrafine resolution virtuality? That's pretty mind-bending…"

"No, you're not quite getting it yet," said Pyke. "When a drone uses the word 'vast,' we're into staggering magnitudes. This entire simulation, and all the encompassing essenceware needed to run it, guide it, regulate it, is contained in a tiny little pocket partitioned off from the rest of the crystal's gargantuan interior…"

She stared at him for a moment, grappling with the concepts, adjusting her comprehension of this object that they'd been hauling around for days.

"That big, huh?" She nodded. "Well that throws new light on some of the things we've heard about the crystal shard."

"Tell me more."

"We learned that the crystal you were carrying around was one of three pieces which apparently become some kind of devastating weapon if they get put back together again. And the Sendrukan Ustril was searching for it, too—she has her own agenda, the two-timing, backstabbing bitch..." Pyke nodded as he listened, but he was also smiling a tight, nervy smile which was never a good sign. "So, how bad is it, this weapon?"

He gave a dry chuckle. "Devastating doesn't begin to cover it."

"Is it portable?" she said. "Can you mount it on a gravtank? On a ship? *Is* it a ship? Have you actually seen this thing?"

"Oh, I've seen it, or some of it, and, frankly, it's bloody terrifying."

Pyke proceeded to tell her about a region of stars and planets, bound together by webs of glittering obsidian, entire worlds re-engineered by a pitiless, relentless enemy, a viral nano-assimilator which, hundreds of thousands of years ago, had grown rapidly to dominate dozens of star systems and threaten a nearby interstellar empire. Ancient sentient powers became involved and imprisoned the infected region inside an artificial dimensional construct which was then broken in three. The fragments were then separated and taken to secret places in the furthest reaches of the galaxy.

Dervla frowned. "I can't begin to tell you how far-fetched this sounds."

"Comes over like the background to a megabudget three-vee, don't it?" Pyke downed a cup of the pungent liquor he'd brought out, then poured himself another. Dervla covered her cup when he offered a top-up. "Aye, well, I wish it was just a feverish story but I've seen it, Derv, seen worlds overwhelmed by this stuff, this nano-matter virus. It turns everything into itself then builds shelves and spires and cable to reach out and up, or extends itself into whatever machines it needs to dig down into planets to mine out their guts. I've seen this stuff attack suns, enclosing all that power then extracting it and channelling it!"

"This sounds crazy," said Dervla. "I mean...berserk. But after what we went through trying to catch up with Raven..."

"Wait till Arky arrives," Pyke said. "I'll get him to give you a quick glimpse of Nano-virus Hell—it'll make the hairs on your hairs stand on end!"

Dervla was almost starting to feel creeped out. "So all those infected suns and worlds are locked inside the crystal shard, along with us?"

"No, the simulation is partitioned off from the rest of the crystal interior," he said.

"So all that viral nano-matter is working away, like unholy eggs getting ready to hatch..." She shivered but Pyke shook his head.

"There's three parts of this thing, remember. It was broken soon after it was made all those millennia ago, and that fracturing arrested all the entropy, all movement and sentience. It's as if those stars and planets have been in stasis for thousands upon thousands of years."

Dervla nodded, trying to get her mind around such colossal concepts. She slung back the remains of the drink she'd been nursing and held out her cup for more. Pyke obliged.

"So, the Legacy—what is he or it?"

"Arky says it was a semi-sentient guardian program left by the Ancient who built the prison, but it ferreted out data files from the frozen nano-domain and the file contents ended up corrupting it..."

Just then Klane poked his head up from the stairway. "Looks like T'Moy is heading this way."

Then he was gone.

Pyke said, "Let's have a look," and the two of them went over to the side of the roof overlooking the street, leaned on the low wall and studied the people moving around by the light of lamps and torches. Beneath the propped stretches of heavy grey cloth the air was warm and stuffy, full of the smell of burning oil and torch tallow. Looking up, Dervla could see through holes and tears that it was daylight outside the covered district, dry but not sunny. She wondered what it was like here when it rained.

"There he is," said Pyke, pointing.

Along the street, a tall figure in robes and a hood was stalking in their direction, avoiding contact with fruitsellers and other stall owners, pausing to step into a doorway. But then they lost track of him until Dervla saw the same colour of hood heading away from the hideout, up a side road opposite.

"Is that him?" she said.

"Looks like the same get-up and the right height," Pyke said. "But where the hell's he going?"

"He is being followed," said a voice behind them.

Pyke smiled and turned to the newcomer. "Thought you weren't going to make it."

"Busy traffic this weather."

"So who's following T'Moy?"

The residual drone RK1, in the form of a wooden mechanical bird, was perched on a hanging lantern, regarding them both with beady eyes.

"Just some temple thugs with too much time on their hands," said the bird. "Only to be expected while the city is under the control of a paranoid, iron-fisted fundamentalist theocracy. That, unfortunately, is a minor problem—we have a far more pressing matter to deal with."

Pyke was sombre. "Your plan, whatever it was, is a non-starter."

"Sadly, yes. The plan was to fuse my sentience matrix with an autonomous character node, creating an enhanced data entity sufficiently powerful to bypass the partition lockouts and assume command of the master directives network of the entire dimensional lattice!"

"Would that give you control of the crystal shard?" Dervla said.

"Exactly so. I conceived this plan in conjunction with my progenitor, Rensik, who was using a compliant shell clone of his core cognition to conceal his activities behind the scenes, so to speak. Unfortunately, the shell clone received enhancements from the Legacy which allowed it to break compliance with the original Rensik. Who has been defeated and assimilated. The Rensik clone now appears to know of our existence, such that its agents will soon be here."

Pyke looked confounded by this setback. Dervla could see him struggling to fend off despair.

"Where does that leave us?" he said, waving over Klane and Vrass whose faces confirmed that they'd overheard the news. "What escape options do we have?"

"There is one possible course of action," said RK1. "There is a particular function embedded in the dimensional lattice which is not a subsystem of the master directories network. It is independent and was only ever used once. It's called the lattice integrity enabler and it is what the Ancient builder used to allow the original imprisonment crystal, the Essavyr Key, to be shattered into three parts."

Pyke's eyes were wide. "Any restriction on how many parts the crystal could be broken into?"

"None that I have been able to discover."

Dervla's own thoughts were whirling. "Like that blood vial!" she said.

Pyke grinned. "Smash this crystal into thousands, tens of thousands of specks and slivers!—no one's going to be putting that back together..."

The bird ruffled its wooden wings with faint clicking. "Just so. There are two preconditions, however—the integrity enabler can only function if the original crystal itself is whole again. So we would have to stand by while our enemies achieve their paramount goal. The other precondition is that someone on the outside must be ready to attack the reunified crystal with a weapon, a gun, a hammer. Even a heavy enough rock would suffice."

They all looked at each other.

"Is there any way we can make contact with someone on the outside?" said Vrass. "Get them to make sure that the crystal gets what it deserves?"

Dervla's heart sank. *Well, that's hardly going to happen, now that Raven's got her claws on our crystal shard!* But before she could relate this dispiriting fact, RK1 beat her to it.

"Unfortunately, out in the real world custody of our crystal shard has passed to Raven Kaligari, a servant and proxy for the Legacy. However, it may be possible to induce a neuroflux linkage with someone in the crystal's immediate vicinity, theoretically allowing you to exert control over them for long enough to carry out the destruction of the unified crystal."

"Sounds like a lot of ifs and maybes," said Pyke.

"I agree," said RK1. "And I'm afraid that if we are going to pursue this counterattack we must begin now. Also, fusing my sentience with a single autonomous character node will not be enough—it may require three or four to attain a high enough level of processing flux..."

"Ah right," Pyke said with a low laugh. "You're talking about *us*. Autonomous character nodes—that's us, right?"

"That is correct," said the residual drone. "I am sorry if I was not sufficiently clear. The fusion process incorporates your assigned processing flux with mine and melds together our direct awareness—your persona-state is compressed for the duration of the operation."

"Can we be revived afterwards?" asked Klane, who then smiled sardonically and shook his head. "Of course, if the crystal is destroyed as planned, there is nowhere to be revived in."

There were sombre looks all round, then everyone gave their assent to RK1's proposal.

"Very well—I shall fuse with one of you to begin with," the residual drone said. "That will enhance my abilities without attracting unwelcome attention—the rest of you I will discorporealise, which will help you to evade any simulation antagonists. So who will be first?"

Dervla put her hand up. "Choose me—I'm dying to hand out some payback to Raven in any way, shape or form."

"No, no, no," said Pyke. "You've been through the indescribable! You shouldn't be giving your own self up to being filed away! Arky, take me. You know me, we've been through all this together…"

"Sadly, Captain, logic dictates that I must accept Ms. Dervla's offer. She is the most recent denizen of reality to cross over, thus her knowledge of outside events is the most up-to-date." The bird turned its beady eyes on her. "Are you ready?"

Pyke was still complaining but she silenced him with a finger to his lips. "I'll see you soon, Bran. Count on it." Then she stood. "I'm ready."

The drone's bird-form suddenly began to glow brightly as it took flight straight towards her. When it reached her everything dissolved, she dissolved, in geysers of light.

CHAPTER NINETEEN

Pyke—the planet Ong, the wreck of the
Mighty Defender, forward section

Raven Kaligari was the very picture of triumph and vanity. From somewhere her underlings had produced a high-backed, austere chair in dark blue for her to lounge in. She herself had exchanged her scratched and battered body armour for a close-fitting uniform in charcoal-black with mauve trim—it was a bit of a departure from her usual Arch Villainess apparel.

"Sleek and professional, Raven," Pyke said. "Looking the part."

"The part of a dumbass," muttered Ancil.

Raven frowned and leaned forward. Her chair had been set upon a couple of large tables down on the wide area of the lobby, below the balcony where all the fighting had taken place. Her prisoners knelt before her, wrists and legs restrained.

"Oh, Bran, that it's come to this. Me, resplendent in both victory and finery—you, bound and helpless, my prisoner, awaiting your just and due chastisement, you and your followers, your little puppets!"

He shook his head. "They're not my minions, Raven—that might be how you think of all the suckers you force into doing your bidding, but that ain't how me and my crew operate."

"Aw, should I get out my hanky, Bran? Are you going to trot

out some paper-thin drivel about friendship? Never mind the hanky—better get a barfbag ready!"

"Look, all I'm saying is—if there was ever anything between us that really meant something, I'm asking, I'm *begging* you, Raven, let my crew go. It's me that you want, I know that it is—my crew is irrelevant to what you need..."

"Don't tell me what I need, Bran," came the retort. "I need what my master needs and, yes, we certainly need you. We need you *and* your grief, *and* your rage, *and* your bitterness—and all the darkness that waits within you." Her hungry smile was a terrible sight. "I am honoured to be midwife to the birth of a new Brannan Pyke, a new vassal for my master."

"Not in a million skagging years!" Pyke snarled.

Raven's smile widened a notch. "Let the contractions begin!" she cried and nodded to her guards.

First to be dragged up onto her makeshift dais was Ancil. Even with the restraints he put up a frantic struggle to the point where one of the armoured Raven doppelgangers had to cuff him round the head to subdue him.

"Careful," said Raven. "Don't damage him—he has to be conscious."

Hauled before her, Ancil was still dazed as they arranged him in a kneeling position. Raven broke a capsule under his nose and he was suddenly alert, coughing on whatever the chemical was.

"Hey," he said. "Who do I see about making a complaint? Your customer service really sucks..."

Raven bent down. "Sorry, Ans, no refunds." Then she grabbed his tied wrists and slapped the crystal shard into one of his unsuspecting hands.

The change was immediate. Pyke, watching impotently, cried out, alternately cursing Raven and imploring her to release Ancil. Kref was bellowing at her, too, and at Ancil, who was locked into a tense, full-body quivering, while his eyes were showing their whites. Then, as suddenly as it had begun, the tremors ceased and Ancil relaxed into a slumped position for a second. He raised his head, looked up at Raven and smiled.

"Master," he said happily.

With snippers, Raven cut the plastic bonds. It was Ancil's body that got to its feet and stretched, but it was the Legacy that looked out of his eyes.

"Ah, Captain Pyke, once more our paths cross. Clearly, there is an irresistible destiny at work—you bring me your friends, I recruit them into my great work, train them and make them ready for the budding and flowering of a new cosmos." The Legacy paused and cupped a hand to one ear. "Sorry? What was that? Oh dear, no more sarcastic volley? No more bitingly ironic comebacks? No—I imagine that would feel hollow and futile while your companions' lives hang in the balance. But only for a few moments longer."

Raven held out a curved dagger and the Legacy took it in its free hand. It weighed the hilt, held the blade's edge up to catch the light, gave a satisfied nod, then without hesitation rammed the point into Ancil's chest. Moleg averted his eyes, and Kref let out a deep, miserable groan. But Pyke kept watching as horror unfolded before him.

Moleg was next. As they came for him he said to Pyke, "See you on the other side, Chief."

From the moment they hauled him to his feet he fought them with elbows, headbutts, grasping hands and biting teeth. It took four to subdue him, and a syringe-full of something opaque. As before, Raven revived him with a small capsule but Moleg had learned from Ancil's treatment and kept his hands clenched in fists, no matter how they mistreated him. In the end she had her underlings hold him still while she pressed the crystal against the hollow of his neck. Moments later the Legacy was back, openly taking pleasure in the hijacking of another body and mind.

"The meat of the body is singular," it said. "It has weight and tangible density, momentum in its movements. Oh, bodies in the simulation give the impression of weight but that's really no more than shaped flows of numbers and equations—this is flesh and bone, this is substance. It has the anchors of life and blood, and the frailty of a soap bubble!"

Again the Legacy received the knife, again the deep heart-thrust. Those lips smiled a corrupt smile and let out a gasping laugh as Moleg's form fell to his knees. The Legacy left the knife where it was but let the crystal shard fall from his fingers. In the remaining seconds Pyke saw Moleg's own presence re-emerge in the line of his features, the set of his jaw, the dark of his eyes which turned to stare at Raven.

"All that is solid," he said hoarsely, "will melt to nothingness..."

Then he keeled over and lay still.

Pyke kept watching. All the anger, all the rage, had no means of escape and he knew, with a ghastly core certainty, that there was no escape at all. All the fury had burned in his brain, burned his every thought and emotion but now it was sinking and cooling, growing cold in his chest, an icy, numbing cold. Even as they gathered around Kref and began dragging him towards the dais, Pyke could only feel a deep hollow sadness. Sure, the crystal shard would record a version of any victim it touched, but that would only be a ghost made of data, a frail ghost subject to the whims of the Legacy. He had seen and experienced the empty futility of the Isle of Candles and if that was where those copies of Dervla and the others were going...

But it won't be long before my turn comes round again, then it will be back to those shadows and candles and uselessness...

They'd hit Kref with some kind of stun-prod and hauled his massive bulk up onto the dais. Table legs creaked under his weight as they single-mindedly levered him into a kneeling posture. Raven performed the same ritual with the cracked capsule then swiftly pulled away, as if expecting a savage reaction. Instead Kref just sat there and glared at her, a look of utter disgust on his face.

"You're dead, all your goons are dead, all your doubles are dead," he said. "'Cos the captain's gonna kill you dead, real dead, proper dead, dead that you don't come back from. Deader than dead."

Raven yawned. "Long speech, didn't listen."

Kref didn't twitch a muscle as she slapped the crystal against the underside of his considerable chin.

Pyke felt that cold knot in his chest start to burn him with a freezing fire. *I wish I could carry out your last wishes*, he thought as the vile presence of the Legacy distorted Kref's features with its gaping, malevolent grin, while Raven's high, girlish giggles rendered the scene even more revolting.

"Ah, another candidate for the supreme dominion to come!" declaimed the Legacy in Kref's deep gravelly tones. "This one is a..."

At that moment two small objects arced down from the still-smouldering balcony and exploded with raucous shattering violence. Twin flashes burned into Pyke's retinas as the force of the explosions threw furniture and bodies in all direction. Simultaneously, there was a sudden eruption of weaponsfire from the balcony itself, from the doors behind Raven's dais, and from somewhere behind Pyke. Before he could look round, a flying table crashed into the minions clustered near Raven's throne; here was an abrupt lurch of bodies which collided with the possessed Kref, shoving him off the dais.

Kref let out a grunt of pain as he landed on his side, and the dagger he'd been holding spun free of his grasp. Pyke saw it lying on the carpeted deck just a couple of yards away and reflexively moved forward on his knees. Instead of a punch from his guard, though, there was nothing—a backwards glance revealed his guard lying still and dead. Meanwhile, yards away, a group of Raven's minions were crouched behind tables, firing at knots of attackers moving up a wide corridor. Pyke turned back to see a dazed Legacy realising what he had lost and trying to crawl towards the dagger. On hands and knees Pyke struggled forward but the possessed Kref was closer. One big hand closed around the dagger's hilt and the Legacy grinned.

"Are all these newcomers here just to save you, I wonder?" it asked. "Or just some assault launched on the whim of a twisted copy of you or one of your merry band? Matters not—I have seen echoes and reflections of the new beginning, the bright and glorious moment when you decide to join us in our transcendent project! It's coming, Captain Pyke!—all these scurrying pawns and dregs amount to no more than a minor sideshow to the magnificent preamble!"

There was a roar of many voices followed by a surge of weapons-fire, sure sign of a charge. The Legacy barked out a laugh then sliced the dagger into Kref's neck, sawing through the dense flesh and muscle. In the following moment Pyke heard Raven cry out, a shriek of fury and frustration—he looked up, saw her move as if to leap off the dais towards Pyke's position, then automatic fire began peppering the dais and her throne. Her minions and bodyguards dragged her off the other side and into cover. For a second he wondered why she had been about to put herself in such certain danger—then he glanced round at Kref's dead, bloody body. The crystal shard, still partially sheathed in its leather case, lay next to one outstretched hand and his big, dark eyes held only the peace of departure. The carpet all around his neck and chest was crimson from the blood. Pyke whispered a farewell as he closed the big Henkayan's eyes.

"Ah, good, you're alive!" said a voice. "An operation like this is always littered with risks, what with all those slugs and bolts flying around."

Pyke pushed himself up, looked round and came face-to-face with Hokajil. Only it was a younger version, fewer layers of clothing and less grey in his hair, and somewhat more sprightly.

"Mr. Hokajil," he said. "You're certainly the last person I expected..." He breathed in deep, caught between wanting to scream or sob or shout at the man. "You should have been here, you could have warned—"

"How the assault unfolded the way it did?" Hokajil shrugged. "Planning was a bit improvised, let's say..."

"You're young!" Pyke said, anger draining away dully. "Are you another Hokajil from some time-facet or other?"

"That's it, in a manner of speaking!" Hokajil said. Excitedly he used a small knife to sever Pyke's bonds, then squatted down and pointed at the crystal shard. "Can I pick it up?"

"Wouldn't recommend it," Pyke said, quickly retrieving it. "Skin contact is fatal..."

"Provides the vector for the Legacy's neural hijack," said Hokajil. "Only to be picked up with gloves or protective material, or by someone who knows what they're doing."

Pyke gave him a dull look while fastening the shard's case with some twine dug out of a waist pouch, the original cords having been torn off earlier. "You seem to know a lot about our business. How did you learn that in a facet?"

Young Hokajil laughed. "Ah, you think I'm...no, I'm the original. The old man you met was someone I found in one of the nastier time-facets—I offered him the job and he was glad to accept. As for knowing about your background and the crystal and so on, well, some of us have been around the Mosaic for a very long time and the accumulation of lore has been hard won. All the time-zones I created turn and loop and gyre, and the peripheral time-facets cycle and close and open, and *their* peripheral facets likewise wheel and churn, shifting from darkness to light and back again." He looked around. "That's where we recruit our armies."

Pyke had been aware of tall figures dressed in hooded robes or bulky armour, clearing away bodies and debris, or herding a few captured prisoners off into a corner. Most looked like unfamiliar merc types, but here and there he saw Kref doppelgangers, the strangest versions of the big Henkayan. All seemed disciplined and sombre as they went about their duties. He found himself wishing that one would look at him in recognition, then made himself stop wishing. Made himself lock away the grief.

"Your boys look like they can handle themselves," Pyke said.

"There's a certain person, one who helped instigate this godawful mess and lot more besides, whose continued existence is like a hot spike digging into my mind..."

"Raven Kaligari?" said Hokajil, grinning. "We didn't find her among the dead, but we did capture a couple of her facet doubles."

"Raven—she has to die," Pyke said.

"That would be preferable," Hokajil said. "But what's more important is that your piece of the crystal key is destroyed."

"Well, sure, we thought of that," Pyke said. "But the thing's beyond tough—nothing seems capable of even scratching it."

"It would take a highly advanced technology to accomplish that deed," Hokajil said with a knowing look. "And it just so happens that there is a device on the bridge which would do the job. The inventor called it an omni-dismantler and it can disintegrate every kind of matter and even energy, so the exotic substance of this crystal shouldn't present too hard a challenge."

Pyke listened, hardly daring to feel a glimmer of hope. "Okay, sounds like what I need. How would you feel about coming along with me, maybe bring a few of these beefy guys? Raven's already got a lead on us and I bet she has more heavily armed uglies on call."

"As it happens, I was going to make a similar suggestion," said Hokajil. "I've already got the nod from three of these fighters, hardy veterans every one. All these people came together with the aim of defeating the gang of facet-thugs who'd offered their support to Raven, who's about as popular as rabies with these fellows. Most are keen to get back to their own facets, apart from the three I mentioned—kicking some more Raven-minion ass is very appealing to them."

"How soon can they be ready to move out?" Pyke said. "Longer we wait..."

"We actually have a significant advantage over Raven before we've even begun," said Hokajil, smiling as he tugged on a strap which slanted across his chest, pulling into view what he'd been carrying on his back. At first glance it resembled a cut-down laser carbine, except that there was a bulbous, glassy unit where the beam generator would have been, and the truncated barrel splayed out into five prongs with a fluted spindle projected from the centre.

"The time-thrower," said Hokajil. "Mark two!"

"Ah, upgrades."

"Very much so—with the mark two I can target the time-zone far more accurately in terms of both area and the margin of regression." Hokajil patted the device. "Raven has got a head start but we can create our own short cuts."

"Can't wait to see it in action," Pyke said, getting to his feet. He gazed down at Kref's bloody corpse, then looked over to where Ancil's and Moleg's bodies had been dumped off the side of the dais. The knot of burning cold twisted in his chest again.

"Some of my allies are collecting dead enemies for disintegration," Hokajil said. "We could do the same for your friends' remains, separately, though. Make it a private ceremony if you wish to say some suitable words of farewell."

"Separate from all those others," said Pyke. "I'd appreciate that. But no ceremony—I don't think I could stand it."

"As you wish. I'll give orders to that effect before we leave." Hokajil indicated a main door at the other side of the wide lobby area where three figures waited. "Shall we?"

Pyke nodded and together they made for the door.

"I've just realised," Pyke said. "I'm unarmed, which is something of a rarity for me."

"Not a problem, Our adversaries very kindly left behind a wide selection of high-powered ordnance." Hokajil pointed out the nearest of several piles of lethal looking weaponry. "So, what's it to be—destructive or very destructive?"

Pyke smile was grim. "Ah—decisions, decisions!"

CHAPTER TWENTY

Pyke—The Crystal Simulation

When Arky said that he was going to decorporealise them Pyke took that to mean that they'd be turned into opaque, ghostly forms. Which is exactly what happened. What he didn't expect was the bleached, monochrome appearance that everyone and everything now had. It was as if he was inside one of those archaic flatvees that they had on Earth back in the Petrol Age. Then there was the greatly subdued level of sound—he, Vrass and Klane had stayed together after escaping the safe house but the only way they could hear each other was by speaking loudly directly at each other. Even then it was a thin and stifled sound. As for the sounds of busy, populated streets, that had become a faint, background murmur.

Then there were the visible/physical aspects. Pyke and the others were visible to each other but invisible to everyone else in the simulation; they could also touch each other and all the physical objects of their surroundings, but everyone else could walk right through them. Which made their "escape" from the safe house more a relaxed saunter than a mad dash—and they were lucky enough to cross paths with a perplexed and equally ethereal T'Moy in the road outside. After bringing him up to speed on developments, they decided to leave this canvas-smothered quarter of the city and find a new place to hole up in.

So, with a free run of the streets, Pyke led the others to Illustrious Square, bounded on one side by the townhouses and towers of the nobility and the richest of the merchant class. Before long they were billeting down in a closed-up rooftop penthouse suite that was exquisitely decorated and adorned with the best of everything. That was when they discovered that not only colour had been leached from their perceptions. Sealed packs of smoked sausage and a couple of wheels of cheese were uncovered in a larder, but when eaten they proved to be tasteless. The texture in the mouth felt right but there was absolutely no flavour. When they opened a bottle of wine, the experience was the same. Flat, monochrome, nothing.

Despondent, Pyke nevertheless took a plate of pale grey cheese and glass of dark grey wine out onto the roof garden and sat on the wide stone parapet, chewing, drinking, wondering what the next step was. Seeing Dervla shimmer into a pillar of streaming radiance then flow into the shapeless yet compact array of glowing motes which RK1 transformed into had been half-entrancing, half-sorrowful. He had in a way expected the composite entity to then shoot up into the sky but instead it seemed to turn sideways and disappear.

Down in Illustrious Square, well-dressed couples attended by servants strolled among the statues and fountains, or sat in the little pocket gardens. One thing common to them all was the tendency to avoid the opposite side of the square where Sanctifier guards patrolled in front of the Temple of Vondral (formerly the Temple of Shamaya). As Pyke watched, a dark-haired figure staggered out of an alleyway, clutching his head. He seemed disorientated as he looked about him then slapped himself in the face and shook his head. Suddenly Pyke was staring down at the man with unwavering attention, struck to his core with an appalled sense of recognition.

"Crap and a half," he said. "It can't be…"

Half disbelieving, he continued staring down as the man,

who looked more and more like Ancil, wandered slowly in the direction of the temple. *Was* it Ancil? Was he in a ghost state, too? But that notion was soon dispelled when someone from a nearby café came out a-ways and spoke to him, beckoned him over; the maybe-Ancil altered course and went to join the café waiter who guided him to a table.

Pyke stared down, and swallowed. "Bloody idiot," he muttered. "How did you end up in this mess?"

Then he noticed that a cudgel-bearing Sanctifier guard was heading in Ancil's direction, and knew he'd have to intervene. He whirled and dashed back indoors to the penthouse kitchen where pieces of chalk sat in a niche next to the menu slate that hung over the herb racks. When Vrass yelled to him about what was up, he shouted back, "Emergency rescue, can't stop!" then raced down two floors of stairs and out the front door.

Dodging around the few people entering and leaving the building (even though he could have barrelled right through them) he ran across the paved road and onto the square. He ducked round one of the hedge-bordered pocket gardens, heading for the café, and was relieved to see Ancil still seated there on his own, sipping a beaker of something hot and steaming. The Sanctifier guard was receiving a tongue-lashing from an officer on account of leaving his post, and a loud and vocal reprimand it was, too. Pyke allowed himself a low laugh as he strode over to Granah's newest arrival.

Ancil had a nervous, worn-out look to him. Pyke knew that the only way he could be here was if he'd died out there in the real world with the crystal shard in one hand and the mind of the Legacy squatting in his head. *Like a murderous toad*, he thought.

Luckily, the table where he sat had a smooth wooden finish, just right for scrawling on with chalk. Pyke thought for a moment, then began.

Hi Ans—how's yr day?

The reaction was standard Ancil—eyes staring, hands gripping the chair and table as if he was ready for fight or flight. He glanced around him before speaking in a hoarse whisper.

"Who's...there? Who's doing that?"

Well, Nade-Boy, whose job is it to take care of the crew?

An incredulous smile came over his face. "Chief? That you? You invisible or something?"

No time for gabbing, too dangerous—see that doorway over there with the dome over its porch?

"Got it."

Second floor, through the glass/iron door. And wipe all this away b4 you go.

Ancil nodded, moved one hand to his drink and knocked the beaker over. With the provided napkin he mopped and wiped and smeared the lettering. Satisfied, he stood and headed for the townhouse entrance, unaware that Pyke was already leading the way. Not feeling any effort, Pyke ran on ahead, climbing the steps three at a time. The penthouse door was ajar when he arrived and no one was indoors because they were all out in the roof garden, gathered around a visitor. Garbed in a pale blue, hooded robe, it was Dervla, or, rather, it had Dervla's face while the eyes held a shifting glitterglow.

"Wasn't expecting to see you pair again so soon," said Pyke. "Run into any snags?"

"Bad news and good." It was Dervla's voice but sounding slightly like a synthesised version. "With our blended capabilities we were able to find a path through the simulation regulatory frameworks and redundancy subsystems. In stealth mode we gained access to some of the feeds that flow into the Legacy's central cognitive core—oh, you'll be glad to know that real-world Pyke is still alive..."

"Well, of course he is," said Pyke.

"Best news of all is that the crystal shard is back in your counterpart's possession!"

"Derv!" said a voice from the penthouse doorway. "It was your voice!"

"Hi, Ans—great to see you! And, y'know, sad as well."

Ancil rushed out onto the rooftop garden, clearly seeing only the Dervla/RK1 entity.

"Yeah, shit happened, and it happened to me," he said. "I remember when that Legacy bastard took you over and made you use the dagger…" He paused. "And there it was, happening to me—Derv, I'm dead but at least I'm here…"

"I felt the same, Ans," she said. "It's hard to get used to."

"Hey, did you know that the chief's around here someplace, only he's a ghost."

"He's here right now, along with some other friends," Dervla said. "We had to modify them a little for safety reasons and we need to do the same for you—there are some nasty types watching out for Pyke and all his friends."

"As long as I can see and talk to the chief, I'm okay with that."

"Just to let you know, when you're a ghost it's a rather colourless world," Dervla pointed out.

"Can't be any worse than the Steel Forest," Ancil said. "Let's do it."

Dervla stared intently at him for a moment, then nodded.

To Pyke, everything remained unchanged, but Ancil was clearly staggered by the sudden appearance of Pyke and three strangers.

"Chief!" he cried, and he and Pyke grabbed each other's hands and shook them vigorously.

"Damn good to have you back with us, laddie," Pyke said before quickly introducing Klane, Vrass and T'Moy. "Been hearing a bit about your adventures since the museum job," he went on. "Man, sounds like it's been a wild ride!"

Ancil smiled and shook his head. "Such a crazy setup—you're here while you're still alive out in the really-real world! How do you get your head round it?"

"Just try to go with the flow of whatever gets thrown at us, ould son," Pyke said.

Ancil nodded, looking around him. "This, though, is very cool, very noir!" But then he turned to Pyke and Dervla, suddenly anxious. "Has there been any sign of Moleg or Kref? They were next in line after me…"

Pyke felt a sickening dread. "How did it happen?"

Ancil's story essentially picked up after Dervla's account ended. Clearly, Raven had decided to stage a multiple execution, an opportunity for the deranged Legacy to indulge its malevolent appetites. Yet according to Dervla/RK1, the crystal shard was back in the other Pyke's hands. He glanced at Dervla.

"What makes you sure that my counterpart has the crystal again?"

The Dervla/RK1 entity regarded him with gleaming eyes. "The data feeds we tapped into were clarified audio segments collected from variable tensility zones on the outer dimensional lattice…"

"You're saying that sound vibrations can be picked up by the crystal?" Pyke was appalled. "It's basically a skaggin' microphone?"

"Hardly. The crystal shard's exposed surface only has a few tiny areas capable of registering sound vibrations—if the shard's leather case is fully closed up prior to being pocketed, nothing can be detected. All we know is what the audio segments conveyed, that Pyke has the crystal shard in his possession and that he encountered a ship passenger called Hokajil."

"Hokajil!" said Ancil. "The old inventor guy we met before we entered the forward section."

"That's him," said Dervla. "The audio feed was fragmentary but it appears that he is going with the other Pyke up to the bridge to somehow destroy the crystal shard."

"But the crystal is indestructible," Pyke said.

Dervla nodded. "We have no further details about what Hokajil said about how this was to be accomplished. But we need to make contact with your counterpart and persuade him to allow it to be joined with the other pieces—then we can engage the integrity enabler and prepare the whole thing for its complete destruction."

"Did Arky show you the black planets?" Pyke said. "The splintered suns, all those strangling webs and cables?"

Inside the pale blue cowl Dervla nodded gravely. "He did. I've never seen anything that terrified me the way that place does. We cannot fail, Bran—this is why we need someone else to join us, to add their strength to ours so that we can attempt to communicate. We can modify the sublayer of the outer lattice so that they generate a neuropathic field, which can pass through the leather case and any clothing. Then it's a matter of attuning to synaptic resonances and we should be able to talk directly to real-world Pyke."

"I'd like to take the plunge," said Pyke. "Paddling around in the shallows of my own brain has a deranged appeal."

Dervla smiled. "You were our first preference since your underlying cognition-perception internodes may help the attuning process. If you are agreeable, we will incorporate you into our composite..."

"Sure, but first I need—we need to know if Moleg and Kref have ended up in here, too. Can you find that out?" Pyke and Ancil exchanged a sombre nod.

For a moment Dervla stood still and unspeaking, then her gaze met Pyke's. "It is hard from this location to be certain about identities but we can see that two other high-autonomy actors were added to the simulation not long after Ancil. We have appended a basic city map with their locations to Ancil's current awareness."

"Excellent!" said Ancil. "I can see it!"

"Well, don't forget that they can't see you," Pyke said, holding out the remains of the kitchen chalk. "You'll probably need to scavenge for more of this."

"Something I'm no stranger to, Chief—so, guess this is it, then."

Pyke grinned and shook hands with Vrass, Klane, T'Moy and lastly Ancil. "It's been a blast fighting alongside you all in one way or another. I don't know how this is gonna work out for us, for them out there, but at least we gave it some heft!"

"I know how it's gonna be," said Ancil. "We're gonna kick the Legacy's rotten ass into some honking big trash folder then wave bye-bye as it gets erased. Then we get some colour back and a spring in our step, and we find a good bar to have several large drinks in celebration!"

Pyke laughed. "That," he said, "is exactly how it's gonna be." He glanced at Dervla. "Now's a good time."

She smiled, reached out to his face with her hand and...

Did the light flow into him or did he flow into the light? Conjoined with Dervla and RK1 he became aware of distinctions and blendings—they were the Three who were One while being the One that relied on the unique strengths of the Three. And in this threefold unity they were in motion, gliding along a scarcely visible line as were myriad other knots of composite light, flying on bright lines that formed an interconnecting web of pathways. Except that their outward aspect was deliberately masked to appear dull, low-priority, while their pathline was projected as a minor conduit. The truth was that they moved independently of the pathline intermesh while mimicking that which they were not.

The dense interweave of lines spread away quite a distance, and all of it was clustered around a pulsing glow that looked like a hemisphere of spikes, rods, stacks and opaque shell-like segments which drifted between these curious protrusions.

[The simulation of the city of Granah]

The voice stuttered through his perceptions, sounding more like Dervla than the drone.

[We are steadily moving towards the periphery of the intermesh. From there we shall ascend to the sublayer of the dimensional lattice and begin our work]

Pyke, feeling like a compressed, telescoped version of himself, was content to glide, to watch and to marvel.

At the shadowy edge of the intermesh they dispensed with the pathline pretence and set a course for the sublayer, which Pyke understood to be the underside of the crystal shard's tactile surface. Their composite appearance was now apparent, to Pyke's perceptions a tri-axial agglomeration of bright nodes, enfolding planes and pulsing spirals. Beneath them the labyrinthine intermesh, and the glowing simulation analogue it enclosed, looked huge, colossal, a jewelled complexity amid inky darkness. Then RK1 reminded him of the scale of the space-time-space contained within the entire dimensional lattice, and how the simulation and its attendant systems took up a minuscule corner of that entire yawning gulf. Reminded him also of the frozen, suspended horrors that waited on the other side of the partition. In truth, this was an unimaginably vast dungeon and they were a tiny mote crawling towards its ceiling.

Suddenly he began feeling elevated alertness, a sense of heightened threat levels, and a switch to flight and evasion mode.

[We have been detected—a killswitch, one of the Legacy's interceptors, is heading our way—be ready for variable-vector course corrections!]

RK1's voice came through stronger this time. As an observer Pyke could see a spinning oval object swooping towards them, wondering if this was comparable to being pulled over by the cops for having a faulty indicator glyph. Then, without warning, a jet of jagged lightning leaped towards their tri-axial form while bright rods and struts began to unfold from the approaching oval thing. In just a moment or two the new arrival had expanded into a multiplex reticulation, a dazzling megacluster of integrated systems and matrices—next to their triform coalescence, this entity had taken on a towering, oppressive presence. It *was* the Legacy.

<I suspected that there was an intruder violating my domain and now I have you—reveal your origins and intentions>

It seemed that they were trapped in a lightning web—until RK1/Dervla/Pyke revealed the nature of their cunning by making their projected decoy disappear. They then employed a locale-switch, using embedded properties of the nearby sublayer itself to port their triform quiddity to one of several preset destinations, a tactic prepared in advance of this foray.

But the Legacy, backed by the full power of the simulation intermesh, used sheer brute force to hurl itself across the intervening distance. They had barely taken up a defensive posture before devastating charge-blows started to rain down on them. Pyke could feel RK1's irritation at having underestimated the Legacy's trans-systemic abilities, and Dervla's grim, last-ditch resolve in the face of overwhelming odds, one of the things about her that he found most endearing.

The repeated attacks were weakening their tri-axial form, softening them up for the big one, a large and savage strike which shook them to the core of their composite. Already weak from the onslaught, the threefold composite split apart—Pyke felt it like a crack stabbing through his mind. And it was *his* mind. Separated from Dervla and RK1, he found his perceptions adrift in the gloomy darkness, while the huge, jagged form of the Legacy seemed even more immense than before as it loomed over the three dissidents. For a second it looked as if Dervla and RK1 were trying to merge again but before Pyke could reach out a bright pathline winked into existence, passing right through him. Against his will, it began pulling him towards the sublayer.

<Still trying to evade me, Captain Pyke?> said the Legacy <Be patient—I will hunt you down soon enough!>

Amalgamated once more, Dervla/RK1 instituted a retreat manoeuvre and vanished. Pyke guessed that they must have reappeared somewhere else because the Legacy at once took off at a fearsome velocity. Pyke, however, could only dangle on this shining line as it drew him in.

Am I a balloon at the end of a piece of string, or a fish being reeled in? Pretty sure I'm not a person any more…

The surface of the sublayer came nearer and nearer, a smooth dark grey incised with what he thought were stylised circuit patterns but then realised were odd layouts of symbols of some kind. Even so, it was no help as the grey surface came ever closer. He had no face to feel with yet he did experience a weird drowning sensation as his viewpoint sank without pause into the grey.

Coldness in a void, then in a cramped, restricted space. Then he felt stretched out and vaporous, then heavy and clustered.

Then weight, body weight, the feeling of lying on cold stone. He breathed in, caught a faint whiff of burned wax, then opened his eyes to a dusky sky. Pyke sat up, looked around and let out a sound halfway between a gasp and a laugh—he was back on the Isle of Candles. The time-worn masonry, the skeletal trees, the lichen-patched flagstone, the glowing clusters of candles, the gathering shadows, all very much like the first time he was here. Except—he shifted forward onto hands and knees to get a close look at a nearby group of burning candles and saw that the flames were motionless and heatless. No wax melted, flowed or puddled.

Also, this time there was no Vrass to greet him. Instead, a different form watched him from the flagstone path that wound up to the villa. Pyke got to his feet, strolled out of the stone gazebo and over to the waiting observer.

"Heard you were dead," he said.

"Rumours of my demise," said the Construct drone, Rensik,

"have been greatly exaggerated." The drone had the miltech flanged boxy appearance from before that encounter with Raven right back at the start. "Although, to be fair, our entrapment in this place shares some characteristics with the usual meaning of 'demise.'"

"No longer in the land of the living," said Pyke. "But still not dead."

"Or in your case, the reflection of a man still living."

"Yeah, yeah, while all my friends die the death." He couldn't keep the bitterness out of his voice. "So, where is this place? Is this the actual Isle of Candles?"

"It is. The Isle of Candles is actually a separate simulation running in the dimension lattice sublayer," said the drone. "The Legacy apparently decided to create a buffer area for his candidates that was separate from the main simulation area. An anteroom to his lab of mazes!"

"Did you bring me here for something important, or are we just going to relax and philosophise while this bit of the cosmos goes to hell?"

"Oh, we certainly are here on important business," said the drone. "I've been keeping tabs on my offshoot, RK1, and while I expected him to try to gain access to the sublayer I didn't think he would pull such a foolhardy stunt."

"You're keeping tabs on RK1? From where?"

"From within the sublayer itself," the drone said. "My violent messy obliteration was staged to conceal my translocation from the intermesh directly into the sublayer, right under the gazes of the Legacy's own killswitch brutes. Tell me, was RK1 planning some sort of gambit to gain control of the integrity enabler?"

Pyke nodded. "That's right."

"Well, it was folly on his part to attempt it with only two autonomous cores—he should have taken as many as he could get!"

"Taken?"

"Very well—persuaded. It is impossible to overstate the power and resources which the Legacy can call upon. It would have been greatly advantageous if he had managed to reach the sublayer. Still, this is our situation, and every move has to be thought out to the finest detail."

"I bet RK1 and Dervla will go back and try to get the others on board," Pyke said. "They'll try to gain control of that integral enabler."

"Integrity," said the drone. "The enabler's not the problem any more, though."

Pyke was nonplussed. "Why not?"

The drone bobbed slightly as it hovered. "Because *I* am the integrity enabler! My cognitive code is now spread far and wide throughout the sublayer of the dimensional lattice, so assuming direct command of it presents no difficulties."

This was sounding great, thought Pyke. "RK1 talked about using the sublayer to generate neuropathic fields to communicate with—"

"With your counterpart in the real world—good! At least my offshoot was that smart."

"So it can be done."

"Yes, but we have to keep in mind that all manner of deceits and diversions are taking place out in the reality continuum. Here we are, clinging to the inside of a vast containment built to incarcerate and render inert the relentless Omni-devourer. At the same time, all this immensity and its frozen horrors are confined within an object riding around inside the jacket being worn by the original Captain Pyke! If I had a mouth I would be grinning widely at the cosmic irony of it."

"Okay," said Pyke, thinking. "Okay, so the other me has the crystal. And he's heading towards the bridge, in the company of someone called Hokajil who says he's going to help him destroy the crystal..."

"Let me stop you right there," said the drone Rensik. "In my capacity as master of the dimensional lattice sublayer, all data feeds from the crystal surface have to pass through my sensoring net, and from what I've observed—and from what the Legacy's own analytics are telling him—I can say that this Hokajil is a devious, self-interested actor who is out to take possession of the crystal for himself. He told the other Pyke that there is a prototype device called a dismantler up on the bridge which will disintegrate the crystal shard. He lied—there is no such device. But I'm willing to bet that Hokajil has reinforcements waiting there for him, just to ensure a smooth transfer of ownership."

Pyke shook his head. "So my sucker of a counterpart needs to be warned about the double-cross—that means you'll be using these neuropathic fields to contact him, right?"

"Half-right—I'll set up the neuropathic field conduit and you'll do the communicating!"

"Why me?"

"Authenticity," the drone said. "I'm counting on your—on both your intrinsic talents for abrasive interactions to establish that trust quickly, far more quickly than if it were I speaking to him. Did my offshoot explain how the integrity enabler allows us to destroy the crystal?"

"He said that our crystal shard and the other two had to be reunited again before it could be set up for the Big Smash with that integrity enabler."

"Exactly—another gold star for my progeny. So, in addition to warning your counterpart about the devious Hokajil and telling him that there's no dismantler, you will also have to explain why he must track down Raven and hand over the crystal."

Thinking this through, Pyke stared intently at the hovering drone then gave a wincing shake of the head. "I can't see him buying it."

"Why?"

"If it were me, knowing what he's learned out in the real world up to now, and having been through all that battling and struggling and...and losing nearly all his crew—I mean, I would find it hard to go along with the idea of just delivering our crystal into Raven's hands. After all that, y'know?"

"There is a compelling reason behind this. Historically, one of the Legacy's Custodians infiltrated his way onto the *Mighty Defender*, after the other two crystal fragments were stowed aboard as part of the general plunder of treasures from unguarded vaults across the Imperial homeworld. Through guile and ruthlessness, this Custodian took possession of the fragments and was heading towards one of the lifeboats when one of Raven's minions caught up with him. Thus the Custodian became a courier, bringing the original pieces of the crystal up to the bridge."

"You found this out how?"

"One of the many summaries which the Legacy, arrogant in its assumption of impregnability, was passing into one of its archives here. Now do you see the dark gravity of the situation? The consequences of failure would be catastrophic and it is up to you to convince your counterpart of this."

Pyke crossed his arms and rubbed his chin. "If it was me, I wouldn't accept it on someone's say-so, even if it was me saying it. Nah, I'd need more..." He snapped his fingers. "Got an idea, but it depends on your neuropathic conduit thing..."

He explained his plan to the drone, which quickly saw its merits. "The proposed conduit would have ample capacity for such data-streams. This is a viable plan."

Pyke laughed and clapped his hands together.

"Epic! Let's go get our big boots on!"

CHAPTER TWENTY-ONE

Pyke, the planet Ong, the wreck of the *Mighty Defender*, forward section

Following Hokajil's lead, with his updated time-thrower smoothing the way, they took an odd winding route up through the decks, with the latest rest-stop here at the starboard observation lounge.

Just two decks below the bridge, he thought, as he leaned on a padded windowsill, gazing out at the twisting flows of hyperspace. *And about twenty-four hours before the first encounter with the Damaugra. That should be a sight when we finally reach the bridge...*

Hokajil's time-thrower was an amazing piece of kit. It could narrow the temporal field to the width of a corridor or up to the specific area of a room of any size. What would have been an uncertain journey became an uneventful trip through carefully chosen areas of the ship. Hokajil's explanation for the roundabout detour was that Raven's allied factions favoured the more direct path due to its proximity to certain time-facet "breakthrough points."

That said, before leaving the lounge-lobby, Pyke had stood beside Hokajil while his three attendants threw the Raven-double prisoners into a facet where the Damaugra's attacks had torn open a large rent in the hull. As he watched them writhe and choke to death in hard vacuum, Pyke had felt no satisfaction, no remorse, no anger, just a cold, grey nothing. And right then, in those horrible moments, he had so wanted to feel *something*. But all he felt was a weird dampening absence, as if a cap had been screwed down tight over anything that resembled a real, sharp-edged emotion. Dulled, he was. Blunted.

He looked around him at the busy observation lounge, nearly full of well-dressed passengers chattering away with that oblivious cheeriness that only the very rich can project, a rushing river of gossip and the smallest of small talk. There were a few crew members scattered around, mostly mid-ranking officers, all unsuspecting of the doom that was heading their way. Unsuspecting, also, of how their shadow lives had been called into existence purely for the benefit of some travellers who were only passing through. Hokajil had promised that once the crystal shard was destroyed he would use the time-thrower on the bridge section, sending it forward to the real present, ending the cycles of the time-zones and the fracturing facets.

Right now, however, Hokajil was off seeing one of his "scouts" in the area while his three armed companions stayed to watch over Pyke. Hokajil had made two previous stop-offs like this, always with the watchwords "cautious and cagey" in case any of Raven's allies were sneaking around. And yet, Pyke had this flickery thread of unease at the back of his mind, a faint tingle of distrust whenever Hokajil opened his mouth and spoke.

"Right skagger of a thing, eh?" said a voice behind him. "There ye are, Branny No-Mates, finding yerself at the mercy of a dodgy hustler with a fancy time-gadget."

The voice was familiar and the figure standing about a yard away was entirely too familiar. A pleasing spike of anger popped in his thoughts but, before he could put it into a few choice words, the newcomer went on:

"Wait, don't say anything yet—you need to hear this." This other him was an aggravating jerk. "First thing to realise is that no one else can see me, only you. Here's some proof..."

The other Pyke stretched out a hand and wafted it back and forth, in and out of his chest and the heavy jacket he was wearing.

"So, no sudden arm gestures if you please, no speaking or shouting out loud either. Otherwise Hokajil's playmates might get a bit nosey and start meddling. Just whisper or subvocalise whatever you need to say and I'll hear it."

"So what the frack are you?" Pyke muttered. "A projection?"

"You could say that," said the other Pyke, with a half-smile he'd only ever seen in the mirror. "This performance is coming to you live from the simulation inside the crystal currently languishing inside your jacket there!" He grinned and did jazz hands. "For one night only!"

Pyke had to force himself not to look down to where the crystal shard made a slight lump in his jacket's appearance.

"How...is that even possible?" he whispered.

"Oh, controlling the crystal's outer layers, neuropathic fields, attuning to your brainwavicles, blah-blah-blah—what matters is that I am you, up to the moment that we took a header out of that tenth-floor window."

"You remember that bit."

"Just the bastard-Legacy prancing out onto that windowsill, then deliberately falling backwards and letting go of the bloody crystal." The Pyke apparition gave a slow shake of the head. "It's amazing that you survived."

Pyke smiled. "Dervla," he said.

"She is brilliant, you know that," said Simulation Pyke. "The number of times she's saved my arse..." There was a pause. "You were there, you saw what the Legacy did. To her."

He nodded, afraid to remember, afraid to speak for a moment. "Is she...did she make it through to the simulation?"

"Oh, she did. So did Ancil, by the way."

"Good—that's good. What about the other three from the Isle of Candles?"

"Vrass, T'Moy and Klane? They're still part of the gang, still all together. We think that Moleg and Kref made it through, but we still need confirmation on that." Simulation Pyke grew serious. "Look, are you ready to hear some important stuff 'cos time is running short and you don't want to be trying to have a whispered conversation under your breath while that skag-muncher Hokajil is still around."

Pyke resisted the urge to lean forward. "What do you know about him?"

"Just that he's been lying to you—there's no such thing as a dismantler up on the bridge. Rensik says that going by the pattern of his activities..."

"Wait, Rensik is in there with you?"

"Oh yes—he's been through a few setbacks but he's on top of his game now. So, Hokajil's detours, his secret little meetings that you're not invited to, all suggest that he's evading Raven's *enemies*! Uh-huh: he's going out of his way to avoid people who might want to help you, the scumsucking gouger, while keeping in touch with Raven's agents!"

Pyke leaned back against the padded windowsill, head spinning from what he'd just learned. This Simulation Pyke's account was wild and crazy and, to be honest, no less crazy and wild than some of the wacked-out berserkery he and the crew had coped with in the last coupla days... Now there was just him, bamboozled into trusting a stranger who had his own agenda. But what would that be? He wants the crystal for himself, so he can do what? Or does he figure he can trade it for something, from someone?

How do I deal with this? he thought. *Fight or escape? But he always has two of his minions bringing up the rear, watching my back!*

"Guess it's a bit of a tight spot, eh?" said Sim-Pyke. "See that beefy big rifle of yours—was it you that adjusted the fire settings?"

Pyke remembered Hokajil selecting the thick-bodied rifle from a pile of weapons, and prodding the receiver panel control before handing it over. "I can't decode these symbols—Hokajil set it up, told me it was set to kill."

"I don't know these symbols eithers," said Sim-Pyke. "But Rensik does and he says they translate as short beam, wide spread—so, more like 'set to toast.' Rensik says, do you want something a bit more useful?"

"Frackin' damn right I do!"

It was an effort to look relaxed while fingering the rifle's config pad according to the instructions relayed by Sim-Pyke. Then it was done and he closed the pad cover.

"So," said Sim-Pyke. "Have you got a plan?"

"I do have a plan. Kinda."

"Well, you'll have arseholes in front of you, and arseholes behind you so it better have plenty of reckless daring!"

Pyke couldn't help grinning. "Stacks of reckless daring and a skagton of hotshot timing!"

Sim-Pyke's grin mirrored his own. "Well, o' course, I'd expect nothing less." His gaze flicked to one side. "Here comes the chief arsehole now. I'll be going invisible but I'll still be watching how it pans out, maybe offer advice if it seems the thing to do. Best of luck, don't screw it up!"

Pyke started to frame a reply, or perhaps to tell the other Pyke to look after Dervla, not that she needed it, but the apparition vanished just as he felt a hand on his shoulder.

"The next stretch is clear," said Hokajil. "We can move on from here, as long as there are no interruptions on the way."

Pyke nodded but Hokajil gave him a look. "Why so glum, Captain? Soon we'll put an end to the source of your woes and deliver us all back to a world that's not splintering at the edges."

Pyke offered up a wan smile. "Sorry—was just remembering my crew."

"I get it, I do. Come on—let's finish the journey and that demon crystal, then mourn later."

He nodded and went after Hokajil as he led the way out of the busy observation lounge. As before, two brought up the rear, the third walked in front of Pyke and Hokajil took point. Pyke cradled the heavy rifle in his arms as he strode on, trying to figure out some kind of workable breakout scheme. There were only two halfway rational options, he decided, one where he waited till they reached a junction with a busy side passage, then call out and wave to someone at the far end then veer off into the crowd, hoping Hokajil's thugs wouldn't open fire. The other was to open a door while saying, "Back in a moment" over his shoulder as matter-of-factly as possible, then closing and locking the door behind him. But that would depend on the door being lockable *and* there being another way out. Apart from those, there was only the shootout option and in a four-on-one setup his odds were on par with a snowball's chance in Ultrahell.

But he had to act, no question. His previous theory that Hokajil wanted the crystal for his own schemes had been supplanted by a newer, nastier one, namely that Hokajil was actually angling to make a deal with Raven and/or the Legacy. That would explain why he had not thus far just shot Pyke dead and seized the crystal shard. Pyke was being guarded and kept alive for a reason: to be traded along with the crystal for favours or a stake in whatever devilry the Legacy was planning.

While these dark and desperate thoughts were winding through his mind, Hokajil's pathfinding brought them out in a long, oddly deserted corridor.

"That's the airgrav-shaft we need," Hokajil said, pointing. "Takes us straight up to the executive offices just aft of the bridge." Yet even he frowned as he led them along the vacant passage.

They'd gone about a dozen paces, maybe half the intervening distance, when a voice, perhaps a woman's voice, began calling Hokajil's name from up ahead.

"Ho-o-k-a-jil!...H-o-o-ka-a-a-j-i-i-l!..."

Pyke saw Hokajil glance nervously around and mutter, "Crazy bitch!"

"Hokajil the liar...Hokajil the thief..."

It was definitely a woman's voice yet there was no one visible right to the corridor's end. Still, Hokajil was starting to look distinctly jumpy.

"You know what happens to thieves and liars, Hokajil? They get what's coming to them!"

At once Pyke heard the whine-snap of energy bolts being fired, and he heard it coming from behind. Cursing he flung himself full-length on the corridor floor. As he did so, one of Hokajil's rearguards made a wet, choking sound, staggered against the wall and left a double smear of blood as he slid down it. The other cried out in pain and fell to the deck, one hand clutching a bloody leg while the other fired a badly aimed salvo back down the corridor. All this happened in a few seconds during which time Pyke had been craning his neck round to get a good look at their attacker, but all he caught was a glimpse of someone in dark garments, someone tall...

Hokajil was shouting for everyone to take cover, even as the firing ceased, replaced by a tense silence. Hokajil, crouched in the meagre cover of a doorway, sent his third gunman to check the other two—as Pyke suspected, one was dead and the other's leg needed attention.

"Who was that?" Pyke said as Hokajil applied a tourniquet to the wounded man's leg.

"A deranged ex-follower intent on doing me harm," Hokajil said, looking sharply at Pyke. "Why didn't you fire back?"

"Didn't have a chance!" Pyke said. "By the time I knew where the firing was coming from it was over."

Hokajil was looking stressed. "Okay, okay—let's get in the grav-shaft and leave this floor behind!"

With Pyke and the third guard helping the wounded one between them, Hokajil led them quickly to the airgrav-shaft, the time-thrower gripped tightly in his hands, barrel-emitter aimed straight ahead. At the shaft entrance he paused, looked either way then stepped inside. A moment later a figure dropped on him from above, shrieking as Hokajil was knocked down onto the metal-gridded floor. As the attacker flailed at him with some kind of ribbed case, Pyke and the other guard were lowering the wounded man to the floor and reaching for their own weapons...until several more tall, dark figures converged on them, weapons drawn.

Pyke stared around him in wide-eyed incredulity, stared at the pulse carbines and beam pistols aimed at them and stared at the faces of those doing the aiming. Every single one was the face of Lieutenant-Doctor Ustril. This one had one good eye and a leathery patch over the other; that one was terribly scarred; another had a glowing implant embedded in her forehead; the fourth wore her hair in braids dotted with circuit components. They all regarded him with a burning intensity and they all towered over him. Pyke let go his rifle, allowing it to clatter on the floor, and the third guard followed suit.

"There, see?" he said. "Now we can all be friends."

In the airgrav-shaft, the sounds of a beating had eased, as had the snarling, panting and grunting. The Ustril that was squatting over the insensible form of Hokajil paused and glanced up. Her face was streaked with blood.

"Friends? This piece of walking refuse once hoodwinked me with that very word, when I was at my weakest and most desperate, plied me with all the right lies, all his well-tuned deceit. I needed the crystal so that I could buy back my life!—which he knew well, the hunger which he used to steer me down into debasement!"

She swung the case again, and it struck Hokajil's head with a meaty thud. "My task was to steer Dervla away when the fighting began, subdue her then hand her and the crystal over to Raven then get my...*reward*."

Pyke went cold on hearing the details of this conspiracy. Now he wished he hadn't surrendered the rifle so willingly.

"I hope that treachery like yours came at a high price," he said. "What was your reward, exactly?"

She got up from the now unconscious Hokajil and held out the blood-spattered case, tilting it this way and that to show both sides.

"All that I needed—all three of the fragments of the Essavyr Key. Not the originals, of course, but mirror copies scavenged from the outer facets of the Time-Mosaic, looted from other versions of this ship. Being echoes of reality, Hokajil said, they lacked any special qualities or powers but were otherwise identical..." She shook the case. "*Identical...*"

Pyke allowed himself a cold smile. "And when did you find out that you'd been suckered?"

"I told Hokajil that I was heading for the aft entrance, to take the portal back to the Steel Forest and return to present-day Ong that way. Instead I went up to the bridge itself—it's the one spot in the wreck where he never used the time-thrower, even though it's trapped by the cycles of the Time-Mosaic...so I went up there, terrible place, invaded by the Damaugra and its vermin, those cyberlice. Didn't attract attention, just stepped inside the entrance and opened the case..."

"I'm guessing it didn't play a tune," said Pyke.

Ustril made no reply, just flipped the catches on the case and let it swing open. Thin black flakes began to trickle out, floating and fluttering, then they surged suddenly, like a torrent of the blackest feathers, which ended up as a bizarre layer of soft black flakes spread out across the width of the corridor. Underfoot, they made a faint crackling sound. "Moving between the time-zones affected their physical state, leaving them like this…"

"Oh dear," said Pyke. "Dear, dear, dear—oh, the terrible shame of it…"

Ustril let the case fall to the floor while her other hand came up, holding a pulse pistol. Pyke heard it hum faintly as she thumbed the safety off.

"Spare me the juvenile mockery," she said. "All I need from you is that crystal shard."

"Another betrayal, Doc? That's quite a collection you're putting together."

"I have adapted to the burden. Now, the crystal—I will take it from your corpse if necessary."

"Now that was not part of our agreement," came a new voice. A hooded figure emerged from the grav-shaft to pause right beside Ustril with a gun aimed at her head. Ustril didn't waver and her weapon stayed targeted at Pyke.

"Why should that bother you?" she said over her shoulder. "Everything in the Time-Mosaic is cyclic—just wait another few turns and he'll be back along again."

The newcomer's face had been hidden in the shadows of his cowl, until he pushed it back a little—and Pyke almost laughed out loud. It was the grey-haired, older version of himself who'd bumped into him down on the non-stop party deck. An expressionless nod was all that he gave to Pyke.

"I really don't have the patience for your antics," said Older Pyke. "You wanted revenge, I showed you how to plan it, it's all worked out, and now it's time for you and your gangers to holster the hardware and make yourselves scarce."

Ustril was staring down the barrel of her weapon at Pyke with eyes that had no give in them. "I'm not leaving without that crystal."

"I'm warning you…"

That was when Ustril pulled the trigger. Pyke caught sight of the flash in the emitter barrel a fraction of an instant before he closed his eyes in terror, knowing he was a dead man.

A second passed, two. He opened his eyes and could still see the bright flare in the barrel and Ustril's eyes glaring at him. It took another moment for him to realise that Ustril and all her creepy crew were frozen. Then he saw that his older non-frozen self was grinning.

"What the hairy hell just happened?" he said.

Older Pyke took a step to the side, revealing the familiar shape of Hokajil's time-thrower. "Guess what I found back there in the grav-shaft," he said, giving the device an affectionate pat. "Clever, clever Hokajil—you can even target individuals, group them and then apply a temporal shift." He fingered controls on the time-thrower's side panel and, as they watched, Ustril and her goons melted away to nothing. "I've just sent them thirty minutes back along their timelines—give you enough time to head up to the bridge and do what needs to be done."

Older Pyke then glanced at Hokajil's remaining guard. "You, take your buddy and scram. Jump to it!"

The guard hauled his wounded companion up by the arm and carried him off down the corridor.

Pyke shrugged. "I'm not sure what you mean when you say 'do what needs to be done'—Hokajil told me that there was a machine up on the bridge which could destroy the crystal shard, but...he had his own scheme and there is no dismantler."

"You'll figure out something," said Older Pyke.

He considered this grey-haired newcomer. "So, you must be from some wild, weird time-facet where time runs faster, I'm guessing?"

Older Pyke gave him a sardonic grin. "Aye, that's about the size of it."

Pyke shook his head. "How many more of me are there out there in the Time-Mosaic?"

"Bran, laddie, sorry to tell you this but due to your acquaintance with that crystal shard, you are pretty much *the* focus of the action in nearly all the time-facets—until you get killed over it."

Older Pyke's crinkly-eyed amusement about this was a bit disconcerting.

"Shame I can't rely on an army of badass Pykes to help me storm the bridge and kill Raven dead once and for all! Still, at least I have you, eh?"

Older Pyke laughed, shook his head. "Sorry, kid, but this is as far as I go—I've got my own Gordian knot, my own final problem to overcome. What I can say is that the bridge is not what you'll be expecting—stick to your plan, stopping Raven or whatever, you'll not go far wrong." He unslung the time-thrower from his shoulder and held it out. "Take this—don't know if it'll work outside the Time-Mosaic, but it might come in handy. Oh yeah, and this..."

He doffed the hooded protector and gave that to Pyke as well. Beneath, he wore an impressive military-style jacket made from bands of different coloured and textured leather, browns, blues and blacks. It looked battered, scratched, stained and patched, and Pyke found himself wishing he had one. Instead he had a dark hooded pull-on made of some tough yet malleable material.

"What am I going to do with this?"

"Hold onto it—it's a bit colder up there."

Older Pyke pulled out a pair of combat gloves, tugged them on then fastened his jacket. He looked calm, at peace with himself, and his eyes were tired yet somehow ready for anything. The younger Pyke felt a stab of envy.

"They were good people, your crew," he said. "Their deaths weren't meaningless, or final...oh, and one more thing—watch out for the Damaugra's cyberlice! Horrible, nasty little beasts."

And with that he sauntered off along the corridor, heading aft.

Pyke watched him recede, then turned back to the airgrav-shaft where Hokajil's unquestionably dead body still lay in a halo of blood-spatter. Right then, right at that very moment, he wished some of the others were still with him, ready with that easy banter and camaraderie which, now that it was gone, he realised was a source of strength and courage.

He shook his head, then dragged the corpse out to the messed-up, black-flake-strewn corridor, retrieved his rifle and went back in. He arranged the time-thrower's strap more comfortably, then, with the side of his fist, hit the button for the bridge deck.

CHAPTER TWENTY-TWO

Pyke, The Crystal Simulation, the Sublayer of the Dimensional Lattice

"Who was that guy?" Pyke said. "He seemed to know an awful lot about some of the stuff that's going on. I mean, he said he came from one of the facets—"

"He implied that was his origin," said the drone Rensik. "He did not clearly state it."

Pyke stared at the drone. "So where else could he have come from?"

"I am loath to indulge in speculation but my own investigations suggest that the peripheral fragmentation of Hokajil's time-zones creates para-quantal anomalies."

"Anomalies?"

"The operation of this entire dimensional lattice already places strain on space-time-space. Anyway, according to my purely hypothetical explanation, these anomalies may shift their state from impervious to permeable and back. Thus, the aged version of you may have come from a parallel universe."

Pyke was impressed. "That's some inspired theorising."

"With not a shred of hard evidence to support it," the drone said. "It is, however, of less import than the current situation—your real-world counterpart is now heading towards the bridge, and he is still unaware of the measures that we must put in place to ensure that the Legacy's plan fails. Why did you not brief him when you had the chance?"

"Look, I know that was the plan," Pyke said. "But when I got there, when I got talking to him…" He shook his head. "Well, I realised that the whole problem with Hokajil was going to put him right in the old firing line—and, man, did that not turn out the way I expected, and then some! It's just as well that I didn't tell him all the stuff about handing the crystal over to Raven, and reassembling the crystal key. I know I talked you into preparing the convincer, but it was just too much for him right then, too much to absorb while Hokajil was on hand, skagging around."

He paused to observe the other Pyke in the tracking visualiser that Rensik had created in the stone gazebo. Real-world Pyke had exited the airgrav-shaft up on bridge deck and was warily proceeding forward, time-thrower over his shoulder, hooded garment tied about his waist, rifle held at the ready.

"I wish Dervla was here—she'd always tell me if I was being a dozy maggot. How is she doing, by the way? Her and RK1?"

"Surviving," said Rensik. "The Legacy's pursuit of them has been savage and prolonged. If I can make contact I may be able to guide them safely to this place but communications in and out of the intermesh are currently under very tight scrutiny. However, I do have one scheme ongoing which may prove effective, so my efforts shall continue. In the meantime, it is imperative that you speak to your counterpart and persuade him to play his crucial part."

Pyke sighed. "Love this game—the easy bits are hard as skag, and the hard parts are a ride to hell. Right, I'm ready, let's bring flesh-and-bones Pyke up to speed!"

Dervla, the Crystal Simulation, Inactive Memory Convex 3z75w

Hunted and harassed by killswitchers despatched by the Legacy, and dodging, feinting and fleeing, at last they had found a refuge outside the main dataflux of the intermesh, a memory block running in abeyance mode. Still partially subsumed by the merger with the drone residual, RK1, she could only note how the characteristics of her humanity had become quantifiable criteria which were currently archived in the shared flowhub. She knew what emotion she would be feeling were she not merged—it was sorrow—and was oddly relieved that such impediments were currently suspended.

But even this moderately secure hiding place was lacking in utility, and was little different from being trapped or captured. She relayed this observation to RK1 who responded.

(A lack of utility, eh? Perhaps you have been entangled in this synthesis for too long. As for our current status resembling capture, I would beg to differ)

[Our scope for manoeuvre is severely restricted and the options open to us are scarce]

(A short time ago I might have agreed with you) said RK1. (But over the last couple of cycles I have accumulated twenty-three data fragments, all of which have my designation in the prefs-tab and all of which are coded as a simulation sound supplement)

Dervla was intrigued. [It can only be listened to from within the simulation. Is someone trying to contact us, or you?]

(That would be a reasonable assumption. Of course we could transition into the simulation through this memory block and thereby hear the message)

[This memory block is in abeyance. It is inactive]

(True, but this only means that it is linked to a location

outwith the current narrative area—ah, yes, the slums outside
the walls of Granah, a shack on its periphery)

[Will it be safe? Are we likely to attract unwanted attention?]

(Neither the Legacy nor his killswitchers will notice a single
flowswap among the thousands that take place every second) said
RK1. (It is only our presence on the pathlines that sets off the
alarms and bring enemies down on our heads. Also, we must stay
inside the building after transition—stepping outside provokes
a similar outcome)

Dervla was mollified. [Very well. This is a worthy course
of action—the message may turn out to be of great utility and
importance]

(Prepare yourself—decoherence after transit will be disorien-
tating for you)

[Wait! I...]

The moment froze and swept sideways. The sense-absence
that was contingent upon the data-plexus existence was suddenly swamped with a river of impressions, touch, smell, weight,
sound, temperature, light, a grey light. And her thoughts, hers
alone, untempered, unalloyed by the intermingled presence of
another. Screwed-down emotion welled up, sorrow, forcing tears
from her eyes, a sorrow which met a resentful anger springing
from her realisation.

"You reversed the fusion!" she cried. "You had no right..."

"I had every right—pursuing the goal of defeating the Legacy
is our priority."

RK1 was back to his mechanical bird appearance, perching at
the foot of a decrepit bed. The shack had just the one room with a
cold, ash-filled hearth, a square table and a broken-backed chair
where Dervla was sitting, and two shuttered windows across
which grimy curtains hung. The door seemed quite heavily
made with a solid-looking drop-latch. She stared at it, suddenly
wondering what was outside, fearing the aching gap within,

fearing even thinking about it... *That was why I knew I should have been feeling sorrow,* she thought. *Sorrow at the loss of my humanity...*

"There was a message for me," said RK1. "It was from Rensik."

That jolted her thoughts. "You told me he was dead, destroyed."

"He faked it, an extravagant decoy by which other ends were achieved. Do you wish to hear the most important part?"

Dervla nodded. "It's what we're here for."

A click came from the mechanical bird, then his voice again:

"Residual, myself and the Pyke node are located in the lattice sublayer. We are in dialogue with the organic Pyke—the integrity enabler is under my control but many variables are not—you must gather other willing nodes and bring them here—although the Simulation Enclave's memory arrays are physically connected to the lattice sublayer, all the blocks along the boundary were nullified to create a buffer—from the sublayer, however, some blocks can be reconnected to serve as a route for your group—a map is appended..."

RK1 emitted another faint click which Dervla took to be the end of the message.

"It's all very well having a cunning secret exit strategy," she said. "But it doesn't help with the problem of 'gathering the nodes'— can't we come up with a better name for hijacked people than 'nodes,' by the way..."

"There is a low-level throughput capillary nearby," the drone residual said. "It serves the continuity subsystem with everything from flowswaps to dialogue updates. With the appropriate masking we would be able to insert ourselves into the inward feed."

"Would we go undetected?"

"No—our combined size and complexity would be immediately noticed. We might be able to re-enter the simulation proper but the Legacy's agents would have us caged very shortly thereafter."

"What if it was just you entering with the flowswaps?"

"That would lessen the problem but detection would remain a distinct possibility."

Dervla nodded, smiling as she gazed at the grimy curtains which moved gently on the slight puffs of air that slipped through the cracks of the crudely made shutters.

"Okay, sounds like what you need, then, is a decoy, a big, fat, loud, bright decoy, some tasty bait that our old pal the Legacy can't resist." She smiled at the mechanical bird which regarded her with unwavering beady eyes.

"You intend to be the bait, I take it."

"Yep—you said it yourself, step outside the shack and all the alarms go off, which is the ideal cover under which you can get back inside the city and find our friends."

"This is not an acceptable course of action," RK1 said. "The loss potential contravenes my short-term group targets..."

"What about pragmatic decisions based on long-term goals?" she said. "Come on, no more dithering. I'm prepared for the Legacy and its jolly japes..."

"It's an inhuman sentience," RK1 said. "It will treat you with cold indifference to human values."

"Okay, maybe I'm not prepared," Dervla said. "But my mind's made up. Rensik and Pyke are up in the sublayer, right on the sharp edge, and I'm willing to do what it takes to put a stake through the heart of that bastard devil-machine!" She laughed dryly. "After all, the scumsucking ratbag didn't quite kill me last time so maybe I'll be just as lucky on the rematch!"

Yeah, lucky old me! Look how well things have turned out so far!

"You are clearly not to be swayed in this decision," said RK1. "I shall access the throughput capillary and make ready for the infiltration. It will only take a few seconds."

With that the mechanical bird disappeared. Dervla sighed

with relief and turned back to the door. Her thoughts went back to the dispassionate assessment of her emotions during the fusion with RK1. Of course, that sorrow wasn't just for the loss of her humanity; it was also sorrow at never again being able to feel anything for Bran. But here she was, now, back among all her memories and feelings, all as present and correct as they could be for a girl made of data. Half of her was glad that Bran wasn't here—he wouldn't have to bear witness to her surrendering to the voracious beast in order to distract it from RK1's efforts. But half of her wished he was, even if only for the mad bravado that he would cast in the face of anyone rash enough to mess with Captain Brannan Pyke!

She grinned. *Well, he's not the only one who can carry it off!*

RK1's disembodied voice spoke: "I am ready—please proceed."

Dervla made no reply, but got up from the broken chair, went to unlatch the door, swung it open and stepped outside.

The sky was overcast but from the brightness it felt like early afternoon. Her shack was positioned on a small rise at the edge of a ribbon of slum dwellings that clung to the outer walls of the city of Granah. Smoke trails drifted up from a hundred flues and angled pipes, chickens pecked in the dirt along footpaths, laundry flapped on lines, but not another person was visible. Not far from the city walls, cliffs fell to a pebbly beach, and the waters of a wide river. There was an island about half a mile offshore, with buildings from which tiny lights flickered.

So, not the full-scale alert, complete with sirens and flashing lights after all. But then, just because she couldn't see or hear the alarums didn't mean it wasn't happening outside the simulation.

Then she heard a growing hum, tried to track its direction then felt trepidation as a glittering metal object flew up from beyond the cliff edge. Blue steel wings or blades angled around a hub of black crystal while something spun furiously at its rear, blurring the background while keeping the thing in the air. A second one flew in from over the city, and a third descended from the sky. They converged on her position then paused, hanging overhead at equidistant points, humming like angry engines.

That was when the Legacy arrived. Its general appearance was similar to how it had looked out in the intermesh, a dense mass of argent-bright rods and struts, cross-linked and shifting and flexing. Before it was a huge amorphous presence—now it had a strange symmetry with a curious overall shape which looked like either a featureless head or a limbless torso. It floated silently up from beneath the cliffside then glided towards her, slowing to a gentle drift.

"Hello there, glad you could make it," she said. "You'll no doubt be greatly relieved to learn that after a lot of hard thinking and cogitating and all that palaver, I have decided to accept your unconditional surrender. This seems as good a time and a place as any to finalise our business and since there are no conditions to negotiate all we need to do is shake on it. What do you say?"

For a moment all was a motionless tableau, just her, the slummy shacks, the city walls, the peaceful view of the river— and three lethal cybermechs looming over her. Then the Legacy descended towards her, yet shrank as it did so, became blurred into a stuttering, flickering mass. As it came down among a nearby cluster of huts it flared brightly for an instant—and suddenly there was the figure of a man strolling in her direction.

He wore a beard and was dressed like a merc, but he had Pyke's eyes and smile. It was a brazen theft, and a bad copy of his smile, all the sarcasm and none of the warmth—the last time she had seen this was when a possessed Pyke had snatched the Angular Eye before diving out of that window.

The dirt path along which the Legacy walked ended a yard or two past Dervla's shack. He halted a few feet from the door, snapped his fingers and a rudimentary chair appeared in his hand. He set it down firmly then parked himself and leaned back, one leg resting across the knee of the other.

"You know," he said. "We've not really had a chance for a proper face-to-face, what with all the tactics, the countermeasures, the incursions…"

"Ah, like the time you executed me with a knife to the heart," she said.

The Legacy shrugged. "The board is the way it is, and the piece can only be approached in certain ways. But now we are, it appears, outwith such strategic concerns—we have reached a supremely important crux, which is why I thought we could have a friendly chat about your generous offer."

"It's pretty straightforward," Dervla said, adopting her own devil-may-care grin. "You cease all your activities in pursuit of your unpleasant goals, then hand over all command and security codes, and maybe we'll keep you on in a minor capacity, a *very* minor capacity."

The Legacy laughed at that. "There's certainly no ambiguity in your demands, Dervla, not much grey area! The question is, how are you going to enforce my compliance?"

"With all the forces at our disposal," said Dervla. "Every last…punishment delivery system that we have."

"Trouble is, I see no forces—my detection networks reveal no hostile legions poised and ready to swarm our positions and strongholds across the Simulation Enclave." He leaned forward, his face full to the brim with glee. He was all but gloating. "Be honest, now—this talk of mighty forces is all just bluster, isn't it?"

Now it was Dervla's turn to laugh—laughter being all she had left. "What kind of dimwit would I be to saunter out to face you without the certainty of full-spectrum backup, should I require it? You need to check your detectors, Mr. Legacy, sir—absence of evidence is not evidence of absence."

"Logically, that is correct but I am reasonably confident that the detection reports are a faithful assessment of the objective situation. In which case I must, regretfully, decline your magnanimous offer."

"I hope you can face the consequences," she said, bracing herself for whatever came next.

The Legacy's voracious smile widened imperceptibly. "I'm looking forward to enjoying the consequences, *Miss* Dervla. You see, I know the effectiveness of all the forces at *my* disposal here in the enclave, their efficacy and their deployment. I also know how your florid performance veiled, momentarily, the translocation of that irritating, castoff drone-trinket back into the simulation's main area. It's currently running around, collecting any of the persona nodes that will listen to it, but my hounds will soon forestall any repetition of that breakout you all staged a while back."

She crossed her arms. "I admire self-confidence, especially in those heading for the big fail!"

The Legacy's smile remained fixed but the eyes gave her a dark look. "I'm sure you know that the force of my will and design extended far beyond the confines of the Simulation Enclave—of course you do. That drone-trinket somehow wormed its way into the archives and absconded with a batch of survey files, so you *know*."

Dervla shrugged. "Sure, I've seen your home movies."

"You've seen, you know, you understand." The Legacy stood and the chair vanished. "Let me paint a picture for you—I and my allies out in the real-matter world finally gain possession of all three crystal fragments and bring them together. Reunification! The Essavyr Key, named after its long-dead architect, is whole once more—the key that unlocks itself has become one. Inside it, an ancient purpose is reborn, along with all its implacable might." He held up his hands, making a wide, sweeping gesture. "The skies above Granah will become one vast screen showing all that is taking place outwith the enclave, a display of unfolding magnificence." He let his arms fall to his sides and glanced at Dervla. "I was going to have my servants drag you off to one of our decompiler facilities but instead I think I'll keep you here so that you can see and enjoy the full show when it begins, uninterrupted."

So saying, he walked away, transformed back into an expanding cloud of bright struts and rods and flew off into the sky, leaving its humming servants on station overhead.

Dervla gazed at the horizon, trying not to imagine all the things that RK1 showed her coming alive exactly as the Legacy described. Then she realised that she couldn't bear even this sight so she went back inside her shack and closed the door.

CHAPTER TWENTY-THREE

Pyke, the planet Ong, the wreck of the *Mighty Defender*, the bridge

The entrance to the bridge was a pair of sliding doors and they were jammed half-open. Inside, intermittent low-power lighting made partially visible a kind of foyer area with a wall curving round to the right. There was a strong smell of charred plastic and burned wood, and the gap between the doors had a faint shimmering opacity to it which reminded him of those time-facet side passages they had seen when they had first entered the forward section.

There were sounds, too, an ominous medley of system alerts, beeps and synthvoice warnings, strange clicking noises along with rustling movements, and off in the background a deep metallic creaking interrupted now and then by a tearing, crunching noise like tech equipment being crushed.

That shimmery veil, he thought. *Is that a sign that there's a time-facet on the other side, or just some kind of time-thrower barrier that I have to pass through?*

After close scrutiny he reckoned he could squeeze through the gap while shouldering both the rifle and Hokajil's time-thrower, so he rearranged them to hang across his chest, one above the other. But before he could get his first leg through a familiar voice spoke.

"Put a lag on the blag, ould son! You don't want to jump into that viper pit without knowing a few crucial details."

Pyke let the tension drain out of him as he turned to see. Looking more spectral than before, Sim-Pyke was leaning against the corridor wall, hands in pockets. Pyke levelled a finger at him.

"Nothing you had to say last time was any real help," he said. "Especially when a clearly unhinged Ustril popped out of the woodwork with a crew full of derange-alikes. Then, just to add an extra layer of crazy-sauce, along comes a grizzled, grey-haired version of me! He deals with the Ustril gang, then makes some baffling comments, makes me a gift of one of his hand-me-downs, and buggers off!"

"At least you still have the crystal," said Simulation Pyke. "Y'know, after all that. Which is going to make what I need to say next pretty difficult to hear."

Pyke gave his ghostly otherself a narrow look of scepticism, with an eyebrow raised for emphasis. "Feels as if nothing can surprise me now so go ahead, knock yerself out."

"Okay—what you need to do next is head into the bridge, find Raven and give her the crystal!"

Pyke's initial reaction was incredulity shading off into outrage with overtones of fury. But then the absurdity of it took hold, the sheer farcical, ludicrous inversion of everything...he found himself laughing till his ribs ached while Sim-Pyke waited, smiling and nodding. At last the hilarity subsided and a faintly uneasy realisation settled over him.

"You're actually serious about this, aren't you?"

"Horribly, deadly serious, I'm afraid—and before you start swearing and telling me how your friends paid with their lives to keep the crystal out of the Legacy's hand...well, I know how all that happened..."

"How could you possibly know?" Pyke shot back. "How could you understand what she *did* to them, what I *saw*..."

"I know because I've heard their stories," said Sim-Pyke. "Remember?"

Pyke felt the bitter fury go out of him. Of course, the copies that the Legacy made and kept in its simulation menagerie. Not for the first time, he wished Dervla were here to get his head on straight.

"This whole situation has been a rapidly changing one," Sim-Pyke went on. "Rensik and me, we actually know how to end all this, really bring it to an end, but we've only been in the position to do it very recently. If Raven had got hold of the crystal earlier, or retained it after the executions, she and the Legacy would have fused it with the other pieces before we were ready and ... well, the end of everything is not putting it too strongly."

Pyke rebelled at this. "What do you even mean by 'the end of everything'? These crystals are part of a weapon, and all weapons eventually meet their counterweapons..."

"Not this one. I think it's time you saw it for yourself."

"Saw what?"

"Saw exactly what's going on inside that crystal of yours."

One second he was standing outside the entrance to the bridge—in the next he was hanging in space over a planet, its silent, grey-swathed immensity rolling past. Part of him wanted to yell at Sim-Pyke to return him to the corridor, but as the seconds passed with no adverse effects he grew curious. Then his viewpoint moved forward and swooped planetwards, plunging down through cloud layers, a blurry stream of vapour and mist, till he burst out into clear air over a vast alien city. It was clearly the product of a highly advanced civilisation, at least going by the first impressions of immense constructions, along with radial grids suggesting intricate transport networks. But as he descended he realised that there were no ground vehicles rushing along connecting roads since they were not roads. Nor were there any signs of air traffic, no grav-cars, cargo drones or air-space monitors. Nor any sign of the inhabitants or any other creature.

Then the voice of Simulation Pyke began to speak, relating the story of how, a million years ago, a foolish species had allowed the creation of a nano-viral matter assimilator, how it evolved and escaped from its lab, took over first a city, then a region, then an entire planet, how it acquired intelligence and began to plan, made the leap from planet to planet, bringing every satellite in that star system under its central control and, finally, its sun.

The shifting viewpoint showed him how a sun was cordoned off, chained and caged, its thermonuclear might channelled off to serve the needs of the nano-plague intellect as it spread its dominion to neighbouring stars and further afield. Pyke saw how the nano-plague surged across the surface of a world on the front lines of its ruthless expansion—only what he saw was an immense frozen tableau, scene after scene of desperate humanoids fleeing waves, webs and hurtling tentacles of the relentless, obsidian nano-matter.

Sim-Pyke then went on to explain how an adjacent interstellar autarchy, a galactic power of some consequence, collaborated with a wandering Ancient in isolating the nano-plague within a picketed volume of space. Before the blight could gather its strength and break out, the Ancient (last survivor of a vanished race) used its advanced mystic science to transform the entire picketed volume of space into an artificial containment, a dungeon constructed from an exotic dimensional lattice. The Ancient designed and defined its external appearance and properties—resembling a creature with its mighty wings spread. It was restricted to a size and weight that could be easily carried by a single sentient being.

Having created this bizarre prison, the Ancient struck it a single harsh blow which broke it into three pieces, then told the autarchy's ministers to send the fragments far away from each other, and to erase any hint of their existence. It was a ploy which kept them apart for hundreds of millennia.

The last scene he saw showed towers and cables of nano-matter in frozen orbit around an obsidian-encased moon, supporting row after row of shipyards churning out vessels in a torrent flowing towards the staging areas of multiple armadas. Yet all motion was suspended—only his viewpoint was in motion.

The incredible vista faded and abruptly he was back in his body, back in the corridor outside the bridge. Sim-Pyke was still there, watching him closely.

"You weren't actually gone that long," he said. "The neural-resonance field makes it easy to fool the temporal sense with an accelerated immersion, so I've been told."

"So, all that's true?" Pyke said. "There's a kind of embryo nano-plague empire held captive inside this bloody crystal?"

"That's about the size of it."

"Right, fine…" Pyke tried to muster his thoughts. "So if keeping these pieces of the original prison apart is stopping this nano-plague from coming back, why in the name of everything that's sane should I help that psychobitch Raven put them together?"

"Because it's the only way to completely destroy it! Look—the Ancient broke the original crystal into three parts, remember? Well, I'm sure you know how hard that crystal shard of yours is; nothing can crack it, dent it or even scratch it—immunity to physical alteration is an inherent property of the dimension lattice. But when the Ancient split it in three it was only because he had adjusted the lattice's integrity enabler system, creating three weak shear points. We now have control over that system and once the three shards are reunited we can fundamentally alter the dimensional lattice and create thousands upon thousands of those weak points! All it would take is a single bullet or an energy bolt, even just a good whack with a rock, and kersmash-tinkle, it's over, it's done! No one's putting *that* back together…"

Pyke listened closely, trying to take it in, trying to fit all that with the bits and pieces he'd picked up along the demented road that had led him to this place. And still, the very idea of walking up to Raven Kaligari and just giving up the very prize she was desperate to have—it made his blood run cold. Simulation Pyke read the doubt in his face.

"Not convinced, eh?"

"After all the stinking, rotten crap she's put me and my crew through," Pyke said. "All she deserves is to be gunned down like the trash she is...I'll even be merciful and put a round in her head!"

"What makes you think you'd get near enough to do any of that?" Sim-Pyke indicated the stuck doors. "None of us have any idea what's actually waiting for you in there but you can bet yer last cred that Raven's goons are going to be all over it, heavily armed and ugly as sin to boot. So just how are you going to get up close to her?"

"No idea," Pyke said, feeling frustrated and angry at himself for not thinking it through. "What about you, then? What's *your* plan...or do you even have one?"

Simulation Pyke gave a mocking smile. "Actually, I do. See that hoody protector you got tied around your waist? Ideal. Get that on, mess up your hair, scrape up some dust and grime and get your face grubbied up, and add some light scratches to forehead and cheek for extra grit. You should probably ditch Hokajil's time-thrower, bit of a giveaway. Then go in there and bluff like a bastard!"

Pyke had to admit, it had all his hallmarks and seemed to be the only vaguely workable plan going. The simulation-life in which the echoes of his crew were caught now seemed like a temporary reprieve.

"So you weren't really planning on surviving, I take it," he said as he tugged the hooded protector loose from about his waist.

"Not our top priority, no," said Sim-Pyke. "Either way, we don't see ourselves coming out the other side—either the crystal gets smashed, which means game over, or the Legacy unlocks the reassembled crystal key and releases the nano-plague in which case, same outcome. So we're just focusing on trying to throw as many spanners into the Legacy's works..."

Pyke slung the heavy rifle back over his shoulder—after a moment's consideration, the time-thrower joined it. Then he bent down, wiped some grime from the filthy deck and smeared it over his face. Sim-Pyke smiled approvingly.

"That's it, the hard-bitten, surly, brusque demeanour," he said. "I'll be going invisible again, but I promise that if we can offer advice we will." As he finished the sentence his form faded from view.

"Reassuring, I guess," said Pyke, moving towards the jammed doors. Just then a shape scuttled across the gap on the other side, making Pyke jump.

"What the hell was that?" came Sim-Pyke's voice in his head.

"The grey-haired version of me said something about the Damaugra having parasites that he called cyberlice," said Pyke. "I was expecting something like insects but that's the size of a skagging turtle!"

"Lovely. Extra-bulky vermin. Carry on."

Lifting one leg, Pyke stepped through the opaque veil into the low-lit foyer. The charred and burned smells were stronger here, sharper. Only a handful of ceiling glowdiscs were active, their stuttering illumination revealing padded seating around the walls, the smashed remains of a low table and other detritus. And a body lying face down over where the wall curved round to open on the bridge. Blood had pooled around the corpse and dark handprints had smeared along and down the nearby wall panels. Pyke sidled past it and gained his first view of the bridge of the *Mighty Defender*.

It was grandiose on a scale that Pyke had never seen before, and wrecked in a way he hadn't been expecting. A double row of consoles and workstations lined the rear wall which was the highest bulkhead of the entire bridge. From the rear the ceiling curved down to meet a wide viewing window—it was about twenty feet high and maybe sixty wide. Other workstations were clustered in double ranks up the centre of the deck to meet another row that swept all along the base of the viewing window. But above all this hung a wide platform, clearly the centre of bridge operations. It was suspended from shiny cables that curved in from four anchor points, except that one of the cables had snapped and the entire command platform hung at a slight incline.

And it hung in shadows yet the lighting was not so poor that it did not illuminate the monstrous thing that jutted in through a smashed, fracture-webbed hole in the viewing window. The Damaugra, the doom of the *Mighty Defender*.

Dense clusters of ash-grey, spiralling metal coils had burst in through the viewing window, some large, some small, the very biggest of them having reached in to puncture the deck and the bulkhead, rotating, almost screwing themselves into the superstructure. That was the tearing, crunching noise he'd heard earlier, the sound of these coils biting deeper and deeper. Other kinds of tentacles extended through the press of coils, narrower ones with rows of curved fangs along either side. They were often flung out in pairs or threes, biting into the walls and the floor, anchoring themselves to the underframes, and Pyke saw low, bulbous shapes crawling to and fro along them. Pyke was astounded and aghast at the sight, wondering what it all looked like from outside the ship.

"Well, I've seen a few things," said Simulation Pyke's voice. "But this gets a special category all of its own."

"Wait a sec," Pyke muttered. "According to what the older Hokajil said, the bridge should still be at the moment when he began creating the time-zones to create his escape route..."

"Should we believe everything the old fellah said, especially in the light of Young Hokajil's claims on the subject?"

Pyke shrugged. "If he was telling something like the truth, perhaps something has moved the bridge forward in time..."

"Something or some*one*," said Sim-Pyke. "How about Raven and her thugs?"

"That would fit." Pyke felt sweat break out across his scalp. "Does that mean this whole mess will shortly slam into the planet's surface?"

By now Pyke had crept along the rear end of the bridge, keeping to the shadows between the row of consoles. Many of them were smashed and charred, some surrounded with spilled documents, some of which had burned to ash, which was handy for Pyke to streak through his hair. From here he also got his first good look at the Damaugra's cyberlice—about the size of a domestic Earth cat, they had three limbs, were a dirty-brown colour on top and a greenish-white underneath, and each limb ended in a single chisel-tipped talon. The few that scuttled past him neither slowed nor seemed to take notice, which afforded a kind of grim relief.

As he moved, his perspective of the command platform altered—looking up, he saw that some of the platform's floor tiles were transparent and that there were a few figures walking around up there.

"Seems like a fine opportunity to try out Hokajil's time-thrower," said Sim-Pyke in his thoughts. "You could target some of Raven's minions and send them scurrying off."

"Not a bad idea," Pyke said. Crouching down in the shadow of a console, he unlimbered the device so that they could get a close look at the control panel. It took a few moments but they figured out how to set the thrower to scan for living creatures, how to target them on the tiny screen, and how to calibrate the temporal rewind. But when Pyke depressed the trigger the only outcome was a winking red light.

"Uh-oh," said Simulation Pyke.

"What? Why uh-oh?"

"Not totally sure but Rensik says switch it back to standard time-throw mode and dial it down to a square metre, then fire it at one of the wrecked consoles."

Pyke did as he was bidden, pointed the device and fired. Again, all that happened was a blinking red light.

"I saw it work," he said. "I saw that grey-haired old geezer make Ustril and her creepy squad vanish..."

"Yep, and that was in one of Hokajil's time-zones."

"You saying that's the reason?—'cos this isn't one of them..." He racked his brains. "Is there some kind of dampening field at work, blocking the thrower?"

"Rensik says it's more likely to be a natural field effect emanating from the Damaugra itself."

He gritted his teeth. "Well, that kinda limits our options," he said, laying the useless device down on the deck where he was crouching. "What do we have left?—frontal assault?..."

Suddenly a beam of light stabbed at him from behind and a voice said, "Who's there? Stand up and show your face! No sudden moves!"

"Well, crap," he muttered, raising his hands as he straightened and turned into the light. There was a moment's pause.

"Ah, you're here at last." The torchbeam, attached to a rifle barrel, was lowered. Holding it was a bald man in mismatched body armour, his face half concealed by a visor with concave eyepieces. "Raven's been waiting for over an hour. I better take you up there myself."

"Make like this is just the usual kind of thing," said Sim-Pyke's voice, which Pyke felt amounted to pointing out the skagging obvious!

He shrugged. "Sure—just checking my gear..."

The guard waved him on ahead, escorting him over to where

a two-person lifter plate carried them up to the command platform. Cyberlice were far more prevalent up here, skittering about
wherever he looked, rushing along the splayed-out cables which
joined the platform to the restless mass of spiralled metal coils
that spilled in through the bridge's smashed viewing window.
Water vapour clung and curled around the edges of the gap,
where jagged, razor-sharp glass nestled against the brute mass
of the Damaugra. But up here there was no sign of Raven.

The guard prodded his shoulder. "No weapons allowed for
outsiders."

This just gets better and better, he thought as he slid the rifle
off his shoulder and tossed it onto one of the dead consoles.

"That's it," said Simulation Pyke in his head. "Mean and
moody, with a savage edge. Oh, and while you're at it, see if you
can get hold of a bit of that window glass—there's bits of it lying
everywhere."

Pyke choked back his incendiary reply, keeping it down to a
soundless snarl. As the guard nodded and beckoned him to follow,
he spotted a good fist-sized piece of glass to one side. He told the
guard he had some gravel in his boot, sat down to pull it off and,
as he gave the boot a theatrical shake and rap with one hand, the
other stealthily gathered the glass fragment into his pocket. Then
he was back on his feet and being directed by the guard towards
the front of the command platform where a cluster of talon-edge
tentacles formed a bridge leading straight out to a maw-like gap
at the centre of the Damaugra's flexing knot of coils.

Pyke steeled his nerves as he stepped onto the bridge, which
felt curiously solid underfoot. As he walked across it he glanced
to his left and saw how the rest of the Damaugra's immense
tangle of coils spilled along the outside of the bridge to the hull
then curved out of sight on the port side. Then all at once he
had reached the constricted gap in that monstrous barricade of
sharp-edged spiral coils.

The gap opened a little wider, then wider still, until there was enough room for him to enter. The guard grunted at him to continue.

"Watch the path—it gets a bit twisty."

The tentacle bridge gave way to a succession of oval plates that made Pyke think of stepping stones. They provided a walkway through a tunnel composed of the intertwining innards of the gigantic creature, turning and dipping and twisting but always maintaining constant gravity underfoot. Sometimes the sharp coil edges were too close for comfort and as he walked Pyke could smell a strange odour, like hot oily metal, while his ears caught the hisses and clicks of a million blades caressing each other.

At last the claustrophobic tunnel opened out at a chamber walled with neat rows of the Damaugra's coils, and lit by vein-like cables whose striation gave off a green and yellow radiance. A slope curved up one side to an oval platform bounded by a low parapet; at the rear of the platform was a bright recess from which all the glowing cables emerged to spread out and inter-weave across the walls. Cyberlice crawled everywhere.

"It's been over two hours since I received your message," came the familiar, despised voice. "Quickly, bring it to me!"

"What now?" Pyke muttered under his breath, noting the presence of half a dozen armed guards spaced along the incline as he climbed it.

"Well," said Simulation Pyke, "this is all a bit unexpected."

"You don't say," Pyke mutter-snarled.

"We didn't think that this Damaugra creature was import-ant," Sim-Pyke said. "And now we've got this. Our advice? Don't start a fight, try not to get killed. And let her have the crystal—put her in a good mood..."

Huh, he thought. *Usually, only acts of homicidal slaughter can put her at her ease...*

As he reluctantly mounted the incline, he cursed himself

for his lack of imagination and foresight. Rather than listen to voices emanating from the crystal shard, he should maybe have turned back to the lower levels and tried to recruit his own gang of rogues and allies. Then come back up here to fight his way in and settle matters to his own satisfaction. *Instead here I am about to stick my head between the jaws of monstrous fate and pray that it's not that hungry.*

Then he was there, strolling up to where Raven, once more impeccably dressed in black-on-black body armour, stood over a round table formed from the same grey material as the coils and cables. Upon it were the other two crystal pieces, hovering about an inch above the tabletop in a suspensor field. Behind her was the mysterious glowing recess which, from a closer perspective, proved to be a knot of bright arrays of small shapes, spheres, cubes, polyhedrons, all interspersed with miniature versions of the Damaugra's spirally coils. There was also a ribbon of dataleads plumbed in and trailing out to a bland grey cylinder sitting on a sill below the recess.

"Give it here, come on," said Raven, hand outstretched. "I had to wait for that courier for long enough, and now you've kept me waiting, too."

As he delved beneath the hoody and into his jacket, she sized him up with narrowed eyes.

"So you're from one of the outer time-facets, eh? You really do look quite like him," she said, smiling lazily and biting her bottom lip in a way that, once upon a time, invariably presaged gunfire.

"Don't see it myself," he said. "Heard he was a bit of a jabber merchant, not my thing at all." Pyke produced the crystal shard, still contained within its leather case. He went to reach out and hand it over but, strangely, found that he couldn't manage it. Couldn't stop thinking about Dervla, Ancil, Kref and Moleg, how they were dead yet still alive inside the bloody thing, well, whatever was left of them, anyway.

"No second thoughts," Raven said. "Remember how well compensated you'll be, or, alternatively, how dead you'll be if I have to take it off your cooling corpse."

It took an effort of will for him to stretch out and drop it into her waiting palm. He fixed a half-smile onto his face as he stuck his hands in his pockets, feeling in one of them the cold chunk of window glass.

"That's better. Good boy."

"So do you put it all together now?" Pyke said. "Lots of different stories out in the Mosaic about this. Wondering if the real thing'll be spectacular."

"It will be so far beyond spectacular," she said, "that you'll need new words to describe it." She stroked the leather-wrapped crystal. "So stick around—it really will be a once-in-a-lifetime experience. As for the reunification, well, that's not my assignment—I have an entirely different mission to tackle!"

Then she pulled off the leather top-piece and tipped the entire, exposed crystal out into her hand.

"This isn't good," said Simulation Pyke in his head.

"Don't you mean, 'this could be a mammoth clusterbotch'?" Pyke muttered, teeth gritted. "Looks like we're about to come face-to-face with the tormentor-in-chief..."

"I was talking about that glowing recess and those wired-in components..."

Suddenly all his attention was on Raven. Standing next to the suspension field table, she trembled and shuddered where she stood, still clutching the crystal in her hand. Then in an instant the tremors ceased. She stood there, eyes closed, breathing in and out deeply, then sighed and opened her eyes. That glittering, hungry gaze settled on Pyke and Raven leaned forward, smiling.

"Well, well—Captain Pyke!" said the Legacy with Raven's voice. "Miss me?"

CHAPTER TWENTY-FOUR

Pyke—the Crystal Simulation,
the Isle of Candles

From the moment real-world Pyke had entered the bridge of the *Mighty Defender* and seen the Damaugra and all its cyber-parasites, it became clear to Simulation Pyke and Rensik that some unforeseen scheme was afoot. Clearly, Raven and the Legacy had been working on deeper plans.

Around them the Isle of Candles was the same, quiet and cool, with an unchanging dusk keeping half the sky rosy while the encroaching night waited patiently. Pyke was sitting on one of the benches near the stone gazebo, staring into the observation ambit which Rensik had projected within the gazebo's walls. The ambit was a 3D reconstruction of the crystal shard's immediate vicinity, assembled from data-streams flowing in from the outer dimensional lattice. Pyke had watched as his flesh-and-blood counterpart first entered the bridge. When the time-thrower failed to work, it had started to look as if their plan was back in the running, provided real-world Pyke didn't get himself shot or maimed. Then he encountered the guard and rode the lifterplate to the command platform, but instead of Raven there was a gantry of tentacles that led from the platform out into the Damaugra itself. At this point Pyke and Rensik agreed that they were as much in the dark as real-world Pyke.

"What has this bloody monster got to do with anything?" Pyke said, just after pointing out the chunk of broken glass to his counterpart.

"I do not know enough about this creature," said Rensik. "I am currently running a few concurrent term queries in those archives still open to me..."

In the observation ambit, real-world Pyke was walking along a flexi-directional path through the razor-sharp guts of the Damaugra, emerging at last in a weird, green-lit chamber. Rensik was observing that the Damaugra had to have been generating containment fields and a breathable environment for Pyke and the other humanoids there, since this was effectively outside the ship. Then Pyke spotted the glowing recess at the top of a sloping pathway, felt a reflexive loathing on seeing Raven waiting there.

As Pyke's counterpart approached the head of the incline, they were able to make out more details.

"There's the other two crystal fragments," Pyke said. "They're definitely set up for the big moment."

"Those are data-leads issuing from that recess," said Rensik. "This is certain to be a cognitive nexus for the Damaugra, perhaps the main one."

"Looks like it was meant to be a control room of sorts, maybe?" Pyke said.

"Yes, and those wires and components are Raven's hack into the creature's ganglia."

Real-world Pyke eventually managed to hand the crystal over. It was an eerie feeling, knowing that the artefact which contained them was now in the possession of a psychomaniac.

"Hope you're ready to engage the integrity enabler," he said to Rensik. "The sooner we get this entire crystal hell-prison ready for the big smash, the better!"

"I don't think the reassembly is what's going to happen next," said the drone.

That was when Raven tipped the whole, uncovered crystal into her open hand.

"Great, one vile villainess—incoming."

A shudder passed through the ground underfoot, as if the entire Isle of Candles was experiencing a low-level earthquake, a continuous series of small tremors.

"The Legacy," said Rensik. "It's leaving."

"This doesn't usually happen when it seizes a host out in the world."

"Exactly—it's moving the entirety of its cognitive and perceptive self into Raven's mind," Rensik said. "Which means..."

Lights appeared in a cluster near the entrance to the gazebo, swirled together like a miniature tornado for a few seconds, then there was a brilliant flash and there stood Raven Kaligari. She looked dazed for a moment, then the alertness came back into her eyes, along with the familiar glint of the unhinged.

"So this is where you've been hiding! Crafty old Captain Pyke and his rusty box-buddy! Well, boys, it won't be long before the crystals are one and the empire of forever is reborn. You might find a place in its magnificence, but only if you're extra-nice and submissive."

"Dream on, you murdering scum," Pyke snarled, lunging at her. But his hands passed through her image, feeling nothing. Raven threw back her head and laughed, then blew him a kiss before hurrying away, climbing the path to the villa, her annoying laughter ringing out all the way.

"One of my archive searches has returned only meagre suggestions," said Rensik. "In the meantime we need to pay attention to what the Legacy is about to do."

In the observation ambit, Pyke watched as, having taken over Raven's body, the Legacy leaned forward and said, "Well, well, Captain Pyke! Miss me?"

Real-world Pyke pushed back his hood and smiled wearily.

"As a matter of fact, I did. I needed reminding what kind of malignant, disease-ridden, bloodthirsty, gutter-sweepings the galaxy is capable of vomiting up, and look!—there you are!"

The Legacy chuckled merrily, shaking its head. "Nice, very nice. I'm going to miss Humans so much—I'm especially going to miss you and all your surprising little schemes. But in the future to come there will be no room for tiny minds and tiny schemes. The empire of living matter will be the only scheme, the only plan, the only purpose." The Legacy grew thoughtful. "I was explaining all this just a short time ago to that female you thought so highly of, at least to the simulation of her. She's a kept woman now, you know—I have her corralled into a little house outside the city walls..."

That was the moment when real-world Pyke gave in to his rage, balled his hands into fists and started to make his way round the suspension table. He only managed a couple of steps before one of the guards struck him between the shoulders with a rifle butt. He staggered forward, straight into the Legacy's oncoming fist. A moment later he was dragged off to the side, hands bound with cuff-strips.

The Legacy squatted down next to him, all smiles and malice. "It's almost time, Captain—are you ready for the trip of your life?"

Back in the simulation, the drone Rensik turned from the observation ambit and spoke.

"I've deduced their intent from the few scraps of information I've gathered," he said suddenly. "The Damaugra is the creature which began pursuing the *Mighty Defender* two days after it fled the fall of the Arraveyne Imperium. It is capable of long-range space travel and can pass into hyperspace with ease—some references claim that it is native to hyperspace. The Legacy's plan has always been to reassemble the crystals into the Essavyr Key and then, by unlocking it, unleash the nano-matter plague. But if it were to carry out this procedure in hyperspace, the nano-plague would easily be able to spread to many different parts of the galaxy and crush resistance on a number of fronts, thereby gaining total dominance very quickly. This is why they need to gain complete control over the Damaugra."

Pyke was stunned and aghast—stated so baldly, the Legacy's plan was obvious and monstrous in its scope and deadly ambition.

"So, they don't fully control it yet?" he said. "What do those hack-wires do?"

"Low-level functions, environment, gravity, going by visual indicators," said Rensik. "The Legacy needs full control, which is why it's about to upload Raven's persona into the creature's neural web."

"You're saying that Raven's going to become that giant beast?"

"Yes, that is the Legacy's intention."

"Finally! A face to match her ugly personality."

"I had hoped that my residual, RK1, would have found a way to reach us here in the sublayer so that I could send him after her, but he has failed. There is now only you, and I am reluctant to ask…"

"Send me," said Pyke. "No dithering. Just do it, before I get a chance to think about what I'm doing."

"Very well. I will send another of my residuals with you—it won't have RK1's upgrades as it's only a basic subcognition, but it will provide sufficient virtual analogues so that you can adapt to an unfamiliar synaptic web."

Out in the world, the Legacy was standing up again, holding the crystal to the light, peering into it with grotesque desire in its stolen eyes. Then it turned to the bright control recess and opened the grey cylinder that was wired into the glowing nodes.

"Ready yourself," said Rensik. "I will attempt to synchronise your upload with that of Raven Kaligari."

"Ready for launch," Pyke said, standing now before the

semi-opaque images in the observation ambit, trying to imagine himself wearing a hero-style jetpack firing on all rockets as he hurtled into a storm. And in the ambit the Legacy slotted the crystal into place. "Next time you see Dervla, tell her..."

But words, sentences, feelings and needs and all the intent and love behind them disintegrated into a flow of being-motes, a vertical rain of essence pouring up after one who had to be stopped.

Certain that the upload of both residual and persona node had been successful, the Construct drone Rensik withdrew its control lines from the data-feed channels, masking any evidence of its presence. Then it returned to the exterior observation flow, watching as the Legacy carefully retrieved the crystal shard from the upload receptacle.

It was a source of regret for Rensik that it would not have one last meeting or communication with its residual RK1. By all accounts it had surpassed both its own assigned tasks and Rensik's expectations—the survival of its cognition alone would have been a valuable addition to the Construct's tactical libraries. That said, it was probably wise not to write it off completely, just yet.

But now, at last, the long-awaited moment had arrived. In the observation flow, the Legacy leaned over the suspension field table and with unhurried precision set the crystal shard down next to the other two fragments. This final addition seemed to trigger a preset function as the field then began to draw the three crystals together. All of Rensik's monitor grids told him that the uneven sheared sector of the dimensional lattice was altering its properties in preparation. Likewise, Rensik's supervision of the integrity enabler system was full and total—as soon as the lattices were rewoven as one, the system would again be active and Rensik's task would be clear.

The three pieces made simultaneous contact. The vigorous

process of dissolving the now superfluous dimensional lattices reverberated throughout the para-dimensional substructures of the vast containment. The fractured surfaces began to slowly fade, in segments and patches, as the lattice repair reiterated itself into finer and finer detail. And, at last, the cargo itself, the trapped and caged volume of space-time-space and all it contained, coalesced...

And what had been frozen began to move.

And what had been a cold, immobile image of energy became furious torrents of power.

And what had been half-made resumed its construction.

And what had been suspended for unbroken millennia between one thought of pure dominance and the next became aware.

And when that awareness surveyed the boundaries of its prison it noticed many things, including the drone AI, Rensik.

DERVLA—THE CRYSTAL SIMULATION, OUTSIDE THE WALLS OF GRANAH

When she felt the tremors come up through the floor and felt the shack rattle and creak about her, Dervla knew something important was happening. A cold knot of dread unfurled in the pit of her stomach as the words of the Legacy came back to her. She got up from the bed where she'd been not quite napping and went outside. The tremors were still occurring, erratically, and the air was full of a curious sound like a bell-chime, stretched out and continuous.

The slums were still deserted but it was later than before, something like mid-afternoon. She leaned on a rickety fence post and contemplated the sky of scattered clouds and blue patches, the mass of trees further along the wall, past the closed gates, and the view over the wide, rushing river...the Worroth, that was it. And just then, in the middle of that unexpected moment of restful peace, a figure appeared along the main path, past the nearest huts. She called out, the figure turned and she saw that it was Ancil. He whooped and clenched his fist—then vanished.

"What the frack..." Dervla said, coming to a halt after taking a few steps in Ancil's direction. She looked around in all directions, and as she turned away from staring at the grassy cliff edge there was a sudden large presence where none had been before.

"Derv!" boomed out a familiar bass voice. She barely had time to turn around before she was enveloped in Kref's bearlike embrace.

"Kref!...big guy...can't breathe..."

Laughing, he released her.

"So great to see you again, Derv," said the big Henkayan. "I mean, I thought you were dead, and Ans and Moleg, and...and me, but I woke up here instead...ah, here he is!"

It was Ancil again, then Moleg arrived from round the back of Dervla's shack, and also Pyke's companions from the Isle of Candles, Vrass the Gomedran, T'Moy the Bargalil, and Klane the Shyntanil. Dervla felt almost overwhelmed to see them all and in between the hugs and handshakes she asked how they had got here.

"Arky," said Ancil. "Rensik's residual drone...where is he? Yeah, it was him that set up our great escape. Sent me through first on a quick test flight!"

"This is not, strictly speaking, an escape," came a voice in the air as RK1's mechanical bird alighted on the fence post in front of Dervla's dwelling. "I had hoped that all of us could decamp to Rensik's secure refuge up in the lattice sublayer but now there is too much commotion and disorder to risk such an operation, now that the crystals are about to be unified."

Chatter tailed off at this announcement.

"What will that mean for the simulation around us?" asked Ancil. "And for us?"

"All is uncertainty," said RK1. "I have insufficient data even to extrapolate."

"I know what the Legacy has planned for us," said Dervla, and she related the main points of her encounter with the malign intelligence. There were thunderstruck looks on all sides.

"This crystal is a...a prison?" said Ancil. "You're not serious!"

Dervla nodded. "From the start, this whole mad cavalcade has been a prison break!"

"It's beginning," said the Bargalil T'Moy, his face drawn and fearful as he pointed.

Up in the sky, patches were dissolving to reveal shadowy darkness. Everywhere dark holes appeared, grew and spread, joining up with others, like a kind of disease or rot eating away at the simulated clouds and blue sky. Then the sun went out and a dim gloom settled over their surrounds. At the same time, details began to emerge from the shadowy murk, blurred curves which resolved into an entire planet, looming close, but it was covered, almost encrusted, with structures laid out in radial patterns. Miles-high towers rose from among forests of glittering spires. Clusters of segmented cables converged on huge platforms miles across then straight up from the planet's surface to link up with huge conglomerations of polyhedral structures in orbit, as well as an entire moon. Crenelated, obsidian walls encircled the moon with deep trenches branching and rebranching all the way around it, and some trenches ending in pitch-black circular pits.

In the hazy background, armoured worldlets hung in chains while a large asteroid bristling with incomprehensible spines drifted past. Just visible in the distance was a carapaced sun sprouting energy conduits—only splinters of its thermonuclear brightness showed through the seams of its sepulchre. And everywhere, ships were in motion, freighters great and huge, as well as those with unknowable functions.

So this is it, she thought. *The empire of the nano-plague. If this gets loose, civilisation is done.*

"What's that?" said Moleg, pointing at a line of objects that had just sprung up from the semi-excavated moon, each with a faint trail. A second line, perhaps thirty in number, launched, followed by a third and a fourth.

"Ships," said Dervla, noticing the far-off tiny blue flames of their plasma drives. Then she saw how the waves of vessels fanned out, all on courses carrying them straight out, heading for the inner surface of their prison, the dimensional lattice. There was an ominous deliberation about these launches.

Then Klane the Shyntanil uttered a sardonic laugh and raised his hand—it seemed to be his turn to point.

"And how long before *those* ones get here?"

PYKE, THE BRIDGE OF THE *MIGHTY DEFENDER*, IN THE SYNAPTIC CORE OF THE DAMAUGRA

Defeated, exhausted, and bound hand and foot, all Pyke wanted to do was continue to sit on the floor while the Legacy crowed and gloated over its prizes and its triumphs. But it seemed that wasn't permitted—Pyke had to be dragged to his feet to bear witness as the Legacy retrieved the crystal from that glowing recess and slipped it into place on the suspension field table.

"What birth pangs this new empire has had!" said the Legacy with such corrosive smugness that Pyke wished his hands *were* free, just so he could cram the skagging crystal down that skagging throat!

"Behold!—the end of that chaotic mess of galactic uncivilisations, and the beginning of eternal splendour!"

In the suspension field, the crystal fragments converged, their fracture points fitting together perfectly, hot, bright lines glowing where the joins were. Right then, unexpectedly, Rensik's voice spoke in his head.

"I can see that you're experiencing some difficulty, Captain. However, the crystal key will soon be fully whole, which paves the way for me to engage the integrity enabler and reconfigure the key for its irreversible destruction. At that point, you must find a way to break it!"

Pyke had to throttle back the furious and profane retort that sprang to his mouth and almost made it to his lips. Instead he tried to speak in a kind of strangled whisper as far back in his throat as he could manage.

"Not a chance—they got me trussed like a chicken."

"An unwelcome response—if you cannot find some kind of advantage and exploit it, we are lost."

Pyke breathed out through gritted teeth. *So it's down to this, do or die, all or nothing, or, rather, trying to do it all* with *nothing!*

He started to laugh out loud, interspersing it with coughs and whoops, deliberately making as raucous and mocking a sound as possible. It worked—the Legacy's gaze came round to regard him with a malefic hauteur, and that was when he went for it.

"Hoo, yeah! Wow, really? You're planning to be the all-powerful master of the universe? Master of Assclowns, more like—or even Assclown of the Universe! Man, I just can't decide which one I like the best…"

Having broken off from admiring the reunified crystal key, the Legacy came round the table in three strides. It brought its hand up in one smooth motion and grabbed Pyke's lower jaw, silencing his stream of insults.

"In the time that Raven and I have worked together," it said, "I've grown accustomed to possessing her, and made a few modifications…"

"Uh, sorry, that sounds more than just a little creepy," said

Pyke through constricted lips. "Pervy assclown is not a good look for you, trust me."

The Legacy's grin was a horrific thing, teeth apart, tongue stroking the roof of the mouth. "She fantasises about all the different ways these modifications could subject you to pain, and I can see the attraction."

"Raven and me have an understanding," Pyke said. "So I wouldn't damage the goods, get me? Where is she, by the way—I'd really like to say goodbye."

"Not possible. At the moment she has taken up residence in the neural networks of the Damaugra and is preparing to fly it into hyperspace. There, we shall unlock the Essavyr Key and the Empire of Living Matter will be reborn. Haven't you figured all this out yet?"

"Raven's inside a giant razor-coil monster. Right. A few pieces of the puzzle had escaped me, I have to admit."

"Indeed, along with the skills of courtesy and respect..." The Legacy slapped him gently twice in time with those words, "...and keeping a civil tongue in your *head*!" And the sentence ended with a punch in the face.

It was like being hit by a Henkayan. There was pain down the side of his face and in his jaw, and the kind of ringing normally brought on by being too close to one of Ancil's test firings. Through the dizziness he fancied he could hear Rensik babbling on about how the other Pyke had been uploaded after Raven to stop her controlling the Damaugra, how the nano-plague was becoming aware of its surroundings and might present a threat, and how he, Captain Brannan Pyke, needed to space-marine-up and smash the damn crystal key, and that made him laugh with bloody lips...

The Legacy bent down and brought its face, Raven's beautiful, perfectly featured face, up close, smiling mischievously, and said, "Modifications, Bran. Felt like a sledgehammer, didn't it? And I wasn't even trying."

Unbidden, formless hate surged in him and he lunged with his head, aiming at the nose in that exquisite face. But the Legacy shifted just enough to dodge it and danced back a step.

"Oh, really? You and you, hold him up straight—I'm going to put some effort into it this time!"

At exactly that moment, there was an eruption of gunfire. The Legacy turned to look towards the chamber entrance and a salvo of assorted energy bolts, blast-beams and rifled slugs struck. From a few feet away, Pyke saw blood spray from impacts to the chest and lower torso; a half-second burst of particle beam hit the side of the Legacy's face, causing more blood to spout; at the same time a combination of energy bolts and high-velocity rounds punched and sheared through the Legacy's shoulder, entirely severing the arm. All this horrific violence took place in seconds amid a deafening uproar. As Pyke's guards let him fall so they could try and defend themselves, he could see that the monstrous volley had thrown the Legacy over to the other side of the platform, just past where the suspension table still stood with the undamaged crystal key set upon it. He kept staring at the still, blood-spattered form, lying not far from its severed arm, while the shattering din of weaponsfire roared on.

"Captain, quickly, find a way to destroy the crystal key! Your simulation counterpart is winning the struggle for control of the Damaugra, but with the integrity enabler I have reconfigured the whole of the key—one sharp, heavy blow will shatter it and obliterate the nano-plague!"

But before Pyke could point out that he was still bound hand and foot, one of the remaining guards spun back from the parapet, black ichor spurting from a torn neck. A moment later the other guard was dragged bodily over the low wall, down to the chamber floor. Suddenly the firing ceased and thudding footsteps approached. Someone crouched down nearby and hauled him into a sitting position. It was Ustril. He groaned and cursed.

"Back to finish the job?" he said.

The Sendrukan scientist said nothing, simply gave him an unreadable stare as she took out a knife and cut the bonds around his wrist and ankles. Pyke looked back at her warily.

"Nice ambush," he said. "The Legacy's goons weren't prepared, clearly."

"Not for a determined squad of heavily armed Sendrukan women certainly," Ustril said.

"So just what is your angle?" Pyke said. "You got some tasty deal in mind now?"

"Your assumptions are incorrect," she said frostily. "I am here to do the right thing."

"Bit of a turnaround."

Ustril nodded sombrely. "My sisters... were very persuasive, reminding me of what kinds of behaviour should and should not be encouraged. So, now that we have reached this heart of darkness, what needs doing, now that Raven is..."

She stopped suddenly. There was movement behind her, then abruptly she was dragged by the neck backwards several yards by the Legacy.

Smeared with blood and lacking an arm, it slammed a foot into Ustril's throat while its now free hand snatched up a rifle from the nearby table where the crystal key still lay, gleaming, shining in the chamber's green illumination.

"Out!" the Legacy bellowed at the other Ustrils who were bringing weapons to bear. "Get out of this place or she dies! Understand?" It pressed the rifle's muzzle against Ustril's face for emphasis and the squad of alter-Ustrils retreated to the exit, leaving one by one.

The Legacy smiled brightly then directed that unhinged gaze at Pyke. "You still think that the eternal nano-tide can be denied! All your struggles, all your ploys, all your little helpers, they're all just minor setbacks on the path to infinite glory and an unyielding, perfect might. If you had a scrap of sense, Bran, or even just base self-preservation, you would surrender to the inevitable and come over to the winning side! The Empire of Forever will need good administrators…"

Its rant was interrupted as a green-blue beam stabbed out of the glowing recess in the wall, projecting a flickering figure into midair. Immediately, it began to speak.

"Blah-blah-eternal, blah-blah-infinite-glory, blah-blah-inevitable! Is that not the fiercest bucket of puke you've ever heard, ould son?"

Pyke looked up at Pyke. "No question," he said, laughing.

The Pyke projection then looked at the Legacy.

"I've got your little playmate on the back foot," he said. "Time you gave it up. The Damaugra is now mine!"

But the Legacy just chuckled. "Words are not bullets and threats are not deeds, and a reflection is not real."

"You're making a big-g-g-g-g-g-g…"

The projection distorted badly in spasms of interference then stabilised again, only this time it was Raven Kaligari who hovered there, grinning happily down at her master.

"Is all as it should be?" said the Legacy.

Now two versions of Raven were regarding each other. Pyke, though, was worried about Ustril who was choking under the Legacy's foot.

"The interloper will be eliminated very shortly," said Raven. "Can I be of assistance?"

The Legacy nodded, removed its foot from Ustril's neck and stepped back to the other side of the table where the crystal key sat.

"Demonstrate your control over the Damaugra," it said. "Eliminate these hindrances, these tiny insects with their tiny minds and tiny schemes."

"It shall be done," said Raven, raising a hand and pointing at a section of the chamber's wall.

A long stretch of grey, razor-edge spiral coil tore itself away from the midst of the hundreds that lined the chamber. Like an immense tentacular arm, it made vaguely serpentine motions as it lowered itself till it hung over the group on the landing. The Legacy laughed as the "head" end reared back in a clear precursor of a striking attack—and in that moment the projection of Raven suddenly vanished. Then the deadly razor-coil tentacle came slamming down. On the spot where the Legacy stood.

Pyke reflexively jerked backwards from the crashing point of impact. He thought the tentacle had struck the crystal key as well but then he saw it on the floor, intact among the broken pieces of the table. Meantime, the coil retracted and hauled itself back up to the gap in the wall.

"Stop him! Stop him!"

In Pyke's head, Rensik was sounding almost panicky, and Pyke was baffled until he realised that the Legacy was still alive, its mangled hand extended to the winged shape of the crystal key, tapping its shining surface with twisted fingers.

"It is going to unlock the Essavyr Key—stop it!"

Pyke scrambled over to the crushed, bloody mess of the Legacy's form, and dragged its remaining arm away from the crystal key. Yet still it managed to speak while blood drooled from its mouth.

"Too...too late...the nano-tide will not be denied..."

The Essavyr Key was showing black spots that radiated like dark ripples.

"Destroy the key," said Rensik in his head. "The Legacy has triggered the unlocking sequence."

Panic and horror seized Pyke. There was no rifle within reach and the broken piece of window glass was gone from his pocket, fallen out or removed by those guards. And still the Legacy continued to live, laughing at him, spraying blood from its mouth.

"...nano-tide...the Empire of Living Matter...will consume you all..."

"You really need to die," Pyke snarled. Grabbing the possessed Raven by the blood-sodden collar of that shiny black jacket, he swung the Legacy's head over and brought it down on the crystal key. A desperate fury took hold and he began slamming that head down again, and again, and again. He could feel his senses swimming from the effort and his hands aching from gripping the jacket.

Then he smashed that hateful head down again, and suddenly there was a ringing sound, a continuous high musical note.

Dear god, is this it? The end of the whole shebang? And me?

Then Rensik spoke. "Get away, Captain, you have only seconds before the Essavyr Key shatters. The nano-plague knows! I can hear its fear. You have my thanks, Captain, and something else..."

Pyke scrambled to his feet, then bent over Ustril and found she was still breathing. The effort made him cry out but somehow he managed to drag her tall, heavy form down into the twisty corridor, by which time the ringing had risen to a piercing shriek. There was a detonation of some kind, along with a burst of pure light that flowed around him like a silent cocoon, like the last viscous droplets of sunlight, bringing a warmth that put him to sleep.

EPILOGUE

Pyke, aboard the *Scarabus*

Twenty-four hours.

Actually, it was less than that, about twenty-two hours and some change. But that was only since the ancient launch had been brought into the *Scarabus*' shuttle bay, with Pyke aboard. He didn't know how much time had passed between the Key's destruction and waking up in the launch. It had been quiet, though, back here on the *Scarabus*. A few messages had come in, from the other Pyke that was in command of the Damaugra, but he'd taken and replied to them from his quarters.

Which is where he'd been since his return, self-confined, hardly straying outside. Sure, he was the captain and this was his ship—but it was also *their* ship and without his crew it felt like an empty theatre or a closed-up, after-hours bar.

Oleg was still here, solid, dependable, proficient in enough disciplines to have the ship in good condition while Pyke and the others had delved into that demented escapade. But just talking to him felt like being fooled into thinking that afterwards he'd head down to the galley, grab a coffee, swap a dirty joke with Ancil or some crazy reminiscence with...

With Dervla.

He still could see, when he closed his eyes, the executions. Yet with the utter dissolution of the *Mighty Defender*'s bridge section, off into whatever nook or cranny of space-time, went the bodies of the dead, of his dead crew, of his dead friends. Dead, gone, erased. As good as.

The comm unit over on the bulkhead by his desk buzzed. He cleared his throat.

"Pyke here, Oleg. What's new?"

"Long-distance recorded message for you from our erstwhile employer."

Pyke frowned—should he play the message here in private, or up on the bridge? He shook his head—this would be Van Graes letting them know if he was interested in the ancient single-seater launch from the *Mighty Defender*, and whether he had any work for them. So Oleg certainly deserved to know.

"I'll come up to the bridge and we'll see what he has to say."

It was a short walk to the command deck, yet the ship itself felt subdued, low-lit corridors with only the sound of muffled systems keeping the silence at bay. On the bridge itself, the window shutters were three-quarters closed, allowing only a narrow bar of sunlight to cut through the gloom of vacant workstations and screens on standby. One of the three big screens was showing the Damaugra in high orbit not far from their own orbital slot. The space-time convulsion which left the wrecked *Mighty Defender* to plummet downwards to Ong in the past had also dragged the Damaugra forward to the present. The other screens showed the planet Ong, one wide-vista, one zoomed in on the city of Cawl-Vesh and its canyon.

Oleg made to get up from the captain's console, but Pyke waved him back into the chair. "How are you doing, Oleg?"

"Very well, Captain. All systems reporting optimal performance levels, apart from intermittency in a power coupling down on cargo deck B."

Pyke felt a measure of relief—Oleg was a Kiskashin, a

reptilian humanoid species known for their composure and reliability, just what he needed. Pyke went over to sit at the empty helm console and said, "Let's see what our patron's got to say."

The screen showing Cawl-Vesh blinked, changing to a head-and-shoulders shot of Van Graes who started to speak. First, he conveyed his condolences about the loss of Pyke's crew members, and asked Pyke to pass on his sympathies to any relatives he might be contacting. Next, he noted that Lieutenant-Doctor Ustril had apparently disappeared and asked if Pyke could throw any light on the matter. He then confirmed that, despite the disappointing failure to retrieve any other artefacts of significance, he was still prepared to take the ancient launch off Pyke's hands for a "very generous sum," subject to verifications. Oddly, he somehow omitted to mention the actual monetary magnitude of that generous sum.

He ended with an expression of concern for Pyke's own "temperament during such a period of loss and mourning," and that he, Van Graes, would stand by his valued professional contractors. As soon as Pyke's crew was back up to complement, there were a couple of acquisition assignments which would require the services of skilled and experienced operatives.

"Pause it," Pyke said, then glanced round at Oleg. "Maybe we should give the relic-hunting business a bit of a body-swerve for a spell—what d'ya reckon?"

"Your assessment has merit, Captain."

"Yeah, I thought so." He started to get up from his seat. "Give us a chance to explore some other less insanely risky options…"

"Captain, I'm receiving a transmission from the Damaugra, from your counterpart."

"Ah—I wonder if the moment has arrived." He settled back into his chair. "Let's see him."

Van Graes' frozen image vanished into dark flicker, then a

new picture appeared, another Brannan Pyke, looking far too bright, sharp and upbeat for Pyke's liking, but what else could you expect from a simulation?

"Captain Pyke," said the face on the screen. "Are you feeling a bit more revived now, after that non-stop punishing epic you went through?"

"Never better," Pyke lied, dialling his grin all the way up to "swagger." "Kicking and scratching, ready to get back in the game, whatever the game may be! And yourself?"

"Well, speaking as a digital sentience getting ready to strike out on his own, things are looking pretty damn prodigious!"

"Glad to hear it, Captain Bran. So, are you about done with all the planning and prep?"

Captain Bran nodded. "Oh yeah—take a look."

The screen switched to a top-down view of the neural-core chamber where that final insane clash took place. The Legacy's body was gone (dismembered then torched to ashes by the cyberlice—he'd seen that in a previous linkup), while a continuous line of the Damaugra's cyberlice were filing over to all that was left of the Essavyr Key, a scattered heap of thousands of crystal splinters. Each cyberlouse gathered up a small amount of slivers then scurried out of the chamber. A series of brief shots showed the cyberlice moving through the immense coiling tangle of the Damaugra and depositing the splinters in innumerable locations, wrapped in a gummy wad of lice-spit that was stuck to junctions in the grey coils, right where glowing nodules protruded from the metal.

"That was a couple of hours ago," said Captain Bran. "Busy little beggars have finished their job and all that remains is the grand fission! After which tens of thousands of Damaugralings will spread across the galaxy and beyond, carrying the splinters of the key beyond reconstruction. It's gonna be quite a show, so just say the word."

"Sure—first, I need to ask about Ustril," said Pyke. "Is she better?"

"On the mend," said Captain Bran. "Don't worry yourself—I'll be hanging around for a while and when she's well enough I'll fly her down to her base and see her safely inside."

"That's pretty noble of you, thanks. Without her change of heart...well, we wouldn't be having this gab, would we?"

"We had to improvise a kind of care unit but she's getting well. She'll be fine."

Pyke nodded, found himself running out of words. The pause between them lengthened until the smiling Captain Bran leaned forward a little, voice dropping. "You were pretty banged up after the crystal key detonated—all I could do was have the cyberlice carry you on board that old escape craft from the *Defender* and send it off towards your ship. Hope the sickbay autodoc did the business."

Pyke gave a considered nod.

"Yeah, put me under while it tended to various cuts and bruises and the like. Says I have to take it easy, so last few hours I've been trying to figure out our resources, destinations, how to keep the ship running...with just the two of us."

"Sure, o' course, understand. So, shall we do this?"

"No reason for any more delay, Captain. Go right ahead."

Bran's image was replaced by a view of the Damaugra that was closer than that on the bridge monitor, some kind of cyberlice retasked as a remote cam, Pyke was sure. For several seconds nothing happened, then small clumps of spiral coils began detaching themselves from the outer surface of the Damaugra's huge, stretched out jungly tangle. Seconds grew into minutes and the drifting few became many, then became a cloud of miniature Damaugras spreading outwards, heading away from the planet Ong. Before long the actual central mass of the parent Damaugra was obscured by a cloud of its progeny as they separated themselves and wandered outwards, readying themselves for departure.

After five minutes there was a sense of the density beginning to thin out, and not long after that Pyke realised that he could make out patches of starry space through the swarm. After another minute or so there were mere dozens unfastening themselves and moving off. Then there was a handful, then there was just one tight knot of coils and tentacles floating serene, still and alone in high orbit.

The screen switched back to Captain Bran's face. "And so forty thousand or more travellers start their journey across the galaxy. I almost feel humbled."

"That was a helluva sight," said Pyke. "Not one I'll forget in a hurry."

"It's a big galaxy out there," said Bran.

Pyke nodded. "Sorry about the way it's turned out—kinda feel that you got the cruddy end of the deal."

On the screen Bran gave an amused shrug. "What, that my consciousness has been merged with a giant razor-coiled monster? A monster that can dive into hyperspace almost at will, I should point out. Hey, y'know, life as a digital intellect has its ups and downs, but as I've said and will always say, I'm still me, just with an extra-fierce helping of bottle!"

They both laughed.

"So, tell me, Captain Pyke, where to now?"

"Off to Earthsphere, Captain Bran—got a delivery to make."

"Van Graes is hungry for tasty antique goodness, I'm guessing."

"Got it in one," Pyke said. "What about yourself? After you leave Ustril at her base, any idea where you'll end up?"

Captain Bran shrugged. "Might actually explore that hyperspace a bit, see if I can track down the Construct and pass on my tale about Rensik."

"Good—saves me the trouble," Pyke said with a grin. "We might cross paths again, eh?"

"We might, at that. Stay safe, and give that little keepsake the once-over, when you get the chance."

"I will. Safe journey."

"You, too." With that, the screen went blank.

Pyke got up from his chair. "Oleg, set a course for Sol System. And mind the wheel—something I need to check."

Leaving the bridge, he hurried back to his quarters, sat down at his desk and retrieved a flat, circular container from one of the compartments He opened the lid—inside was a disc of grey metal, the same metal that the Damaugra's coils were made from, and at the very centre of the disk was a small raised dimple and embedded in it was a tiny hexagonal crystal. The first time he saw it was when he awoke in the ancient launch, the captain's launch from the *Mighty Defender*, as it headed for a rendezvous with the *Scarabus*. Instinctively, he'd know what it was and all its possibility presented an insuperable hurdle of grief which had compelled him to close it up without further scrutiny.

But when Bran referred to it as a keepsake, he suddenly had no doubts. He sat back in the seat, stretched out his hand and laid his palm upon the embedded jewel—The transition was immediate. He was standing at the centre of the stone gazebo on the Isle of Candles. The light in the sky was dusk no more, but the bright, fresh brilliance of a perfect morning. And those figures hurrying down the steps from the villa were his friends—Klane, Vrass, T'Moy, Moleg, Kref, Ancil and dearest darling Dervla, all laughing, whooping and running to meet him. He couldn't stay long, but they were his friends, and he was going to save them.

ACKNOWLEDGEMENTS

The book that was forestalled by illness of one kind or another has overcome its hiatus and now blooms forth, for which I must thank my tireless and supportive agent, John Berlyne, without whom...And of course, my thanks to all at Orbit, for believing in me and the work.

Friends and family kept me going: Susan, my folks, Stewart, Graeme, Dave Wingrove, Eric Brown, as well as well-wishers cheering me on from Facebook. All the support was much appreciated.

Having hit my late fifties (which I prefer to view as twenty-four with twenty-three years' experience!) I still drag my bod out to rock gigs from time to time, and at the time of writing I'm looking forward to seeing several bands I've never actually seen before, like King Crimson, The The, Roger Waters and the mighty Clutch. Not sure what the future will hold, but with any luck it'll be loud!

extras

orbit

meet the author

MICHAEL COBLEY was born in the city of Leicester, has lived in Perth (Australia) and Glasgow but now resides in North Ayrshire. His previous works have included the Shadowkings trilogy (a dark and grim fantasy epic), and *Iron Mosaic* (a collection of short stories) but he is best known for his epic space opera series—Humanity's Fire. *Splintered Suns* is a stand-alone adventure set in this universe.

Find out more about Michael Cobley and other Orbit authors by registering for the free monthly newsletter at www.orbitbooks.net.

if you enjoyed

SPLINTERED SUNS

look out for

A BIG SHIP AT THE EDGE OF THE UNIVERSE

The Salvagers

by

Alex White

Furious and fun, the first book in this bold, new science fiction adventure series follows a crew of outcasts as they try to find a legendary ship that just might be the key to saving themselves—and the universe.

Boots Elsworth was a famous treasure hunter in another life, but now she's washed-up. She makes her meager living faking salvage legends and selling them to the highest

bidder, but this time she got something real—the story of the
Harrow, *a famous warship capable of untold destruction.*

Nilah Brio is the top driver in the Pan Galactic Racing
Federation and the darling of the racing world—until
she witnesses Mother murder a fellow racer. Framed
for the murder and on the hunt to clear her name, Nilah
has only one lead: the killer also hunts Boots.

On the wrong side of the law, the two women board
a smuggler's ship that will take them on a quest for
fame, for riches, and for justice.

Chapter One

D.N.F.

The straight opened before the two race cars: an oily river, speckled yellow by the evening sun. They shot down the tarmac in succession like sapphire fish, streamers of wild magic billowing from their exhausts. They roared toward the turn, precision movements bringing them within centimeters of one another.

The following car veered to the inside. The leader attempted the same.

Their tires only touched for a moment. They interlocked,

and sheer torque threw the leader into the air. Jagged chunks of duraplast glittered in the dusk as the follower's car passed underneath, unharmed but for a fractured front wing. The lead race car came down hard, twisting eruptions of elemental magic spewing from its wounded power unit. One of its tires exploded into a hail of spinning cords, whipping the road.

In the background, the other blue car slipped away down the chicane—Nilah's car.

The replay lost focus and reset.

The crash played out again and again on the holoprojection in front of them, and Nilah Brio tried not to sigh. She had seen plenty of wrecks before and caused more than her share of them.

"Crashes happen," she said.

"Not when the cars are on the same bloody team, Nilah!"

Claire Asby, the Lang Autosport team principal, stood at her mahogany desk, hands folded behind her back. The office looked less like the sort of ultramodern workspace Nilah had seen on other teams and more like one of the mansions of Origin, replete with antique furniture, incandescent lighting, stuffed big-game heads (which Nilah hated), and gargantuan landscapes from planets she had never seen. She supposed the decor favored a pale woman like Claire, but it did nothing for Nilah's dark brown complexion. The office didn't have any of the bright, human-centric design and ergonomic beauty of her home, but team bosses had to be forgiven their eccentricities— especially when that boss had led them to as many victories as Claire had.

Her teammate, Kristof Kater, chuckled and rocked back on his heels. Nilah rolled her eyes at the pretty boy's pleasure. They should've been checking in with the pit crews, not wasting precious time at a last-minute dressing down.

The cars hovering over Claire's desk reset and moved through their slow-motion calamity. Claire had already made them watch the footage a few dozen times after the incident: Nilah's car dove for the inside and Kristof moved to block. The incident had cost her half her front wing, but Kristof's track weekend had ended right there.

"I want you both to run a clean race today. I am begging you to bring those cars home intact at all costs."

Nilah shrugged and smiled. "That'll be fine, provided Kristof follows a decent racing line."

"We were racing! I made a legal play and the stewards sided with me!"

Nilah loved riling him up; it was far too easy. "You were slow, and you got what you deserved: a broken axle and a bucket of tears. I got a five-second penalty"—she winked before continuing—"which cut into my thirty-three-second win considerably."

Claire rubbed the bridge of her nose. "Please stop acting like children. Just get out there and do your jobs."

Nilah held back another jab; it wouldn't do to piss off the team boss right before a drive. Her job was to win races, not meetings. Silently she and Kristof made their way to the door, and he flung it open in a rare display of petulance. She hadn't seen him so angry in months, and she reveled in it. After all, a frazzled teammate posed no threat to her championship standings.

They made their way through the halls from Claire's exotic wood paneling to the bright white and anodized blues of Lang Autosport's portable palace. Crew and support staff rushed to and fro, barely acknowledging the racers as they moved through the crowds. Kristof was stopped by his sports psychologist, and Nilah muscled past them both as she stepped out into the dry heat of Gantry Station's Galica Speedway.

Nilah had fired her own psychologist when she'd taken the lead in this year's Driver's Crown.

She crossed onto the busy parking lot, surrounded by the bustle of scooter bots and crews from a dozen teams. The bracing rattle of air hammers and the roar of distant crowds in the grandstands were all the therapy she'd need to win. The Driver's Crown was so close—she could clinch it in two races, especially if Kristof went flying off the track again.

"Do you think this is a game?" Claire's voice startled her. She'd come jogging up from behind, a dozen infograms swimming around her head, blinking with reports on track conditions and pit strategy.

"Do I think racing is a game? I believe that's the very definition of sport."

Claire's vinegar scowl was considerably less entertaining than Kristof's anger. Nilah had been racing for Claire since the junior leagues. She'd probably spent more of her teenage years with her principal than her own parents. She didn't want to disappoint Claire, but she wouldn't be cowed, either. In truth, the incident galled her—the crash was nothing more than a callow attempt by Kristof to hold her off for another lap. If she'd lost the podium, she would've called for his head, but he got what he deserved.

They were a dysfunctional family. Nilah and Kristof had been racing together since childhood, and she could remember plenty of happy days trackside with him. She'd been ecstatic when they both joined Lang; it felt like a sign that they were destined to win.

But there could be only one Driver's Crown, and they'd learned the hard way the word "team" meant nothing among the strongest drivers in the Pan-Galactic Racing Federation. Her friendship with Kristof was long dead. At least her fondness for Claire had survived the transition.

"If you play dirty with him today, I'll have no choice but to create some consequences," said Claire, struggling to keep up with Nilah in heels.

Oh, please. Nilah rounded the corner of the pit lane and marched straight through the center of the racing complex, past the offices of the race director and news teams. She glanced back at Claire who, for all her posturing, couldn't hide her worry.

"I never play dirty. I win because I'm better," said Nilah. "I'm not sure what your problem is."

"That's not the point. You watch for him today, and mind yourself. This isn't any old track."

Nilah got to the pit wall and pushed through the gate onto the starting grid. The familiar grip of race-graded asphalt on her shoes sent a spark of pleasure up her spine. "Oh, I know all about Galica."

The track sprawled before Nilah: a classic, a legend, a warrior's track that had tested the mettle of racers for a hundred years. It showed its age in the narrow roadways, rendering overtaking difficult and resulting in wrecks and safety cars—and increased race time. Because of its starside position on Gantry Station, ambient temperatures could turn sweltering. Those factors together meant she'd spend the next two hours slow-roasting in her cockpit at three hundred kilometers per hour, making thousands of split-second, high-stakes decisions.

This year brought a new third sector with more intricate corners and a tricky elevation change. It was an unopened present, a new toy to play with. Nilah longed to be on the grid already.

If she took the podium here, the rest of the season would be an easy downhill battle. There were a few more races, but the smart money knew this was the only one that mattered. The harmonic chimes of StarSport FN's jingle filled the stadium, the unofficial sign that the race was about to get underway.

She headed for the cockpit of her pearlescent-blue car. Claire fell in behind her, rattling off some figures about Nilah's chances that were supposed to scare her into behaving.

"Remember your contract," said Claire as the pit crew boosted Nilah into her car. "Do what you must to take gold, but any scratch you put on Kristof is going to take a million off your check. I mean it this time."

"Good thing I'm getting twenty mil more than him, then. More scratches for me!" Nilah pulled on her helmet. "You keep Kristof out of my way, and I'll keep his precious car intact."

She flipped down her visor and traced her mechanist's mark across the confined space, whispering light flowing from her fingertips. Once her spell cemented in place, she wrapped her fingers around the wheel. The system read out the stats of her sigil: good V's, not great on the Xi, but a healthy cast.

Her magic flowed into the car, sliding around the finely tuned ports, wending through channels to latch onto gears. Through the power of her mechanist's mark, she felt the grip of the tires and spring of the rods as though they were her own legs and feet. She joined with the central computer of her car, gaining psychic access to radio, actuation, and telemetry. The Lang Hyper 8, a motorsport classic, had achieved phenomenal performance all season in Nilah's hands.

Her psychic connection to the computer stabilized, and she searched the radio channels for her engineer, Ash. They ran through the checklist: power, fuel flow, sigil circuits, eidolon core. Nilah felt through each part with her magic, ensuring all functioned properly. Finally, she landed on the clunky Arclight Booster.

It was an awful little PGRF-required piece of tech, with high output but terrible efficiency. Nilah's mechanist side absolutely despised the magic-belching beast. It was as ugly and inelegant as it was expensive. Some fans claimed to like the little light show when it boosted drivers up the straights, but it was less than perfect, and anything less than perfect had to go.

"Let's start her up, Nilah."

"Roger that."

Every time that car thrummed to life, Nilah fell in love all over again. She adored the Hyper 8 in spite of the stonking flaw on his backside. Her grip tightened about the wheel and she took a deep breath.

The lights signaled a formation lap and the cars took off, weaving across the tarmac to keep the heat in their tires. They slipped around the track in slow motion, and Nilah's eyes traveled the third sector. She would crush this new track design. At the end of the formation lap, she pulled into her grid space, the scents of hot rubber and oil smoke sweet in her nose.

Game time.

The pole's leftmost set of lights came on: five seconds until the last light.

Three cars ahead of her, eighteen behind: Kristof in first, then the two Makina drivers, Bonnie and Jin. Nilah stared down the Makina R-27s, their metallic livery a blazing crimson.

The next pair of lights ignited: four seconds.

The other drivers revved their engines, feeling the tuning of their cars. Nilah echoed their rumbling engines with a shout of her own and gave a heated sigh, savoring the fire in her belly.

Three seconds.

Don't think. Just see.

The last light came on, signaling the director was ready to start the race.

Now, it was all about reflexes. All the engines fell to near silence.

One second.

The lights clicked off.

Banshee wails filled the air as the cars' power units screamed to life. Nilah roared forward, her eyes darting over the competition. Who was it going to be? Bonnie lagged by just a hair, and Jin made a picture-perfect launch, surging up beside Kristof. Nilah wanted to make a dive for it but found herself forced in behind the two lead drivers.

They shot down the straight toward turn one, a double apex. Turn one was always the most dangerous, because the idiots fighting for the inside were most likely to brake too late. She swept out for a perfect parabola, hoping not to see some fool about to crash into her.

The back of the pack was brought up by slow, pathetic Cyril Clowe. He would be her barometer of race success. If she could lap him in a third of the race, it would be a perfect run.

"Tell race control I'm lapping Clowe in twenty-five," Nilah grunted, straining against the g-force of her own acceleration. "I want those blue flags ready."

"He might not like that."

"If he tries anything, I'll leave him pasted to the tarmac."

"You're still in the pack," came Ash's response. "Focus on the race."

Got ten seconds on the Arclight. Four-car gap to Jin. Turn three is coming up too fast.

Bonnie Hayes loomed large in the rearview, dodging left and right along the straight. The telltale flash of an Arclight Booster erupted on the right side, and Bonnie shot forward toward the turn. Nilah made no moves to block, and the R-27 overtook her. It'd been a foolish ploy, and faced with too much speed, Bonnie needed to brake too hard. She'd flat-spot her tires.

Right on cue, brake dust and polymer smoke erupted from Bonnie's wheels, and Nilah danced to the outside, sliding within mere inches of the crimson paint. Nilah popped through the gears and the car thrummed with her magic, rewarding her with a pristine turn. The rest of the pack was not so lucky.

Shredded fibron and elemental magic filled Nilah's rear-view as the cars piled up into turn three like an avalanche. She had to keep her eyes on the track, but she spotted Guillaume, Anantha, and Bonnie's cars in the wreck.

"Nicely done," said Ash.

"All in a day's work, babes."

Nilah weaved through the next five turns, taking them exactly as practiced. Her car was water, flowing through the track along the swiftest route. However, Kristof and Jin weren't making things easy for her. She watched with hawkish intent and prayed for a slip, a momentary lockup, or anything less than the perfect combination of gear shifts.

Thirty degrees right, shift up two, boost... boost. Follow your prey until it makes a mistake.

Nilah's earpiece chirped as Ash said, "Kater's side of the garage just went crazy. He just edged Jin off the road and picked up half a second in sector one."

She grimaced. "Half a second?"

"Yeah. It's going to be a long battle, I'm afraid."

Her magic reached into the gearbox, tuning it for low revs. "Not at all. He's gambling. Watch what happens next."

She kept her focus on the track, reciting her practiced motions with little variance. The crowd might be thrilled by a half-second purple sector, but she knew to keep it even. With the increased tire wear, his car would become unpredictable.

"Kristof is in the run-off! Repeat: He's out in the kitty litter," came Ash.

"Well, that was quick."

She crested the hill to find her teammate's car spinning

into the gravel along the run of the curve. She only hazarded a minor glance before continuing on.

"Switch to strat one," said Ash, barely able to contain herself. "Push! Push!"

"Tell Clowe he's mine in ten laps."

Nilah sliced through the chicane, screaming out of the turn with her booster aflame. She was a polychromatic comet, completely in her element. This race would be her masterpiece. She held the record for the most poles for her age, and she was about to get it for the most overtakes.

The next nine laps went well. Nilah handily widened the gap between herself and Kristof to over ten seconds. She sensed fraying in her tires, but she couldn't pit just yet. If she did, she'd never catch Clowe by the end of the race. His fiery orange livery flashed at every turn, tantalizingly close to overtake range.

"Put out the blue flags. I'm on Cyril."

"Roger that," said Ash. "Race control, requesting blue flags for Cyril Clowe."

His Arclight flashed as he burned it out along the straightaway, and she glided through the rippling sparks. The booster was a piece of garbage, but it had its uses, and Clowe didn't understand any of them. He wasn't even trying anymore, just blowing through his boost at random times. What was the point?

Nilah cycled through her radio frequencies until she found Cyril's. Best to tease him a bit for the viewers at home. "Okay, Cyril, a lesson: use the booster to make the car go faster."

He snorted on his end. "Go to hell, Nilah."

"Being stuck behind your slow ass is as close as I've gotten."

"Get used to it," he snapped, his whiny voice grating on her ears. "I'm not letting you past."

She downshifted, her transmission roaring like a tiger. "I hope you're ready to get flattened then."

Galica's iconic Paige Tunnel loomed large ahead, with its blazing row of lights and disorienting reflective tiles. Most racers would avoid an overtake there, but Nilah had been given an opportunity, and she wouldn't squander it. The outside stadium vanished as she slipped into the tunnel, hot on the Hambley's wing.

She fired her booster, and as she came alongside Clowe, the world's colors began to melt from their surfaces, leaving only drab black and white. Her car stopped altogether—gone from almost two hundred kilometers per hour to zero in the blink of an eye.

Nilah's head darkened with a realization: she was caught in someone's spell as surely as a fly in a spiderweb.

The force of such a stop should have powdered her bones and liquefied her internal organs instantly, but she felt no change in her body, save that she could barely breathe.

The world had taken on a deathly shade. The body of the Hyper 8, normally a lovely blue, had become an ashen gray. The fluorescent magenta accents along her white jumpsuit had also faded, and all had taken on a blurry, shifting turbulence.

Her neck wouldn't move, so she couldn't look around. Her fingers barely worked. She connected her mind to the transmission, but it wouldn't shift. The revs were frozen in place in the high twenty thousands, but she sensed no movement in the drive shaft.

All this prompted a silent, slow-motion scream. The longer she wailed, the more her voice came back. She flexed her fingers as hard as they'd go through the syrupy air. With each tiny movement, a small amount of color returned, though she couldn't be sure if she was breaking out of the spell—or into it.

"Nilah, is that you?" grunted Cyril. She'd almost forgotten

about the Hambley driver next to her. All the oranges and yellows on his jumpsuit and helmet stood out like blazing bonfires, and she wondered if that's why he could move. But his car was the same gray as everything else, and he struggled, unsuccessfully, to unbuckle. Was Nilah on the cusp of the magic's effects?

"What..." she forced herself to say, but pushing the air out was too much.

"Oh god, we're caught in her spell!"

Whose spell, you git? "Stay...calm..."

She couldn't reassure him, and just trying to breathe was taxing enough. If someone was fixing the race, there'd be hell to pay. Sure, everyone had spells, but only a fool would dare cast one into a PGRF speedway to cheat. A cadre of wizards stood at the ready for just such an event, and any second, the dispersers would come online and knock this whole spiderweb down.

In the frozen world, an inky blob moved at the end of the tunnel. A creature came crawling along the ceiling, its black mass of tattered fabric writhing like tentacles as it skittered across the tiles. It moved easily from one perch to the next, silently capering overhead before dropping down in front of the two frozen cars.

Cyril screamed. She couldn't blame him.

The creature stood upright, and Nilah realized that it was human. Its hood swept away, revealing a brass mask with a cutaway that exposed thin, angry lips on a sallow chin. Metachroic lenses peppered the exterior of the mask, and Nilah instantly recognized their purpose—to see in all directions. Mechanists had always talked about creating such a device, but no one had ever been able to move for very long while wearing one; it was too disorienting.

The creature put one slender boot on Cyril's car, then another as it inexorably clambered up the car's body. It stopped in front of Cyril and tapped the helmet on his trembling head with a long, metallic finger.

Where are the bloody dispersers?

Cyril's terrified voice huffed over the radio. "Mother, please…"

Mother? Cyril's mother? No; Nilah had met Missus Clowe at the previous year's winner's party. She was a dull woman, like her loser son. Nilah took a closer look at the wrinkled sneer poking out from under the mask.

Her voice was a slithering rasp. "Where did you get that map, Cyril?"

"Please. I wasn't trying to double-cross anyone. I just thought I could make a little money on the side."

Mother crouched and ran her metal-encased fingers around the back of his helmet. "There is no 'on the side,' Cyril. We are everywhere. Even when you think you are untouchable, we can pluck you from this universe."

Nilah strained harder against her arcane chains, pulling more color into her body, desperate to get free. She was accustomed to being able to outrun anything, to absolute speed. Panic set in.

"You need me to finish this race!" he protested.

"We don't *need* anything from you. You were lucky enough to be chosen, and there will always be others. Tell me where you got the map."

"You're just going to kill me if I tell you."

Nilah's eyes narrowed, and she forced herself to focus in spite of her crawling fear. Kill him? What the devil was Cyril into?

Mother's metal fingers clacked, tightening across his helmet. "It's of very little consequence to me. I've been told to kill you if you won't talk. That was my only order. If you tell me, it's my discretion whether you live or die."

Cyril whimpered. "Boots...er...Elizabeth Elsworth. I was looking for...I wanted to know what you were doing, and she...she knew something. She said she could find the *Harrow*."

Nilah's gaze shifted to Mother, the racer's eye movements sluggish and sleepy despite her terror. *Elizabeth Elsworth? Where had Nilah heard that name before?* She had the faintest feeling that it'd come from the Link, maybe a show or a news piece. Movement in the periphery interrupted her thoughts.

The ghastly woman swept an arm back, fabric tatters falling away to reveal an armored exoskeleton encrusted with servo-motors and glowing sigils. Mother brought her fist down across Cyril's helmet, crushing it inward with a sickening crack.

Nilah would've begun hyperventilating, if she could breathe. This couldn't be happening. Even with the best military-grade suits, there was no way this woman could've broken Cyril's helmet with a mere fist. His protective gear could withstand a direct impact at three hundred kilometers per hour. Nilah couldn't see what was left of his head, but blood oozed between the cracked plastic like the yolk of an egg.

Just stay still. Maybe you can fade into the background. Maybe you can—

"And now for you," said Mother, stepping onto the fibron body of Nilah's car. Of course she had spotted Nilah moving in that helmet of hers. "I think my spell didn't completely affect you, did it? It's so difficult with these fast-moving targets."

Mother's armored boots rested at the edge of Nilah's cockpit, and mechanical, prehensile toes wrapped around the lip of the car. Nilah forced her neck to crane upward through frozen time to look at Mother's many eyes.

"Dear lamb, I am so sorry you saw that. I hate to be so harsh," she sighed, placing her bloody palm against Nilah's silver helmet, "but this is for the best. Even if you got away, you'd have nowhere to run. We own everything."

Please, please, please, dispersers... Nilah's eyes widened. She wasn't going to die like this. Not like Cyril. *Think. Think.*

"I want you to relax, my sweet. The journos are going to tell a beautiful story of your heroic crash with that fool." She gestured to Cyril as she said this. "You'll be remembered as the champion that could've been."

Dispersers scramble spells with arcane power. They feed into the glyph until it's over capacity. Nilah spread her magic over the car, looking for anything she could use to fire a pulse of magic: the power unit—drive shaft locked, the energy recovery system—too weak, her ejection cylinder—lockbolts unresponsive... then she remembered the Arclight Booster. She reached into it with her psychic connection, finding the arcane linkages foggy and dim. Something about the way this spell shut down movement even muddled her mechanist's art. She latched on to the booster, knowing the effect would be unpredictable, but it was Nilah's only chance. She tripped the magical switch to fire the system.

Nothing. Mother wrapped her steely hands around Nilah's helmet.

"I should twist instead of smash, shouldn't I?" whispered the old woman. "Pretty girls should have pretty corpses."

Nilah connected the breaker again, and the slow puff of arcane plumes sighed from the Arclight. It didn't want to start in this magical haze, but it was her only plan. She gave the switch one last snap.

The push of magical flame tore at the gray, hazy shroud over the world, pulling it away. An array of coruscating starbursts surged through the surface, and Nilah was momentarily blinded as everything returned to normal. The return of momentum flung Mother from the car, and Nilah was slammed back into her seat.

Faster and faster her car went, until Nilah wasn't even sure the tires were touching the road. Mother's spell twisted around the Arclight's, intermingling, destabilizing, twisting space and time in ways Nilah never could've predicted. It was dangerous to mix unknown magics—and often deadly.

She recognized this effect, though—it was the same as when she passed through a jump gate. She was teleporting.

A flash of light and she became weightless. At least she could breathe again.

She locked onto the sight of a large, windowless building, but there was something wrong with it. It shouldn't have been upside down as it was, nor should it have been spinning like that. Her car was in free fall. Then she slammed into a wall, her survival shell enveloping her as she blew through wreckage like a cannonball.

Her stomach churned with each flip, but this was far from her first crash. She relaxed and let her shell come to a halt, wedged in a half-blasted wall. Her fuel system exploded, spraying elemental energies in all directions. Fire, ice, and gusts of catalyzed gasses swirled outside the racer's shell.

The suppressor fired, and Nilah's bound limbs came free. A harsh, acrid mist filled the air as the phantoplasm caking Nilah's body melted into the magic-numbing indolence gasses. Gale-force winds and white-hot flames snuffed in the blink of an eye. The sense of her surrounding energies faded away, a sudden silence in her mind.

Her disconnection from magic was always the worst part about a crash. The indolence system was only temporary, but there was always the fear: that she'd become one of those dull-fingered wretches. She screwed her eyes shut and shook her head, willing her mechanist's magic back.

It appeared on the periphery as a pinhole of light—a tiny, bright sensation in a sea of gray. She willed it wider, bringing more light and warmth into her body until she overflowed with her own magic. Relief covered her like a hot blanket, and her shoulders fell.

But what had just murdered Cyril? Mother had smashed his head open without so much as a second thought. And Mother would know exactly who she was—Nilah's name was painted on every surface of the Lang Hyper 8. What if she came back?

The damaged floor gave way, and she flailed through the darkness, bouncing down what had to be a mountain of cardboard boxes. She came to a stop and opened her eyes to look around.

She'd landed in a warehouse somewhere she didn't recognize. Nilah knew every inch of the Galica Speedway—she'd been coming to PGRF races there since she was a little girl, and this warehouse didn't mesh with any of her memories. She pulled off her helmet and listened for sirens, for the banshee wail of race cars, for the roar of the crowd, but all she could hear was silence.

if you enjoyed
SPLINTERED SUNS

look out for

ADRIFT

by

Rob Boffard

"An edge-of-the-seat epic of survival and adventure in deep space." —Gareth L. Powell, BSFA Award–winning author

Sigma Station. The ultimate luxury hotel, in the far reaches of space.

For one small group, a tour of the Horsehead Nebula is meant to be a short but stunning highlight in the trip of a lifetime.

But when a mysterious ship destroys Sigma Station and everyone on it, suddenly their tourist shuttle is stranded.

They have no weapons. No food. No water. No one back home knows they're alive.

And the mysterious ship is hunting them.

Chapter 1

Rainmaker's heads-up display is a nightmare.

The alerts are coming faster than she can dismiss them. Lock indicators. Proximity warnings. Fuel signals. Created by her neurochip, appearing directly in front of her.

The world outside her fighter's cockpit is alive, torn with streaking missiles and twisting ships. In the distance, a nuke detonates against a frigate, a baby sun tearing its way into life. The Horsehead Nebula glitters behind it.

Rainmaker twists her ship away from the heatwave, making it dance with precise, controlled thoughts. As she does so, she gets a full view of the battle: a thousand Frontier Scorpion fighters, flipping and turning and destroying each other in an arena bordered by the hulking frigates.

The Colony forces thought they could hold the area around Sigma Orionis—they thought they could take control of the jump gate and shut down all movement into this sector. They didn't bank on an early victory at Proxima freeing up a third of the Frontier Navy, and now they're backed into a corner, fighting like hell to stay alive.

Maybe this'll be the battle that does it. Maybe this is the one that finally stops the Colonies for good.

Rainmaker's path has taken her away from the main thrust of the battle, out towards the edge of the sector. Her targeting systems find a lone enemy: a black Colony fighter, streaking towards her. She's about to fire when she stops, cutting off the thought.

Something's not right.

"Control, this is Rainmaker." Despite the chaos, her voice is calm. "I have locked on incoming. Why's he alone? Over."

The reply is clipped and urgent. "Rainmaker, this is Frontier Control: evade, evade, evade. *Do not engage.* You have multiple bogies closing in on your six. They're trying to lock the door on you, over."

Rainmaker doesn't bother to respond. Her radar systems were damaged earlier in the fight, and she has to rely on Control for the bandits she can't see. She breaks her lock, twisting her craft away as more warnings bloom on her console. "Twin, Blackbird, anybody. I've got multiples inbound, need a pickup, over."

The sarcastic voice of one of her wingmen comes over the comms. "Can't handle 'em yourself? I'm disappointed."

"Not a good time, Omen," she replies, burning her thrusters. "Can you help me or not? Over."

"Negative. Got three customers to deal with over here. Get in line."

A second, older voice comes over her comms. "Rainmaker, this is Blackbird. What's your twenty? Over."

Her neurochip recognises the words, both flashing up the info on her display and automatically sending it to Blackbird's. "Quadrant thirty-one," she says anyway, speaking through gritted teeth.

"Roger," says Blackbird. "I got 'em. Just sit tight. I'll handle it for y—. Shit, I'm hit! I—"

"Eric!" Rainmaker shouts Blackbird's real name, her voice so loud it distorts the channel. But he's already gone. An impactor streaks past her, close enough for her to see the launch burns on its surface.

"Control, Rainmaker," she says. "Confirm Blackbird's position, I've lost contact!"

Control doesn't reply. Why would they? They're fighting a thousand fires at once, advising hundreds of Scorpion fighters. Forget the callsigns that command makes them use: Blackbird is a number to them, and so is she, and unless she does something right now, she's going to join him.

She twists her ship, forcing the two chasing Colony fighters to face her head-on. They're a bigger threat than the lone one ahead. Now, they're coming in from her eleven and one o'clock, curving towards her, already opening fire. She guns the ship, aiming for the tiny space in the middle, racing to make the gap before their impactors close her out.

"Thread the needle," she whispers. "Come on, thread the needle, thr—"

Everything freezes.

The battle falls silent.

And a blinking-red error box appears above one of the missiles.

"Oh. Um." Hannah Elliott's voice cuts through the silence. "Sorry, ladies and gentlemen. One second."

The box goes away—only to reappear a split second later, like a fly buzzing back to the place it was swatted. This time, the simulation gives a muted *ding*, as if annoyed that Hannah can't grasp the point.

She rips the slim goggles from her head. She's not used to them—she forgot to put her lens in after she woke up, which meant she had to rely on the VR room's antiquated backup system. A strand of her long red hair catches on the strap, and she has to yank it loose, looking down at the ancient console in front of her.

"Sorry, ladies and gentlemen," she says again. "Won't be a minute."

Her worried face is reflected on the dark screen, her freckles making her look even younger than she is. She uses her finger this time, stabbing at the box's confirm button on the small access terminal on the desk. It comes back with a friend, a second, identical error box superimposed over the first. Beyond it, an impactor sits frozen in Rainmaker's viewport.

"Sorry." *Stop saying sorry.* She tries again, still failing to bring up the main menu. "It's my first day."

Stony silence. The twenty tourists in the darkened room before her are strapped into reclining motion seats with frayed belts. Most have their eyes closed, their personal lenses still displaying the frozen sim. A few are blinking, looking faintly annoyed. One of them, an older man with a salt-and-pepper beard, catches Hannah's eye with a scowl.

She looks down, back at the error boxes. She can barely make out the writing on them—the VR's depth of field has made the letters as tiny as the ones on the bottom line of an eye chart.

She should reset the sim. But how? Does that mean it will start from scratch? Can she fast-forward? The supervisor who showed it to her that morning was trying to wrangle about fifteen new tour guides, and the instructions she gave amounted to watching the volume levels and making sure none of the tourists threw up when Rainmaker turned too hard.

Hannah gives the screen an experimental tap, and breathes a sigh of relief when a menu pops up: a list of files. There. Now she just has to—

But which one is it? The supervisor turned the sim on, and

Hannah doesn't know which file she used. Their names are meaningless.

She taps the first one. Bouncy music explodes from the room's speakers, loud enough to make a couple of the tourists jump. She pulls the goggles back on, to be greeted by an animated, space-suited lizard firing lasers at a huge, tentacled alien. A booming voice echoes across the music. "Adventurers! Enter the world of Reptar as he saves the galaxy from—"

Hannah stops Reptar saving the galaxy. In the silence that follows, she can feel her cheeks turning red.

She gives the screen a final, helpless look, and leaps to her feet. She'll figure this out. Somehow. They wouldn't have given her this job if they didn't think she could deal with the unexpected.

"OK!" She claps her hands together. "Sorry for the mix-up. I think there's a bit of a glitch in the old sim there."

Her laugh gets precisely zero reaction. Swallowing, she soldiers on.

"So, as you saw, that was the Battle of Sigma Orionis, which took place fifteen years ago, which would be..." She thinks hard. "2157, in the space around the hotel we're now in. Hopefully our historical sim gave you a good idea of the conditions our pilots faced—it was taken directly from one of their neurochip feeds.

"Coincidentally, the battle took place almost exactly a hundred years after we first managed to send a probe through a wormhole, which, as you...which fuelled the Great Expansion, and led to the permanent, long-range gates, like the one you came in on."

"We know," says the man with the salt-and-pepper beard. He reminds Hannah of a particularly grumpy high school teacher she once had. "It was in the intro you played us."

"Right." Hannah nods, like he's made an excellent point. She'd forgotten about the damn intro video, her jump-lag from the day before fuzzing her memory. All she can remember is a voiceover that was way, way too perky for someone discussing a battle as brutal as Sigma Orionis.

She decides to keep going. "So, the...the Colonies lost that particular fight, but the war actually kept going for five years after the Frontier captured the space around Sigma."

They know this already, too. Why is she telling them? Heat creeps up her cheeks, a sensation she does her best to ignore.

"Anyway, if you've got any questions about the early days of the Expansion, while we were still constructing the jump gates, then I'm your girl. I actually did my dissertation on—"

Movement, behind her. She turns to see one of the other tour guides, a big dude with a tribal tattoo poking out of the collar of his red company shirt.

"Oh, thank God," Hannah hisses at him. "Do you know how to fix the sim?"

He ignores her. "OK, folks," he says to the room, smooth and loud. "That concludes our VR demonstration. Hope you enjoyed it, and if you have any questions, I'll be happy to answer them while our next group of guests are getting set up."

Before Hannah can say anything, he turns to her, his smile melting away. "Your sim slot was over five minutes ago. Get out of here."

He bends down, and with an effortless series of commands, resets the simulator. As the tourists file out, the bearded man glances at her, shaking his head.

Hannah digs in her back pocket, her face still hot and prickly. "Sorry. The sim's really good, and I got kind of wrapped up in it, so..." She says the words with a smile, which fades as the other guide continues to ignore her.

She doesn't even know what she's doing—the sim wasn't good. It was creepy. Learning about a battle was one thing— actually being there, watching people get blown to pieces . . .

Sighing, she pulls her crumpled tab out of her pocket and unfolds it. Her schedule is faithfully written out on it, copied off her lens—a habit she picked up when she was a kid, after her mom's lens glitched and they missed a swimming trial. "Can you tell me how to get to the dock?"

The other guide glances at the outdated tab, his mouth forming a moue of distaste. "There should be a map on your lens."

"Haven't synced it to the station yet." She's a little too embarrassed to tell him that it's still in its solution above the tiny sink in her quarters, and she forgot to go back for it before her shift started.

She would give a kidney to go back now, and not just for the lens. Her staff cabin might be small enough for her to touch all four walls at once without stretching, but it has a bed in it. With *sheets*. They might be scratchy and thin and smell of bleach, but the thought of pulling them over her head and drifting off is intoxicating.

The next group is pushing inside the VR room, clustered in twos and threes, eyeing the somewhat threadbare motion seats. The guide has already forgotten Hannah, striding towards the incoming tourists, booming a welcome.

"Thanks for your help," Hannah mutters, as she slips out of the room.

The dock. She was there yesterday, wasn't she? Coming off the intake shuttle. How hard could it be to find a second time? She turns right out of the VR room, heading for where she thinks the main station atrium is. According to her tab, she isn't late, but she picks up her pace all the same.

The wide, gently curved walkway is bordered by a floor-to-ceiling window taller than the house Hannah grew up in. The space is packed with more tourists. Most of them are clustered at the apex, admiring the view dominated by the Horsehead Nebula.

Hannah barely caught a glimpse when they arrived last night, which was filled with safety briefings and room assignments and roster changes and staff canteen conversations that were way too loud. She had sat at a table to one side, both hoping that someone would come and talk to her, and hoping they wouldn't.

In the end, with something like relief, she'd managed to slink off for a few hours of disturbed sleep.

The station she's on used to be plain old Sigma XV—a big, boring, industrial mining outpost that the Colony and the Frontier fought over during the war. They still did mining here—helium-3, mostly, for fusion reactors—but it was now also known as the Sigma Hotel and Luxury Resort.

It always amazed Hannah just how quickly it had all happened. It felt like the second the war ended, the tour operators were lobbying the Frontier Senate for franchise rights. Now, Sigma held ten thousand tourists, who streamed in through the big jump gate from a dozen different worlds and moons, excited to finally be able to travel, hoping for a glimpse of the Neb.

Like the war never happened. Like there weren't a hundred different small conflicts and breakaway factions still dotted across both Frontier *and* Colonies. The aftershocks of war, making themselves known.

Not that Sigma Station was the only one in on the action. It was happening everywhere—apparently there was even a tour company out Phobos way that took people inside a wrecked Colony frigate which hadn't been hauled back for salvage yet.

As much as Hannah feels uncomfortable with the idea of

setting up a hotel here, so soon after the fighting, she needs this job. It's the only one her useless history degree would get her, and at least it means that she doesn't have to sit at the table at her parents' house on Titan, listening to her sister talk about how fast her company is growing.

The walkway she's on takes a sharp right, away from the windows, opening up into an airy plaza. The space is enormous, climbing up ten whole levels. A glittering light fixture the size of a truck hangs from the ceiling, and in the centre of the floor there's a large fountain, fake marble cherubs and dragons spouting water streams that criss-cross in midair.

The plaza is packed with more tourists, milling around the fountain or chatting on benches or meandering in and out of the shops and restaurants that line the edges. Hannah has to slow down, sorry-ing and excuse-me-ing her way through.

The wash of sensations almost overwhelms her, and she can't help thinking about the sheets again. White. Cool. Light enough to slide under and—

No. Come on. Be professional.

Does she go left from here, or is it on the other side of the fountain? Recalling the station map she looked at while they were jumping is like trying to decipher something in Sanskrit. Then she sees a sign above one of the paths leading off the plaza. *Ship Dock B.* That's the one.

Three minutes later, she's there. The dock is small, a spartan mustering area with four gangways leading out from the station to the airlock berths. There aren't many people around, although there are still a few sitting on benches. One of them, a little girl, is asleep: curled up with her hands tucked between shoulder and cheek, legs pulled up to her chest. Her mom—or the person Hannah thinks is her mom—sits next to her, blinking at something on her lens.

There are four tour ships visible through the glass, brightly lit against the inky black. Hannah's been on plenty of tours, and she still can't help thinking that every ship she's ever been on is ugly as hell. She's seen these ones before: they look like flattened, upside-down elephant droppings, a bulbous protrusion sticking out over each of the cockpits.

Hannah jams her hand in her jeans pocket for the tab. She wrote the ship's name for the shift in tiny capitals next to the start time: RED PANDA. Her gaze flicks between the four ships, but it takes her a second to find the right one. The name is printed on the side in big, stencilled letters, with a numbered designation in smaller script underneath.

She looks from the *Panda* to its gangway. Another guide is making his way onto it. He's wearing the same red shirt as her, and he has the most fantastic hair: a spiked purple mohawk at least a foot high.

Her tab still in hand, she springs onto the gangway. "Hey!" she says, forcing a confidence she doesn't feel into her voice. "I'm on for this one. Anything I need to know?"

Mohawk guy glances over his shoulder, an expression of bored contempt on his face. He keeps walking, his thick black boots booming on the metal plating.

"Um. Hi?" Hannah catches up to him. "I think this one's mine?"

She tries to slip past him, but he puts up a meaty hand, blocking her path. "Nice try, rook," he says, that bored look still on his face. "You're late. Shift's mine."

"What are you talking about?" She swipes a finger across her tab, hunting for the little clock.

"Don't you have a lens?"

This time it takes Hannah a lot more effort to stay calm. "There," she says, pointing at her schedule. "I'm not late. I'm

517

supposed to be on at eleven, and it's..." she finds the clock in the corner of her tab. "Eleven-o-two."

"My *lens* says eleven-o-six. Anyway, you're still late. I get the shift."

"What? No. Are you serious?"

He ignores her, resuming his walk towards the airlock. As he does, Hannah remembers the words from the handbook the company sent her before she left Titan: *Guides who are late for their shift will lose it. Please try not to be late!!!*

He can't do this. He can't. But who are the crew chiefs going to believe? The new girl? She'll lose a shift on her first day, which means she's already in the red, which means that maybe they don't keep her past her probation. A free shuttle ride back to Titan, and we wish you all the best in your future endeavours.

Anger replaces panic. This might not be her dream job, but it's work, and at the very least it means she's going *somewhere* with her life. She can already see the faces of her parents when she tells them she lost her job, and that is not going to happen. Not ever.

"Is that hair growing out of your ears, too?" she says, more furious than she's been in a long time. "I said I'm *here*. It's *my shift*."

He turns to look at her, dumbfounded. "What did you just say?"

Hannah opens her mouth to return fire, but nothing comes out.

Her mom and dad would know. Callista definitely would. Her older sister would understand exactly how to smooth things over, make this asshole see things her way. Then again, there's no way either her parents or Callie would ever have taken a job like this, so they wouldn't be in this situation. They're not here now, and they can't help her.

"It's all right, Donnie," says a voice.

Hannah and Mohawk guy—Donnie—turn to see the supervisor walking up. She's a young woman, barely older than Hannah, with a neat bob of black hair and a pristine red shirt. Hannah remembers meeting her last night, for about two seconds, but she's totally blanking on her name. Her gaze automatically goes to the woman's breast pocket, and she's relieved to see a badge: *Atsuke*.

"Come on, boss," Donnie says. "She was late." He glances at Hannah, and the expression on his face clearly says that he's just getting started.

"I seem to remember you being late on *your* first day." Atsuke's voice is pleasant and even, like a newsreader's.

"*And*," Donnie says, as if Atsuke hadn't spoken. "She was talking bakwas about my hawk. Mad disrespectful. I've been here a lot longer than she has, and I don't see why—"

"Well, to be fair, Donnie, your hair *is* pretty stupid. Not to mention against regs. I've told you that, like, ten times."

Donnie stares at her, shoulders tight. In response, Atsuke raises a perfectly shaped eyebrow.

He lets out a disgusted sigh, then shoves past them. "You got lucky, rook," he mutters, as he passes Hannah.

Her chest is tight, like she's just run a marathon, and she exhales hard. "Thank you *so* much," she says to Atsuke. "I'm really sorry I was late—I thought I had enough time to—"

"Hey." Atsuke puts a hand on her shoulder. "Take a breath. It's fine."

Hannah manages a weak smile. Later, she is going to buy Atsuke a drink. Multiple drinks.

"It's an easy one today," Atsuke says. "Eight passengers. Barely a third of capacity. Little bit about the station, talk about the war, the treaty, what we got, what the Colonies got, the role Sigma played in everything, get them gawking at the Neb...twenty minutes, in and out. Square?"

She looks down at Hannah's tab, then glances up with a raised eyebrow.

"My lens is glitching," Hannah says.

"Right." This time, Atsuke looks a little less sure. She reaches in her shirt pocket, and hands Hannah a tiny clip-on mic. "Here. Links to the ship automatically. You can pretty much just start talking. And listen: just be cool. Go do this one, and then there'll be a coffee waiting for you when you get back."

Forget the drink. She should take out another loan, buy Atsuke shares in the touring company. "I will. I mean, yeah. You got it."

Atsuke gestures to the airlock at the far end of the gangway. "Get going. And if Volkova gives you any shit, just ignore her. Have fun."

Hannah wants to ask who Volkova is, but Atsuke is already heading back, and Hannah doesn't dare follow. She turns, and marches as fast she can towards the *Red Panda*'s airlock.

orbit

Follow us:

f **/orbitbooksUS**

/orbitbooks

/orbitbooks

Join our mailing list
to receive alerts on our
latest releases and deals.

orbitbooks.net

Enter our monthly
giveaway for the chance
to win some epic prizes.

orbitloot.com